STAY CALM AND AIM FOR THE HEAD

BELINDA DUNFORD

Acknowledgements

Thanks to all my family and friends for your continual support; I'm grateful to have so many people behind me.
And more specific thanks in no particular order to:
Kevin Dunford for his belief in me, for aiding me in gun research, and for beta-reading.
Shelley Trigg for believing in me and for beta-reading.
Natasha Levesque-Glanville for being my original beta-listener for any and all drafts, and for her willingness to help with brainstorming whenever needed. Ghost friends forever!
Kyle Dunford for his help with brainstorming about various parts in the story (especially the lake scene and lab layout) and for helping me make it make as much sense as a zombie story is ever going to.
Diane Arnold for always believing in me, for beta-reading and for her aid in brainstorming sessions.
Jim Arnold for his support and his help developing the synopses for this book.
Allison Dunford for her support.
Chris Huston for aiding me in gun research and for beta-reading.
Ashley Knight for her continuous support and positivity.
Dennis and David Fell, Gianna Magliocco, Johanna Hunt and all of my other awesomely helpful beta readers.
asofterworld.com where I got my actual "during a zombie attack please follow me" bag.

Chapter One
The Ominous Situation

Elliot

"BRRAWKK-SKLANKK!"

The noise sounds like a zombie chicken mating with one of those metal lawn flamingos that had been brought to life.

"BRRAWKK-SKLANKK!"

The sound invades my dream, making it even weirder than it already was. It takes me a few more sleep drunk moments before I realize that it's the alarm crashing through the speakers, and what that means.

"BRRAWKK-SKLANKK!"

The alarm is insistent, as I shake off the last of the dream involving chess, and those girls from that magazine the security guards gave me. They suddenly started talking like the alarm, and with that surreal image still in my brain, I try to wrap my head around the reality that, yes, the alarm is actually sounding.

My brain is still confusedly trying to process why the alarm would be going off at all in a vitamin research facility. I tug on my favourite corduroys, the nearest t-shirt, and my slightly too small lab coat. Gregory's idea of a joke, I think. However, as I head towards the door to go investigate why the alarms are going off, I finally notice that I can't see all that clearly. I can't put my finger on why, but in the back of my still sleepy mind, I can't help but think of those urban legends wherein mega corporations drug their employees for nefarious purposes. Or of a half-remembered storyline from a *Twilight Zone* episode involving sudden blindness.

I ground the palms of my hands into my eyes trying to clear my vision, but it's no help. I can still see only vague shapes around the room. I'm not going to lie. I can feel the beginnings of a panic attack. The alarm's continuous screams from overhead exacerbates my fright, and I begin making my way over to the fuzzy, silver shape that I'm pretty sure is the door before panic sets in fully, and I freeze up, which has been known to happen. I seem to have something in between a fight-or-flight response, wherein, I simply freeze and do nothing at all—it can be pretty inconvenient.

On the way to the door, I run into a few things and send something crashing, but I eventually make it relatively unscathed. I try to grab the door handle, but I can only make out a blur that's slightly more distinct than the bigger blur of the door itself.

"BRRAWKK-SKLANKK!"

I can't quite hold back a whimper and that helps me to get angry at myself long enough to calm down before yelling out for help.

"Hello!" I cry out, my voice breaking in the middle of the word. I shake my head, clear my throat, and try again. "Hello! I'm in, um, in need of assistance, here!" I slam my hands on the door and clarify, "I'm in need of assistance in room forty-two! I, um, I can't see!"

"BRRAWKK-SKLANKK!"

I wait until there's a pause in the screaming alarm before continuing with my explanation, the scientist in me not wanting to leave any details out that could be important. Describing my symptoms also has the side benefit of calming me down and returning my voice to its normal pitch, so I carry on, even though it's unlikely anyone could hear me through the thick, metal door.

"Well, that is, I can see, but my vision is blurry and I assume that's not a good thing, especially since I don't know the reason. So, um, if anyone's out there, I'd really appreciate it if you could let me out and tell me why the alarm is going off."

I bang on the door some more and I feel my left hand slip as it finally finds the handle. I open the door, stumbling into the apparently abandoned hallway, glancing from side to side.

"What is this, a fire drill?" I ask, mostly to myself since I seem to be alone.

"BRRAWKK-SKLANKK!"

"Uh, Doc?"

Or maybe not alone. I jump at the unexpected voice in the sudden silence following the alarm burst, and turn to see a large, blurred figure standing in front of me. I think it's one of the security personnel. I can't tell which one, but judging from the size, I would guess it is Terry, because he's the biggest of the guards—not to mention my least favourite. I try to regain my composure as I respond, "Yes, hello, um, do you think you might be able to help me? I am unable to see very well for some reason."

The blurred form is silent for a second before he asks, sounding like he's trying to suppress a laugh, "Don't you usually wear glasses, Doc?"

I can feel my face burn red as I answer, "Oh. Yeah, well…normally. The alarms woke me up and confused me. Um, could you help me find my glasses?"

The blurry head nods and he leads me back into my room, handing me my glasses after a few moments of searching. Once my surroundings are back in their proper focus, I can clearly see that the guard is indeed Terry in all his muscled and smirking redneck glory. I'm used to him laughing at me, so it hardly bothers me and at least he helped me with barely a comment.

"Do you have any idea why we're having a fire drill right now? This *is* a fire drill, right?" I grin and chuckle a little. "What am I saying? Of course, it's a fire drill. All we make is vitamins and supplements. What could've gone wrong?"

"BRRAWKK-SKLANKK!"

Terry glances up in the direction of the speaker and shakes his head as he looks back at me. "Sorry to disappoint, Doc, but no, this ain't no fire drill."

My heart thuds with a blip of fear as I try to make sense of what he's saying, before I realize that he's teasing me, a favourite pastime of the guards. "Ha-ha, very funny, Terry. Now where is everyone?"

Terry frowns at me. "I'm not screwin' with you, Doc. We're evacuatin' the building. Something's happened. I'm not sure what, but it's bad and we gotta get you out ASAP. I was just comin' to get you when you ran into me." He looks at me expectantly as he finishes chuckling at the memory. "So are you ready to go?"

My heart is beginning to pound, but I try to remain calm in case it is all an elaborate prank thought up by the guards, since that's not an unlikely scenario. "Come on, Terry, I know I'm gullible, like when you guys convinced me that Jordan's birthday was a costume party and I came dressed as C3P0, but this is just going to extremes. I'm not going to fall for it this time." I start straightening up the mess I made of the room with my blind clumsiness, but pause when I hear Terry let out an annoyed sigh that is soon lost in the renewed screeching of the alarm.

"BRRAWKK-SKLANKK!"

"Dude, get your squint head outta your ass! This ain't no drill. This ain't no prank. The building is *not* safe and if you don't come with me willingly, I have orders to whoop your ass into submission and drag you out." Terry pauses as he looks scornfully at my skinny frame and snorts contemptuously at my admitted lack of muscle matter (except for the brain area, of course) "Which, I'm guessin' would not be that difficult but would still be damn annoying. So move your skinny ass, get whatever's important to you and let's get the fuck outta here!"

"BRRAWKK-SKLANKK!"

I stand still, blinking disbelievingly for a few seconds before I start moving quickly around the room, gathering my stuff as fast as I can. The expression on his face, as well as the threat of violence scared me more than I would like him to know. I grab my battered, green duffle bag from the corner of the room and start stuffing things into it. I keep waiting for Terry to burst out laughing at my gullibility, but he just stands in front of the door, waiting impatiently with his massive arms crossed over his massive chest.

I can hear the thundering of my heart in my ears as I realize that this is very likely not a prank, and I begin to move even faster. I grab my laptop, glasses case, stuff some extra clothes in and head towards the bookshelf. I'm putting my books and comic books, including my favourite series of graphic novels by Pete Moon in the bag, when I hear Terry sigh in annoyance again.

"What?" I ask as he walks over to me.

"Just hurry it up, Doc, we really gotta get outta here, and damn quick. Just leave the books. They can't be that all-firin' important!"

"They are 'all-firing' important to me," I protest awkwardly, but I start packing the books more quickly and finally end up just shoving them into my bag. "Okay, I think that's all I need. We can go."

With all of my books inside, my duffle is now quite heavy. I figure it's probably better to suffer in silence, than to ask Terry to carry it for me and risk another scathing look in the general direction of my generally under developed upper body. However, it seems Terry figured I would just slow him down anyway, so he grabs the bag and my upper arm roughly. His hand almost closes entirely around it and I try not to gulp too loudly. He then begins marching me into the hallway.

"BRRAWKK-SKLANKK!"

I pull my arm out of his grasp, saying, "I can walk fine now that I have my glasses. Thanks, though." Terry grunts and continues down the hallway at a fast clip. After walking for a few moments in silence, minus the alarm, which is still "brawk-sklanking" loudly around us, we approach the elevator. I reach for the button, but Terry swats my hand away.

"Nuh-uh, Doc, we gotta take the stairs. Don't you know it's safer in an emergency? Besides, we gotta go up to the roof, and the elevator doesn't go all the way up there."

"Okay, but I think the hand slap was a bit unnecessary," I can't help retorting. I wish I was able to keep the whine from my voice, because Terry just grins wider as he punches a strange type of key-card I've never seen before into the electronic key-pad beside the stairwell door and we start up the stairs.

"BRRAWKK-SKLANKK!"

Terry takes the stairs two at a time as we head up to the roof, and I have to struggle to catch up, apparently much to his delight as he breaks into yet another grin and finally responds to my comment about him slapping my hand.

"Unnecessary? Maybe. Fun? Hell yes."

I decide not to respond in order to protect my safety, since annoying Terry would probably be akin to poking a sleeping bear. Actually, I think I would prefer my chances with an angry ursine rather than an angry Terry. We reach the roof and as Terry opens the door, I feel the bite of the cold instantly. He doesn't seem to notice the chill, but then he does have all that muscle to insulate him. As my eyes adjust to the brightness of the sun reflecting off of the snow-covered mountains, I notice the helicopter for the first time.

I can see a strange man sitting inside it at the controls. Mitch, Gregory's personal assistant, is perched on the edge of the door-less opening in the side of the helicopter, apparently waiting for us. Finally, I see Gregory standing beside the helicopter, looking impatient as he smokes his pipe. I barely notice his impatience since it's his usual expression. What catches my attention is that his hands seem to be shaking, as he tips some of the ash out of his pipe. I've never once seen Gregory's hands shake and that, more than anything, is what finally makes it sink in that something very bad has happened.

Lucy

"PARTY!" Lia screams over the music she's head banging to.

I shake my head at her boisterousness, giving in to a smile, even though I still can't understand her level of excitement about going to meet guys we hardly know for a bush party in the mountains. I don't know about you, but as far as I'm concerned, this scenario has ominous written all over it. I should not have agreed to go with her this weekend. Honestly, *Deliverance* much?

I say as much to Lia while turning down the music, and I'm not sure which annoys her more. The look she gives me could either have to do with music possessiveness, or her oft-repeated complaint that "I don't get out enough lately," which she blames on my "obsessive paranoia" from watching "one too many horror movies."

To be fair, I have seen more horror movies than I can count, so it's not exactly implausible that my admittedly sometimes hermit-like existence is caused by a fear of someday getting stalked by a psycho killer or zombies or whatever other monsters keep people up at night. But like they say (and I'm not even going to get into the paranoid person's catnip that *that* statement contains), just because you're paranoid, doesn't mean that they're not out to get you and that you won't find yourself in a horror movie type of situation one day. Just look at Randy from *Scream*, he was paranoid and he still got all kinds of dead. I just think that it's better to be safe than being disembowelled or dismembered or any other type of fate beginning with the prefix "dis" which I think we can agree, never leads to anything good. Yes, my definition of safe might mean being overly suspicious at times, but it just might save your life one day, so I think it's worth the occasional funny look.

A much beleaguered sigh shakes me out of my paranoia reverie, and I finally realize that I'm in the midst of a mild Lia Glare, as she awaits a response to something I hadn't noticed she was saying.

"Um, what?" I ask, rather eloquently.

Lia sighs again, but repeats herself in a wheedling tone of voice, "Come on, Luce, I know you aren't really sure about this weekend, but I think you'll have fun and it's been forever since

7

we've had an adventure. Besides, the guys are magically delicious."

"And surprisingly nutritious?" I ask as I roll my eyes. I don't feel like arguing though so I wave off her coming protest at my sarcasm and simply say, "Yeah, yeah, I know. But you gotta admit, going camping in the woods, where there's actually a lake named Crystal Lake, by the way, for a weekend of frivolity has '80s horror movie written all over it. And I don't really feel like running into Jason...or his mother, for that matter. Do you?"

Lia sticks her tongue out at me and then says, "I admit it's a bit creepy, but at least *I'm* willing to set aside my mild case of paranoia for a swoon-worthy boy from time to time. Anyway, if we *are* in '80s horror-movie-land, then we might run into crazy Ralph, which would be awesome. Besides that, we're well armed in case Mrs. Voorhees decides to make a special one-time cameo appearance. With or without her son, I'm pretty sure we could take 'em."

I can't help but smile at the mention of crazy Ralph, our favourite character from the original *Friday the 13th* movies, and I definitely cannot hold back a laugh at the mental image of the crazed mother and son, also from said movies, bonding by stalking and killing sex-crazed co-eds together as we fight back, matching them machete for machete. Not that we're sex-crazed co-eds or anything, but you know what I mean.

In light of my amusement and Lia's reassurance that we're well-armed enough to take on anything that might attack us, I almost feel bad about switching her music while she was extolling the virtues of giving up paranoia for love...or for lust, anyway. Instead of hip-twist worthy dance music, low notes better suited to the various ominous scenarios flitting about my head pound out of the ancient speakers of her equally ancient shaggin' wagon. Said wagon is affectionately referred to as Brown Sugar and painted that shade of brown that people in the '70s somehow convinced themselves was cool. Although who can blame them, what with all of the drugs floating around in that era, their collective style judgment was hardly up to its fighting best. For more examples, see bellbottoms, platforms with goldfish inside, and afros with combs stuck in them.

The unexpected music change causes Lia to exhale loudly in consternation once again. "What. The. Hell. Lucy? What is this anyway?"

Shrugging, I simply reply, "It's more befitting of the situation."

The Lia Glare returns and at a much higher power level to boot. "The Situation? Like on Jersey Shore?"

"Ew, no...I'm talking about the ominous situation we're currently heading into, not that oompa-loompa, steroid-abusing freak. I can't believe you watched that show."

"If you say 'ominous' one more time," Lia growls in what is actually a rather ominous manner, obviously choosing to ignore my joke about her fondness for the mysteriously famous, overly tanned Guidos and Guidettes.

Smirking, I say, "Ominous," much to Lia's visible chagrin, as she makes a strangled noise in her throat and she pulls the van over to the side of the road.

"That's it," she growls again and turns down the music, then pinches the bridge of her nose while sighing and turns to face me. She frowns, her face all serious as she attempts to get me to be more cooperative and less paranoid. (Like that'll happen.) Her blue-green eyes are earnest as she says, "Okay, so just do me a favour and picture this: that perfectly wavy hair the colour of warm caramel, those eyes that make you feel like you're drowning—"

"Huh, never noticed that myself," I interject, unable to keep the grin out of my voice. It's just so fun to tease her.

"Alright, do me two favours: picture this *and* shut up," she says, her facial expression threatening to morph back into a full-on Lia Glare, until I do the clichéd shutting-up zipper motion over my lips and make my own facial expression as innocent as possible. Seemingly satisfied, Lia continues, "Okay then...so the drowning pools that are his eyes—"

"Drowning pools? I'm pretty sure that's the name of a band you know...I wonder if they named it after him," I interrupt again, powerless to stop myself until she makes a noise disturbingly close to a snarl, and I raise my hands in acquiescence. "Okay, okay. I'm just saying you're gettin' a little poetic on me."

"Ahem," Lia clears her throat pointedly and glances at me to see if I'm about to start up again, but I keep my mouth shut this time and wave my hand to tell her to get a move on with the description of her prospective lover boy. She makes a satisfied "hmmph" noise and faces the windshield again, hands moving as if she's painting a picture while she stares off into the distance, picturing Carson, no doubt.

"So, we start off with great hair, move down to amazing eyes, a mouth that has me very curious about its potential, broad shoulders, generally rippling muscles, and we move down again, to an area I'm even *more* curious about, because it has been way too damn long and he is very fucking hot. And hopefully hot at fucking—a possibility which I would love to explore, because yes..." With this thought, Lia trails off as though picturing said exploration and it's my turn to clear my throat and return her attention back to Earth. She shakes her head and carries on with her sales pitch.

"Besides, his cute friend that you seem to like will be there," she says in what I'm sure she assumes is a tone of voice which will convince me to jump on board, and perhaps the friend grenade for that matter. "What's-his-name...Rocky *Horror* guy, Brad! Carson told me that he asked about you," she finishes in the same girl-talk co-conspirator tone of voice.

I fight off the urge to respond with a sarcastic and bitchy, "Oh joy! He asked about me? Now my life is complete." Instead I reply with, "'Kay, first of all, objectification much? Secondly, it's now gonna be really hard to resist doing the whole 'Janet, Brad, Dr. Scott, Rocky, blank stare' bit, thanks to you calling him *Rocky Horror* guy." Lia attempts to interrupt me with a disgruntled noise, but I press on, "However, because I love you and also tend to be guilty of objectifying guys myself and well, I do love me some *Rocky Horror*, I shall attempt to be a somewhat less paranoid 'party girl.'"

Lia groans. "Did you actually just use air quotes? What have I said about using air quotes?" Nevertheless, she seems pleased with my promise of attempted normalcy.

I try to smile like a "normal" person. It hurts my face just a bit, but I'm pretty sure she doesn't notice.

Lia

A pained smile stretches the corners of Lucy's mouth and it looks so awkward, I swear she looks like a Borg or some other *Star Trek* creature doing an impersonation of a human being smiling.

"Jesus," I mutter as I push fallen strands of my dark brown, shoulder-length hair behind my ears and sigh again, loudly. She can be so tragic sometimes. "It's just a party with a couple of guys, possibly some bad soft-rock and Mike's Hard Lemonade." I hold up my hand in the universal sign of shut-the-hell-up as I attempt to rebuff the outburst that's bound to come. "Now look here, missy, I realize these aren't the greatest selling points, but it's been forever since we've done anything like this and it'll be fun. And Carson is so damn pretty!"

She snorts in response but says nothing, so I soldier on, gesturing out the windshield, my arm movement more reminiscent of Vanna White than I would like as it encompasses the breathtaking mountains surrounding us, emphasized by the cloudless blue sky that is evocative enough of Carson's eyes to motivate the continuation of my gung-ho speech. "It's a beautiful day: the sun is shining, there's not a cloud in the sky. What could go wrong?"

"Goddammit, Lia. You just jinxed us! Something's definitely gonna go wrong now," Lucy says, sounding both amused and exasperated. I can't see her full reaction because half her face is hidden behind her oversized sunglasses, but her mouth twists into a pained grimace. The girl is seriously paranoid.

"Calm down, nothing is gonna happen—" I begin.

"Oh, my God, you need to stop before you get us both killed," she cuts me off abruptly.

"Alright, I'm officially banning you from watching horror movies for a whole month when we get home, maybe two."

Lucy snorts, "Yeah, like we have any hope of getting home now that you've jinxed us twice. We're double jinxed. Which is definitely gonna lead to horrific and possibly ironic deaths, depending on what type of monster-villain we encounter, so thanks for that."

"Okay, you're now veering into total crazy-town, lady. You need to take a breath," I say, feeling exasperated myself. Although it's combined with a surge of affection as she runs one hand through her long, auburn hair, while gripping her omnipresent necklaces in the other, a familiar stress gesture that makes me want to hug her, even when other parts of me want to smack some sense into her.

"Whatever, let's just go and get this doom over with," she says.

"Oh, it's doom now is it?" I ask incredulously. She really needs to lay off the scary movies. I watch my fair share, too (which you can blame on her), but I can handle it.

"Yes, doom! The doom of the ominous situation."

"There is no ominous situation. Everything will be—"

"If you finish that sentence, I'm gonna tuck and roll right out this van and I will walk home."

I throw my hands up in frustration. "Okay, fine. It won't be alright, we'll encounter pure evil and will probably die. Better?"

"Yes. You're just lucky you have all this junk in your trunk, because we're definitely gonna need it," she says.

I give up on trying to bring her back into reality and just say, "Nothing like a Claymore sword to end a psycho's killing spree!" Complete with a strange gung-ho arm movement that I seem to have picked up from my dad.

She snorts at my arm-motion then retorts, "Actually, I prefer the machete. They're good for fending off psychos and zombies, too!"

"Heck yes. Bitches be scared of my machete," I add with a gangster head bob that has Lucy snorting again.

The road courses by us, mountains growing ever larger as we ascend the pass. I flick the volume on the stereo back up and the Dropkick Murphys flood out through the speakers, almost drowning out the clanking sounds my weapon collection makes as it clatters around in its crate.

They're purely for academic purposes.

"Hey, what would happen if we were pulled over by the cops?" Lucy asks suddenly, glancing back at my assortment of swords, axes, spears, bows, knives, and other various lethal instruments comprising my collection of some of the deadliest weapons from throughout history, and are thunking around against the sides of their crate.

"It's purely academic," I protest, "I swear." I add, making the Eagle Scout sign with my right hand.

"I don't know if the educational nature of your weapon collection will really matter to Officer Friendly," Lucy points out, raising a teasing eyebrow just above her oversized sunglasses.

"I have the necessary permits. They're for my thesis!"

I swear.

"Well, at least you're getting your story straight for the cops," she jokes as she continues to admire my collection.

"You're one to talk, always carrying your knife with you no matter where you go" I remind her.

"Pff, that's just being practical," she retorts in a voice that I'm sure is accompanied by an eye-roll, even if I can't actually see her eyeballs to confirm this. "Now, shut up and drive. I'm starving. Oh, and just so you know, I call the machete in case of emergencies."

"And what, I get the cell phone?" I whine, deciding to bypass the practicality comment and move onto the much more dire discussion of who gets which weapon in case we need to turn into our badass alter-egos for some reason.

"Yeah, 'cause there aren't a billion other weapons to choose from. Besides, I thought the axe-thing was your favourite?" she reminds me.

"Well, that is true; it's light weight and still deadly. Plus, it can double as a hatchet in a pinch!" I can't seem to stop myself from swinging my fist up in the same gung-ho manner as before, and she snorts once again at my expense.

On that note, I glance into the rear view mirror and notice the heavy, dark clouds suddenly making an appearance across the horizon, casting looming shadows over the foothills behind us. I decide not to point out the portentous looking weather shift, fearing Lucy's film-student adherence to the concept of pathetic fallacy...she's said the word "ominous" enough times today already.

Lucy

I shake my head again at Lia's insistence that everything will be fine in the face of obviously imminent doom—that she made so much worse by uttering the banned phrases. To soothe the anxiety of my inner horror movie addled beast, I return my focus to admiring all of the deadly and awesome weapons in her collection. Thanks to the research required for her thesis, she has some of the most badass weapons ever recreated from history, which could turn out to be very useful…especially in case of zombie attacks; something I truly can't help but think about, like all the time. Almost every time I enter a new building, I consider the safety of the premises in relation to the possibility of a zombie attack. Okay, so maybe I *am* something of a paranoid freak, but I figure it's probably better to be paranoid than to be caught unaware, and thereby be the first one to end up as bits of human McNuggets being masticated by a decaying zombie jaw. Or maybe I have seen one too many movies, but either way, at least I'm prepared, like a Boy Scout. Or Max Brooks.

Whoops. Lia's looking at me like I've missed something again.

"Are you still obsessing about weaponry over there?"

"Um…no?"

Lia sighs at the apparent hopelessness of my condition and turns down the music so we can talk. "Aren't you even the least bit excited to finally get some quality time with Brad? You do think he's hot, don't you?"

"Well, yeah…" I lie, because it's easier and I have other things to worry about right now than if some popped-collar dude-bro likes me or not. "But I'm a bit nervous, 'cause we've barely ever talked. I mean, it was really only that one time at Carson's luau party and I was pretty tipsy so…I dunno. But I'm sure it will be great?"

"Okay, you said that like a question."

Crap. "It's just…" I pause for a second, trying to think. I don't want to waste time thinking about this worthless guy. I need to be devoting my brainpower to coming up with exit strategies from the numerous scenes of bloodied horror that are filling my brain.

So I just say the first thing that comes to mind. "It's just that he is very…good looking and…it's been a while so…" I trail off hoping that did the trick and that she will mercifully ignore my long pauses, and I can go back to mentally running through my favoured and most likely to be useful defence and/or escape tactics (depending on the scenario that arises).

"Aw, Luce, don't worry about that. I got the vibe from Carson that Brad really likes you. Everything will be fine." I'm glad that she took the bait, but, bah, she did it again!

I shoot her a mutinous look. "Do you want me to make an emergency exit from a moving vehicle? 'Cause I will if you don't stop saying that."

"Oh, geez, I was talking about guy stuff, not"—she throws me a dirty look—"ominous things. You know, when we meet up with the guys, it might be best if you try to tone down the horror movie paranoia just a little bit. Like just a smidge."

"Well, I never! If I have to tone down zombie stranger danger, you have to tone down the pros and cons of certain bladed instruments from the 15th century, 'cause you might scare your yummy boy away all by yourself."

She makes a mock-outraged sound and retorts, "How can you tone down the intense death-dealing power of a Claymore sword? It simply can't be done."

"Well, if you go on about the weaponry too much, Carson might be worried about getting certain appendages divided from his person if he steps outta line, and that would probably put a damper on things."

"Meh, I don't think he's really smart enough to come to that conclusion. But I guess you're right, the topic of bladed instruments doesn't usually make for terrific pillow talk, and since I *do* want him to *come* to a certain type of conclusion—"

"Dirty," I interject.

"Damn straight. I have needs," Lia affirms.

I turn the music back up and smile. Now I can go back to indulging in my emergency fight or flight plans in peace—I have a feeling we're gonna need them. Especially once the restaurant that Carson recommended we stop at on the way comes into view.

It's tucked into the side of an isolated rest-stop area, and the only thing that stops me from flat-out refusing to enter the premises is that its parking lot abounds with various trucking vehicles. So at least there'd be many witnesses should something untoward happen…unless they're all in on it together.

As we pull into one of the few empty parking spaces, I notice the vacancy sign for a motel attached to the diner. I can't help commenting, "Oh, goody, there's a motel attached to it, too, just in case we get tired of hanging out with weirdo truckers and feel like staying in a place that I'm pretty sure even Norman Bates would find creeptastic."

Lia glances at the motel and grimaces, but says, "Yeah, it's not ideal, but you were the one who said you were starving, can't we just go in, ignore the possibly creepy trucker guys, eat, and get to the campsite with the pretty, pretty boys?" She pulls a respectable pouting face and looks at me with puppy eyes.

"Fine. I am hungry. Let's just go in and get it over with, but I'm not going anywhere near that motel. I am in no mood to get my face ripped off along with contracting the salmonella we're bound to encounter in there. If we're lucky, it'll only be salmonella. And I'm bringing my knife."

"How is that different from anywhere else we go?" She asks as we get out of the van and head to our doom…or at least a likely stomach ache. I concede her point because she is right about the knife thing.

We enter the restaurant, which can be called this only in the loosest definition of the word, and a prickling sense of creepiness crawls along my skin, as all around the old-school diner space, truckers turn to gaze at us, making me really regret agreeing to wear my black halter-top. I usually stick to band shirts or things with skulls on them, but I at least wanted to look like I was making an effort so Lia would be less likely to have a stress meltdown. One guy in particular is staring hard enough to make me feel like I'm wearing nothing at all, I stare back hard until he starts to get uncomfortable and looks away. I return my attention to the diner itself and quietly start humming the theme to *Deliverance*, while glancing around the wood-paneled walls, "Dur nuh nur nur nur nur nur, dur nuh nur nur nur nur."

"Quit with the 'Dueling Banjos,' alright? Let's just sit down. It'll be fine, I promise. It's busy, so that means it's got to be at least decent," Lia chastises me as we head towards a booth.

I roll my eyes, but say nothing as I sit down at one of the only torn, red pleather booths still available, swiping my hand across the sticky, blue Formica table top to rid it of the crumbs, looking accusingly up at Lia, who studiously ignores my glare as she sits down and opens up one of the coffee-stained menus.

"Y'all want coffee?" Lia and I both look up at the sudden sound of the voice, which turns out to belong to Gert, according to her name-tag, a steel-haired, almost morbidly obese woman in a blue and red uniform that matches the décor, if you can even call it that. The uniform pulls tightly around the rolls of fat covering her body and her cankles feed into sensible, white shoes that squeak as she shifts her considerable weight, impatient for our answers.

"Um, yes?" Lia answers, almost like a question as she tries not to stare impolitely at our waitress.

I shake my head no and ask for a Coke instead, but am disappointed as she responds, "Sorry, darlin', we only got Pepsi; do you want that?" Now, I'm often called "sweetheart" or "hon" or some such thing by waitresses for whatever reason, but the way Gert says "darlin'" makes it sound like an insult.

I make a face as I sigh, "I'll just have water then, thanks."

Gert snorts derisively and shifts again, shoes squeaking, as she glances at our open menus. "Well, are y'all ready to order?"

As we shake our heads, Gert is already walking away, surprisingly quickly for her size. I make a face at her back.

"They don't even have Coke; of course they don't." Lia opens her mouth, but I pre-emptively wave away her optimistic protests. "Never mind, maybe the food will be good at least." Lia looks more content since I'm trying to be positive about the creepy (not to mention sticky) diner.

Lia starts talking about Carson some more as I scan the menu for anything that might possibly be somewhat edible. I don't trust random diner meat, so I decide just to have the garden salad, before finally realizing that Lia is expecting me to participate in the conversation.

"Sorry, what?" I ask, articulate as always.

Lia makes an annoyed face at me and says, "I was just saying that I hope Carson has an air mattress or something. I don't really want to do the pleasure grind with him with rocks and twigs ramming into my back. Heh, the only thing I want ramming into me is his—" Lia breaks off, flustered, as Gert arrives back at the table smirking at Lia's embarrassed expression. I don't know how she keeps sneaking up like that; she's like a fat ninja in squeaky shoes that mysteriously go silent when she approaches.

"Y'all decide what you want yet?" she asks, cheeks and chins dimpling with a badly suppressed smile.

Lia shuts her menu, not meeting Gert's amused, muddy brown eyes, as she stutters with embarrassment through her order. "Y-yes, just a s-salad, please." Then she sips her coffee as she pretends nothing happened.

I try not to laugh, considering the plethora of weapons in her van that she could use against me if I piss her off too badly. Continuing to stifle a laugh, I say, "I'll just have a salad, too, please," while ignoring the look of amused condescension that Gert gives us both before waddling away.

Chapter Two
So many goddamn horror movie survival rules are being broken here, how on Earth can I be expected to relax?

Daphne

Tif's hot pink beetle convertible rolls to a stop, the big colour-coordinated flower (so cute!) in the tiny vase on the dash shaking as the tires crunch over gravel.

Ugh, gravel? This is gonna play hell with my new Manolos…well, they're knock-offs, but they're still too good for this nasty-ass dirt that Tif's actually expecting me to walk on. Ew times, like, a gagillion! At least, the guy Blaine is bringing is supposed to be totes hot, but still, why did we have to meet them in the mountains? All my cutest boy-enticing clothes are gonna get totally mussed! Not hot! What self-respecting trust-fund boy would ask to meet a girl in the woods, anyway? Don't they know Amelia Posts or whatev would totally frown on this? Tif says it'll be totes romantic. Like, I'm so sure.

"Tif…" I whine, but she's gotta understand. I mean, her Manolos are *real*, how can she not be freaking out right now?

"I know, I know, Daff, but this guy is definitely delectable, trust me; I've seen his pic. And we can get our shoes cleaned when we get home. Besides, they've got trust funds, remember? So Nate could finally buy you *real* Manolos."

I pout my lower lip at her dig at my knock-offs. At least they're good knock-offs, not like those nasty things she got from Chinatown that she wore in high school. I would say so, but her reminder about the hot boys, especially hot boys with money makes me focus on the end game, like my mom taught me.

"Tif!"

We both turn at the sound of Blaine's voice and I'm totes excited (in more ways than one) to discover one of the yummiest munchables I've ever laid eyes on (and later, hopefully other parts of my awesome bod) standing beside him.

My blind date is tall (and I do like 'em tall) with yummily broad shoulders straining a bit at the seams of his totes retro leather jacket. He's got surprisingly great brown hair that's, like, all wavy. I usually prefer other blonds like my gorgeous self, but I can definitely make an exception for him. 'Cause his face is, like, one of the best I've ever seen in person. But it would be even more luscious if he wasn't all frowny (he's totes gonna need Botox early if he keeps up with that scrunchy angry-boy face). Maybe he's worried that Tifani is his blind date. I'm way hotter so I wouldn't even blame him if he was. Not that I'd ever tell her, 'cause she's my BFF, but seriously, my boob job turned out way better than hers did. I'm much tanner, and my extensions look totes more real than hers do.

"Blainey!" Tif exclaims as she saunters up to him and immediately starts making out with him. I walk over to my date, waggling my definitely superior assets on the way. He's still all frowny, which makes no sense 'cause it should be obvi by now that I'm his date, and not Tif, but whatev, I'll be makin' him smile for all kinds of reasons in no time. I'm not, like, a slut or anything, but I *definitely* know how to make a man happy in, like, every way.

"Hey there, I'm Daphne, but you can call me Daffy, 'cause, like, everyone does." I smile my best come hither smile. I know it's my best one, 'cause I've practiced them all in the mirror and taken Facebook pictures of them all and this one always gets the best responses from hotties on the net. I stop in front of him just before my boobs brush his chest—one of my best guy-grabbing moves. The gorgeous sampler of man-cake in front of me shifts his mouth-watering muscles as he glances towards the still lip-locked Blaine and Tif, probably totes jelly of the action and picturing us doing the same (and more). Like, how could he not be?

"You must be Nathan? You're, like, even hotter than Tif said you were!" I grin up at him again and step even closer, my boobs definitely brushing against him now. He steps back, probably worried he might jizz in his pants from standing so close to me.

"Yeah, uh, I'm Nate. Hey." He looks sorta anxiously at Blaine and Tif, probably wishing they were elsewhere so we could *really* get to know each other. I guess he's just not a public guy like Blaine, what a total gentleman!

Nate

Jesus fucking Christ. I don't know why the hell I let Blaine talk me into meeting this chick. She's so vacuous and shallow, my head's starting to hurt just from listening to her talk, not to mention all the pink she's wearing. That her nickname is so ridiculously apt can't even strike me as funny, because I'm just trying so hard not to throttle her so she'll just shut the hell up already.

Who would actually choose to be called "Daffy" anyway? Someone stupid enough not to realize what it means, I guess. Blaine's been trying to convince me that the soul-sucking vapidity of this chick is worth it because she's hot. Sometimes, I don't know how we've stayed friends this long 'cause it's like he doesn't know me at all. I couldn't care less about her so-called "hotness." She's such a goddamn dumb-ass and she keeps batting her eyelashes at me like that, as though with one wink from her make-up laden eyes, I'll get a raging hard-on and not be able to resist her womanly wiles.

Fuck that...or really, I'd rather not.

"...don't you think, Nathan?" Daffy finishes asking something inane, batting those stupid eyes at me and sticking her obviously fake tits in my face again.

God, if her general idiocy and skankiness weren't enough for me to dislike her instantly, her calling me "Nathan" would sure do it. I hate being called that. It's what my mom used to call me. Seriously, shouldn't the fact that I introduced myself as Nate give her some clue that I would like to be called Nate? Though I'd prefer just to be called nothing by her. The best thing I could imagine would be if she were just to go the fuck away.

I grunt and shift even further away from her. She doesn't get the message. Not surprising considering her stupidity, but it is still very goddamn annoying.

"Don't you think it would be cool if, like, every girl had a matching butterfly tattoo? It could be like a beautification project or something?" She sidles closer to me as she finishes this idea that is bad enough and bordering very closely on retardation, but she's a fucking up-talker, too? Kill me now. Or her...yeah, definitely kill her instead. Somebody...anybody, before I do it myself.

Jesus Christ. Even Blaine has to hide a smirk at that tattoo idea and he actually thinks she's hot, or at the very least fuckable, to use his term for girls like her and Tifani. Personally, I don't see it. They're both chicken fried all over from so much bleach in their hair and UV rays on their skin. Tifani's face has a strange hardness to it that makes her look way older than twenty-two, something that is only made worse by the couple of pounds of make-up she has caked all over her face. Her obviously thin lips are outlined strangely to make them look bigger, but she just looks like she slathered it on without looking in a mirror. And Daffy...God, she's just awful. It's possible she might actually be pretty under all her modifications, but it's impossible to tell, she's tweaked so much that she looks like nothing so much as a human Barbie doll. I think I'm going to have nightmares.

I grumble something vague about getting more beer from the truck and walk away. I can hear Blaine stumble after me, making polite excuses, not because he's actually polite, but because he doesn't want to hurt his chances of getting laid by Tifani. ("That's with one 'f' and an 'i', hun.") I can't decide whether I want to punch something or vomit, maybe both. I can't bring myself to sympathize with his predicament, because looks aside, she's as awful as Daffy, if not worse. If that's even possible, she could accomplish it. For one thing, she has those fuckin' creepy eyelash things over the headlights of her stupid pink car. How the hell can Blaine like this chick?

"Dude!" Blaine catches up to me and cuffs me on the back of the head—a dangerous move for anyone but him. "What are you doing? She is *totally* into you."

"Do you honestly think I give a shit, Blaine? I thought you knew me at least a little better than that. For Christ's sake, where do I even start? She's an up-talker, she's a moron, she called me Nathan, she looks like a mandarin orange mutated with fuckin' silicone, which is objectively impressive from a scientific standpoint, but is torture to be around...and butterfly tattoos?"

Blaine pats my arm. "Dude, look I know, but come on, just come back—"

"Collective butterfly tattoos, Blaine?"

"I know, but..."

"Come on."

"Okay, yes, she's stupid," he finally concedes.

"Thank you."

"But, please, man, I need this. Tifani is so hot and if Daffy's distracting her, I won't be able to…work my magic."

I pull a face. Daffy is excruciating to be around and I can't help being disgusted at the thought of Blaine "working his magic" with Tifani. That is not a mental image I need. I'm definitely going to have nightmares tonight.

"God, did you actually just say 'work my magic'? What is wrong with you?"

Blaine frowns, pretending to be hurt. "Nothing's wrong with me." Another fake pout. "I just really wanna slip Tif my man meat." He punctuates this charming declaration with a series of pelvic thrusts that are worryingly close to my truck. "Like *that*," he finishes, gesturing at his crotch in case I might not understand what he's getting at. "C'mon, Nate, help me out here. I just gotta tap that paradise cove."

"'Paradise cove'? What are you, a pirate?"

"Well, I do wanna get me some booty." I walked right in to that one.

I sigh and look up to the heavens as though asking for help (as if I actually believe that works). "Good Lord, I should not have asked."

Seeing that I'm still unconvinced, Blaine drops to his knees in supplication. Drama queen. "Come on, Nate, pleeeasse? Pretty please with a naked hot chick on top, preferably with whipped cream? Just give me this? It's one weekend and—"

"Oh, Jesus H. Fine, just get up, you drama queen, but if that orange freak tries to make a move on me, I'm sleeping in the truck with the doors locked."

Blaine gets up and throws his arms around me like a little kid. He's only allowed to hug me because he's like a brother. Otherwise, I'd have knocked him on his ass by now, I don't much like being touched. He exclaims, "Thank you, thank you, thank you! And I prefer the term drama king. By the way, what does the 'H' stand for?"

"What?" I ask.

"The 'H' as in 'Jesus H.' As in what you just said? What does it stand for?"

I hadn't even realized I'd said it. It's an expression my mom used to use. "I don't know actually…Horatio?" I shrug, trying to ignore the memories of her that are trying to surface from where I usually suppress them in the back of my mind.

Blaine laughs, and still grinning, finally releases me before walking back to those tangerine things—I mean, the girls…no, I really don't, they don't deserve even that amount of my respect. This weekend is going to be torture.

Lucy

I swear, I could be a psychic or something, because it's ridiculous how right I was about this weird and disturbing diner. Old-school country twangs out of the speakers at one of those uncomfortable volumes, making it too loud to talk easily but too quiet to be able to reasonably ask that they turn it down. The lyrics seep into my head where they are certainly not welcome. The singer is whining all about how "My woman ran away and my dog followed her, when I tried to follow them my truck died, and the saddest thing in the world to me was losin' that truck. It made my heart break inside."

I want to punch the radio in its non-existent face.

I try to ignore the insipid music and go back to picking at what can only very loosely be called a garden salad. I don't know whose garden they expect us to believe this terrifying concoction came from, but it's certainly nowhere from this plane of existence. I give up on the "salad," pushing it away from me and looking around the diner to distract myself, and to make sure that all my exits are still clear.

Just then, Gert appears by the tableside. She sets two mugs down in front of us and says dispassionately, "Those gentlemen sittin' at the counter there wanted me to bring this hot chocolate over to y'all." If I didn't know her better, I would swear Gert was trying not to laugh. After depositing the drinks, she waddles away, squeaking with every step.

Lia stares at the mugs for a moment before looking up at me with almost panic in her eyes at the disturbing offering. "Escape Plan A?" I ask, grabbing my bag.

Lia pushes her own mostly untouched "salad" away from her and grabs her oversized leopard print purse at the same time. "Definitely."

We throw our money on the table, and book it out of there before someone tells us that we have pretty mouths.

We hop into Brown Sugar and speed out—as much as the old van can speed—and neither of us can stop giggling with the creepiness-induced adrenaline.

"Man, what do you wanna bet that hot chocolate was laced with something nefarious?" I ask, shuddering.

Lia glances over at me, still laughing, before cranking the stereo again and driving onwards to the campsite at which we're supposed to meet the guys. "Kiss Me, I'm Shit-faced" pounds out of the speakers and we both sing along, my phobic thoughts about psycho killers and zombies fading into the back of my mind while we recite the hilarious lyrics and head higher into the beautiful mountains surrounding us.

Lia

We finally arrive at the edges of the make-shift campsite. The scene outside the windshield is unfortunately, as Lucy had anticipated, pretty ominous, especially now that night is getting close to falling. The trees are massive; it looks like their arms are reaching out, just reaching, trying to grab hold of something...or someone—damn it, now I sound like Lucy. I feel a sudden twinge of panic, something deep in my gut, but I push it away. There's no reason for it and there's no way I'm sharing my sudden misguided intuition. She'd enjoy being right way too much.

"Why couldn't it have just been in the main campground? What is it with guys and being in the wilderness?" I ask.

"It makes them feel manly and tough...like cavemen," Lucy answers with a shrug.

"Hot," I deadpan, watching the firelight flickering in orange-yellow slivers through the web of branches in front of Brown Sugar's hood, as I pick up on strains of some basic soft-rock and the distinctive smell of pot filtering through the thick stand of pine trees separating us from the campsite.

"Great," Lucy mutters in an irritated voice, leaning over to undo her seatbelt, "the sweet smell of pot. It should be an awesome party; I sure do love them potheads."

"If it really sucks, I promise we'll go. It's just the guys, at least," I reply, offering a compromise to what I'm sure would be her preferred course of action: leaving immediately.

"Yeah, I guess, but there's no way any *Rocky Horror* action is happening with what's-his-face now, I don't care how hot he is."

"What?" I ask. "You don't want to see his creature of the night?" I ask as I lower my tone suggestively.

Lucy barks out a laugh. "Nope, I sure don't wanna see his 'little Nell,' but at least we can get drunk and forget those truckers and their creeptastic audition for the remake of *Deliverance*."

"Heh, nice," I respond, glad she's not insisting we turn around right now before something evil decides to attack us, or whatever she imagines is going to happen.

Lucy smiles and stretches, then rubs her hands over her face. She then takes her sunglasses off the top of her head where they were holding her bangs in place since the sun started going down and the tinted lenses became superfluous, and deposits them in her zombie-themed bag. Is it any wonder she's obsessed? She looks as tired from the journey as I feel.

We unlock our doors and step out of the van in unison causing another mild wave of giggles. Man, we really are tired…or else that pot is ridiculously strong. Lucy pauses to text her parents, letting them know we arrived safe and sound because she's a "good girl, who doesn't let her parents worry needlessly"— according to my mother, anyway. After she's done being responsible, she heads around to the back of the van and I lean back into the driver's seat, grabbing my giant purse; my cell phone slides into view and it displays two missed calls from my mother.

I groan loudly, my hands over my face, which distorts the groan into something along the lines of "Blargha," causing Lucy to poke her head out from behind the van, mild concern written on her face.

"What?" she asks.

"Rosalind called." I stick out my lower lip in a mock pout. "I hate when my mom wants to talk right before I wanna have sex. I swear it's like she has a seventh sense for these things. Her sixth sense, of course, is for detecting weaknesses in her children that she can use in her damn guilt trips."

"Of course," Lucy replies, smirking as she disappears behind the van again.

"Oh, shut up. You don't know, your parents aren't crazy," I grumble in her direction then try to ignore her sarcastic "Ha!" as I continue to contemplate my phone. Sadly, despite my best psychic efforts, the missed call and voicemail indicators continue to mock me with their continued existence.

"It's not the same type of crazy; she's like an artist when it comes to guilt. Do you want to know how she guilt-tripped me last time?" I persist, switching to my Roz impersonation voice, "'You want that I should die? Alone and unloved by my children, found two weeks later, dead and burst all over the floor only discovered by an Alsatian dog?' They don't even have a dog! I don't know what dog she thinks is going to be discovering her or where she thinks my dad will have gone, or why her body has apparently burst for some reason. Ugh! She is so over dramatic," I growl, shaking my fist at the cruel heavens above for sticking me with such a tiring mother, just as Lucy leans around the back of the van again.

"Hmm, can't imagine what having someone overly dramatic in your life is like," she remarks, her voice dripping with sarcasm.

"Oh, hush. Just go back to what you're doing. I guess I should call her back or she'll probably call in the damn army or something," I gripe as Lucy chuckles and disappears again. I don't know what the hell she's doing back there, but I'm too busy with the distressing thought of talking to my mother to worry about it right now. Just as I'm thinking this and trying to find some way around it, the damn thing rings again, the strident sound of Stewie from *Family Guy* ("Curse you, vile woman!") drowning out the quiet music drifting over from the campsite as the screen flashes the picture of my mom's caller ID, the one she made me re-take about ten times before she let me assign it.

Figuring it's the lesser of two evils, I just take a deep breath and put the phone up to my ear. "Hi, Ma."

"I thought we agreed that now that you're an adult, and for some reason refuse to ask my permission when you go out of town that you would at least call your poor mother when you are taking your life into your own hands and leaving town, instead of letting me find out about your escapades from one of your brothers or your father."

"And a normal and functional hello to you, too, Ma. We made it safely, in case you were wondering."

"I should hope so. Gallivanting at all hours of the night, two young women, alone, without protection, in the wild!" She whispers "wild" as though it's a four-letter word and I roll my eyes skyward.

"How very forward thinking of you, Dr. Lafontaine. Way to be a feminist, Ma. And you know very well that I can defend myself, and so can Lucy."

"That women's self-defence class can only take you so far. I don't want you getting grand ideas about yourself, thinking you're invincible and ending up hurt—your father and I tried to keep your feet on the ground, but *no*—head always in the clouds. Why can't you be more like your dear brothers?" she sighs, exasperated.

I can hear her nails clicking against the phone as she lapses into one of her patented guilt-inducing silences, and I notice Lucy finally emerging from the van with our bags. I make a face at her, showing my annoyance with my mom and she rolls her eyes and mouths that she wants the keys to lock up the van; I toss them to her, take another deep breath and resign myself to continuing this painful conversation. I start talking again, interrupting the flow of my mother's expert guilting power of disappointed silence.

"Ma, listen, for one thing, it was *not* just a women's self-defence course, but whatever, never mind that, I'm *not* like my 'dear' brothers, and I'm never going to be, you're just going to have to accept that one of these days. Now, Lucy and I are here and we're kind of late so…"

I'm forced to trail off as my mother begins anew with yet another diatribe. "Well, now! I never knew you harboured such resentment towards your brothers, Ophelia, and as for your tone, there are no words for how disappointed I feel. I cannot believe that a child I birthed—after fourteen hours of brutal labour—from my very own loins, cannot find it in her heart to listen to the woman that has been there all her life. The woman who's guided and raised her to make good, positive decisions—"

"Ma!"

"It just breaks my heart…I'm surprised you can't hear it cracking all the way up in God only knows where you are—"

"MA! Enough! I love my brothers and I'll try to be more like say, Samson, in the future and have lots of beautiful babies. A plan I aim to get on with in, oh"—I glance at the time on my phone's screen—"about two minutes, notwithstanding the end of this seemingly eternal conversation." I take a calming breath and think about Carson, think about Carson shirtless. It works well, almost too well…okay, that's way too weird with my mom on the phone. I shake my head to clear it and reluctantly allow her voice to come back into clarity.

"I'm just glad that you seem to have finally come to your senses," she says, completely ignoring my innuendo and obvious reluctance to continue the conversation.

I try again, deciding just to be as clear as possible. "I have to go, tell Daddy I love him."

"Murray, your wayward child is saying she loves you, even though she has neglected to include me in that sentiment. Murray? Murr—"

"Ma! I really do have to go. We're meeting people, okay?"

"Fine, fine. I know I'm just a nuisance to my only daughter—it breaks my heart constantly. Give my love to Lucy...as much as I can give with a broken heart anyway."

"Bye, Ma. We love you and your broken heart, too." I roll my eyes and finally, mercifully, hang up the phone.

"Shall we?" Lucy asks as she comes up to me carrying her black canvas duffle bag over her shoulder and handing me my overnight bag.

I tuck the cell phone back in my purse and swing my quilted brown and turquoise flowered bag over my shoulder, briefly wondering if it's weirdly heavier than I remember, or if I'm just imagining things because I'm tired. "That woman is insane. And exhausting. Can you carry me? I'm now heavy with guilt-trip induced complexes; I don't know if I can walk."

Lucy laughs and says, "Let's go, drama queen," and starts heading towards the music, crouching down a bit to make it unscathed past the branches.

I am not a drama queen! But I'm too tired to argue so I let it drop and turn to follow her, jerking to a halt when Lucy comes to a sudden stop in front of me, growling, but sounding more tired than actually angry as she says, "For Christ's sake!"

Lucy

"You okay?" Lia asks as I stop abruptly in front of her.

"No." I pivot slowly, a Barbie-pink stiletto in my hand—the item responsible for the sudden stop and the newly unimpressed tone in my voice. "Unless they're secret drag-queens, we've got company. Sex kitten company, judging from the shoes."

"Shit," Lia breathes. She's obviously pissed off, too, but I know she's just as exhausted as I am and I know that she's really looking forward to seeing Carson, so I'm guessing she'll want to continue on anyway. I just wish that it wasn't so late so that there were other options for where we're gonna be sleeping tonight, other than at the skeevy motel attached to the diner from hell or with the sexed-up, pot-smoking strangers in the woods. So many goddamn horror movie survival rules are being broken here, how on Earth can I be expected to relax?

"I thought it was just going to be the guys," I say as I drop the shoe on the ground where it lands with a dull thud.

"That's what Carson said!" Lia replies, her voice turning into a whine as she contemplates the shoe on the ground. "I don't know what happened," she continues, her voice small now.

I feel a bubble of fresh anger rise up in my gut. I literally could not care less if *Rocky Horror* guy Brad is banging some other chick, but no one gets to make Lia's voice sound like that. I'm gonna kill Carson.

Lia glances down at the offensively pink shoe I found and shakes her head. "At this point, I am hoping for secret drag queens..." she trails off and the angry bubble in my stomach grows.

"I'm sorry, Li. I didn't realize you liked him so much."

"I don't! I just really wanna do the pleasure grind!" She whines and I pull her into a hug, laughing, feeling slightly better now that I know it's not real feelings, but just lusty ones on the line. But I still might have to kill Carson.

"I know, and it sucks, but at least if he is a two-timing asshole, which unfortunately seems like it's the case, you can have the pleasure of grinding his ass into dust with your sheer badassery, not to mention whatever chick cunt-punted you," I say, trying to comfort her.

"It's not the same," she protests, "and 'badassery' is not a word."

"Well, it should be. Now come on, maybe Janet, Brad, Dr. Scott, Rocky, blank stare is the only one two-timing here," I say and receive a blank stare in reply. "What? I told you, I couldn't resist doing that since you made the reference. This is your fault."

She rolls her eyes and throws the straps of her bags over her shoulder again. "You're really weird, you know that?"

"I know."

"Just checking. Let's go." And with that she sets out in front of me and we soon enter the clearing with the camp fire, complete with Janet, Brad, Dr. Scott, Rocky, blank stare sitting in a chair with some random blonde chick straddling his lap and stuck to his face.

Lovely. Although, honestly, better her than me. He wears pastel shirts with popped collars. As far as I'm concerned, I dodged a bullet.

"Nice," Lia says, taking in the sight of the two sucking face, which hasn't slowed at all upon our arrival.

"Indeed," I answer, then pat her on the shoulder, saying, "Good luck with Carson." Lia frowns at me and I feel the need to clarify, "I'm not being sarcastic, I swear. Just trying to be supportive."

"Oh. It's hard to tell sometimes."

"Yeah, I know. But seriously, good luck," I say then head over to the cooler, fishing out a Mike's Hard Pomegranate something-or-other from the wide selection of girly drinks floating amidst icy water. I nod at Lia and make a fist with my free hand—the gesture of support we've adopted from our shared love of Korean dramas.

She briefly smiles and looks off into the woods, as if wondering where to go to search for the wayward Carson. I sit in a vacant chair as far from the coupling of Brad and random girl as I can get, and take my iPod out of my bag, plugging in my ear buds and getting ready to keep myself occupied while Lia goes in search of one type of pleasure grind or another.

Chapter Three
I do like horror movies, but it's not so fun when it's so goddamn real

Connor

The fluorescent bulbs buzz overhead as we watch the two scientists up front discuss something, their faces anxious as the two security guards they brought with them finally return, muscling in an old TV and VCR set on a rolling stand. I shift in the uncomfortable chair, looking at Luca for direction as the others shift in displeasure, too, but he's just sitting with his eyes forward, back rigid with his always perfect posture, looking completely unflappable as usual.

I roll my eyes and rub a hand over my face, pulling my cheeks and mouth downward until I make the expression my mama always says makes me look like a fish. I feel like a beached fish, just waiting for the scientists to tell us what they're doing here.

We were just in the middle of a training exercise all the way out here in the middle of Jesus-fucking nowhere, freezing our asses off back home in the Great White North, when the scientists and the guards dropped in with their chopper and the order from on high that we were to "lend them our assistance." I just wish we knew why.

We'd all—except for Luca, who, as far as I can tell, has no opinion—prefer if the scientists would just tell us what the fuck happened, who or what we've been called on to contain or fight, but they just avoided the questions, saying it would be better if we saw it for ourselves. So we've just been sitting here for an hour while their 'roided-up lackeys went in search of ancient video equipment, 'cause for some reason their security tape is still on VHS.

There's a rumbling of restlessness throughout the guys as the steroid junkies try to figure out how to set everything up, only silenced when Luca turns in his chair and glowers at us for a few seconds. It's enough; if he's not asking questions, we shouldn't be either.

Finally, the muscle-heads seem to have figured out all the necessary plug-ins and the TV sparks reluctantly to life. I hope it's a good movie. Not like those ones I used to have to watch in Catholic school about how God would smite you if you masturbated, which was pretty much the extent of our sex ed. Who were they kidding, anyway? What teenage guy do they think wouldn't believe it's worth it to get smited...smote? Smoten? Anyway, I guess I should probably start paying attention, 'cause it looks like the movie's about to start and I don't wanna get Luca mad at me.

The old scientist, Gregory—who has a look on his face like a combination of sucking on a lemon and smelling something bad, which judging from his generally persnickety behaviour, I wouldn't be surprised to learn was his normal expression—walks forward and puts the tape in the VCR saying, "What you will see here are some test subjects for a new appetite suppressant pill we were developing. One of the test subjects reacted...badly, as you will see." He makes a harrumphing noise as he walks back toward the other, geeky-looking scientist named Elliot and takes out a pipe, leaning against the wall and going on to act like we don't exist.

Stuffy old British dude.

The tape starts to roll with a quiet hum, the screen turning from blue to grey before finally settling on a black and white image of what I'm guessing were the sleeping quarters for the test subjects. Three chubby chicks are sleeping on a set of bunk beds placed against the far wall of the room; one of the bottom bunks is unoccupied, probably belonging to a fourth chick who's pacing the room, looking just a bit crazy. She walks toward the intercom on the other side of the room and punches it, hard, then stands in front of it, shifting her weight as she waits for a response.

"Yes?" the voice on the intercom crackles in response to her buzz.

The chick shifts again, more aggressively, like she just can't stand still, before growling, "I'm hungry. I thought you said this pill was supposed to suppress my appetite, not make it worse. I'm fucking starving!" With this, she pounds the wall again and resumes pacing as the others move around in their sleep, responding to the ruckus she's making.

"The pill will work differently for different people and that's why we have to do these tests, to work out the last few bugs. Just give it some more time," the voice from the intercom crackles again before going silent. The chick looks enraged and starts mumbling to herself, pacing faster.

"So we were called in here to round up some fuckin' hungry, hungry hippos? I really don't think you need us Doc—you need a damn Twinkie! Feed her ass before she goes on a rampage," Locklan pipes up, ever the smart-ass. Well, dumb-ass is more accurate, but he's being a smart aleck, as my mama would say.

Luca turns in his chair again and from the look on his face, he would obviously agree with Mama. But Locklan seems immune to the power of Luca's glower. I honestly don't know how this is possible, it gives me chills when it's not even directed at me, but he just stares back at him before asking the scientists again, "Seriously, man, what's the fuckin' problem?"

"Man, those girls are hungry alright, but they're hungry for more than food—they're hungry for some sausage! And I would be happy to oblige; I don't mind my girls having some meat on 'em!" Marco declares, gyrating in his seat before bumping fists with Locklan, and then shutting up as Luca turns the glower on him.

"Just keep watching," Elliot says, looking sick, though whether it's from the comments or the events to come in the video, I can't tell. "You'll see," he finishes, tugging at the neck of his Pearl Jam t-shirt nervously and one of the juiced-up guys, the biggest one, pats his shoulder. I wonder if they're, like, a couple or something—not that I have a problem with that sort of thing.

Locklan grunts scornfully but shuts-up, at least for now, as the cantankerous chick flops down on the unoccupied bed and seems to try sleeping for a few moments before she suddenly bolts back up into a sitting position, making Preacher jump a bit in his chair.

I admit, it's pretty damn eerie. She peers around like she's looking for something, and then she suddenly grabs her chest and collapses back down on the bed looking like a rag doll my baby sister used to have, which is messed up; healthy people aren't usually reminiscent of rag dolls.

I hear Preacher grunt in surprise, echoing my unspoken concern. "Did she have a heart attack?" he asks, alarmed.

"No, it was the hand of God," Locklan says, maintaining his asshole tendencies even in the face of death, which is a surprise to no one.

I laugh, trying to calm my fears by helping Locklan make Preacher's seem unreasonable. I'm not proud of this and I'm treated to instant karma when I feel a slap on the back of my head. I look over at Luca, who glowers at me. I force a grin, which is hard, 'cause like I said, his glowers are powerfully intense and scary.

To try to appease him, I scoot forward in my seat—it always used to pacify the nuns at school if you at least looked like you were riveted by whatever was going on. It works pretty well with Luca, too, and he turns back to face the screen again, giving me a warning look as he does so. Chills, I tell ya.

"Just keep watching, please," Elliot repeats, his voice shaking. I take a good look at him. It's an understatement to say he does not look good. He's so close to the same shade of green as our shirts, he could blend with the forest right now and his face is all sweaty like he might ralph at any second. He actually kinda reminds me of E.T. right now, which, given his name, makes me suppress a chuckle, even though I'm guessing he's already seen what happens next and by the look on his face, it won't be pretty. I wish I wasn't sitting in the front row now, just in case he does yak everywhere. I just washed my greens.

While I'm worrying about having to do emergency laundry, I notice the angry chick start to move again, and at first, I silently join Preacher as he breathes a sigh of relief, but it's soon obvious that something is still very wrong with her. She slides off the bed and onto the floor, moving like this snake I caught when I was a kid, then she crouches there and almost seems to sniff the air. Even in black and white, something about her colouring seems way off, and her movements are all jerky, just plain wrong.

My heart speeds up a little in spite of myself. I lean forward again in my desk, really intrigued now and not just faking it. It's no Coppola, but it has potential. There are chicks at least. And I have always loved horror movies.

I lean across the aisle to Luca, eyes still glued to the strange video and whisper, "Dude, do you know what would make this shit even better? If I had some skittles. Or kettle corn. I fuckin' love kettle corn, man, it's all sweet and salty. You know what else is good like that? Pretzels and chocolate. I mean—" I break off as I feel the chills start, seeing a severe glower contorting Luca's face.

Uh-oh.

I try to fix it by backtracking fast as I can. "Though this is good all on its own, too, I do love horror movies, you know that, and—" I break off again as Luca finally speaks, and let me tell you, his voice...it matches the glowers.

"Hey, Connor?"

Oh, man, he used my real name. I am in trouble.

"Yeah, bro?" I ask, trying to lighten him up with a grin.

"Shut the fuck up, *idiota*." He glowers at me until I wriggle, feeling all fish-like again. Man, if they could bottle that glower, parents would never have to worry about disciplining their children again...unless they had kids who were immune like Locklan, of course, but how often would that happen?

Jesus, I better apologize or he might never stop glowering at me. "Oh. Sure, Luke. Sorry, man."

"Just pay attention and sit still," he orders menacingly before shifting his attention back to the events happening on the screen. I shudder a bit—after affects—then do the same.

The weird chick is shifting her weight, still in that bizarre looking crouch. She rolls her head lazily, stretching her neck, when all of a sudden, the chick in the bunk above her moans in her sleep. Crazy chick suddenly jerks to look up and backwards at the girl sleeping above her. The angle of her neck looks like it would be so many kinds of painful but she doesn't even seem to notice, she just twists her body till it's facing the same direction, still on all fours. She sorta skitters toward the bed, moving like a spider, and I can feel the others shifting behind me, all of us starting to wonder what's gonna happen next. Except for Luca, he just sits there, calm as can be, staring straight ahead, completely focused on the screen.

And then it gets worse than I could've imagined. I do like horror movies, but it's not so fun when it's so goddamn real. The chick hops up onto the top bunk and is staring at the sleeping girl there like she's the meal she's been waiting so long for. She skitters forward, pausing for a second as the other girl finally wakes up, opens her eyes and mumbles, "What's going—" before the crazy chick pounces on her, mouth going for her throat.

"Alright, girl-on-girl! Even if it's fat chicks, it's still hot," Locklan chuckles. Marco and Jimmy laugh in agreement. I grin, slapping Luca on the shoulder. I want it to be true, just something funny they're showing us and not what I actually think is happening.

"Dude," I say to Luca, "it's so true." I grin at him again, wishing he'd play along so I wouldn't have to worry that I'm right. But he doesn't grin back; all he does is silently put his index finger to his lips, looking as impassive as Darryl or Carl. He's not gonna be calming me down anytime soon, so I take the hint, clearing my throat among the only sort-of whispered conversations going on around the room.

"Listen up, you Whiskey Tango fucks!" When I'm sure I have their full attention, I mimic Luca, and put my finger in front of my mouth. "SHHHH!"

"Who the hell you callin' Whiskey Tango, gingerbread?" Link growls. Rafe murmurs his commiserative annoyance and glowers at me. I throw a pen lid at Link's head and when he snarls in reply, I blow him a kiss. In response, he shouts, "Down in front you carrot-topped homo!"

I flip him off as the others laugh and I sit back down next to Luca. "How was that, Sarge?" I whisper across the aisle.

"*Bueno,* Mac. *Gracias.*" He's sarcastic, but at least he's back to using my nickname, so he can't be too mad at me anymore. Which is good, because angry Luca...not exactly a day at the park.

"No problem, boss. Anything for you." I reply, grinning as I twist back to the front, just in time to see the carnage.

On the screen, the insane chick (who I'm pretty sure is some kind of zombie at this point) pulls away from the unfortunate girl on the bed, who's throat is now torn open. The majority of her face is gone, too. It's apparently what the zombie chick was craving judging from how enthusiastically she's cruncha-munching on it. The skin is sticking out a bit between her teeth, blood's running down her jaw and onto the sterile looking white outfit she has on, staining it instantly. She continues to chomp happily on her face for a few seconds, and bends down for a second helping before jolting back upright as the girl in the next bunk over wakes up and starts screaming when she sees what's happening.

Her screams wake up the chick sleeping on the bunk under hers and she yells, "Jesus, Mary! What the hell is going on?" But when she sees the blood, she just starts screaming, too, and tries to run for the door, which turns out to be a big mistake. The zombie, having finished her appetizer, joins in on the screeching. She makes a fucking ungodly noise as she leaps off the bed and lands on the running chick, a move I bet she wouldn't have been able to complete before she turned into whatever the fuck she is now. As she enjoys her entrée of the second chick's face and neck, there's a pounding on the door.

It's obviously too little too late; the third girl starts screaming all over again, still paralyzed in her bed as the first victim suddenly sits up and turns her neck almost backward to look at her, blood pouring from her skinless face. Her throat is torn wide open and even on the shitty screen, we can see her windpipe—her fucking windpipe!

But she's somehow still alive...or alive enough. She shifts into the same position the first chick had been in before she pounced, and then she skitters across the beds over to the screaming girl, shrieking that same awful noise the whole way. She jumps on the other chick and starts to have herself a little snack, not wanting the first chick to have all the fun of tearing people's faces off, I guess.

The door finally bursts open, two security guys stopping short when they see the blood-soaked room. The two undead chicks stare at them for a second before they both screech again; sounding like nails on a chalkboard, and every noise you can't stand rolled into one. Leaping and skittering towards the guards, they finally tackle them and go to town all over again. Those undead bitches are sure greedy when it comes to their food. Those appetite suppressing pills really did *not* work.

I've never seen anything like that before, outside my collection of Romero movies, of course. I try to wrap my brain around what we just saw, and find myself coming back to the word "zombie" again and again. They were definitely goddamn zombies. Nothing else enjoys facial meat that much, except maybe Hannibal Lector, but that's a way less likely thing to turn into, so it's gotta be...

"Zombies," Rafe suddenly pipes up. He loves those movies as much as I do, so it's not surprising he's reached the same conclusion I have. "Those chubsters turned into fuckin' zombies! Jesus, they were chowing down on each other like it was their fucking job!"

Gregory steps forward and hits eject, tapping his pipe out over the floor before replacing it in his mouth, his hands shake a little as he does this. Elliot looks so close to puking, I'm surprised he hasn't fled the room yet, and even the steroid junkies look fully freaked. The room is quiet as everyone contemplates what we just saw. I notice Preacher's head is down as he mouths a silent prayer to himself. I feel like doing the same thing and I gave up Catholicism years ago. I make the sign of the cross anyways. A little good mojo never hurt anyone, right? Spectacles, testicles, wallet and watch, I think as my hand traces the still-familiar pattern.

Gregory harrumphs again, calming himself, and takes his pipe out of his mouth, saying, "We are not able to define exactly what happened to those women as of yet, however, as you can see, it is a very serious situation as anyone who is attacked, becomes...like that—"

"Like a zombie," Rafe pipes up again, and I feel myself nodding in agreement.

What else could they be?

Gregory pretty much ignores him, just clears his throat loudly before continuing, "They become like *that* within two hours at most, depending on the person and possibly the locale of the injury or attack. Sometimes it only takes a few minutes, as you saw. We could have told you what was happening, what the symptoms were, but we did not think that you would you have believed us without witnessing it."

"All I wanna know is how do we kill the nasty motherfuckers? I don't give a good goddamn what the fuck they are, just how do we kill 'em?" Link asks, his deep voice rumbling with the intensity of readying for a fight.

"Hoo-ah," a couple of the guys agree quietly.

The intensity's useful; it helps us switch back into soldier mode. Better to be intense, bordering on angry, than scared, and Link's right, once we know how to kill them for sure—based on the movies, it'll be all about damaging the heads, but it'd be good to be certain—what more will we need?

"How many are there?" Luca asks.

Oh, right. We might need to know that, too.

Elliot steps forward, seeming to have his urge to purge under control for now. "Unfortunately, on both counts, we're not quite sure," he continues to talk while a few more guys mumble and grunt in the background, soldier sounds, gearing up for battle, whether or not we know the odds. "It got out of control so quickly and there were so many people in the facility...those deemed most important were evacuated, the rest were left. We didn't have time to figure out how to kill them." He sounds sad and angry as he says this last part.

It's a combination of emotions we can all understand. The idea of leaving people behind isn't exactly something we're comfortable with.

Elliot takes a breather, collects himself and carries on, "But judging from how many people were likely in the facility and how quickly it spreads...there could be hundreds." He swipes a hand over his face, almost knocking his glasses off, he rights them, and then turns away, crossing his skinny arms over his scrawny chest. The bigger of the 'roid freaks pats him on the back again before crossing his own much bigger arms over his much brawnier chest. I really think they might be homos—not that it matters.

"What we need you to do," Gregory says, arrogantly taking over the conversation, "is to work on containment, elimination, and evacuation. Judging from how quickly they move, their constant appetite for fresh food sources and their resistance to death"—now that's a euphemism if I ever heard one—"none of the people in the area are safe; therefore, all of the surrounding campgrounds *must* be evacuated as quickly as possible. However, it is of great import that the citizens do not know what is really going on. You will tell them there are bears loose or some such thing, whatever it takes to get people to leave without telling them what has actually happened.

"The Mithras Corporation, our parent company, wishes this to be dealt with as swiftly as possible, with as few people knowing the truth as possible, as it would be quite damaging to them if this issue were to become public knowledge. If you encounter any of the..." Gregory pauses, apparently at a loss for a word to describe the zombies; he clears his throat and continues, "the afflicted, dispose of them in whatever way possible, do not under any circumstances allow yourselves to be bitten, as all victims have a 100% turn rate, no survivors."

No shit.

"I have another question," Luca says. Gregory's face gets contorted with annoyance but he nods his permission for Luca to continue.

Man, Luca's gotta be boiling up at the way this imperious bastard is treating him.

"How would the 'afflicted'"—you'd have to know Luca to pick up on it, but as he uses Gregory's word for the zombies, his disdain and irritation are obvious—"have been able to get this far south? Isn't your lab pretty far from here? And if they are likely to be in the area, shouldn't we quarantine everyone here instead of evacuating potentially "afflicted' persons that could spread this thing further?"

Gregory's face gets even more pinched—he almost looks like that old Barq's Root Beer guy now—and in a tight voice he says, "In regards to the possibility of the afflicted being present in the area, we had an incident on our way here that quite guarantees they'll be nearby. And as for setting up quarantine, the order from Colonel Flemming is to evacuate, so I would suggest you do just that." With this name-drop of a dude very high up in the ranks, he turns and suddenly heads toward the door, not giving anyone a chance to ask what kind of incident would bring the zombies down here from the lab, only pausing in the threshold to turn back and say, "Elliot," in a voice that makes it clear he's supposed to follow. He does, accompanied by the juiced-up lackeys, the smaller of whom says, "Good luck," before shutting the door behind them, leaving us alone.

I'd be annoyed that we don't know what "the incident" was but, like the others, I'm used to not asking questions. So we put the mysterious "incident" to rest and just move right along. "*Bueno*," Luca says as we all focus on him, awaiting our orders. "We have the map of the grounds and everyone has their comms?" he asks, receiving varied grunts from everyone in response. He nods then continues, "The best bet for a confirmed kill will be to go for the head—"

"Wow, thanks Sergeant Obvious," Locklan interrupts like the asshole we all know and love...oh wait, that's not right...like the asshole we all know and barely tolerate.

"Your mouth is open, Private Gates," Luca says, his voice cold and controlled—it's the tone that could almost give me nightmares...okay, it has occasionally given me nightmares before, I'll admit it. "You might want to see to that."

Chills again, and I'm not even the one in trouble! I don't know how Locklan is unaffected.

Locklan looks like he's about to say something flippant again, but Link cuffs him on the side of the head, almost knocking his stupid wigger-ass off his chair. "You shut that mouth, or I'll shut it for you—around my big donkey-dick."

"Keep dreamin', Link, it ain't never gonna happen, no matter how much you crave it," Locklan retorts, rubbing his head where Link smacked him.

"You are both such homos, why don't you just get it over with and make sweet, sweet love to each other already?" I say as I turn around. They're both glowering at me, but neither has the power of one of Luca's angry stares, so I don't even blink. They grumble a little and Locklan smacks Link across the face before turning around in his seat again. Link punches him hard in the back of the shoulder and Locklan winces, then we all finally focus on Luca again.

His gaze passes between the three of us and I give him my best "good little boy" face. I was just trying to help, so I should *not* be in trouble. Luckily, Luca just shakes his head and moves on. "The head will be our main target in the event of a sighting. Try for decapitation or a head shot and don't let them anywhere near you. We'll break into teams and begin the evac before it gets dark."

"Dude," I say, awe in my voice as I think about what's coming up. It was disconcerting to watch but this thing is actually kinda exciting. "It's like that game 'Deerhunter,' but with zombie chicks instead. Zombie-Chick Hunter. I can't wait to get some!"

"Necrophiliac," someone—Carl, I think—mutters.

So impolite. I flip him off and chuck the rest of my pen at him, earning a low intensity glower from Luca. He ignores Carl and says to me, "*Sí*, Mac, it's totally like an arcade video game. I'm sure none of those zombies are going to try and rip your throat out and make you one of their undead horde while you piss your *pantalones* in fear. It's just like 'Deerhunter.'" He grins, clapping a hand onto my shoulder.

"Bro, you are such a buzz kill," I whine, pulling away. He's a good leader, but he always has to ruin the fun.

"Hey, Mac?" he says with only a bit of a warning sound in his voice so I'm not too worried yet.

"Yeah, Luke?"

"Shut the fuck up." He's smiling as he says this, though, so I'm not hurt or anything; he says it all the time anyway…well, lots of people do actually, but in this situation, it's best just to follow orders.

"Sure, Luke."

"*Bien*, let's get the geeks and the other two back in here, so we can brief them on comms."

In an effort to keep Luca happy with me, I leap up quickly to volunteer to call the scientists back in and some of the guys snigger behind me. I ignore them, opening the door and looking out into the hall. I can't see them, so I head to the storage rooms they'll be sleeping in. On the way, I can't help freaking myself out a little while walking the empty hallway alone. This is always where someone would bite it in the movies, wandering off by themselves and ending up as the munchies for some rogue zombie who snuck in somehow.

"Um, hey?" I jump at the sound of Elliot's voice, scaring him and myself. "S-sorry, I didn't mean to sneak up on you. Did you want something?"

"No worries, man, just spooked a bit from the video, I guess." I laugh, a little embarrassed to have been caught freaking out. I'm just glad it was Elliot who found me and not one of the guys. He looks less like he's gonna be puking all over the place and his skin doesn't match our greens quite so closely anymore, so I'm not worried about standing next to him now. "We wanna brief you guys on our comm system, so you can reach us and vice versa if we need to while we're evac-ing the camps."

"Um, yeah, no problem. I'll just grab them." He disappears into the room I just passed and returns with the others. We walk back to the briefing room in uncomfortable silence. I'm glad it's a short walk. Luca nods at them as we enter and I sit back down in my chair.

"*Bueno.* These are our teams: Donahue, McCoy, Kane, and myself are team Alpha; Church, Cooke, and Cantolena are Team

Bravo; and Halley, Cho, and Gates will be team Charlie. The leads will be Church, Cho, and myself."

A few of the guys grumble about their placement—I wouldn't be surprised if Darryl and Carl were grumbling internally, but they're good soldiers, they never question orders and besides, they're the best at keeping Locklan in line so their position is no surprise—but Luca continues, talking over anyone protesting to make it clear there will be no arguments. "We'll be on comm channel 0082. Stay on that channel. When on comms, my call sign is 'Charlie Actual.'"

"Um," Elliot says, his hand raised, one finger pointing up, "What does 'Charlie Actual' mean?"

A few of the guys snort at his ignorance, not to mention his raised hand. I don't. I feel kinda sorry for the little guy. I just wanna give him a cookie or something and tell him to go take a nap and let the big boys handle this mess.

"It just means I'm team leader," Luca responds seriously, giving Locklan the evil eye while doing so to warn him once again to keep his mouth shut. "Our rally point will be the main campground check-in area. It's outlined in red on your maps. It's eighteen hundred now, so we'll have one hour to canvas the area and an additional hour and a half to clear it before it's completely dark. We meet back at twenty one hundred no matter what. If you're somehow detained, use your comms. Now move out, we've got some civs to evac and some zombies to deep-six," Luca growls as he heads for the door, nodding at the scientists as he exits.

Hoo-ah.

Elliot

As the soldiers leave to evacuate the surrounding campgrounds, I feel my head swim again. It's been hard to focus all afternoon since Gregory told me, and then showed me what was happening with the crappy cell phone video he took of the security monitors. Not to mention everything that happened in the helicopter on the way down from the lab. How Mitch hid his bite until we were already in the air, well away from the lab.

We were flying over Crystal Lake when Terry noticed the blood. Mitch must have been hoping we wouldn't realize that he had been bitten, but Terry saw the blood and made him roll up his pant leg and we saw it. The memory still makes me queasy. That wound was one of the grossest things I've ever seen, all pus and blood and torn, greenish skin. Terry was going to shoot him, but Gregory panicked and just pushed Mitch out of the chopper. I never even saw him hit the ground. We were flying so fast that Jake, the pilot Mithras sent down with the helicopter, didn't even notice, just continued on until we landed on the roof of the fort a couple of minutes later. Then he was surprised to find Mitch gone.

And, God, that video. No matter how many times I see that video, I'll never get used to what happens on it. Never get used to that noise they make. It's like the most terrifying things you can think of made into one dreadful sound. And I can't bear to think of all those people we left behind today, even though Terry told me it was more than likely that they'd all mostly been turned by the time Gregory and I were evacuated, I still can't help picturing all those people I worked with turning into…those things…zombies.

I try to remember how I felt earlier today when I was sure Terry was playing a prank on me, but now, with everything that's happened, I just can't. I try to remember how I felt just the other day, re-reading Pete Moon's graphic novel series, *Shadowlands,* for about the hundredth time. I was re-reading the first one, *One Bright Day in the Shadows*, where there's World War III and in the post-apocalyptic world following it, humans have to defend themselves from those who mutated from the nuclear weapons used. It used to be my favourite series, but now, I can't remember the excitement I used to feel as I read about the main human character, Hunter, leading his small band of remaining humans in the fight against the mutants. I just can't. Now that it's sort of real, or on its way to it, I can't regain that feeling. It's not exciting, it's terrifying and I can't think straight no matter how hard I try.

It was bad enough seeing it happen to the women in the study, whom we'd only worked with for a couple of weeks, but to think of it happening to people I've worked with for years, it's almost unbearable. My hands won't stop shaking. They just keep twitching like they're not even attached to my body anymore. It's a nervous tic attached to emotions so crazy I never even knew I had it before.

Gregory says that the only reason I'm not some sort of flesh-eating zombie is because when the facility went into lockdown, I was sleeping late, so I was the only one left on the floor. I never knew sleeping in could save my life.

Lucky me.

Gregory's still human (or as human as he gets) because he was monitoring the women when it happened. He immediately put the compound into the emergency lockdown protocols, which simultaneously sets off the alarms, locks all of the hallways, stairwells, and entry doors, as well as wiping the system's electronic memories (to protect the company's reputation in the event of a mishap). That's why we only have a VHS tape to demonstrate what happened. The VHS tapes are a safeguard against losing all info, in case a lockdown is initiated accidentally. After the lockdown was in place, Gregory headed straight for the heli-pad and told the security guards to retrieve me. Terry was the only one who made it, but he didn't realize what had happened until later; they'd split up early on because they weren't sure where I was.

Lucky Terry.

He's surprised me since we've found out what's going on. I would've thought he'd be more like Jake, laughing it off and acting all tough, like he isn't scared. But instead, he's the most human I've ever seen him. He's lost a lot of friends today, too; saw two of them get eaten on that goddamn tape, and he seems to be attached to the familiarity I represent. I don't blame him; Gregory is acting completely unaffected, completely inhuman as always. It makes me think that he wouldn't even be turned if he did get bitten, I just don't think there's enough humanity in him to be turned into something else. He's obsessed now with us (mostly him though, I'm sure) not taking the blame once Mithras reviews everything that went wrong. It's a good defence mechanism I suppose, though with Gregory, it's probably just what it seems to be: self-centred concerns about self-preservation above all else. I'm sure the only reason that he's shaken at all isn't because of what happened to everyone else, what could happen to others if they're not evacuated in time, but of what could have happened to him. Selfish jerk.

I wish Mithras had been able to send us more soldiers. I doubt very much that the ten guys who were in the area will be enough, but Gregory said that the people at Mithras didn't really seem to believe him when he told them what was happening, even after he sent them the cell phone video, so they just sent us to these guys and told us to make do. At least most of the soldiers seem to realize the gravity of the situation. That's why I insisted on showing the video to the soldiers first, before explaining the situation, because I really want them to know what they're up against so they have the best possible chance of fighting it.

"You okay, Doc?" Terry asks now, looking concerned.

What a difference the threat of an apocalypse makes.

"I don't think I'm in danger of throwing up anymore; so that's something," I say, trying to hide at least a bit of just how scared I am. Not that Terry cares anymore. He's scared, too. Like I said, a post-apocalyptic world seems cool in *Shadowlands*, but in real life? I can barely breathe, I'm so terrified. "I'll feel better when I know the campgrounds have been evacuated," I continue and Terry nods his agreement as we walk back towards the room the soldiers set up for us in one of the bigger storage areas. Terry, Jake, and I are all sharing one room, but Gregory insisted on having his own, of course. He's such a jerk; he doesn't even care what might happen in the worst case scenario, it's still all about him.

Chapter Four
I think that something, like, bit me...

Blaine

I do feel kind of bad about forcing Nate to come out here with me; Daffy is really a piece of work, and I know Nate hates her already, but what choice did I have? Tifani is so goddamn hot and she said she'd only come up here with me if I brought a friend to distract her friend. Daffy's distracted alright: she hasn't left Nate's side since they met. Nate's distracted, too... distracted by forcing himself to stop thinking of ways to kill her in her sleep, maybe, but he's distracted. So while Nate continues to fend off Daffy's advances, I grab Tif's hand and we slip away into the woods for a little private time, so I can finally make my mojo work for me.

We find a little clearing not far from the camp, and I set down a blanket and turn on the sexy mix I made on my iPhone to put Tif in the mood and about fifteen minutes later, the private time is going great, Tifani's totally under my spell, judging from how quickly she slid her tube top off, not to mention that we're already horizontal on the blanket. But as we're making out, a weird shrieking sound echoes through the trees, just loud enough to be heard over the music and she pulls away from me, looking scared.

"What's wrong?" I ask, hoping she'll get over it quickly so we can get back to magic-time.

"Did you, like, hear that?" she asks. Jesus. I'm tempted to say something mean, but I don't want to ruin my chances of having sex.

"It's probably just a coyote or something, sweetie," I reply, aiming for soothing. It seems to work and we get back to business. Unfortunately, a few minutes later, as we're finally on our way to the really good stuff, there's a loud rustling in the bushes near us, then Tifani yelps, kicking out and pushing me away again, looking even more frightened than before. I don't know what could have spooked her so much, it's not like she's a virgin.

"What's wrong now?" I ask, trying to sound concerned and not exasperated.

"I think...um..."

This is the one drawback to dating chicks like this: more often than not, they could just barely beat a sack of hair in an I.Q. test and it takes them forever to tell stories.

"I think..."

Jesus.

I zip my pants back up as Tifani continues falteringly. The magic show seems to be definitely put on hold now, so I rock back on my heels and get comfortable as I wait for her to finish.

"I think that something, like, bit me? Or something?" She lifts up her right leg and points to her foot, which is, for some reason, now shoe-less. "And it stole my shoe!" she finally finishes, exclaiming indignantly.

That was painful.

I hand Tif back her shirt, resigned to listening to her blather on about whatever she thinks just happened. "I'm sure nothing stole your shoe, Tif," I say in an attempt to reassure her. Then I ask, "What kind of bite was it? Like a mosquito or a spider? What?" In the meantime, I look around the surrounding area for her missing shoe that is both ridiculously expensive and ridiculously pointy, especially for camping, but it's not as if I'm in this for her brains or her practicality. Tifani just shakes her head as she puts her shirt back on.

Damn.

"I don't think so? It really hurt, like a lot? Maybe you should, um, look at it?" She tries to pull up the leg of her skinny jeans to show me the alleged bite, but she can't quite do it because they're so damn tight, which is normally a good thing, but not so much right now. She's giving me a head ache. She probably scraped her leg on something and scared herself...women.

"Alright, well let's go back to the campsite, then, where there's more light, and Daffy can help you with it, okay?" I suggest and Tif nods, sniffling as she reaches up to take my outstretched hand.

"Thanks, Blainey, you're, like, such a sweetie?" she says as she stands up, kissing me on the cheek while standing on one leg.

Yeah, that's what I was aiming for tonight.

I pull her up into my arms so she doesn't injure her bare foot and as we get back to the fire pit, I spot Daffy, but Nate is nowhere to be seen. I wonder if he really was serious about locking himself in the truck if Daffy was too forward with him. I tell the girls I'm going to look for him since Daffy has no idea where he went almost a half hour ago. As I head towards the truck, I can hear Tif telling Daffy about her ordeal, and so many question marks are happening in that conversation that it's not even funny anymore, especially since whatever "bit" Tif totally cock-blocked me.

Nate's not in his truck and I'm about to call his cell when he appears from the direction of the john, looking both annoyed and relieved to see me at the same time, an expression he seems to get a lot lately.

"Hey, man, magic-time get cut *short* this evening?" he asks as he approaches the truck, fishing a beer out of the cooler in the bed.

"Oh, fuck you, man. It wasn't *my* fault; Tif said that something 'bit' her. I have no idea what," I protest, resenting his taking my current blue-balled condition so lightly, not to mention blaming it on me. "All I know is that it was sadly *not* the one-eyed snake."

Nate laughs then takes a sip of his beer before asking, "What did the bite look like?" If it was someone else, I would think it was concern for Tif's health that incited his question, but the more likely scenario is that his survival instincts are kicking in, just in case something actually dangerous is on the loose.

"I don't know. I didn't get a look at it; she couldn't pull her jeans up high enough." I can't help laughing at the memory of this, in spite of what it cost me, and Nate chuckles, too, handing me a beer as he does so. "It was probably just a spider or something. Or for all I know, a twig." I laugh again, drinking my beer, thinking if I can't get laid, I can at least get drunk.

"Or maybe it *was* a snake, just not yours." Nate jokes, laughing at the offended look on my face. The nerve, I tell you; if he wasn't so much bigger and stronger than me, I'd totally...oh, who am I kidding, he'd still be able to kick my ass. I'm a lover, not a fighter. Although, sadly, tonight it looks like I won't even be a lover.

Time for a subject change, I think. "So, what were you doing in the john for so long? Daffy said you were gone for 'like, an hour,' were you hiding from her?"

"Yes," Nate replies bluntly. "I didn't feel like dealing with her giant salad of stupidity anymore, so I told her I had to 'shoot one out to make room for dinner' and left."

I chuckle at the mental image of the look on Daffy's face when Nate said this. "Yup, it worked well," Nate says, confirming that Daffy was horrified at his behaviour.

"I guess we should probably head back," I say, then at Nate's disgusted expression continue, "I know man, but if we aren't back soon, they'll probably come looking for us and then what?"

He sighs and says, "I guess," then he chugs the rest of his beer, tossing the can in the back of the truck.

"Let's go then and get it over with." He starts back towards the camp, then thinks better of it and grabs another couple of beers from the cooler. Good idea. I follow his lead and grab another couple for myself. "You owe me big for this, by the way," he gripes as we walk towards the campsite.

"That's why I bought your favourite beer," I say, grinning.

"Doesn't even begin to cover it, man, at this point we're talking—" Nate falls silent suddenly and turning to follow his gaze, I see why: an army-type truck is driving away from the other side of the campsite.

"'The hell?" I ask, looking at Nate, who shakes his head, looking just as confused as I feel.

"What was that about?" Nate asks as we approach the girls.

"Um, something's apparently, like, loose around here or something? They said that we should pack up? Because it's totes dangerous or whatev?" Daffy ends this scholarly statement with a shrug. I really do owe Nate huge for refraining from killing her.

Nate sighs and rakes his hands through his hair, tugging on the strands—a sign of him being seriously pissed off. I don't blame him; getting actual information out of chicks like this is worse than pulling your own teeth without anaesthetic.

"*What* did they say was loose? And *how* dangerous is it supposed to be, *exactly*?" he asks, through gritted teeth.

"Um, well," Tifani begins replying as Nate removes his hands from his hair only to ball them into fists. "I think, um..."

Oh, Jesus, here she goes again, trying to think—definitely not her strong suit.

"They said something about a pack of bears...or something?" she finishes, looking confused, then victorious for some reason. "Maybe that's what, like, chomped me? And stole my shoe?"

Oh God.

"You think a pack of bears bit you...and stole your...shoe?" Nate asks, not unfairly since that's what it sounded like she said.

"No, silly. Just, like, one...maybe? Or something?" Tifani replies, waving his apparently ridiculous question off.

"Tif, sweetie," I begin, gently, since there may still be some chance of me having sex this weekend, and I don't want to screw it up by being obviously rude like Nate. Not that it would likely matter since they don't even seem to notice how agitated he is. "I don't think you'd be walking if a bear bit your leg. Did you tell the army guys that something bit you?"

"No, I forgot. They were, like, so totally cute, I just blanked." Tif says, grinning.

Bitch.

"Mmhmm, except for that one that kept, like, talking about God. But the other two were totes yum," Daffy confirms, looking to see if she's making Nate jealous. Of course, he doesn't even notice, just pulls his hands through his hair again and begins to pace.

"Are you sure they said it was bears that are on the loose?" He asks, trying to get Daffy to focus.

"Totes! Sort-of. Like pretty sure?" Daffy replies, in a very inept demonstration of the verb. She then looks at Tif for verification of this sentiment.

"Okay." Nate sighs again, pinching the bridge of his nose in exasperation. "How sure would you say? Like 80 percent? 70? What?"

"Well," Daffy replies, looking tired from all the exhausting thinking she's trying to do. "I'm, like, 70/40 percent sure they totes said bears." Nate makes a strangled noise at this, suddenly turning and stalking away, back in the direction of the truck.

Huh. I know they're annoying, but I'm not sure what caused that.

Daffy looks at me. "What's his problem? Is he, like, afraid of bears?"

"Something like that," I say, then turning to Tifani, I notice that she was finally able to roll her pants up high enough, so I continue. "Hey, Tif, why don't you show me that bite now?"

"'Kay," she says, plopping onto one of the chairs surrounding the fire and removing the Kleenex bandage they made, and shows me the wound.

Okay, so maybe she wasn't exaggerating. I inhale sharply when I see it, to which Tif responds, "I know, gross, right?"

Definitely gross. The skin is peeling away from her ankle, the wound swollen and full of yellowish-white goo. Bite marks are clearly indented, looking way too deep considering they would have had to get through her jeans; speaking of, I take a closer look at them. Whatever bit her had enough jaw strength to puncture and tear right through the denim. Spooky.

"Geez, Tif that looks pretty bad, you should've told those soldiers about it so they could get you to a doctor," I say, actually feeling pretty worried now that I know how bad it is.

"No need to worry about that," Nate declares as he suddenly arrives back in the campsite, dark green duffle bag over his shoulder and big, scary rifle in hand. "We're going to them," he asserts, handing me my leather satchel.

"What?" Tifani, Daffy, and I, all ask in unison, which, I don't think I have to tell you, is fairly disturbing. Tif and Daffy laugh, again in unison, as Nate explains.

"I know these woods really well. I grew up here, and there's never been more than a few bears around here, if any, at this time of year. Besides that, if there was for some reason a bear or two—they don't travel in packs—still around, they wouldn't be telling us to evacuate, just to be careful and keep our eyes open. They're not much to worry about if there's only a couple. Something else is going on here, and I'm going to find out what it is." Nate's face is determined, and even if I didn't trust his judgement on things like this, I'd be going with him, because the look on his face is serious enough to let me know that even if nobody else goes with him, he's going after the soldiers.

Besides, if there is something really dangerous on the loose in these woods, I definitely want to be with Nate; he always has a small arsenal of weapons with him—something left over from the "training" his dad made him endure when he was a kid—so whatever's going on in these woods, being with him is probably the safest place to be right now.

Connor

"You're telling me there's a pack of rabid bears traipsing through these mountains?" The very belligerent and very fat man asks as his equally fat and only slightly less belligerent wife snorts at her husband's apparent wit. Luca growls and swipes a hand over his face, looking at me expectantly to indicate I should take over before he decks the guy.

"Sir, listen, they are very dangerous, very rabid bears and we're trying to contain them, but we're not sure how many there are, so, for the sake of your family's safety, please just cooperate and evacuate from the area. Please don't mistake my easy tone for this being something about which you have a choice. This is not a suggestion. It's imperative that you—"

He cuts me off abruptly, raising his voice over mine, his giant moustache twitching with his indignation. "You know, you sure use a lot of big words for someone who doesn't seem to realize that bears don't travel in packs," he says, looking at me smugly as his wife snorts again and pops another roasted marshmallow into her fat face.

I knew we shoulda gone with a different story but, no, Gregory said bears were the simplest explanation. What an idiot; this is all his fault.

"Besides that," the fatty starts up again, "what does the army have to do with rabid bears?"

Damn. A good point and yet another flaw in Gregory's "master plan." However, no good could come of abandoning this ship completely, so I'll have to stick it out...though that doesn't mean I can't tweak it a little to try and make it sound a little more convincing.

"Like I said, sir, we're here for containment and evacuation purposes; however, you're right, we didn't get called in just for that. It's not just bears you need to worry about," I begin, lowering my voice conspiratorially.

"Mac," Luca says warningly from behind me, but I hold up a hand telling him to back off.

"They deserve to know the truth," I say, looking back at him and winking so he knows I'm not gonna disclose the zombie info.

The fat couple looks smugly at each other, satisfied that they got me to divulge the truth of the situation.

Morons.

I clear my throat before leaning closer to them like I'm revealing a big secret before continuing, "It's coyotes, wolves, and all sorts of other animals, too. Apparently, some crazy scientists have been experimenting with different strains of rabies, and they stumbled on one that makes any animal incredibly vicious and attracted to human blood.

"Not only that, but when a human contracts this strain after they're bitten, they go insane before dying very quickly and painfully. The body basically haemorrhages from the inside out, causing muscles to liquefy, including the eyes and brain until they burst out various orifices before finally resulting in death.

"We didn't want to reveal the true nature of the problem because we don't want to cause a panic, but you seem capable of handling the truth," I finish, adding a bit of flattery for good measure and I'm pretty pleased with the results. The man looks pretty fucking worried now, and turns back to his wife who's finally stopped eating and is looking out into the surrounding woods as though something is going to come flying out at any moment and sink its teeth into her, which could be possible given the situation.

"Hon, I think it might be best if we just head on home then," the man says and his wife nods without even looking at him, her eyes still fixed on the trees. "Thanks for finally telling us the truth, son," he says to me, still looking pompous, but mostly just freaked out.

Ha. I win.

We move onto the next site as they begin packing up their things, pretty damn fast, too, if I do say so myself. I always was pretty good at telling horror stories...it's why my sisters refuse to ever go camping with me again.

As we're walking over to the next site, we all heave a collective sigh of annoyance. That one ended pretty well, all things considered, but otherwise, this evac has been very fucking irksome. I've already lost count of how many people we've told our "rabid bears on the loose" story to, and I've lost track of how many people were completely unimpressed by said story. These are hardened Canadians (with the occasional American tourist family thrown in for variety and extra persnikitiness) determined to enjoy what is likely the last opportunity for camping before the cold really sets in. They aren't afraid of bears, even rabid ones, and most of them are just curious about why soldiers are relaying the news and evacuating the camp instead of the park rangers.

See, I told Luca we shoulda dressed up like park rangers; almost no one believes the army is involved with an evac of the area because of some random rabid bears, but no, he always did have something against costumes for some reason, even on Halloween. So we're stuck with this shit-show.

I wish we could just tell them the truth, even though that most likely wouldn't help anything anyway, since no one ever believes it's actually fucking zombies until they either see them chowing down on some unfortunate bastard, or become the unfortunate bastard who's chowed down upon themselves.

I guess we're basically fucked. They're leaving, but reluctantly, and it's taking a hell of a lot longer than originally anticipated. We've already been at it for an hour. Pretty soon it's gonna be full dark out, and there's still a lot of people left in the park. Luca's completely frustrated now and I feel his pain. I really wish these people would just fucking cooperate, stop asking fucking questions, and just get the fuck out before they get attacked by fucking zombies, and we have an even bigger fucking mess on our hands.

Speaking of zombies, we haven't run into any of the undead ghoulies yet, which I guess is a good thing, though I wouldn't mind some practice killing the bastards. I definitely wouldn't mind making sure head shots and/or decapitation works as well as it does in the movies (except, for instance, in *Return of the Living Dead* or *Cabin in the Woods*, perfect examples of bucking tradition that illustrate why I wouldn't mind having some test subjects just to be sure a head shot will be as effective as we hope). But I guess it's probably for the best that we only have to worry about evac-ing the civs at this point, considering that's definitely proven difficult enough.

Jesus H. I'm so exhausted, I wish I could just go and take a nap in that abandoned looking van we saw a little while ago, but I'm pretty sure Luca would notice if I randomly wandered off. Not to mention, even though he's awesome at keeping his composure in high stress situations, for some reason, dealing with civs just makes him crazy irritable and stressed out, so it's probably safer for everyone involved if I stick with him and use my non-threatening charisma to our best advantage.

Chapter Five
Zombies? Yes, zombies!

Lia

I watch Lucy settle into the chair, slip her iPod headphones into her ears, and take a sip from the drink in her hand. She gives me another supportive smile and nods in an encouraging way. I sigh and start walking towards the far edge of the clearing before I realize I don't actually know where I'm going.

"Hey, Brad!" I call out, trying to keep from chuckling, because in spite of my growing annoyance with the Carson situation, I can't help picturing Lucy quoting *Rocky Horror* again, but I press on as he glances in my direction through his haze of smoke and around the girl on his lap and ask, "Where's Carson?"

He gestures in the general direction I was already walking in, and then goes back to making out with the stoned-looking blonde on his lap...lovely. I feel a twinge of guilt for dragging Lucy along on this clearly useless journey, but Lucy doesn't really seem to care so I carry on.

Once I exit the clearing, the light of the fire dims and I blink in the low evening light for a few moments while my eyes adjust. As I'm adjusting, I hear rustling beside me, emanating from the woods to my right, and just as I'm cursing myself for not acting like Lucy and grabbing a knife or something before I ventured off alone in the woods, a very inebriated chick comes stumbling out of the trees. Jesus, it's another blonde, I'm starting to worry that I may not be Carson's type. And if that's the case, and he is screwing some other girl, we really are outta here.

The drunk blonde stumbles into me, looking startled to see a person and not another tree, an observation she confirms with a slurred, "Oh...you're not a tree...you're a girl." She ends this obvious statement with a hiccup and a giggle.

Could this day get any worse? The disturbing diner, our unexpected extra guests, and now I'm probably going to get puked on if I don't get away from this chick soon…seriously, what next?

"Uh, yeah I'm not a tree, so if you're gonna puke, do you think you could do me a favour and aim away from me? Thanks," I say sarcastically, though she's probably much too drunk to pick up on it.

"Oh, you're funny." She drunk giggles again.

Ugh.

"Do you think you could help me get back to the tents?" she asks, gesturing in the same direction Brad did. Damn, well I am going that way anyway…but if she pukes on me, she's on her own. "I really need to lie down," she finishes, swaying on her feet.

"Okay, fine, but seriously…do not throw up on me," I warn, speaking slowly so she has a better chance of getting it through the layer of alcohol that's blurring her synapses.

She nods seriously, grabs onto my arm, and looks at me in a "lead the way" manner. So even though I don't really know the way, I do just that, listening hard for any indications that the alcohol is about to mutiny and crawl back up her esophagus.

As we carry on down the little path we're on, I can see a bit of light up ahead, thank God; I really want to get rid of this girl before she blows chunks all over me and just get down to the good stuff with Carson, finally. But as we get closer to the make-shift camp, I can hear moans that sound all too pleasurable for my liking coming from the only tent that looks occupied. I am so gonna kick his ass if he's screwing some other girl. What a shitty, no good, very bad day!

I walk faster as we get closer, and in the light that remains I can clearly see two bodies contributing to the pleasured moaning. Damn him.

I whip open the tent flap to find Carson with yet another blonde writhing on top of him. What is this? Attack of the Blondes? Upon seeing me standing in the entrance of the tent with the now silent blonde hanging off my right shoulder—she really drank a lot, Jesus—the chick on top of Carson shrieks and covers herself with a sleeping bag. I lower the drunken girl onto the other sleeping bag, then standing up straight again, I cross my arms and do my very best look of utter loathing, straight at Carson.

"Who the hell are you?" the naked blonde asks angrily at the same time Carson anxiously says, "Lia! I didn't think you guys were gonna make it." The girl looks annoyed that he actually knows who I am, but says nothing. Carson has the mild decency to look shamefaced—for about a second—before the look on his face turns much more lascivious. "Now that you're here, you should join us." He winks and slicks his tongue across his lips, patting his still exposed lap.

I cannot believe I actually thought he was hot. What an asshole douche-bag. "You know what, Carson?" I begin, my voice quietly wrathful. Carson doesn't pick up on the simmering anger, just cocks his eyebrow mischievously. Ugh. I really do want to kick his ass, but he is so not worth it. "Go to hell! You're a waste of fucking skin and I hope you get gonorrhea!" I'm shouting now and Carson flinches. The blonde he was screwing cowers behind him as he leans back away from me, covering his quickly deflating dick with his hand, probably in case I decide to kick him there. Although making him unable to bring children into this world does have a certain appeal, he's not worth the effort, so I just give him the finger and stomp back towards the main clearing. Behind me, I can hear the blonde yelling something about how crazy I am, and that she does not have gonorrhea. She's just lucky I didn't kick her either.

Jesus, she's really shrieking now…maybe the drunk chick threw up all over them, which would be lovely poetic justice.

The shrieks fade a bit, as I re-enter the bigger clearing; Brad and the first blonde are now on the ground and horizontal, and Lucy is still listening to music, nursing her drink, and staring at the fire. The news that we're leaving ought to cheer her up at least. "Hey," I say, nudging her shoulder with my hip as I come up beside her, making sure I get her attention. She removes her headphones and looks up at me quizzically. "We're leaving."

"What happened?" she asks, her voice concerned.

"Carson was screwing another chick so I'm pretty much ready to go."

Her face changes, sympathetic anger flowing into her voice, "Oh, Li, I'm sorry…with a name like Carson, I guess we could've expected douche-monkey behaviour, but I know you liked him." She twists her mouth down in an apology.

"Thanks, but we can talk about it later, I kind of just want to get out of here," I say, waving her sympathy off.

"Yeah," she agrees, "let's go." She doesn't ask any more questions and I'm glad. I really don't feel like talking, especially since I'm frustrated—in more ways than one—and I don't know how I'm going to release the tension, but I don't want to take it out on Lucy.

These worries quickly disappear as a sudden terrifying shriek echoes out of the nearby woods. "What the fuck was that?" Lucy asks.

"I don't know, but I think it's time to get back to the van." She nods in agreement and swings her bag over her shoulder. I do the same and we start walking away from the camp quickly. We're only about halfway back to the van when the shrieks sound again, much closer now.

"So...we should run," Lucy asserts, glancing at me for confirmation.

"Yeah, we should definitely run," I agree.

We both start jogging, and I notice again that my bag seems much heavier than before. I'm about to ask Lucy why, when suddenly, the shrieking comes from right in front of us. A crouched figure is separating us from the van.

Lucy's right, I really have to stop asking if things can get any worse, because they really do keep getting worse every time I ask that.

Lucy peels off to the left, sprinting into the trees. I follow suit, the screeching thing scampering along quickly behind me.

Shit.

We sprint for a while; I lose track of how long, all I know is I'm now really glad that Lucy always insists on doing cardio when we work out. I weave around the tree branches that keep snatching at my dress and hair, trying not to lose sight of Lucy, while simultaneously trying to shake whatever the hell is chasing us.

All of a sudden, Lucy stumbles across a fallen log and into a small clearing. She gets up quickly and looks around for me. I jump over the log and gracefully lurch right into her. She steadies me, and then looks behind me, I whip around and do the same, but for the moment, I don't see anything menacing there. I can still hear the shrieks though, and they're not far away. And thanks to our sprint in the wrong direction, I now have no idea where the van is.

"Open your bag!" Lucy commands.

"What?" I ask incredulously, still trying to process what could be chasing us.

She just sighs and opens her bag first, and then mine in quick succession. I am more surprised than I probably should be to see lots of bladed metal glinting up at me.

"Wow, you're paranoid!" I exclaim, then, seeing her indignant face, amend, "I mean, thank God, but still." She mutters something and shakes her head as she crouches down and picks out—what else?—the machete.

I hear a shriek very close by and pick out my own weapon, my favoured double edged axe. We remove the protective sheaths from the blades and stand back to back, waiting for whatever it is to come out, come out wherever it is.

When it does come out, I'm genuinely surprised. It's not an animal; it's the chick Carson was screwing. She's still naked, but she now has an enormous wound decorating her neck, blood covering her torso, and she's looking at us like we're some kind of Atkins-friendly meal.

"Huh," I say, glancing over at Lucy, because I honestly don't know what to say. What do you say at a time like this?

Lucy glances back at me and then quickly returns her stare to the bloodied blonde, who suddenly screeches like a banshee again and launches herself at Lucy. Lucy exclaims, "Oh, good God, man," as she quickly drops to one knee and slices her machete across the naked chick's belly. She spins up and away back onto her feet in one quick motion. I feel my heart squeeze in fear as she barely escapes the chick's grasping hands, but this probably isn't the time to lecture her about it.

Lucy nods nonchalantly at me saying, "So…that's a zombie."

"Why didn't you aim for the head then?" I ask, as the chick's zombiness is made even more obvious when something red and gooey and distinctly organ-like slips out of the open wound across her belly and she steps on it, squishing it up between her toes.

Lucy opens her mouth to respond, but the zombie launches herself at us again, still screeching in that awful way that makes me feel like every hair on my body is standing on end. She's coming at us so fast; I do the only thing I can think of, my movie knowledge ingrained so deep that I barely think before swinging my axe at her head.

My swing is a little off and the blade comes up on a diagonal, her face turning into an incomprehensible mess, as the top half of her head comes loose and drops onto the grass by my feet. The whole gory process takes only a few seconds, and sprays Lucy and me with blood and some kind of gore I can't easily identify and don't really want to, anyway. Thankfully, her re-corpsified corpse finally crumples, the force of the impact causing the majority of her remaining organs to slip-slide out of the widening slit in her stomach, staining the grass around her even more intensely.

"Ew," I say, my brain stuttering as it tries to comprehend what just happened. I feel my gag reflex being seriously tested as I look at my blood-drenched axe, then at my gore-spattered best friend who's just staring at the headless, crumpled corpse. She turns to look back at me, eyes wide, with a "what the fuck?" expression that I'm sure mirrors my own.

Lucy

My heart is pounding furiously, thudding a loud bass beat in my chest, playing to the tune of being terrified. "I cannot fucking believe what just happened."

"Me neither," Lia replies, voice shaking only slightly.

Huh, didn't think that I said that out loud, apparently shock wreaks havoc on my ability to keep my thoughts inside. Oh well, moving on.

"Of all the things to ever be right about!" I shout, raking my hands through my now blood-coated hair. Ick. "I can't fucking believe I was fucking right about there being fucking zombies one day!"

"I know, right?" Lia replies.

Okay, she is officially being way too cavalier for what just happened. "How are you not freaking out right now?" I ask. "I'm freaking out and let's be honest, I was prepared for this. How are you not freaking out?"

"I don't know, shock maybe?" Lia shrugs as she examines her blood-splattered axe. "Plus, to be honest, I was dealing with quite a lot of pent up aggression just now, so I actually feel a little better. Is that wrong?"

I do love this crazy, slightly sociopathic chick. I laugh and throw my arms around her, starting to calm down a bit. And luckily, I'm still wearing my leather jacket, so the amount of blood actually on my skin isn't as bad as it could've been; my hands and chest got the worst of it. I still feel sick, something that intensifies as the blood starts to dry in dark, sticky globs, contrasting intensely against my pale skin, but I don't feel like I'm going to hyperventilate, so I suppose that's something.

"Okay, so there are zombies, 'cause that was definitely a zombie, right?" I ask, still breathing hard. Lia nods in agreement. "So now what?" I say, uncertain, because even if you plan for something, if you don't totally believe it'll ever happen, if it ever does happen, you can still have absolutely no idea what to do.

"Well," Lia pauses, thinking of a game plan, "we could go back to the van and grab some more weapons—good thinking, by the way, weird, but good; they definitely came in handy—to be on the safe side...um...should we call the police, or something?" Lia wonders as she inspects the small arsenal of weapons I put in our bags. "Who do you even call at a time like this?"

"Ghostbusters?" I joke. "But, seriously, folks, there's no point...in calling the cops, I mean, they either won't believe us or won't get here to help until it's too late; it's one of the rules. Getting more weapons, however, is always a good idea. So...uh, where's the van from here?"

Lia's about to respond to one of the first things I said, when she suddenly contemplates my question about the van's whereabouts. "Huh, good question. Kinda lost track of where we were when we were running...not to mention slicing and dicing."

"Ba dum bum pshh," I respond. "Stupid forest," I continue tetchily. I have no idea where we are either, other than in some sort of clearing. This isn't surprising, considering my very shitty sense of direction, but it is still really annoying, especially under these circumstances. I mean, of all the times to get lost and separated from one's means of transportation, when there are zombies running amok in the forest, it really fucking sucks.

"We may as well start walking, I guess; just standing here sure won't help us find the van." And with this, Lia flings her bag over her shoulder, axe still in hand, looking rather badass, indeed.

I adjust my grip on the machete and move to stand up with my bag, but I drop back down into a defensive crouch when I hear twigs snapping and branches moving. "We might have to fight our way out," I say as Lia notices the noises of impending arrival— probably of something sinister—as well.

She drops her bag, adjusts her stance, and tightens her grip on the axe, grinning down at me. I smile back, but it feels like mine sits more grimly on my face. I know it's not exactly the best survival attitude to have when there are hungry undead things about, but I just want to go home, I feel sick enough already.

"Let's do this!" Lia says, looking much more energetic than I feel. Apparently, she still has some rage issues to work out.

Unfortunately for her pent up aggression, however, what finally hacks its way through the trees into our clearing doesn't seem very sinister. First of all, they're much better looking than zombies and second of all, they are also standing upright, which is always a definite plus with strangers.

A group of four is now standing across the small clearing from us, staring at us, or more specifically, our raised weapons, not to mention our general bloodiness, I'm sure. The group is led by easily the most gorgeous guy I've ever seen—all broad shoulders, rippled muscles, and basic drool-inducing-ness. He stands at the front of the group, carrying some kind of rifle that's strapped across his chest, his lovely, lovely chest.

The others—consisting of another guy, not as big or as striking as the leader, but still quite cute, and two chicks, one of whom looks rather sick, is missing her right shoe, and is hanging off of the guy's shoulder (say it with me now: ominous) and both of whom are blonde and look rather orange—stand behind him unarmed and looking scared.

Well. This should be interesting.

"Hey," says the less attractive guy, "uh...we come in peace?" The delicious one rolls his eyes, flips the rifle backwards over his shoulder and walks towards us. I stand up, setting my machete down by my bag. Lia lowers her axe but doesn't put it down.

Now who's paranoid?

"Hi, I'm Nate, that's Blaine, Tifani, and Daphne," he begins, gesturing to the others behind him. "Do you have any idea what's going on here? Some soldiers came to our camp telling us to evacuate, but they weren't clear on what the supposed danger is, exactly," he finishes, raising an eyebrow as he takes in the amount of blood decorating our weapons and clothes.

I'm having trouble focusing on anything other than his sumptuous lips or his eyes, which, not to get all poetic on you, look like the sky just before it rains. I look down, see the blood staining my clothes, give myself a mental shake, and return my concentration to what really matters right now.

"I'm Lucy, this is Lia. And yes, we do know what's going on...zombies."

He glances between us, incredulous. "Zombies?"

"Yes, zombies!" Lia barks, rather defensively, if you ask me. Nate raises his eyebrows again, looking surprised at her tone. "We just finished killing one, so don't you dare look at us like we're crazy!" She gestures angrily at the mutilated body behind us and Nate's eyebrows rise even higher at hearing, and then seeing the proof that we've killed someone.

Great, now he probably thinks we're psycho-killers or something. Not that I care what he thinks about me...anyway, moving on to try to convince him that we're not gonna slaughter them senselessly. "Sorry," I say, patting Lia's arm comfortingly, "she's still in battle mode; however, there are indeed zombies around, so technically, the person we killed was already dead. Anyway, you should be on your guard." Damn, I don't think that helped, he still looks somewhat worried that he may be our next victim.

"Zombies?" one of the orange blondes, the one dressed head to toe in hot pink, not the sick-looking one, suddenly asks. She'd walked over without me even realizing it.

Damn, this stupidly hot guy is really throwing my attention span for a loop. I grab my machete again to focus myself, which might not have been the best idea, since it probably makes me look a tad aggressive...even more so than the blood that's starting to dry and make my skin feel tight. I drop my machete once more and try to look innocent and not at all deranged.

"Are you, like, crazy, or something? 'Cause there's no such thing?" The tangerine skinned, bleached blonde chick continues, looping her arm around Nate's as she does so. She takes in our bloodied demeanours and wrinkles her nose.

Alright, so maybe I was right about the sinister thing, ick. Luckily, Nate seems to agree with this sentiment as he shakes her off, looking rather disgusted. Not that I care. I give myself another mental shake to avoid feeling happy that he's not into the oompa-loompa airhead.

Miss tangerine blondie suddenly screams, as she sees the body behind us. She grabs Nate and hides behind him, screeching, "Oh, my God, they really are, like, mental! They killed someone!"

"A zombie!" I protest. "We killed a zombie!"

"Yeah, a zombie," Lia echoes, sounding both disdainful and indignant at the same time. "But believe what you want. Come on, Luce, we should go find the van." With this, she grabs her bag again and looks at me expectantly. I force myself to shrug.

I am not sad at the thought of leaving Nate's presence, I'm not.

Anyway, that one chick looks pretty bad and would only slow us down if we were to band together. I mean, I wouldn't even be surprised if she'd been bitten, the way she's hanging off Blaine, looking almost asleep...uh-oh. "Um, before we go, can I ask you kind of a weird question?" I ask Nate. He looks wary, but he nods. "Has that girl been bitten by anything?"

71

Both Nate and the oompa-loompa look surprised and confused and they tear their attention away from the semi-decapitated body behind us.

"How'd you know that?" Nate asks, not unreasonably.

Lia and I share a look.

"Uh-oh," Lia says. Then she sighs and drops her bag again.

"Uh-oh, indeed," I reply, picking my machete back up.

"Wait, what 'uh-oh'?" Nate asks. "What the fuck is going on?"

I'm about to reply when the sick-looking chick suddenly collapses, sliding off of Blaine, who crouches down beside her, looking concerned.

"Tif?" The one I now know is Daphne cries and runs back over to Blaine and Tifani.

Lia and I sigh in unison and share another look. This is what happens when you aren't well educated by zombie movies.

"What the fuck is going on?" Nate repeats, but he follows our lead, flipping the rifle back into his hands, the movement almost seeming involuntary; still, smart boy.

Lia leaves me to explain and walks the short distance across the clearing, saying, "Get away from it," as she does so.

Nate looks at me, a question mark all over his gorgeous face.

"If she was bitten by a zombie, which, judging from the look of her, she was, any minute now, she'll *be* a zombie. That's how it works." Nate still looks skeptical, so I figure showing is better than telling, and I start to follow Lia, saying, "Come on," over my shoulder as I do.

In the short time it takes us to reach them, Daphne and Blaine have become completely freaked out, unsurprisingly. "She's not an *it*, she's my *girlfriend*!" Blaine says angrily, trying to get to Tifani, who now looks rather dead. However, he's deterred by Lia's raised axe, so he just shouts, "What the fuck is going on?" Then he looks at Nate helplessly, but since Nate doesn't know what the fuck is going on either, he just silently pats Blaine's shoulder while looking down at Tifani with a tense expression.

"Would you just let us help her already? There's something totally wrong with her!" Daphne exclaims.

"Yeah, no shit, but you can't help her now," Lia replies harshly, moving closer to what was Tifani, probably getting ready to take her head off in a pre-emptive strike before she changes.

"Lia, wait," I say, stepping forward in case she needs back up when that thing reanimates. "Perhaps a demonstration would be more useful?"

Lia considers this, nods, and steps back a bit, coming to stand beside me. "Get ready though," she warns.

"Pff, born ready." I retort, more out of habit and to distract myself from the gruesomeness that I know is coming, rather than because of any urge to actually joke around right now.

"'Kay, seriously—" Daphne begins.

"Just wait," Lia says abruptly, cutting her off.

I saw it, too; little dead girl started to twitch. "Let's back up," I say and Lia and I move backwards in tandem, arms spread, forcing everyone else back with us.

Oh, and she's up. What's left of Tifani sits up suddenly, looking at us but not really seeing us, her eyes glazed and empty, a weird bluish-grey color, the pupil just a dot.

"Tif!" Daphne squeals with excitement, trying to move forward. I stop her with an outstretched, machete-wielding arm.

"Not anymore," I say, quietly as the bimbo formerly known as Tifani shifts onto all fours and cocks her head at us for a moment, and then begins sniffing the air around her.

"What's she doing?" Blaine asks, sounding scared and confused.

"Getting ready to hunt," Lia responds, tightening her grip on the axe. I do the same on the machete and breathe deep.

"But she's, like, a vegan!" Daphne exclaims.

Jesus, that one's a freaking genius.

"Not anymore," I repeat—habit again—but it's much to Lia's apparent enjoyment as she laughs loudly. Lia's laugh recaptures zombie Tifani's attention and her head shifts back towards us quickly. Suddenly, she throws her head back and makes a ghastly noise, same as the first zombie chick we took down. It sounds like a mix between someone gasping for air and a Velociraptor. Instant goose bumps rise on my skin and I feel Daphne jump behind me. In this case, I don't blame her. It's the worst and most horrifying sound I've ever heard. It makes my skin feel like it's trying to crawl away from itself.

Following her shriek, zombie Tifani skitters forward so goddamn fast, she leaps into the air and tackles Blaine before anyone can move.

Goddammit, they move so fucking fast!

Nate fires his rifle, the shell spiralling through the air as the bullet leaves the gun with a loud crack, making me jump involuntarily, and Daffy squeak in fear behind me. The bullet tears through Tifani's throat, snapping her strand of pearls and changing her shriek to something of a distressed gurgle. It would no doubt be a killing shot…if she weren't undead.

"Nathan!" Daphne chastises even though zombie Tif barely seems to notice, even with the blood now spurting out of her throat, she just continues trying to chow down on poor Blaine. Nate gets ready to fire again, bringing the butt of the rifle up to his shoulder and squinting through the sights, but Tif's head is hidden behind Blaine's and he can't get a clear shot. He growls in frustration as he lowers the rifle and Lia jumps into action, kicking Tif in the stomach to dislodge her from her Blaine-shaped snack. Blaine, meanwhile, is just trying to pull her snapping jaws away from his shoulder and neck. Even from about twenty feet away, I can see that his neck looks awful; the skin is bloody, torn, and bitten…worst hickey ever.

Zombie Tifani shrieks again, enraged as she's rolled off of Blaine by Lia's foot. She snaps back into action quickly, though, screeching like a demon—well, as well as a demon that's been shot through the throat can still screech anyway—she claws at Lia's boot and tries to bite her.

I feel completely useless and my heart is pounding like mad as Lia kicks out, trying to disengage zombie Tif from her ankle. She hacks at Tif's head, but it's no use, she can't get enough momentum and zombified Tif is hanging on for dear after-life, trying to bite through Lia's boot.

"Nate!" Blaine shouts as he rolls out of the way, clearing the line of sight for him. A second later, it's all over, as Nate shoots again, the loudness making me jump once more as the bullet enters and exits Tif's head with surprisingly little bloodshed.

Daffy screams and rushes over to the thankfully now completely dead Tifani. She pretty much shoves Lia out of the way as she cradles Tif's head in her lap, sobbing and not seeming to notice that she's getting blood all over herself.

Lia looks at Daffy, shakes her head and mutters, "Thanks," to Nate as she walks by him. He just grunts in reply and walks over to Blaine, kneeling beside him, trying to stop the bleeding with some balled up cloth. A valiant effort but, sadly, it won't matter.

I walk over to Lia and she smiles weakly at me. "You okay?" I ask, my heart still pounding painfully in the face of her near zombification.

"I'm fine," she answers, and I open my mouth to press her further, considering the close call she just had, but she waves me off, saying, "Really, Luce, I'm fine, she didn't even scratch me," she assures me, showing me her unharmed leg.

"That's not really the point," I say, but she just waves me off again and heads over to the others, so I have no choice but to follow her.

"Man, I've dated some real blood-sucking bitches," Blaine says ruefully, sitting up while pressing the cloth to his neck, "but she's definitely just made the top five." He grimaces in pain as Nate smiles grimly, helping him up.

Once Blaine is standing, Nate turns to us. "So...zombies."

"Zombies," I confirm.

"Okay then." He rubs his hands over his face, and then drags them through his hair, not realizing he's smeared blood all over himself (though that's a hazard one just has to accept in the midst of a zombie battle, I suppose). He takes a deep breath then asks, "So now what?"

Blaine

"Now what?"

My thoughts exactly. The zombies just start coming out to play and I get bitten by my stupid and now twice-dead girlfriend. That's just fucking awesome. The only way you could think this might have a happy ending, is if you'd never seen a zombie flick. It won't be pretty, I can tell you that much. God, my neck hurts.

I press the t-shirt Nate retrieved from his duffle more tightly to my wound, as I make an effort not to fall over. Nate's face scrunches with worry and I grin at him, willing myself to stand up straighter so he's not so worried.

God this sucks. That stupid bitch. I didn't even get laid, and now I'm going to turn into a fucking zombie because of her. This is definitely the worst camping trip I've ever been on.

"Now, I'm sorry to tell you, your friend is going to turn into a zombie," the one with the axe says. I think her name is Lia, but it's kind of hard to remember the names of people you've just met when your recently deceased girlfriend is sucking on your neck and not in a good way.

"Lia!" The one with the machete—Lucy—admonishes. I guess I was right.

"It's true. No point in sugar-coating it. Saying it more nicely won't save his life, nothing will," Lia retorts defensively.

Ouch, but good point, I guess. "That's true," I say, rubbing my free hand over my face. "Before long, I'm going to be craving human flesh and brains and have really bad posture and worse grammar. There's no positive way to spin that."

"What are our options then?" Nate asks, bless him. He's being either really loyal, or really stubborn, but probably both. I'm really going to miss him...or I guess I actually won't, because I'll either be dead or zombified, but in theory, I'm really going to miss him.

"Our options are either killing him now, or killing him later," Lia responds.

Again, true, but still, ouch.

"Lia!" Lucy admonishes her again, and I notice her suddenly stop trying to wipe some of the blood off of her hands as she does so.

"Come on, Luce, there's no point trying to be nice about this situation. There is nothing nice about it. It fucking sucks, but so it goes, remember? We're officially in a war now. Who knows how many more of those things are in these woods? It's time to be blunt," Lia finishes this little speech and looks contemptuously at Daffy, who's still on the ground by Tif's body, rocking back and forth and crying loudly. Lia then starts examining the clearing as if to get her bearings.

Decisions, decisions. Should I die now, or die later?

"So what's it going to be?" Lia asks suddenly, staring at me. "Do you want us to kill you, or do you want to do it yourself?" she continues as though she thinks I didn't understand what she meant. She waves her bloodied axe as if to punctuate her question.

"Hang on, no one is killing Blaine!" Nate snaps angrily before looking at me helplessly.

Oh, man. I can't ask Nate to off me. He'd do it if I asked, but it would kill him, so there's no way. And I don't really want Lia or Lucy doing it either because no matter how illogical, Nate would hate them for it, if he doesn't already hate Lia for being honest about how screwed I am and they should probably stick together for safety. So it looks like it'll be a do-it-myself kind of job.

"Nate," I begin, my voice soft, trying to calm him.

"No!" he replies angrily. "There's got to be something we can do." He raises his rifle some in Lia's direction as though she's going to suddenly run at me, axe flailing.

I actually wouldn't put it past her, but it's still a bit much. "Nate," I try again, "dude, you saw what happened to Tif. I don't want to turn into that, and I certainly don't want to risk attacking you or anyone else. So just give me one of your guns, and I'll do it myself, after you guys leave. Look, stop shaking your head. I'm not going to ask you to do it for me and there's no point in you guys waiting around for me to turn all gross and dead, so this will be for the best." Nate still looks livid and anxious, but he doesn't seem to be able to argue anymore. He just looks down for a second, and then silently crouches by his bag and pulls out a handgun. He hands it to me wordlessly as he stands up. His eyes look wet and it's all I can do not to shove the gun back in his hands and beg him to help me, save me somehow.

"Thanks, man," I say instead, even though it sounds utterly moronic, thanking someone for giving me a gun so I can off myself, but there you go, screwed up situations call for screwed up responses.

"What should I tell your parents?" Nate suddenly asks and my stomach sinks; in my freaked out state, I pretty much forgot about them. I'm never going to see them again. We were never touchy-feely close, but they're good people, good parents.

"Shit," I exhale with the word and shake my head. "I don't know man, just, the truth I guess. It's pretty unlikely this will stay contained and I don't want them thinking I killed myself for no reason, so, just tell them the truth."

"Okay" he says, his voice low and heavy. I give him the best smile I can. It feels grim around the edges, so I give up and drop my gaze down.

As I'm staring down at the gun now in my hand, another shriek suddenly sounds from the edge of the clearing and everyone tenses up—except for Daffy, who doesn't even move—waiting for the attack.

Even though we've all had to accept that there are zombies around, I don't think we're ready for what comes slithering out of the trees a few seconds later. It's a zombie, alright, and it's the first one that looks the most like a legitimate horror movie zombie. It's lurching towards us, using only its arms for propulsion, since it has no legs at all; it's really just a torso with arms and a head…but, even with stubborn strings of intestines dragging on the ground behind it that's not the weirdest part. It also has a bloody, black stiletto sticking out of its face—out of the left eye socket to be exact.

Nate reacts first, shooting it through its remaining eye, the weapon resounding with a loud bang; the bullet goes right through its head and neutralizes the zombie with only a little blood splatter. No one says anything for a minute. I think we're still trying to process just how insane this all is; I know I am.

I walk over to the decimated torso and examine the stiletto adorning its face. "I think we solved the mystery of Tif's missing shoe," I say, pointing at it with my gun.

Lucy quips, "I guess high-heels are more useful than I thought."

"Not useful enough. It didn't even kill it," Nate counters, not humorously, but not in an antagonistic way either.

"Good point. I'll just stick with flat shoes—makes it easier to run anyway," Lucy says.

"We should go," Lia says abruptly and I notice Nate's anger flare again. I walk over to him, hoping I can calm him down before they leave. I'm worried about what he might do, what his reaction will be to my death—I'm pretty much all he has, and I can't believe I'm going out like this. I don't know if he can take it.

"Maybe you should just leave Daffy with me," I joke, bringing a weak smile to Nate's pained, angry face as he closes his bag and throws it over his shoulder.

He looks at me, jaw clenched tightly. "Good luck...or something. I'm sorry I missed," he says, his voice sounding odd and choked out. I feel a pain deep in my chest at how bleak his voice sounds. I haven't heard him sound like this since we were kids and his dad went completely bat-shit crazy.

"I would never blame you for that, man, you tried, but Jesus H., zombie Tif was fuckin' fast. It was *not* your fault, please don't think it was," I plead, borrowing his expression, hoping it'll make him smile at least. He sort-of grunts but won't quite look at me. "Besides, you hit her on the second shot," I add, but he just shakes his head like it doesn't even matter.

Zombies ruin everything.

I look over at the girls. Lucy and Lia are arguing quietly. Daffy is sitting up, mostly, but is still pretty slumped over on the ground beside them. I think about how long it took Tif to turn, and I know they don't have much time before they'll have to kill me, too, if they don't leave soon.

So I simply say, "Goodbye." Then, to lighten the mood, I squeeze his shoulder and continue, "'I don't know how I'm gonna quit you.'"

Nate laughs involuntarily again. "Shut up, man." His smile fades quickly, though, and he warns me, "Remember, if you see any of those things before you...you know...just aim for the head. If you can take any of 'em with you..." He trails off, his voice breaking. He clenches his jaw and takes a breath, and then says, "It's better to go out swinging if you can."

"Good point," Lucy says, having come up beside us after she left Lia to watch over the shell-shocked and now blood-covered Daffy—Lia seems delighted with this, as I'm sure you can imagine. "Sorry," Lucy says in response to the look on Nate's face before she continues on, saying gently, "I was just coming to see if you were ready, and also to apologize for Lia's bluntness. She means well, she's just..." Lucy trails off as though not sure how to explain her friend's behaviour.

"'In battle mode'?" Nate offers and Lucy nods, half smiling. He looks back at me, and then pulls me into a bear hug.

"I love you, man," I fake choke out. I do mean it, though. He's like a brother to me, but normally if I say it, he just pulls a face and shoves me, shaking his head at my effusiveness.

This time, he just says a muffled, "You, too," before letting me go. Then he rakes his hands through his hair and I just now notice that he's got my blood all over his face and hands, but this probably isn't the time to tell him. Turning to Lucy, he says, "Let's go," in a gruff voice, his jaw clenched tight again. Lucy tries to smile at me, but it keeps falling off her face.

"I'm sorry," she says again, sounding like she means it. "This just...sucks. I'm sorry we weren't fast enough."

"Yeah, it does suck," I reply, "but it's not your fault. We'd *all* be on our way to zombie-dom if it wasn't for you guys. Besides, I'd rather it was me instead of Nate, so there's that. You just take care of him, ya hear?" She smiles again, a bit easier this time and nods her acquiescence before turning to join the others. She picks up her bag and her machete on the way, glancing back at me once. I wave and smile encouragingly.

"Don't wait too long or you'll turn," Lia advises. Nate glares at her, but says nothing.

What is there to say? It's true and it's good advice. I smile at him, telling him it's okay and he nods in compliance, backing down. "Don't worry, I won't. Good luck and everything. Stay safe. Stay human. Stay alive." I wave the gun to punctuate my promise and my warning, and grin at Nate reassuringly again.

"Goodbye, Blaine," he says and I wave one last time, Lucy waves back as they exit the clearing, leading the still mostly catatonic Daffy behind them.

Once they're gone, the smile fades quickly from my face. It was easy enough to act brave in order to reassure Nate, but now that I'm alone, aside from the mutilated bodies decorating the clearing—the evidence of what I'll become—I have to forcefully fight off panic as I contemplate the gun in my hand.

Maybe I'll just wait a little while.

My hands are shaking like crazy. I know I need to do it soon or it'll be too late. But I'm scared, I'm really, really, fucking scared. I've never thought I was as brave as Nate, for example, but I thought I at least wasn't a coward. But now, when I have a chance to help the cause by taking my soon to be zombie self out of the equation, I can't do it.

I've tried about ten times. I've put the gun to my head, all around my head: in my mouth, to my temple, under my chin, in the middle of my face. I've even tried pointing it at my heart, thinking if maybe I couldn't see it as well, it wouldn't be so fucking terrifying. That didn't work either. I've walked around this stupid clearing so many times, I'm dizzy. But I can't sit still. The mangled bodies—especially Tif's—freak me out, but I'm scared actually to leave the clearing. I'm afraid of running into more things like what Tif turned into. Zombies, I guess. I love the movies, the books, Nate's graphic novels, but in real life…all I want to do is go home and pretend this never happened.

That's not possible, of course. I'll be turning soon. It's already been almost as long as it took Tif to turn. I sweated through my shirt about ten minutes ago and I'm having trouble catching my breath. My heart is pounding like I just went running or had sex, even though we all know that didn't happen thanks to Tif and the fucked-up torso zombie that apparently turned her. I feel like I'm going to throw up or pass out or something. I'm not sure if it's because the change is imminent, or if it's because I'm panicking about the change being imminent.

I'm trying to think of Nate, reminding myself that I don't want him to have to possibly kill the zombie version of me, and thereby realize that I'm such a goddamn coward. But I can't do it, I just pussy out every time I try, pulling the gun away or taking my finger off the trigger just before I can pull it. And now, I'm starting to get hungry and that alone terrifies me, because before she passed out…died, I guess, Tif was going on and on about how hungry she was, begging me to give her something to eat.

Goddamn that stupid bitch for doing this to me. Seriously, if she had to bite anyone, why couldn't she have bitten Daffy and done the world a favour? Because we really don't need another vapid blonde adding to the stereotype and getting in the way. But no, she had to bite me, turn me.

Fuck, I'm hungry.

Goddammit, if I'm going do this before I turn, I better do it now.

Okay...now.

I raise the gun up to my head once more, telling myself I can do this, thinking about Nate having to kill the zombie version of me...the possibility of me biting him or anyone else...okay, now...

Now...

NOW...

Goddammit, Blaine, just do it, you fucking pussy! Just pull the goddamn trigger and stop being such a fucking coward!

I start to squeeze the trigger...my hand feels weak, like the gun is suddenly too heavy, the trigger impossibly stuck.

Is   it   just   fear or......or..

hungryhungryhungryhungryhungryhungryhungryhungryhungr yhungryhungry

hungryhungryhungryhungryhungryhungryhungryhungryhungr yhungryhungry

hungryhungryhungryhungryhungryhungryhungryhungryhungr yhungry........

Nate

I have to force myself to keep going, because every couple of steps, all I want to do is turn back for Blaine. He's my best friend, my brother. He's always been there for me since we were kids; even if he sometimes annoyed the hell out of me, I knew could always count on him. I can't believe that I have to lose him, especially like this. I can't believe I missed the fucking shot and didn't shoot Tif in the head the first time. I never miss.

I can't believe I'm just leaving him there to die alone in that clearing with only those corpses for company, just to save myself the pain of having to kill him. After all we've been through. He was there when no one else was, he kept me sane (or mostly sane) when all I had otherwise was my father. I have to keep reminding myself what Tifani turned into, telling myself I don't want to see Blaine turned into an undead freak like something out of my graphic novels.

He wouldn't want me to see him like that either. He could be shallow, but I certainly never had to question whether or not he cared about me. I don't want to have to kill him myself, but with every step, I'm dreading hearing a gunshot ring out, announcing his death. I don't know if I can make it.

I'm so focused on not turning back that it takes me a good minute to realize Lucy's trying to talk to me. I turn my head in her direction, glad for any kind of distraction. Especially one that looks like her; she's all breasts and hips with a tiny waist, and all this long, dark-red hair; she's definitely a welcome distraction right now.

"What?" I ask, trying to clear my head enough to focus on her properly.

"I was just asking how you were doing. It's a stupid question, I know, but I don't really know what else to say and I feel like I have to say something, at least," she finishes in a rush, looking flustered, her dark brown eyes clouded with concern.

Rage washes over me, not at her, just at everything that happened and how I couldn't do a fucking thing to save him. I let all the fury I feel at Tif for biting him and not Daffy, at not being able to save him, at Lia for making it obvious that I couldn't, at myself for leaving him behind, at everything, wash over me. It's the only way I won't turn back.

"I'm fine," I say, my voice harsh with the wrath coursing through me. Lucy nods and twitches her mouth sympathetically, and then slows down to walk with Lia and Daffy again. She's got a look on her face like maybe she's afraid of me. This thought barely even registers, though, because I can feel the humming in my chest, the sound of static in my ears and I know what's coming, what I have to do. The longer we go without hearing a shot, the more certain I am that he won't be able to do it himself.

The world is reduced to the static in my ears and the hum in my chest, and I stop walking. It's such a certainty that it almost feels like I've already done it, that feeling I always get, which always makes it easier, because if I've already done it then it's not a choice. It's the feeling I get every time just before I kill something, the feeling that makes me certain there's no turning back, just like my father always taught me.

"Nate?" The static abruptly cuts off in that way it has and I look to my left to see Lucy standing beside me looking worried.

"I have to go back," I say, my voice sounding empty, even to my own ears. The decision is already made. It's out of my hands.

"What? Nate, I'm sorry, this situation is beyond terrible, but there's nothing we can do," she protests, trying to reason with me, not understanding that this has nothing to do with saving him, at least not in any way that counts. But it's all I can do, and it's out of my hands.

"He won't do it himself. I know him, he can't. I have to go back and finish it."

"Nate, no, if that's what you think, then let Lia or me do it, you don't have to be the one."

She doesn't understand of course, I doubt anyone but dear old Dad would. "It has to be me, it's all I can do for him now," I say. Feeling my heartbeat slow down to match the timing of the hum in my chest, I turn around and head back for him.

I barely notice Lia, Lucy, and Daffy following me. They're not important right now, so I focus my instincts on what is. I feel my senses get stronger, clearer, like they always do, picking up small sounds I normally wouldn't notice as much, like the ragged sounds of Daffy breathing through the tears that are still flowing down her face, the sound of the three of them snapping twigs and making so much noise behind me.

I walk quickly, shifting to the rhythm my father taught me, moving as silently as possible and watching for any traces of movement around me. I step back between the line of trees into the clearing with the bodies of the zombies. And Blaine. He's sitting on the ground, staring at the gun in his hands. As I watch, he presses the gun to his temple and I wonder if, for the first time ever, the killing feeling was wrong. But after a few seconds, he pulls the gun away from his head quickly and stares off into the distance, looking scared and frustrated, and then something else. Something I can't quite identify at first before I realize that it was the same look Tifani had on her face before she turned. It's almost time. The humming increases in intensity, and I slow my heartbeat down even more, feeling my body relax into the familiar patterns of a hunt.

Blaine's face transforms suddenly, the gun dropping from his grasp, as he becomes something else. I wait for the quiet space that comes in between heartbeats and stare through the sight, not letting anything penetrate the static that's filled my ears again, my thoughts focused solely on the kill. My heart beats, synced with the hum, and in the pause before it beats again, it's time.

The shot pushes my SKS into my shoulder with a familiar pressure, and the bullet leaves the chamber with the loud crack that wipes the static away, and is the cue for the humming to finally cease and my heart rate to speed up again, returning to normal.

I take a breath and cross the clearing quickly, ignoring the shocked sounds of the girls behind me. I reach Blaine's body and make sure the kill was good and clean, like always. The hole is straight through his temple, my bullet having made almost no impact as it travelled through his skull. At least he didn't die with his face mutilated.

I drop to a crouch and retrieve my handgun, clicking on the safety and depositing it in my duffle. I turn back to Blaine and stare down at him. "Goodbye, Blaine. I'm sorry," I say quietly. I stare down at his slack, deadened face, and I make a decision. I can't change what happened, but I can preserve his body as much as possible and give his parents closure. They could even have an open casket if they covered up the bite from Tifani.

I drop my duffle bag on the ground and crouch beside it, opening it up and digging through the contents until I find my collapsible shovel. I unfold it, snap it into its extended shape, and then pick a spot and start digging.

"What are you doing?" Lia asks.

"I need to bury him."

"Do you want help?" Lucy asks.

"Just keep a lookout for more zombies," I say. Then I turn my attention to creating a safe space to leave Blaine until I can come back and retrieve his body, so I can give him back to his parents when all this is over.

It takes a while, I don't really keep track of how long, but it's long enough for it to get almost dark and for the girls, Lia mostly, to start getting anxious to leave, but the hole is finally deep enough that he'll be safe and it won't take me too long to dig him back out when the time comes. I heave myself up out of the grave and walk over to Blaine's body. I pick him up and walk back over to the grave. I set him on the edge and drop back down into the hole. I lean over the edge and pull him towards me, and then I roll him into my arms and lower him to the bottom of the grave.

I haul myself out again and start piling dirt on him. A knot of panic and grief tightens in my chest as the earth covers his face, but I push it away; there's so much more that I need to focus on right now.

When I'm finished covering him up, I place his bag as a temporary headstone, more as a marker than anything else. This won't be his permanent resting spot, so there's no need to place something symbolic and meaningful there.

Then it's time to go. I stand up and turn around to face the girls, all of whom are staring at me. "We should go," I say, "it'll be dark soon."

"Right…yeah," Lia says hesitantly, and then glances at Lucy.

"I'm sorry you had to do that," Lucy says.

"It had to be done," I answer matter-of-factly.

"We could have done it for you."

"No," I state simply, and flicking the safety back on my SKS, I walk past them and head out of the clearing again. After a few seconds, I hear them beginning to follow me, talking in low voices. I ignore them and continue forward, not letting my mind wander to his lifeless face, there's no time for that now.

Before long, we reach another clearing and I feel a hand on my arm. I turn around slowly, to see Lucy standing close to me. "What?" I ask calmly.

"We should probably figure out where we're all going," Lia begins, looking concerned about my behaviour. "Lucy and I were headed back to my van, but we really have no idea where it is from here, so that's probably not our best option. Like you said, it'll be almost completely dark soon, so we should probably try to find somewhere to hole up for the night where we could fend off any zombies more easily."

"Um, weren't we going to try and find the yummy army boys?" Daffy offers helpfully. Lucy and Lia just look at her, then at me, confused. Looks like I'm going to have to break my focus to explain things. Stupid, fucking, useless Daffy. Why couldn't Tifani have bitten her? I wouldn't have given one flying fuck if I had to kill Daffy. I hate her so much; I think I would even have enjoyed it.

"We were following the soldiers that came to our camp because I wanted to know what was going on in the woods. I guess we know what that was now. Anyway, there's a fort off in this direction, which I'm guessing, is where they were headed," I explain.

"Huh," Lia says, unsure, not taking her eyes off me. She looks at Lucy then says more decisively, "That's probably our best bet, then. We should just continue in this direction until we find them."

I grunt and nod, getting ready to continue on as Lucy grabs my arm again. I look down at her and she smiles kindly. "I'm sorry about your friend. I'm so sorry that you had to kill him," she says this so quietly and gently that it actually makes an impact on my aura of numb calm, making me feel slightly more normal—or as normal as I get, anyway.

"Thanks," I say, and she nods once, like she's made up her mind about something. "We should go," I continue and she nods again, adjusting her bag on her shoulder and walking forward.

I head towards the wall of trees once more, but pause when I hear that sound again. It's the same sound I heard at the camp. I didn't think anything of it at the time, but then I heard Tifani make the same one. That god-awful howling noise they make before attacking.

"We've got company," I say. Lia and Lucy nod in agreement, as it shrieks again, closer this time and they hear it too. Daffy's heard it too, and she's collapsed again, bawling. Stupid and fucking useless.

I step back from the edge of the trees, my SKS in hand, waiting. There's another howl and a zombie bolts suddenly out of the trees, screeching the whole way. He's naked, but covered with blood and something that could be vomit—it's hard to tell for sure in the near-dark. He has a chunk of flesh missing from his right arm where he was bitten. He looks like a tool even in zombie form, so I feel even less bad than I would've about putting a bullet in his brain. No hum or static accompany this kill, just like with Tifani, it makes me feel nothing. Maybe it's something about them being already dead, maybe it's something else.

I bring the SKS up to my shoulder, barely needing any time to aim through the sights after all my training. I flip the safety off and squeeze the trigger, feeling the familiar slight recoil while the gun blasts and the shell spins up into the air a few feet. The bullet pierces his skull easily and he drops to the ground instantly. I walk over to him to make sure he's dead, even though it's unnecessary, target practice with Daddy ensured that I'd never miss a shot…or, I guess, almost never since I missed Tif's head. Can't think about that.

My father also taught me to always check my kills, and the accident with the deer ensured that I'd never fail to again. I feel a little better now that I've had the chance to kill something meaningless. I hate that about myself. I hate my father for instilling that in me, but it works. This kill has finally returned my breathing to normal and I feel like I'm in control again. The images of dead Blaine slide into the background for now, and my layer of calm numbness recedes. I kick the zombie in the head, my steel-toed boot landing with a crunch and I feel even better.

I breathe a sigh of relief and move to exit the clearing again, pausing when I hear Lucy breathe behind me, "Jesus, Li, it's Carson."

Lia walks over to check the twice-dead thing and nods her agreement. "Huh, well I guess that makes sense since the chick he was screwing zombified and came after us, too. That girl I thought was drunk was obviously bitten…oh well." With that, she kicks the zombie in the head, too, and says, "Let's go," before crossing through the barrier of trees in front of us.

Lucy glances at me and I can't help but smile.

"Feel better?" she asks, the idea not seeming to alarm her. In fact, from her expression, I'm pretty sure she understands completely, which is new.

I nod. She nods in response and we have kind of a moment.

"You guys coming?" Lia shouts from somewhere in the trees.

"We should go," Lucy says a bit sheepishly, taking Daffy by the wrist in her free hand and leading her behind her as we head off through the trees, weapons at the ready.

Daphne

I can't even believe what's going on. I mean, I don't even know what's going on. My hair is all stiff from Tif's...ugh...blood. I can't even think about it. I can't believe she bit Blaine. Not hot! She should really know better. She's a pro at getting guys, so I can't believe she was, like, so forceful. And I really can't believe Nathan shot her...twice! He totes killed my BFF! I am so furious with him! I know she was kind of having a PMS moment, but, like, how rude! That's no reason to shoot someone in the face. I'm sure I could have, like, calmed Tif down if they had just let me, but they didn't even listen to me.

And then he went and killed his own BFF! This is the craziest day I've had since the Hair Disaster of 2007...actually it's probably even worse than that, although the Hair Disaster of 2007 did mean I had to, like, constantly wear hats, which is totes not my best look and I had to do it for, like, a year, so it's a toss-up.

But you know what's even more upsetting? What those two bitches are wearing. A dress and combat boots? Hello, Lia, the '90s are so over! Unless they come back in again...but they so haven't yet, so yeah! As for the ho in the black halter top, leather jacket, and skinny jeans? Can you say goth? And I can't believe the way she's, like, throwing herself at Nathan. Does she have zero self-respect or what? I know he has a trust fund and he's gorgeous, but she, like, just met him and she's so flirty. What a slut.

For serious, he's mine!

I totally saw him first and anyways, we're basically still on a date, so he's just being rude by ignoring me and talking to her, like, all the time. I know our date was kind of interrupted by Tif going all cray-cray and breaking her vegan diet, but come on, I came all the way up this gross mountain with all these nasty dead-type people who obviously have no concern for noise pollution with that icky noise they make and he's not even appreciating me! So rude! I will totally not let him have sex with me now...well, at least not tonight. Unless I really need to teach that tramp, Lucy, a lesson by showing her how much Nathan totally does like me. And not her.

One yay thing, is that we're going to see those yummy army boys again. Then I can show Nathan what he's missing out on by showing him how much all those other boys appreciate my fantastic bod, golden skin, and gorgeous hair. He's ignoring me for a redhead...ugh. Does he not understand that blondes are just better?

"Are we there yet?" I ask and receive lots of unfriendly looks. It's not like it's a stupid question. It's totes almost dark out and my feet hurt from all this walking. My shoes were made to be admired, not, like, all covered in dirt and blood. These aren't combat boots—thank God! Not that anyone cares, meanies.

"How many times do I have to tell you that it's going to take a while? So either suck it up and shut up, or go away," Nathan says in this totally rude tone of voice. I was just asking. It's not like they were talking about anything interesting, just different ways to kill those things. Ew.

"I still don't know we couldn't have just driven here, I mean, the army boys did."

"Like I already said, it's faster if we don't have to follow the road. Now seriously, shut the hell up."

Ugh. I am for sure not having sex with him tonight.

We find a couple more of the gross things wandering around being all rude, shrieking, and trying to bite us. But they kill them, which I guess is good since I'm way too hot to die, and bite scars would so not be hot. But it's still so nasty. Lucy tried to give me a knife, but, like, I'm abstinent. I totally believe in no violence. I know the gross people started it, but still.

"My feet hurt," I announce, hoping maybe Nathan will, like, finally get the message and carry me.

"Then you shouldn't have worn high heels! Just be quiet, we're trying to focus," Lucy snaps very meanly.

"At least my clothes and shoes are, like, fashionable, unlike you two," I retort. So there.

"Yeah, 'cause we really care about that when we're fighting off zombies, you useless idiot," Lia growls at me.

So rude.

"Although, that other chick's stiletto did make a halfway decent weapon," she says and the others laugh.

Ugh, I do not understand them. I was just trying to help them by letting them know their sense of fashion is completely off. I'm trying to think of a good insult to get back at them for being so rude to me when someone starts, like, shouting a little way in front of us. It doesn't sound like one of the gross people, so I just go back to trying to think of an insult.

"Hey, can we help you with something?" Yay! Two of the yummy army boys are now standing, like, right in front of us...mmm mmm good.

"Oh, thank God," Lia mutters and we walk towards them. And even though I'm all sleepy and sore, I make sure to waggle my assets on the way; I've got to get something out of this totes horrible trip.

Two seconds later, I finally think of a good insult. "Yeah, well, you look like a goth!" I say as we reach the army boys. Everyone just looks at me, but I am way too busy checking out the army boys now to care.

"Anyway..." Nathan says in a harsh tone of voice. Whatever, I'll just go back to flirting with the yum looking army boys. "We've encountered some of the...zombies, and we could use a place to stay for the night so we don't end up getting turned."

"Uh, zombies?" one of the yum army boys asks. "I don't know what you're talking about, sir, but if you wouldn't mind putting down your weapons?"

Now who's dumb? Seriously, people do not give me enough credit. "The gross people wandering around being all rude and totes getting in people's personal space and yelling for, like, no reason?" Everyone stares at me again, but I'm used to it, I just grin at the army boys and one of them winks back at me.

Hah, take that, Nathan.

"Right, well, I'm not sure what you're talking about, miss, but there's no such thing as zombies. Now if—"

Nathan suddenly, like, cuts off the army boy, "Then why are you evacuating the campgrounds?"

"Yeah!" I agree, showing support for my man. I know that one army boy is into me for sure, but a girl's gotta keep her options open.

"There have been several rabid bear sightings, sir, and—" the army boy is cut off again, but not by Nathan this time. Two of the gross people come at us shrieking all loud. It hurts my ears. Nathan shoots one in the head and the army boy who was, like, trying to tell us there were no zombies, shoots the other one and it's quiet again. Thank goodness, 'cause my poor ears are totes ringing like a phone from all the screaming and those stupid loud guns.

"So were those the bears you were talking about?" Nathan asks.

Silly boy. "Those were, like, the zombies?" I say, hoping I don't make him feel stupid by correcting him.

"Oh, shut *up*, Daffy," Lucy and Lia say at, like, the same time. They are such total bee-yatches.

"Sir, I really don't know what you think you just saw—" the army boy tries to convince us again that there's no zombies. Geez, even I figured it out faster.

"You mean what I think I just killed?" Nathan asks, his voice getting all angry and huffy. It's kinda hot.

"Sir—" the army guy tries again, and he sounds nervous now.

"Alright," Lucy interrupts now, "I think we can all agree that people have been coming back from the dead and snacking on other people, so can you just help us out here?"

The army boys are, like, looking back and forth at us then, like, back at each other. "Come on, man," the one who winked at me says, "we should just bring them back to Luca, let him figure out what to do."

"Fine," the other yummy one replies, and then says to us, "We're not saying anything is or isn't going on, but you should come with us."

So we follow them through the trees, which gives me a very nice view of their totes yummy and muscly bums.

Chapter Six
Like some kind of macabre hors d'oeuvres before the zombie jamboree

Connor

"That was fun," I say to Luca when we finally get back to the fort after the painful evac process that took way fucking longer than it should have. What happened to the good old days when people would just believe what a man in uniform was telling them and follow orders without a fuss? Nowadays, people always wanna know the reason for every little thing that's happening; it's exhausting. I blame the internet, with all its free information about everything you never cared about before. It was so much better when everyone just used it to search for porn.

Luca grunts in response to my sarcasm and doesn't look up from the map of the campground and the surrounding areas that he's studying. He's been like that since we saw the video and the evac went all FUBAR. It's what he does when he's freaking out but doesn't want anyone to know; he usually comes out of it when he thinks of a plan so I'm not worried. I'm freaking out, too, but with all the zombie movies I've watched over the years, I feel like I was more prepared than the average bear for this kind of thing to happen. Luca always resisted when Rafe and me wanted to show him the movies, he always tried to get out of it, 'cause he never really appreciated them. Which you think he would considering his granny's all up into that Santerian voodoo business and I'm pretty sure there's some type of zombie folklore involved in that wackness.

Before I can descend any further into pondering the difference between voodoo zombies and Romero zombies, a very ticked off and very feminine voice shatters the relative silence of the surrounding woods. "No, really, I don't think you understand my point—there are face-eating zombies just hanging out, waiting to gnaw on any unarmed idiots who have the bad luck to wander within chomping range," the voice asserts angrily, and Luca finally looks up from his map.

He glances at me with a "what the hell?" expression on his face and all I can do is shrug as he turns to stare at the location the voice is coming from. When he sees it's where Locklan and Darryl are supposed to be patrolling, his expression darkens, coming dangerously close to turning into a full-on glower. Anger works pretty well for pulling him out of his freak-out spirals but I almost never resort to causing it since I don't handle those glowers so good. Which is why I'm thinking it's a good thing for once that Locklan never seems fazed by them. Luca works better when he's not freaking out.

The strident female voice continues, loudly, "Logically, wouldn't the intelligent course of action be to, oh, I don't know, *arm* the random civilians you wander into? Or at least let them keep their own *goddamn battle axes*!"

What the hell is going on?

"'Battle axes'?" I repeat, looking over at Luca to see his reaction to this surreal development.

Luca's eyes are trained on the place from which the voice is emanating, confusion messing with his glower power, giving his face a weird expression, like it can't decide which emotion it wants to show. If I weren't worried his glare would win out and become directed at me, I don't think I'd be able to suppress a chuckle at the sight.

"Let *go* of me!" The person belonging to the voice finally exits from the trees, wrenching her arm from Locklan's grasp as she does so. Once she's freed herself, she shoves the bangs of her dark hair out of her eyes and adjusts her black, cat's-eye glasses so that she's now glowering up at Locklan without any obstructions.

"You want to help me? Help me? You can *help* by giving me back my damn axe! This"—she gestures to the, yup, battle axe, now in Locklan's possession, and then holds up her empty hands—"is not protection. This is…endangerment…and just stupid. I know what I'm doing!" she finishes in a huff and puts her hands on her hips.

Locklan sneers at her and tries to plow past her, but she's not intimidated, and she is *not* moving. Locklan gets a pained look on his face and shifts his weight. He looks over her head in our direction, a helpless look mixing with the discomfort in his expression.

I can't help snickering a little as I watch Locklan squirm. It's a hell of a sight: 6'4", 210 pound Locklan looking completely discomfited as this diminutive pit-bull of a girl fumes up at him...for taking her battle axe away. I can't help being impressed even though I've got a gut feeling this chick is gonna be nothing but trouble. And my gut feelings are almost always right...no matter what Luca or my mama says.

Locklan glances over at Darryl, looking for help, but Darryl looks as impassive as always, and maybe even a little amused for once. Locklan's on his own and it is very entertaining. Even Luca is smiling a little, so distracted by the scene in front of us that he hasn't even put the map away yet, he's still just holding it out in front of him as he watches the show.

"*Lia!*" I only now notice a shorter chick with long, curly, reddish-brown hair as she grabs the angry chick's—Lia's—hand and yanks her back hard enough to make her lose her footing. Lia stumbles in her combat boots. "Are you trying to get yourself shot?"

Locklan chuckles, saying, "Yeah, why don't you just shut up and listen to your hot little friend, ya crazy bitch?"

"Oh, hell no, you did not just say that!" the smaller chick growls, now almost as indignant as Lia, and Locklan's laughter is cut short by the twin pissed off looks on the faces of these crazy chicks. He squirms for a couple more seconds in the face of their glares before turning to Luca, saying, "Shit, these gems are all yours, Sergeant."

The group accompanying him and Darryl—which, besides the fuming Lia and the slightly more reasonable shorter chick, includes a tall dude with a rifle and a hot blonde chick who seems to be unarmed—notices us for the first time as Locklan calls attention to us.

"Good riddance," Locklan growls, then spits, the loogie landing inches from Lia's boots. She looks ready to punch him, but she's held back by the shorter chick, who now looks pretty goddamn enraged herself. It's a good thing she's holding Lia back, from the way Locklan talks about chicks, something tells me he wouldn't have much compunction about hitting a girl.

It's the loogie that does it. Luca shakes his head and the glower wins out over confusion as he hands me the map and says, "Private Gates. *Ven aca!*"

Uh-oh. Spanish. That's never a good sign when it comes to Luca's temper.

I struggle to fold up the map as Locklan swaggers over, swinging the battle axe a little as he walks. He smirks at me fighting with the map as he walks up and I wrangle it into one hand and flip him off with the other.

"What?" Locklan asks, his voice filled with arrogance as he shifts his attention to Luca. Luckily, his lack of respect has Luca so annoyed with him that he doesn't notice my struggles with the map, or how I finally give up trying to wrestle it into its original folded shape and just kinda crumple it up and shove it into one of my pockets where it immediately expands and makes the pocket bulge funny…'cause I am just that smooth.

Luca glowers even more intensely at Locklan and growls emphatically, "What, *sir*." Luca stares Locklan down until even he can't stand it and he breaks off and glances to the side.

"Sir, what, sir?" Locklan mutters, eyes flashing at the reprimand.

"What part of the mission did you not understand? We're supposed to leave the civs out of this, and you're definitely not supposed to disrespect them so they act even more disagreeable." His voice is tight with frustration making his accent more noticeable than usual.

"It's not *my* fault, they just stumbled onto us; apparently they got lost, and now they refuse to leave without some answers. They figured it out on their own, which should be obvious, but I'll let you fill them in on the rest, *sir*. I can't deal with that crazy bitch for one more second." He hefts the battle axe up, and shakes his head in disbelief.

For once, I'm inclined to agree with the prick. I saw a lot of weird, bad shit in the Middle East, but this is a new one—or, I guess, an old one, medieval, even. "They say they were camping, but who the fuck brings a battle axe to go camping?" He raises his voice so Lia can hear him. I hate to admit it, but he does have a good point. Luca seems to think so, too, since his glower lessens a little and he stares at the battle axe more closely, then at its owner.

"I didn't bring it to camp with! It's for my thesis! God, I've only said it five times!" Lia protests loudly. I glance over at her as she's about to speak again, Luca does the same and she meets his gaze with her own and holds it. Her face is flushed and her eyes are bright, but she closes her mouth without a word, still looking furious as she crosses her arms over her chest, a move which seems to capture Luca's attention more than I would've thought, considering how he's usually so obsessed with being "professional." The redhead looks between the two of them, looking as surprised as I feel.

The moment is over quickly, though, as Luca shakes his head and returns his attention to Locklan. "Private Gates, never mind the goat rodeo you've dropped on my doorstep like a gift wrapped pile of *mierda en fuego*, or the civs you've put in serious fucking danger, you are a professional soldier. Behave as such or I will see to it you're on cleaning detail for the rest of your career.

"And if you continue to antagonize the *chica*, I'll make sure she gets this"—he takes the axe from Locklan's grip—"back. I'm not sure you'd like to see where she might bury it." He points to the northwest quadrant. "Relieve Church from patrol. Double rotation. I don't want to see your face or hear your voice until zero-dark-thirty, you hear me, *cabrón*?" Luca orders, his Spanish slipping out again the way it always does when he's pissed.

"Yes, sir," Locklan mutters, giving a half-assed salute and turning on his heel.

Asshole.

Luca mutters something else angry and Spanish then goes back to examining the axe and the strange group still accompanying Darryl. Noticing Darryl, Luca says, "Cho, join Gates, make sure he doesn't do anything else stupid and you can relieve Donahue while you're at it."

"Yes, sir," Darryl answers—with the appropriate amount of respect, might I add—before jogging off after Locklan. Darryl has always been a good soldier, he's one of those people who's just born to follow orders and not ask questions.

Luca nods at me and we walk over to the group, which is eyeing us warily, except for the hot blonde, she's just staring into space like she doesn't even realize she's in the middle of what could very well be the zombie apocalypse, or the zompocalypse, if you will.

Suddenly, Lia clears her throat, and reluctantly taking my attention from the blonde, I look back at her and ask, "So what kind of thesis are you writing, exactly?"

"I'm a historical anthropology grad student with a concentration in ancient combat and weaponry—I have permits. I swear. I'm not just some crazy girl with an axe," she answers, her hands punctuating everything she says, her voice just one step down from being out-right rude and hostile.

Luca raises an eyebrow at her but says nothing. I look over at him and I can tell he's not ready to talk yet; he hates dealing with civs, so it usually takes him a while to actually talk if he has to deal.

"It's not fair; he let Lucy keep her machete." I glance at the shorter chick—Lucy, I guess—who holds up a machete in confirmation.

Who are these girls?

My attention goes back to Lia as she continues her invective, "He called me 'sweetheart,' so I said that I was neither his girlfriend nor his daughter, so he could shove his sweetheart shit and to tell us why the fuck there are zombies skittering about, and then he just took it away. He's completely unreasonable," she explains, crossing her arms over her chest again and huffing angrily, reminding me a little of a dragon.

"*You* have a battle axe in a provincial campground, which you refused to lower even in the face of a direct order to do so, and *he's* completely unreasonable?" Luca breaks his silence to ask, the puzzled expression from earlier having overthrown the glower for now. Lia's own glower, however, turns furious again and she opens her mouth to begin what I'm sure would be another rant, but Luca holds up a hand to silence her and turns to me asking, "Corporal McCoy, is this *chica* serious?"

I give her a once-over, as she fumes silently. I glance from her combat boots and her torn leggings to her awkwardly buttoned sweater and blood-spattered flowery dress, face and neck, and clear my throat, preparing to answer as Luca plays his civ game. Since he hates dealing with them, when he's around civs and they piss him off or he thinks they're gonna cause trouble, he starts to act like his asshole alternate self.

I don't like playing, but he's my C.O. so I answer like I know he wants me to: "In the opinion of this soldier, sir, I'm gonna have to say yes."

I try not to wince as Lia looks even angrier, something that seemed impossible a minute ago, but somehow she does it with a complicated movement that thins her lips to a fraction of their original size and the balling of her shaking hands into fists. I can almost see her vibrating. Lucy's calming hand doesn't seem to be working so well anymore; Lia looks like she's either going to throw a punch or cry. I honestly don't want to be on the receiving end of either.

Having achieved his goal of annoying her and putting her off balance, Luca switches back to professional soldier mode and goes for soothing. "Listen, ma'am," he says, exaggerating the Latino lilt in his voice to calm her down.

"Lia," she insists, her voice low and dangerous, not at all impressed by his accent.

"Lia. I am Sergeant Luca Ortiz and I apologize for Private Gates. This is a stressful situation we're involved in, as I'm sure you've noticed, and reactions are bound to be volatile. I'm sure that in his opinion, your safety with a dangerous weapon was a valid concern. You need to understand that in this instance, weapons should be the sole concern of those properly trained by the military," he ends this little speech with the smile that almost always has the ladies swooning over him and doesn't bother apologizing for either his behaviour or mine.

Her hands unclench slowly as she gears up for another lecture, clearly not taken in by his charms. "We were attacked by no less than six zombies within the hour it took us to leave my van and get here. Without that axe, my friends and I would very likely be numbering among the undead—"

"Um, we helped a little, you know," Lucy says indignantly and I can't hold back a smile.

Lia sighs, looking disgruntled to have been interrupted during her rant. "Not what I meant, okay? I was just trying to make a point." Lucy grumbles and rolls her eyes but doesn't say anything else. Lia takes a deep breath, focuses her attention back on Luca and continues with her speech as though nothing happened. "Military trained or not, I'd rather have the ability to protect myself than wait around for someone else to do it for me. If I followed your advice, I'd be dead at least three times over by now." There's a tiny tremor in her voice. She's more scared than she's letting on, hiding it beneath her bravado and angry speeches. Not that I can blame her, I may love the movies, but that doesn't mean they don't occasionally give me nightmares.

Luca lowers his voice to an intimate level, rolling his r's even more, hoping to ease her mind with flirtation if nothing else, I guess. I don't blame him, we don't have much time, and it's been a proven tactic with women in the past, battle zone or not. "Listen, Lia, we'll be happy to return it to you once we get you on your way and we know you're safe. My men are well trained and well armed. Let us do this for you." He smiles at her again, his tone of voice doing its best to make it seem like they're alone.

It doesn't faze her for a second, which obviously flusters and irritates him.

"Our safety is your main concern, right?" she asks. I suspect a logical argument and Luca frowns in annoyance like he suspects a trap, but he nods in assent anyways and waves for her to continue her diatribe. "I'm safer when I'm armed. I know how to use my weapons." She looks hard into his eyes, willing him to understand.

Even if he does understand, I know it won't bother him any less. She's an uncontrolled element. Our unit has been drilled and trained to work as a seamless combat unit...well, except for Locklan, who tends to make things go awry, but right now he's not the point. The chaos factor of this girl, the zombies, and other untrained civs wielding rifles and machetes—it's too many unknowns, and I can tell it makes him uneasy. He is one heck of a control freak and at this point, he probably *will* give back her battle axe just so he can get rid of them and regain complete control.

Luca makes a face, then smiles again, seeming to decide trying the reasonable yet flirty tactic once more. It usually works much better for him, and he can't seem to help stubbornly trying to get positive results in this situation, too. "You know most *chicas* would be happy not to have to hold a weapon at all—most people even."

Before Lia can respond, the hot blonde pipes up, and gives credence to the jokes...not that it makes me any less attracted to her. "Yeah, Lia, weapons are, like, super dangerous and so nasty. Plus, they are terrible accessories...they're so heavy! It would be so much better if you would just, like, accessorize with bangles.

All that blood and stuff does nothing for your complexion. You're pretty pasty anyways so it's probably not something you want to, like, draw attention to?"

Wow. I mean, I usually like 'em a bit dumb, but wow.

"Okay, you have five seconds to get the hell away from me," Lia announces, not bothering to turn around; she's still focused on Luca, her determined glower fixed in place, her mouth still folded up into that thin little line.

"I'm just trying to give you some fashion advice, Lia, you don't have to get all snickety," the blonde pouts. It's actually kinda impressive how dumb she is.

However, Lia does not seem to agree with me. "I don't even know or care what word you're trying to say. You have two seconds," she growls, eyes still fixed on Luca. They look like they're in a really intense staring contest.

Lia's low growl finally makes the hot blonde reconsider giving her fashion advice and she hobbles away on her impossibly high heels. Lia takes a deep breath and holds out a shaky hand towards Luca. "I promise I won't be a problem. Please," she adds softly, her voice both imploring and fierce as she continues to hold his gaze. He takes her in for a moment, breaking the staring contest as he looks her over. He rubs his jaw with his free hand and continues to study her, pausing longer at her tits than he normally would in professional soldier mode.

"Please," she repeats, obviously ignoring his wandering eyes in the interest of retrieving her axe.

Luca shakes his head, looks skyward and seems to decide that we have to attend to more pressing matters. Like zombies chowing down on people's limbs and faces like pop-tarts in a ration-pack, for example.

He pulls himself completely back into soldier mode, and finally passes over her battle axe with a stern, "Zombies only, or I confiscate it for good." She smiles as she takes her axe back, her mouth finally returning to normal as she grips the handle happily.

Strange, strange chick. I mean, it's a badass weapon and all, but it's still weird that she threw such a hissy fit just for having it taken away. Luca told her we'd protect her, so I don't know what she's got her panties all in a wad for.

Before I can go back to checking out the blonde discreetly (to avoid the wrath of Luca; I know he thinks we should just be completely focused on the impending zombie apocalypse, but come on, I'm just a formerly Catholic man, I can't help it! Besides, it's not like he wasn't doing his share of checking someone out), Luca calls my attention back to him with a sharp nudge to my arm...not to sound like a pussy, but ow. Guess I wasn't being so discreet after all.

"Connor."

Uh-oh, warning tone and my real name, I better start paying attention. "Sorry, Luke," I say, eyes downcast to portray the proper amount of chagrin, which is a time-tested move I perfected to get the nun's wimples out of a bunch when they'd catch me doing something ruler-smack worthy back in school.

Luca just grunts in my direction, but as far as I'm concerned, that means the move worked so no chills pop up for the time being. "Where were you heading when you found us?" Luca asks the group.

"We were actually trying to figure out how to get to you guys to find out exactly what's going on. Failing that, we were going to try to get back to Lia's van since, with all the other weapons she has in it, it's probably one of the safest places to be right now," Lucy responds before Lia can start up with yet another outburst. Girls like Lia are why I actually prefer the dumb ones; they're way less trouble.

"*Qué es el problema?*" Luca asks. "Just go back to your van so you can exit the area and leave the zombie-killing up to us." Luca still has his "oh, aren't I just so charming and Spanish" voice on and I can't stop myself from rolling my eyes.

"Well, we would," Lucy begins patiently, "but we don't know where it is, exactly. We got lost when we were fighting off the first zombie we ran into."

I remember the abandoned looking van I saw while we were evac-ing the campground. "Hey, is it kind of a Scooby-doo Mystery Machine type of van?" I ask and Lucy and Lia both suddenly look a lot happier.

"You've seen it?" Lia asks, and for the first time since we met her, she doesn't sound like she's going to decapitate the next person she sees with her newly returned axe.

"Yeah. You remember, Luke?" I ask and he nods in response, looking distracted again, his mind probably already strategizing ahead. "I could take them to it," I offer, mostly thinking about winning the gratitude of the willowy blonde who keeps winking at me.

I can't really tell if it's on purpose or if she hasn't quite figured out how to work her eyelids, but I figure it's probably a good sign either way since at least her gaze is directed at me.

"*Si. Buena idea*, Mac, but find Kane *primero* and get him to accompany you, you might need back-up on the way. I'm going to reconvene with the geeks and let them know how the evac went."

I don't bat an eye when he doesn't call Elliot or Gregory by their names; he never bothers to remember anyone's name unless they impress him in some way and earn his respect. When I first started serving under him, it took a whole six months before he stopped calling me "Freckles" and actually troubled himself to learn my real name. The guys would still tease me about it if everyone else's early nicknames from Luca weren't just as unflattering. We all just have a silent agreement never to use them on each other.

I notice Lia getting all huffy again, probably 'cause Luca implied she and her battle axe weren't enough back-up.

Seriously strange girl. And again, this is why I enjoy the simple (in every definition of the word) girls like the blonde chick; they're docile and they tend to do what you tell them to without question.

Luca nods at all of us, reminds me to keep my comm on, like I'm gonna forget that again, it was one time, but he never lets me forget it, and then walks back to the fort.

"Alright," I say smiling at the group, Lucy and the blonde smile back, Lia and the big guy, whose name I didn't catch, don't. "I'll just call Lincoln and then we can get you folks out of here."

Why did I just say "folks"? Who the hell *ever* says "folks"? It's not cool. Luckily, the blonde doesn't seem to have noticed.

Lucy smiles again, shifting her machete from hand to hand. Gotta respect a girl who brings the weapon favoured by the Voorhees' for chopping up camp counsellors to a zombie fight. Not to mention her awesome and now, weirdly appropriate bag, which glows dimly in the dark and says, "During a zombie attack please follow me." If I didn't have a thing for dumb blondes, she'd definitely be on my radar.

Reminding myself that I've gotta call Link, I click on my comm unit, saying, "Link, it's Mac, just called to say I miss you, and I feel so alone without you here beside me so get your sweet November ass over to the main entrance in the truck 'cause we gotta escort some civs back to their vehicle. Alpha 2-1 out." I grin at the running joke between Link and me.

Link's voice crackles over the radio, "Talkin' 'bout missing me, you damn faggot? I'll be right there…so I can kick your homo ass. Alpha 2-2 out."

I turn back to the group, who all have matching puzzled looks on their faces. Right. I sometimes forget that some people don't understand the homoerotic jokes between us soldiers.

"Um…" I begin just as Link drives up to us, leaning out the window and smacking me on the back of my head as he rolls to a stop. "Right, well, anyway…we should probably all get introduced before we go. Everyone, this is Master Corporal Lincoln Kane, but you can call him Link, I'm Corporal Connor McCoy, but you can call me Mac. Link, this is Lucy and Lia and, uh—" I break off and step closer to the blonde "—I didn't quite catch your name."

"I'm Daphne, but you can, like, call me Daffy?" The blonde says, turning it into a question and Link raises his eyebrows at me.

I don't even care, she's still hot.

"You got a name?" Link asks the big guy who's staring at Daffy with a disgusted look on his face. Not all guys appreciate the charm of the dumb ones like I do.

"I'm Nate—" he begins, but he's quickly interrupted by Daffy saying, "but you can, like, call him Nathan?"

"No, you can't," he argues, irritated. "My name is Nate, that's it."

"What no last name, like Cher?" I ask.

"Or Madonna?" Link adds and Nate glowers at us. Wow, his glowers are almost as powerful as Luca's; I've got, like, baby chills going on.

"It's Townshend," Nate says, his voice tight with annoyance.

Geez, dude should really lighten up. I know there are zombies around, but come on, you gotta retain your sense of humour in crisis situations or you'll go bonkers.

"Really? As in Pete?" Lucy asks, sounding excited. That *is* a pretty awesome person to share a last name with, I gotta admit.

Nate glances at her, smiling. "Yeah, it's the only good thing my father ever gave me." His words are bitter but his voice isn't as he looks at her.

Hmm…could be a bit of bow-chikka-chikka-wow-wow going on there. Daffy looks between the two of them, a persnickety look on her face. Hmm…or a triangular type of situation, maybe.

"Who's Pete?" Daffy asks, her snotty voice matching the expression on her face.

"Never mind," Nate says, ignoring her, which distorts her face even more as she pouts. It makes her just a little less hot.

"We gonna go anytime soon, ya carrot-headed fag-sucker?" Link asks.

Good point—except for the fag-sucking thing, that's just rude. "Right, right," I say, ignoring his insult and switching my comm unit back on, saying, "Hey, Luke, just lettin' you know we're Oscar Mike. Alpha 2-1 out." Turning to Link, I say, "Let's go," just as Daffy pipes up asking, "Who's Mike? Is he hot?" I stifle a laugh, but Link doesn't bother, which isn't surprising 'cause he doesn't seem at all interested in getting in her pants.

"What, you don't want to know if Oscar is hot?" Lia asks as Lucy and Nate grin and don't bother stifling laughs themselves as they pile into the truck.

"No," Daffy begins and I'll admit I have a morbid curiosity as to the rationale. "He sounds, like, grouchy for some reason." She turns to me, winking again and pouting her lips, which seems to make talking difficult so she returns them to normal before asking again, "So who's Mike?" and hopping into the truck, too. I walk around the front, getting in the shotgun seat and shutting the door behind me.

"There's no one named Mike," Link responds, rolling his eyes. "It means we're on the move."

"That makes no sense," Daffy protests. "There are definitely people named Mike, I've met some." She looks thoroughly confused, which I hate to say I actually find a little endearing, but don't judge me, it's been a while since I was around chicks, especially one this hot.

I open my mouth to explain things to her, but I feel a tap on my arm before I can say anything. I look back and Lucy says, "Don't bother, trust me." I shut my mouth again. She's probably right.

"Oh, before we head out, do any of you have flashlights, by any chance?" I ask. "Link and I have a couple and some night vision goggles, but only a pair each. It'll be fully dark once we get away from the lights of the fort, so we should probably get this sorted out now."

"I have one," Lucy answers, pulling a small black flashlight out of her zombie bag. "I'm night-blind so I always carry one."

"Why don't you guys take our flashlights," I say, offering mine to Daffy as Link offers his, first to Nate, who just looks at him, and then to Lia who declines, saying, "I'll just follow Lucy's, I can see pretty well in the dark." Link shrugs and puts the flashlight back in his pocket.

After figuring out the flashlight situation, we drive in the direction where I remember seeing Lia's van. The journey is mostly silent, only interrupted by an occasional outburst from Daffy about still not understanding who or where Oscar and Mike are and Lucy answering our questions about the zombies they've encountered so far. After about five minutes, we arrive at the small clearing where Lia's van is still sitting and they all exit the truck.

Lucy opens her mouth to say goodbye when those ungodly shrieks suddenly ring through the air, announcing the imminent arrival of zombies. I feel chills similar to those from Luca's glowers, since I haven't seen any in person yet and I'm half scared and half excited to fight some off. I grab my night vision goggles out of one of my pockets and hop out of the truck. Link does the same and we join the others. I wish we had more NVGs for everyone, but we couldn't grab extras without pissing Luca off for taking too long; he wants these civs gone, now.

"Now aren't you glad I got my axe back?" Lia gripes, completely unfairly.

"Hey, I wasn't the one who took it in the first place, so hush," I say and she grumbles but just adjusts her stance, gripping her axe tight, getting ready.

Lucy drops her bags and shifts her machete to her right hand while easing Daffy to the ground with her left. "Just stay here and don't move, okay? Unless you wanna fight?" she asks as she does so, laughing at the horrified look on Daffy's face.

"Alright everyone, let's circle up, protect our sixes," I order, ignoring Daffy's query about what exactly we're protecting. This chick is seriously hot, but she could also get us all killed if we're not careful so I think ignoring her is probably best for now.

Nate flips his rifle into his hands and Link and me both get our pistols out. We form the circle around Daffy, facing outward so our sixes are protected, ready for combat. The screeches rip through the night air again and I'm glad for the NVGs giving me a better sight line. Lucy shines her flashlight around the trees, the light flickering as it catches on branches and what is possibly the occasional zombie.

And then suddenly they're on us, at least seven of the scary monsters, looking even fucking scarier awash with the green tinge of the NVGs. I don't wait for them to get closer, I just start shooting, landing mostly torso shots because they're so goddamn fast. I saw it on the tape, but in person, it's just insane how quick they move, besides that, it's dark and even with the NVGs it's hard to get a good line of sight on the undead bastards.

Link is having similar luck, shouting, "Goddamn you motherfuckers, just die!" while he shoots into the trees. Somehow, Nate seems to land every single shot and soon we're down to just three zombies. The remaining undead howl loudly before rushing us. Nate takes down one easily, his bullet seeming to sluice through its head as it collapses. Link and I take care of a second, leaving Lucy and Lia to hack apart the third before it bites them or Daffy. Lia swings the axe hard, just missing the zombie's head as it moves quickly out of the way, still howling.

"Damn it, Luce, shine the goddamn light!" she shouts angrily.

I try to get a clean shot at the thing, but can't without risking hitting Lucy or Lia. Link and Nate both hold back from shooting, too, seeming to have the same problem.

"I'm fucking trying!" Lucy retorts and, finally catching the zombie in a stream of light, she swings her machete hard, up and into the side of its head, slashing so hard that it almost splits the skull horizontally in half. Chunks of brain mixed with blood and pieces of bone spray out around Lucy's machete, splattering her and Lia anew. It's gonna be hell to wash all that blood off.

"God, those bastards are fast!" Lucy exclaims, removing her machete from the cleaved head with some difficulty.

"Everyone okay?" I ask. "No one was bit?" Everyone answers in the negative, which is a relief.

"God, you're so useless!" Lia shouts at Daffy, who's only just gotten up.

"I told you, I'm abstinent!" Daffy snaps, causing pretty much everyone to snort with laughter despite what just happened. Even with zombies trying to eat your face, stupid people are still entertaining. And like Tallahassee says in *Zombieland*, "You gotta enjoy the little things."

"Yeah, I'll just bet you are," Lia growls and seems to be gearing up for more when Lucy steps in saying, "Okay, okay, can we just get in the van please, where it's at least safer than it is out here, and then get the hell outta here?" Lia grumbles but agrees.

I agree too; I hate being out in the open like this, with those things coming from nowhere, it's giving me chills *worse* than one of Luca's glowers, which is definitely saying something.

"Thanks for the escort," Lia says, possibly sarcastically, as she takes out her keys and unlocks the doors of the van, opening the side ones so Nate and Daffy can get in. Daffy holds her hand out for Nate to help her, but he ignores it, getting in ahead of her and whistling over Lia's admittedly impressive weapon collection residing in a crate behind the second row of seats.

"You're welcome," I say, taking the opportunity to help Daffy into the van as she seems incapable of doing it herself. "Just get out of here and don't worry about the zombies, we'll take care of them. Just remember, if you do see any more of them, 'in the brain and not the chest, head shots are the very best.'"

Lucy grins at me, but Lia disdainfully says, "Yeah, we know."

Feeling uncomfortable, I shift the direction of my attention, saying to Nate, "You can come back for your truck after it's all clear," since he seemed kinda reluctant to leave it behind. He just grunts at me from inside the van, not even bothering to look at me; I don't know what Daffy sees in him, he is so persnickety.

Link adds, "Yeah, we'll take care of those nasty undead fuckers, don't worry your pretty little heads."

Lia scowls at this, but Lucy smacks her in the arm to pre-emptively shut her up, "Let's just go alright? I'm all sticky and gross."

"Fine. We're going," Lia consents, then nods at Link and me before getting in the driver's seat. Lucy deposits her bag on the back bed-type thing above the weapons crate, before shutting the doors and going up to ride shotgun, saying, "Thanks again," over her shoulder as she does so.

Once they're all in the van, Lia starts it up, honking the horn once then driving away. Link looks over at me. "Let's head back, carrot-cake. I hope we get to take out more of those undead fucks on the way."

"Hoo-ah," I agree. After a second I add, "I hope they make it out okay." Link grunts in response and we hop back into the truck before any more zombies can attack us and I contact Luca on the comm letting him know we're Oscar Mike again.

Lucy

I try to run my hands through my sticky and blood-matted hair but my fingers keep getting stuck in the knots...I really wish I could take a shower. My face feels tight from all the zombie blood that's sprayed onto it tonight and my arm is getting sore from hacking at undead things with my machete. So it goes when there are zombies about, I suppose, but it's rather unpleasant, to say the least, and I am ready to go home.

"Uh-oh," Lia says quietly as the van starts with a low rumble.

"What now?" I ask, fear and exhausted annoyance mingling in my voice.

"We're almost out of gas," she replies.

Of course we are.

"Did anyone notice a gas station anywhere nearby?" Lia asks, sounding as tired as I feel, but luckily, I can answer in the affirmative.

"Yeah, I think I saw one near the creepiest motel since the Bates were in business," I reply, earning some laughter from Lia and Nate. Daffy is silent, probably trying to figure out the reference...or just playing the circus song over and over again in her head, who knows?

"Good," Lia responds, "let's go home. I'm so done with zombies."

Nate and I murmur our agreement and the van falls into silence as we head towards the campground's exit. Despite how ready I am to go home and sleep this nightmare off, I can't stop thinking about how we're just going home with nothing to do but hope that this is all taken care of without us. The horror movie obsessed, film-student part of my brain is shrieking at me that this is a mistake, jumping up and down saying that characters splitting up and heading for the hills, hoping everything will be hunky dory when they come out of hiding is a plot point that almost always ends up with things being far, far worse when they return from the hills. I can't stop my brain from picturing scenes from *Dawn of the Dead*, *Night of the Living Dead*, et cetera, picturing this thing spreading until they outnumber us; isn't that always the fear?

"Hey," Lia says, catching my wandering attention and rescuing me from picturing having to fight off zombies everywhere we go in the near future. I look over at her and she pats my hand saying, "I'm sorry I yelled at you, just the stress of fighting off a zombie in the dark and—"

"Lia, stop," I interrupt, "it's so not a big deal, and it's not like I didn't yell back, so don't even worry about it. We're totally fine." I smile at her to show I mean it and squeeze her hand once before letting go.

Honestly, at the time, I barely even noticed her yelling at me, I was just freaking out about fighting off something I could barely see...damn my shitty night vision. Not to mention I was trying to stop the thing from gnawing on Daffy, though Lord knows why; that girl is so useless, we'd probably be in less danger if she were actually a zombie.

Lia smiles back at me then glances into the back of the van, frowning at something she sees back there. I follow her gaze, twisting around in my seat to see Daffy typing something on her phone. I wonder if she's updating her Facebook status to something like "OMG just, like, totes got attacked by, like, zombies? RIP Tif." I stifle a laugh at this mental image and Nate glances over at me, smiling a bit and I feel my stomach flip a little...I can't believe I'm getting a crush on this guy, who's possibly a bit psychotic, when there are zombies...

Holy shit!

"Holy shit!" Lia cries suddenly as we come to an abrupt stop near the exit gates.

"I was just thinking that," I say and Lia smiles briefly before returning her gaze to the carnage visible through the windshield.

"Why did we stop?" Daffy asks from behind me then she leans forward to see what's going on. "OMG!" she exclaims at exactly the same time Nate says, "Fuck," in a low voice as they both see what's happening right in front of us.

There are at least twenty zombies out in front of the van gathered near some abandoned cars. The zombies are in the middle of a feast. Several recently deceased and dismembered persons are being passed around like some kind of macabre hors d'oeuvres before the zombie jamboree.

"I'm gonna guess some people who were bitten escaped the attention of the soldiers and turned in the car," Nate offers, leaning forward so he can see better and I hate to admit that my brain momentarily blanks out as his arm brushes mine and my God, he smells so good even spattered with blood...like wet cedar...mmm.

"Well, that makes that whole thing make more sense," Lia's voice breaks into my crush oblivion and I shake my head, looking to see what she's pointing at. Two small, child-sized zombies are munching quite happily on what I'm really hoping isn't their parents, but, let's face it...probably is.

"That's just rude," Daffy pipes up and I snort back a laugh.

I will say this for her, she certainly helps keep the whole zombie situation light, intentionally or not.

"Are we just gonna drive through them or what?" Nate asks.

Good point. How are we going to get out? The gates are locked, the attendants likely having been turned into tasty morsels long before we arrived, and there are cars and a whole passel of zombies to get through before we're free and clear, as well.

Huh. "Hey, what do you call a group of zombies?" I ask, causing both Lia and Nate to look at me in disbelief. "Come on...if they had a name for a group of them, what would you call it?"

"A murder?" Nate offers.

"That's crows...or is it ravens? Either way, it's one of those. I don't think there *is* a name for a group of zombies," Lia replies.

"Right. I guess we could just call it a pack, like wolves," I suggest and receive another dubious look from Lia that I would have thought she'd reserve only for Daffy-isms.

"Zombies don't really hunt in packs, Luce. They're not that smart. I mean, they're dead," she says and glances back out of the window at the contested subjects.

"I'm not so sure that's true," Nate begins, and Lia twists around in her seat to shoot him the Daffy look now. "I know they're dead, I just mean I'm not so sure they aren't starting to hunt in groups. You know that sound they make? I think other ones respond to it, like wolves howling. When we were on our way here, more kept coming after they howled. I think they can call to each other. And look at how they're sharing food; they may be dead, but they seem to still have some instincts intact." He has a point: that screeching sound they make does seem to attract others, like it's some sort of battle cry, letting each other know that they found food.

Lia looks at me, then at Nate, and then just shakes her head. "That's impossible. They can't communicate...they're dead."

"Is it more impossible than the fact that there *are* zombies...eating people...right in front of us?" I ask and Lia punches my arm.

"You know what I mean," she says. "They can't talk to each other in any of the movies."

"'You mean the movies *lied?*'" I say, clutching a hand to my chest in mock outrage as I quote *Return of the Living Dead*. Lia gets a weird look on her face, like if she could look at herself incredulously, she would.

She shakes her head, saying, "I can't believe I just said that."

"And they do communicate in *Land of the Dead* and *Return of the Living Dead*, so there you go." I pause as I contemplate an experiment we could do to find out for sure whether they are communicating or not. "Look, let me try something. We should find out for sure if they're starting to communicate because the soldiers should know; it might help them and let's face it, we're not getting through that wall of undead anytime soon so our only option is to go back to the fort."

"What?" Lia asks angrily.

"Do you have a better idea? I love Brown Sugar, but I don't think it's up to ramming through about twenty-five zombies and then taking out the gate. And if we total the van, we're screwed." I say and Lia growls something about "chauvinistic, sexist bastards," but doesn't argue.

"I definitely vote for going back to the yummy army boys," Daffy says and Lia glares at her in the rear-view mirror.

"What are you gonna do?" Nate asks.

"Why do you suddenly care?" Daffy demands snippily.

"I don't," Nate says acidly. "I was asking Lucy."

I hear Daffy sniff unhappily as I answer, "I think I could probably imitate that noise they make, but if it works, we're gonna have to *move*, Li, fast as the van can go." I start to roll down my window. Lia grabs my arm, stopping me. "What?" I ask, confused.

"One, this is a terrible idea, and two, if it works, an incredibly dangerous one," she replies.

"One, it's really all we can do to test our hypothesis, and two, just get ready to drive if it does work and we'll be fine," I retort and she growls but lets me go. I finish rolling down the window, looking to either side to check for zombies before sticking my oh so edible head out the window. I lean out, but not too far—I can just hear imaginary movie audiences screaming about this being a bad idea.

I clear my throat, take a deep breath and then do my best impression of their shrieks by inhaling and trying to make a loud, high-pitched noise at the same time. It works pretty well, if I say so myself. The others seem to think so, too: Lia looks surprised and Nate looks awed.

"That's freaky. Are you, like, part zombie or something?" Daffy contributes from behind me.

I look at the pack of zombies in front of the van and notice quite a few of them staring in our direction now. I make the noise again, louder. Okay, that definitely got their attention. All of the zombies are looking at the van and the majority are shrieking in response. They start skittering towards the van and I turn to Lia saying, "Now would probably be a good time to go."

"On it," she replies, throwing the van into reverse just as I feel a hand clamp down hard on my arm. I'm suddenly thankful once again that I'm wearing my leather jacket because it is, you guessed it, ladies and gents, a zombie. It shrieks at me and I shriek back, and man, if the undead can be confused, that's what happens, causing it to pause long enough for me to hack its hand off with my machete, made somewhat more difficult because I have to use my left hand, so it takes a few tries, which is as enjoyable as it sounds. I'm finally successful and Nate pulls me back into the relative safety of the van.

I yank the now unattached hand off of my arm and throw it out the window, before quickly rolling it back up as Lia speeds away from the gathering zombies in reverse gear.

"I think we can safely say it works," I say, laughing and rubbing my arm where the zombie grabbed me. I can already feel a bruise starting to form, those things are sure strong.

"Yay for experimentation," Daffy pipes up and I can't help laughing again as I put my machete back down between my feet.

"You okay?" Nate asks and I nod in confirmation.

"Thanks for pulling me back in," I add, smiling.

"Anytime," he replies, causing my stomach to do a rather acrobatic double back flip. Like I said, it is possible he's a bit insane, killing your best friend can do that to a person, but he is still majorly gorgeous.

Lia is silent as she focuses on driving away from the ravenous horde of undead trying to follow the van. She manages to shake them and about five minutes later, we're back at the army base again. Lia slams on the brakes just in time to avoid smushing Mac, the rather hot ginger (even if he has the bad taste to find Daffy attractive) who escorted us back to the van. To say he looks surprised to see us would be something of an understatement, especially considering he was almost a ginger pancake.

"Sorry about that," Lia says as she opens her door and gets out of the van. I do the same, going around to open the side door for Daffy and Nate. Nate hops out, holding his rifle and pack. Daffy pauses, waiting for someone to help her down.

Mac obliges while asking, "What...what are you doing back here? And why were you driving backwards?"

"Zombies, is the answer for both questions, I'm afraid," I answer, leaning into the crate to join Lia in gathering more weapons.

"The gates were blocked by a massive amount of zombies. It seems like some people who were bitten made it past you guys. We even saw some zombie kids eating what was probably the remnants of their parents," Nate adds, shaking his head at the memory.

"Geez, 'when I was a kid, we fuckin' respected our parents, we didn't fuckin' eat 'em,'" Mac replies, quoting *Undead*—a fantastically ridiculous Australian zombie movie. I burst out laughing and he grins, seeming pleased that I know the quote. I get it; I too love bonding with people over a shared love of horror movies.

Lia has grabbed a plethora of weapons from the van and hands them to Mac, saying, "These should do for now." Then, upon seeing his confused face, she clarifies, "Since we can't leave, we're staying here because there's safety in numbers and besides, we can help with the whole zombie extermination thing, so I'm bringing my weapons."

"I better, uh, bring these in, I guess, and go tell Luca what's happening," Mac says, looking awkward with his arms full of various bladed instruments.

"Oh, one more thing to tell Luca," I add, "they're starting to communicate."

"Who?" asks Mac, looking even more confused.

"The zombies," Nate replies, taking some of the weapons from Mac before he drops them in shock.

"But...in the movies..." Mac starts, then trails off as he thinks about what he's saying and instead just asks, "How do you know?"

"I made the noise they make and they responded, shrieking back and dropping their munchables, to check out what was making the noise. We think they use it to tell others they've found food," I answer and Mac's mouth drops open as he considers the ramifications of the zombies being able to communicate, even to this primitive degree.

"Wow," he says, looking quite pale, making his freckles stand out sharply in the bright fluorescent light flickering above the door. "We should get inside so we can tell Luca and the others what's happening."

Lia reaches back into the van to retrieve her favourite sword, the Claymore, as Nate nods and follows Mac inside with Daffy prancing along behind them...I don't know how someone can still prance when covered in blood and general ick, but somehow she manages it. This is a bit impressive in a sort of disturbing way.

I'm about to follow along behind them when Lia grabs my arm, holding me back.

"What's up?" I ask her and finally notice that she looks rather pissed off. "Are you mad at me?" I ask incredulously, not understanding why she would be.

"Yes. You put yourself in a lot of danger back there, and you just can't Luce; I can't lose you." Her voice gets quiet at the end and her eyes look teary. She suddenly turns away, slams the doors shut on the back of the van and storms inside, Claymore in hand.

Well, that escalated quickly.

Chapter Seven
All they have left is the animal instincts of survival and finding food

Lia

I stalk away from Lucy, gripping my Claymore tightly, feeding my frustration into the grip and wishing there was a handy zombie around for me to decapitate. It just makes me so crazy how she'll take stupid risks like that, not even seeming to realize she could get hurt or worse. I hate when she does something dangerous and doesn't even seem to be scared, like slashing this afternoon's first zombie without worrying she might be getting too close. It's a zombie attack; the potential for risk is high enough without her helping it along. And I can't lose her. It just hurts my heart so much to even think of the possibility of her getting bitten and turning into a zombie and the idea that I might have to kill her the way Nate did Blaine...no matter the situation, I don't think I could do it. I can't even imagine how it's affecting Nate, having done that to his best friend—mostly because he doesn't actually seem all that affected. Maybe it's a defence mechanism of sorts, but it's got me worried, especially since he seems to have caught Lucy's eye, and she, his, which is even more worrying. I can't fault her for it completely, he *is* damn pretty, but the possibility for psychosis is enough for me to draw the line at any kind of lustful situation. I do not pleasure grind with crazies; it's a rule.

I turn the corner and push through a set of doors and I'm suddenly in what looks like a cafeteria and am in the presence of several soldiers that are standing around Mac, gawking at my weapons laid out on a table. The soldiers notice me standing in the doorway and switch to gawking at me. For a second I can't think of why they would be doing that and then I remember that I'm wearing a dress, I'm covered in blood, and I'm holding a big-ass sword.

Mac, who really seems unable to stand any kind of awkward silence, steps forward saying, "Uh, guys, this is Lia—the battle-axe chick." The soldiers grunt a hello and continue eyeing the Claymore sword. I can see a couple of them smirking, making me wish even more that there was a zombie around because their expressions are really making me want to kill something again.

"Lia," Mac continues trying to fill the awkward silence as I catch sight of Nate by one of the back tables, a pained expression on his face as Daffy chatters in his ear. Poor guy. It's possible he's crazy, but I still feel for him. "This is Corporal Harold Church—everyone calls him Preacher—Private Jimmy Cooke, Private Marco Cantolena, Corporal Rafe Donahue, Corporal Carl Halley. Uh, you already met Link…and Private Locklan Gates and Master Corporal Darryl Cho—they're out patrolling right now." He gestures to each man in turn; his mouth curling with distaste as he finally names the sexist asshole soldier who took my axe away. It's comforting to know I'm not the only one he infuriates. In fact, judging from the way Mac's distaste is mirrored by all the other soldiers, I'm guessing he pisses everybody off. Surprise, surprise. I'm relieved that he's not here right now, or the blade of my Claymore might just have found a home…in his face.

I notice the soldiers glance behind me at the same time I hear a noise, and I turn to see Lucy walk in, still gripping her machete. She looks at me uncertainly, barely seeming to notice the others. Damn, when she looks at me with that face like she's a little puppy that got in trouble and doesn't know why, my anger just melts away. I can never stay mad for very long when she starts pouting. It's vexing.

I sigh and am about to give in and reassure her that we're fine when Sergeant Ortiz—Luca—walks into the cafeteria, trailing four guys behind him: two in lab coats and two who look like they've lifted one too many dumbbells.

Nate walks over towards Lucy and me. Daffy trails along behind him, though her progress is slow because she keeps getting sidetracked by winking at whichever soldiers she deems cute enough to be worthy of her attention. To my disgust, several of them wink back and look her slowly up and down in a completely lecherous way that makes me glad I never finished that sad, little salad at the diner, because if I had, I think it would be attempting to crawl back up my throat right about now.

Lucy comes up beside me, I notice a similar expression on her face, and I reach out, squeezing her upper arm, silently telling her we're okay. She looks over at me, smiling happily. I can't hold back a sigh. Sometimes I think she must practice her pouty look in the mirror; she can turn it on and off so quickly.

"*Bueno*, you're all here," Luca says, "we can get on with the introductions and then find places for everyone to sleep."

Ugh, Luca. Chauvinistic ass. I really can't stand people that know just how sexy they are and use it to get whatever they want. I can't believe he tried to flirt with me to get me to calm down about the axe thing. Like I would fall for that. His accent isn't even *that* cute. Seriously, he infuriates me almost as much as that Gates asshole. And the only reason it's not *as* much is that he did eventually give me my axe back.

Mac repeats the names of the soldiers and then continues with the introductions and I'm distracted from that train of thought. "So this is Gregory Thrushfield III, Elliot Frink, Jake Matthews, and Terry Morgan. Everyone, this is Lia, Lucy, Daffy, and uh, Nate Townshend. Sorry girls, I don't know your last names," he finishes apologetically and awkwardly. I can't believe the skinny, nerdy dude's last name is actually Frink, that's just unfortunate. And of course, the stuffy looking, grey-haired guy has a numbered name. He hasn't yet deigned to speak to any of us; he's just standing there smoking his pipe. Ugh.

"Mine's Malone, Lia's is Lafontaine...no idea what Daffy's is though," Lucy says, a shrug of apathy in her voice.

"What my what is?" Daffy asks, and I gain a little respect for Luca as he snorts in disdain. Seriously, how can someone be so vapid and still remember to breathe all day, every day?

"Your last name," Mac explains patiently. God, it's so obvious he just wants to get under her skirt.

"Oh," Daffy titters moronically, tossing her blood-stained hair over her overly-tanned shoulders. I'm pretty sure I'm losing brain cells just standing this near to her. "It's Simpkins." God, I can practically hear the drool pooling and the wood forming in the pants of the idiots staring at Daffy like she's naked, instead of clothed in that headache inducing shade of pink and covered with blood and gore. It's not just the soldiers, either. It's the skinny dude and the two big guys, as well. Even the snotty old guy is taking a peek now and then.

Elliot is actually the worst of them, if only because it looks so pathetic. He's looking at Daffy like she's the answer to his prayers, which just makes me want to blow chunks even more, not to mention hit him upside the head and knock some sense into him. She's so goddamn awful.

I glance at Nate and Lucy, who look as quizzical as I feel at all the attention Daffy's getting, just for standing there giggling like an idiot—though I am actually impressed that she remembered her own last name and didn't have to check the label on her Hello Kitty suitcase or something first.

"*Bueno.* Now that we're done with that, we should get you civs to bed, it's late," Luca interrupts the mindless gazing of the idiots—a completely different type of zombie problem. The fact that he seems to be unaffected by Daffy, as well, makes me dislike him a little less...but only a little, he's still an ass.

Mac shakes his head and has the decency to look shame-faced as some of his blood returns north and he nods at Luca. "Right, Sarge, on it." He turns his attention back to us. "There's an empty barracks that all you girls can sleep in."

Oh joy, we get to share a room with Daffy.

"And Nate, there's a good sized storage room that you can crash in; we can set you up with a free cot from our barracks." Nate nods in response, not seeming very concerned about the sleeping arrangements. Of course he's not, he's lucky, because he doesn't have to share with the bleached blonde bimbo.

"Um, can I just ask a question before we're sent to our rooms?" Lucy inquires, earning a dirty look from Luca for not being quietly complacent. I'm surprised he *doesn't* like Daffy since she's easy to control and he seems like he'd like that.

"*Qué?*" Luca asks.

"Um, who are these guys?" She gestures to the lab coats and the dudes who look like their bodyguards.

"We just told you," Luca answers, irritated.

"You told us their names, not who they are or what they're doing here," Lucy points out and Luca's frown deepens.

"Yeah," I add, "they don't exactly look like soldiers."

"We're scientists from SymbioVitaTech," Elliot responds and Gregory smacks him on the head with his pipe, causing him to wince. The bigger guy, Terry, suddenly hits the pipe out of Gregory's hand, sending it across the room and into the wall, where it snaps in two. Gregory looks enraged and stalks out of the room without a backward glance. Elliot looks thunderstruck. Jake, the other big guy, just laughs and returns his attention to Daffy's boobs. Everyone else is quiet, staring at Terry like they don't know what to say.

"Um, yeah, kinda got that you were some type of scientists or whatever from the lab coats, but why are you here?" Lucy continues hesitantly, looking a little unsure after the mildly violent exchange that just happened.

Elliot sighs. "SymbioVitaTech is where this whole thing got started. We were the lead research scientists there." His voice is so sad, even with his pathetic Daffy lust, I kind of want to just go over and give him a hug; he looks so defeated.

"So what happened?" I ask.

"It's a long story—" Elliot begins before abruptly interrupting himself. "The short version is we don't exactly know yet."

"But how—" I start to ask just as Lucy inquires, "Did you know that they're communicating...and hunting in packs?"

The look on Elliot and Terry's faces is enough to let us know that they weren't aware of this little tidbit yet. "P-please excuse me," Elliot stammers, walking quickly out the door Gregory left through, Terry following behind him.

The door shuts for a moment then Terry sticks his head back in and says, "Jake," in an authoritative voice. Jake tears his eyes away from Daffy, who giggles—lowering the collective I.Q. in the room even further, I'm sure. Jake grumbles but follows Terry anyway, letting the door slam behind him.

"Huh," I say glancing at Lucy.

"Yeah," she agrees.

Luca shakes his head and makes a hand motion at Mac, who nods and turns back to us.

"Alright, folks," he stops for a second, suddenly getting a pained expression on his face, then he shakes his head and continues, "uh, alright, *everyone*, come with me and I'll show you where you'll be bunking till we can figure out how to get you outta here."

It's obvious we won't be allowed any more questions tonight and I really need a shower so I decide to let it go. For now.

Elliot

I can't believe that the zombies are starting to communicate. I guess that it makes a sort of twisted sense: because they're the reanimated dead, all they have left is the animal instincts of survival and finding food, but it just makes them that much scarier and there's a part of me (I won't tell you how big a part) that just wants to go and hide under my bed until it's all over. I'm even more anxious now that there are civilians involved. I don't want to be responsible for any more deaths—or undeaths—of innocent people. I wish that they'd been able to escape, even though they did bring valuable information back with them. If the zombies are starting to hunt in packs and communicate, that means that they have at least enough sentience to know how to improve their chances of survival, which is even more terrifying than them simply reanimating.

I've been pacing in Gregory's room since Lucy told us what the zombies have been doing, trying to figure things out and trying to calm down. I am trying to think about the problem instead of having my mind wander back to thoughts of the amazingly lovely Daphne. I've never seen anyone so beautiful and exquisite. Even covered in blood, I couldn't take my eyes off of her. She's even prettier than those girls in the magazines that Terry and his friends gave me...probably because she's real. She's even more dazzling than Brittany Jones, my long-term high school crush and fantasy girlfriend. From her golden blonde hair to her bright blue eyes to...everything else, she's just...distracting me. I'm supposed to be brainstorming.

I don't know where the heck Gregory went after he stomped off like an angry child when Terry broke his pipe—which I still can't believe he did—so while I'm waiting for him to come back, I'm brainstorming about what on Earth could have caused the mutation in the first subject. I can't think about her by name or it's too hard to cope with what she turned into.

I have no idea what may have caused the subject to have the complete opposite reaction to the pills. They were supposed to help suppress one's appetite; it was going to be sold by Lady Slim workout and diet centres across the continent. We even had a name for the pills already; the trials were going so well, until they...weren't. We were going to call it Inner Thin (and our ad company had even come up with a slogan: *Inner Thin: helps bring out the inner, thinner you*).

We had such success with the trials in the beginning: the subjects were less hungry, they could eat less and still be full, and they had fewer cravings...and then subject Four. It never really took with her. At first, we weren't worried because vitamin supplements and medications work differently in everyone and in some people, not at all. But for it to have had the complete reverse effect than it was supposed to have. For it to make her crave...people. For it to make her so darn hungry that she ate another woman's face...that's something the research could never have predicted. Honestly, in what of the possible negative side effects would anyone have predicted: "this product may turn you into a zombie"?

I just have no idea what could have caused it. And without that, we can have no idea how to possibly fix it...or, rather, counteract it, I suppose. We obviously can't cure those already turned, because they're basically walking corpses, so if we did figure out a way to reverse the reanimation process, they would just give in to the natural processes and decompose and fully die. But that, at least, would be more efficient than destroying the brain of every single zombie, and that's something.

I wonder...the main chemical in Inner Thin pills targets the part of the brain that works to make people think they have to eat more. It basically kind of suppresses the animal instinct survival centre of the brain. So, what if, in subject Four, it didn't suppress it? What if it supplemented it...overloaded it? What if it made the animal instinct for survival overload so much that it overtook the human reason part and just killed it off? Thereby basically killing the host, just leaving it alive enough to be able to feed the survival needs. And once it was in the system...the mutated body chemicals could easily be transferred via saliva or other bodily fluids into the next victim's bloodstream.

If that's what happened...all we'd really need to do to counteract the effects would be to counteract the main chemical, to come up with a different chemical that would negate the effects.

Oh, my God, I really need to find Gregory...we need to get back to the lab.

Nate

It feels good to finally be alone, even if it's in the tiny storage closet that Mac put me up in. For the first time all day, I don't have Daffy yammering in my ear about one moronic thing or another and I finally feel like I can breathe. Then again, without the distraction of everyone else, my thoughts keep turning back to Blaine and how he looked after I killed him. How it felt to bury him. There's a small part of me that wishes I had just let him become a zombie and left him alone because then at least there'd be a part of him that's still alive in a way. I know it's selfish and illogical and I'd hate to have seen him that way permanently—it was hell just seeing him as a zombie for the few seconds I did before I killed him—but thinking about him being completely gone, forever...it kills me.

Never mind. I felt it. It wasn't a choice. It had to be done. I know what that feeling means. My father made sure that I knew. It's never a mistake when I feel that buzzing, hear that static. Because it's not a choice anymore, it's out of my hands, so how could it be a mistake?

Despite this knowledge, I still feel a little shaky. Blaine's dead face keeps flashing across my eyelids. To calm myself down and divert myself from the memories, I decide to clean my SKS and try to distract myself as much as possible. I sit down on the cot Mac hauled in here for me, take out my servicing kit and pull out a patch. As I open the solvent, the familiar smell brings back more memories than I was counting on.

I keep having flashbacks from when we were kids, when we first met at that private school my mother had me in before she left us and my father pulled me out. Blaine was so different from the others, even back then. He was definitely the product of money, but, back then, so was I. But it was like it was just this thing that was a part of his life; he never lorded it over people or thought they were less than him if they didn't have as much. Point in fact, after my mother left and my father pulled me out of school, Blaine stood by me, even when things got weird. When I got weird.

After my father started home-schooling me, training me; after he made it so I hated almost everything, just like him, so I looked forward to the training sessions...even after all that, Blaine stood by me. He kept me sane...or as close to sane as it would have ever been possible for me to be. He never turned his back on me, no matter what. He was my best friend and if Tif wasn't already dead (or twice-dead, I guess) I would kill the bitch for what she did to him, how she doomed him to one of two awful fates. How she caused the situation where I didn't have a choice but to kill my dead best friend. Fucking bitch.

I can't think about this anymore or I'll go crazier. I get up off the cot, grab some clean clothes out of my duffle and head out towards the communal bathroom I'll be sharing with the soldiers. The girls get their own, right down the hall. After the weird exchange with the scientists, we were basically exiled to our rooms to clean off the blood covering all of us and get some sleep. We're supposed to reconvene in the morning and strategize or whatever. All I care about is killing more of those things, since that seems to keep the static at bay, the way Blaine used to.

In the hallway, I almost run right into Lucy, who's heading for the showers, too, judging from the clean clothes and the towel she's carrying.

"Oh. Hey," I say, feeling awkward for some reason.

"Hi," she replies, half-smiling.

"How's it going?" I ask, which is a stupid question considering not only the circumstances, but also the fact that I last saw her about fifteen minutes ago. It's weird that things are less awkward when there are zombies around. But Lucy makes me feel things I never really have before, and while that might partly because of how good she is at killing stuff, I figure that's not the worst thing that could attract me to a person. I could be attracted to Daffy, for example, and that would be way more disturbing.

"It's fine," she says, chuckling a little, then continuing, "I think I'm gonna hit the showers, though"—I'm not going to get into how this mental image affects me—"I'm all gross and bloody."

"Right, uh, same here," I reply as she smiles again and heads into the bathroom. That's definitely the way I wanted that interaction to go. I go to pull my hands through my hair in frustration, but stop myself when I remember that it's matted with Blaine's blood. I head into the bathroom myself, glad to see that's it's completely empty, at least for now, and set my clothes down on a bench before looking in a mirror.

My face is streaked with zombie blood, and, worse, Blaine's. My hair is sticking up in weird spikes, gelled in place by yet more gore. I look like I'm dressed up as a mass murderer for Halloween. It's drying in rusty flakes around my fingernails, too, and I'm suddenly grateful for the chance to shower. Hopefully, it'll be easier to stop thinking about Blaine's dead face when I'm not covered in his blood.

First things first, though: there are a couple of old-fashioned electric razors on the counter and I learned a long time ago from my training sessions that when going into a situation where a lot blood will be a factor, it's just better not to have hair.

I plug in one of the razors and it whirrs to life—unenthusiastically, but it'll do. I start along the top of my head. I have to work harder on the sections really permeated by gore, but it's all gone in about fifteen minutes. Having a shaved head when there's going to be blood flying around is efficient, but I always hate how I look with it because it reminds me of growing up with my father.

I stare at the memory inciting reflection for a few more seconds before turning away and heading for the bay of showers. To take my mind off Blaine's blood disappearing down the drain, I focus instead on thoughts of killing zombies tomorrow. With every single one I take down, it'll feel a bit like I'm getting revenge on Tif, because I'm going to picture every single one with her face. With possible exceptions for the occasional Daffy or my father...or maybe even that asshole soldier who gave Lucy such a hard time; just thinking of that guy and his smug face...my heart starts pounding and for a second, I can't tell whether or not that's static I hear, or just the sound of the water hitting the tiles of the shower.

And then I know.

Lucy

I am so excited to finally have a shower and wash away all the ickiness covering my face, hands, torso, hair, and—yeah it's pretty much just everywhere at this point. Don't mind me while I shudder violently.

I shake my head at myself as I get undressed and get ready to shower, feeling embarrassed about the awkward exchange with Nate out in the hallway. It's been so long since I've had a crush. I forgot how tongue-tied and ridiculous they make me, especially when I'm also not sure if I should be afraid of the object of my affections or not. I give my brain another mental shake, reminding myself that this is *so* not something to be worrying about right now...well, possibly the part where he might be dangerous is a valid concern, but still.

I step into the shower stall, wincing at how cold the water is—though the fact that there's water at all is quite the luxury so I guess I shouldn't complain. I stand under the tepid spray until the water is no longer a brownish red, trying to keep my thoughts off how Nate is probably also showering right now. I pull my hands through my hair and scrub my face until I'm content that I'm probably as clean as I'll get and I step out of the shower, wrapping a towel around myself as I do. I head to the mirrors to make sure that I got all of the blood off my...well, yeah, almost everything considering all of the gore that I was splattered with today. I see a few stubborn flecks remaining and sigh. I head back to the shower, and then change my mind, figuring it'll be easier if I just do it in front of a sink with the aid of a mirror instead or I may be continuing this dance all night.

I drop my towel and pull on my bra and panties, so I'm not just standing around naked in case someone walks in. Luckily, my legs are clean since they didn't get too bloody in the first place, thanks to my pants and boots, so I tug on my sweat pants, too. Like I've said, I've seen my share of horror movies, and probably other people's shares, too, and the naked chicks never fare well, so it's probably better to try and remain as clothed as possible until this horror movie scenario is dealt with.

Honestly, if I wasn't so coated with blood and guts, I'd have skipped the shower scene altogether. I mean, if nakedness is a bad decision in horror movie situations, then participating in a shower scene is an even worse idea. Everyone knows that if you take a shower in a horror movie, then you will very likely not ever be dry and alive again, and getting clean is really not worth it if you're just gonna die. Especially considering you'll likely be covered in blood soon, so it's all just a waste of time anyway.

I continue to mull over various horror survival versus death scenarios in my mind as I scrub at the most resistant bloodstains on my skin. I'm just scraping at a patch on my neck when Lia walks in, obviously getting ready to take her own shower.

"Hey," Lia says as she walks up beside me and I grunt in response, focused on blood removal. "Having a hard time getting clean?" she jokes with innuendo heavy in her voice.

"Dirty," I mutter and shoot her a half-smile in the mirror before returning my attention to my task, now working on some blood left at my right temple, hanging on to the roots of my hair. "It's harder than it looks," I say off-hand.

"That's what he said," she counters and I snort a laugh, scraping my skin with my thumbnail. "Ow," I pout and Lia rolls her eyes. I stick my tongue out at her and return to my scrubbing.

"I see you braved the shower despite the horror movie situation we currently find ourselves in," Lia says as she turns on the tap in one of the shower stalls.

"You know me way too well," I say, then continue, "besides, I didn't have much choice. One: I was seriously icky. Two: there are way too many cute guys around here to continue walking around like Carrie post-pig's blood, even if the ick factor wasn't enough to motivate a cleansing."

"And you call me boy-crazy," she says, smiling.

"Pff, I have never denied my own boy-crazed tendencies," I retort.

She pauses for a second before responding, checking the water temperature in the shower with an extended wrist at the same time. "Speaking of boys and craziness," she begins, "you might wanna be careful about that crush you're cultivating on Nate. Seeing what he did to Blaine...he might not be all there, you know?"

"I am so *not* 'cultivating a crush,' this could be the zombie apocalypse for all we know, it's hardly the time," I argue. Then, seeing her wholly unconvinced face in the mirror, I sigh heavily. "Damn, you really do know me too well. Anyway, we can't expect him to be normal after having to kill his best friend, even if he was a zombie," I can't help defending Nate, he's just so pretty.

"But he *didn't* have to kill him. We offered to do it so he wouldn't have to. That's the weird part. Seriously, would you be okay with killing me, even if I zombied out on you?" she asks.

"No! Of course not!" I answer emphatically.

"Exactly. I couldn't kill you either, even then. That's why it's weird and why I'm pretty sure he's a bit of a psycho."

"But he's so hot!" I whine, drawing out the "o" sound.

"What does that have to do with anything?" she asks.

"Hot guys aren't supposed to be psychos. It's not fair! It's confusing to my lady parts!"

Lia laughs and shakes her head at me. "I'm sorry to break it to you and lady town, but beautiful people can be crazy, too. Freaky looking people with mullets and strange lumps don't have the market cornered on being loony-tunes, you know."

"Yeah, well, I'm still gonna wait for more evidence that he's stark raving before I give up on him, 'cause, not to sound like Daffy, but, yum," I say as I finally eradicate what I'm pretty sure is the last vestige of zombie blood on me.

"Fine. Just be on the lookout for any behaviour that's overtly craze-balls, okay?"

"Agreed. Is there any blood left on my back?"

She turns from the shower where she's testing the temperature again and inspects my back. "Nope, you're good. Does this water ever heat up?"

"Thanks. And nope, sorry, it's cold showers all around."

"Huh. And yet yours didn't seem to put a damper on your lust for Nate. Strange."

"Ha-ha. I'm going to bed," I say, crossing to the bench and pulling on one of the many Who shirts I have in my collection. "Enjoy your shower."

"Mmhmm," she grunts then begins staring intently at the shower spray as if she can heat it up by sheer power of will.

"Are you trying to make the water warmer with your mind?" I ask, innocently.

"It's worth a try. I hate cold showers."

"Well, good luck with that," I say and she raises her middle finger in response.

"Love you, too," I say and flounce out of the room, ignoring the water she flicks at my retreating back as I go.

Lia

I attempt to splash water at Lucy as she heads out of the room but she's already too far away. I really hate cold showers. Bracing myself, I undress, remove my glasses, and step into the spray quickly before I can change my mind. I hold back a shriek at the icy temperature of the water that's finally sluicing away the blood and ichor staining what feels like my entire body. Seeing the gore start to swirl down the drain, I am able to remind myself that the coldness will be worth it in the end and far preferable to the alternative of remaining covered in zombie remnants. I scour myself as best I can with just bar soap and no loofah, but I figure I'll probably have to mimic Lucy and get the rest off over the sink, where I'll have a better vantage point.

The water flowing off me is finally clear so I decide it's time to get out. I put my glasses back on and locate my towel. I dry off, trying to warm myself back up. I change into my Betty Boop pyjamas, wishing they were a bit less sexy (not to mention warmer...brr) since we're surrounded by chauvinistic, sexist soldiers, but since I had been planning on having sex with Carson, they're all I brought. So it goes, as Lucy says.

As I turn to the mirrors and strategize about how best to attack the remaining blood clinging to my skin and hair while trying to warm up at the same time, Daffy prances into the bathroom. Seriously, she prances everywhere; I don't think she ever just walks normally.

Upon seeing me, she comes to halt and pulls a pouty face. "Oh. Hi, Lia," she says.

I simply growl in answer and go back to scrubbing myself, redoubling my efforts so I'm not trapped in here with her any longer than I absolutely have to be.

"Ugh, this stuff is, like, so gross!" Daffy gripes as she looks at herself in the mirror. "It's totes gonna mess with my skin regiment!"

"Yeah, that's definitely the real tragedy right now," I mutter.

"I know, right?" she says and it's probably a very good thing, or not, depending on your perspective, that I'm unarmed right now. Daffy doesn't notice the murderous expression on my face, not that she'd be appropriately scared even if she did. She just turns around and prances over to the row of shower stalls. She turns the water on and immediately undresses.

Oh yeah, that's just what I need to make this weekend from hell complete. I shudder and work on ignoring her, scratching at a particularly obstinate bit of blood that's on the edge of my collarbone. However, when Daffy calls over the noise of the shower, "Lia, do you think you could, like, help me get some of the blood off my back?" I decide the rest of the blood still on me can stay for now. It's just not worth it.

Grabbing my bloodied clothes and a fresh towel for some extra warmth, I hightail it out of there and head to the barracks that I'm sharing with Lucy, and sadly, with Daffy. Another involuntary shudder passes through me as she calls my name again.

This weekend really sucks balls.

Chapter Eight
Leaving us to come up with a Plan B

Elliot

My face is pressed tightly against my thin pillow as I wake up slowly and for a few seconds, before I'm fully awake, I feel normal. I think about the work that needs to be done that day for the remaining trials before I'm jolted back into the awful reality by looking around the room, seeing Terry sitting up on a nearby cot—looking like he hasn't slept all night and Jake passed out on the cot beyond him.

When Terry notices me looking at him he attempts a smile, but it doesn't stick. "Mornin', Doc," he says in a gruff voice as he runs his hands over his tired face. The motion makes his words come out garbled, but I get the gist.

"Good morning, Terry," I reply with a wry smile. "I was hoping that this had all been a dream from reading too much of *Shadowlands* lately," I continue, smiling weakly at him.

"I wish it was all in our heads too, Doc," he answers then pauses for a moment before asking, "What's *Shadowlands*?"

"It's one of the graphic novels series that I read," I reply sheepishly, half expecting him to start teasing me like he used to, but he just looks at me expectantly like he's waiting for a more detailed explanation.

"Um, they're by this guy, Pete Moon, and, um, they're about a nuclear apocalypse following World War III. It basically comes down to mutants versus remaining humans. They're really good; one of my favourite series," I finish in a rush, a part of me still ready to go on the defensive in case Terry suddenly morphs back into the old version of himself, but he doesn't, he just nods his head and looks out the window.

"They sound pretty cool," he says, startling me, not just because it's an unexpected thing for him to say but also because it seemed like he'd stopped listening to me. "Did you bring them with you?" He asks, surprising me further.

"Yeah," I reply, "I bring them everywhere. They're good books to re-read because they seem different every time. Why?" I ask.

"Could I maybe borrow them?" He asks, and I have to fight my body's natural reactions to keep my jaw from falling open because I've never seen Terry read anything that didn't have women who were at least half-naked on the cover. "Some escapism would probably be good, even if it's a similar situation, I could use a distraction."

"Um, sure. Of course. I'll grab them for you," I answer haltingly because I still can't believe how different Terry has become in less than twenty-four hours. I get up out of bed, almost half-heartedly hoping that Terry will make fun of my "chicken legs" poking out of my boxers because it would at least make things seem a little bit more normal, but he's silent, just staring out the window again as he scratches his growing stubble.

As I cross the room to my duffle, I hear Jake mumble something as he turns over in his sleep. I don't know how he can sleep so well in this situation, but I guess maybe ignorance really is bliss, because in the short time that I've known him, Jake seems like one of the most ignorant people I've ever met...except maybe for that one soldier, I think his name is Locklan, they're pretty much tied.

I fish the books out of my bag, grabbing some fresh clothes while I'm at it; I'll never be able to impress Daphne in wrinkled clothes. Tucking the clothes under my left arm, I balance the five books making up the *Shadowlands* series so far between both hands (Pete Moon is supposedly in the midst of writing the newest one and despite recent events, I'm still really excited to read it when it comes out...I just hope that I don't get eaten by zombies first).

"Here," I say, handing the stack to Terry. "The first one is *One Bright Day in the Shadows* and well, they have the numbers on them, so I guess the order is self-explanatory," I finish awkwardly while Terry examines the covers silently. "Alright, well, I'm going to go shower and then find Gregory. We should probably get ready to strategize with the soldiers and the others as soon as possible," I say, heading for the door.

"Thanks, Doc," Terry says from behind me and I look back to see him already reading *One Bright Day*. Will wonders never cease?

"You're welcome," I reply, smiling as I leave the room.

On the way to the bathroom, I pass a couple of the soldiers and they nod at me silently. I do the same back, knowing that I don't look nearly as cool as them while doing so. I hope none of them are in the bathroom when I get there, that would just be awkward and uncomfortable, not to mention damaging to my self-esteem; they're all so much bigger than me and it'll just remind me how Daphne won't stop staring at them but probably doesn't remember my name. But I'm in luck: the bathroom is empty when I go in and I can't help but breathe a sigh of relief. I really don't need to add to my self-esteem issues about my scrawny physique.

Once I've finished showering—it took longer than I originally planned because thoughts of Daphne kept popping into my head and well...yeah—I dress quickly in my best pair of brown corduroys and my faded Pearl Jam concert tee. I pull a white button up on over my t-shirt because Daphne strikes me as the kind of woman who likes her men to dress well.

Oh. It's a little wrinkled...I hope she doesn't notice.

Anyway, now to find Gregory and get the soldiers to gather everyone for a meeting so that we can tell them what we've figured out. Well, what *I've* figured out, Gregory says my plan is stupid. But he's wrong, it's going to work. It has to.

I know that I should be focusing solely on the zombie problem, but I still can't help hoping that Daphne remembers my name today.

Connor

Ah, morning; the sun is shining, the sky is blue...there are zombies in the trees...or at least that's what it sounds like; there must be tons of them around now. I heard them screeching to each other all night. They're like fucking howler monkeys! It's ridiculous. I know we missed a bunch of people during evac, but, Christ's tit, there's a lot of 'em out there and I'm guessing we're probably one of the few food sources left out here 'cause they are movin' in like nobody's business.

It's a good thing we're well stocked with weapons, even more so now than we were before since the civs couldn't leave, so we've got Lia's entire weapon collection to help us out. Plus, Nate's a hunter or something so he's got a ton of weapons, too. Now, if only there were more of *us*, that would be great, but I guess being in a zombie scenario, you can't expect to outnumber them for long since lots of people don't know how to kick zombie ass successfully so they do tend to multiply quickly.

Luca sent me to round the civs up so I'm heading for the barracks we set the girls up in, while he calls in the remaining guys from patrol. It's getting too dangerous for them to be out there anymore so we're just going to have to start patrolling from inside the relative safety of the fort. Luca's in a snit, with full on Glower Power happening, 'cause Locklan didn't check in this morning, which isn't too unusual, but Luca's still majorly pissed off.

The scientists apparently had a breakthrough last night and have something of a plan, so once everyone is together, we're gonna have a strategy meeting. Gregory's not happy about the civs getting full disclosure, but Luca figures at this point, we need all the help we can get so they may as well know everything we know. Which I think is a smart move and besides, this way I get more face time with Daffy.

I run into Nate just as he's coming out of the guys' bathroom. Whoa.

"Jesus H., man, you look different!" I exclaim, taking in his newly shaved head. He looks completely ready for battle...except for his quizzical smile.

"Heh, you say that too, eh? Do you know what the 'H' stands for?" he asks.

Not a bad question.

"Well, when I was in school, I used to say it stood for homeslice, as in 'Jesus is my homeslice,' but that really seemed to annoy the nuns for some reason. I got smacked with a yard stick more than once for saying that. They seriously have no sense of humour," I reply, smiling at the memory. Man, it was fun irritating the nuns even if they always smacked me afterwards, it was totally worth it.

"Shocking," Nate says, then, in response to what I assume is my own quizzical expression, elaborates, "nuns not having a sense of humour."

"Oh, right," I laugh, "I guess not. Anyways, I don't know what it really stands for. What's your theory?" I ask, but before Nate can respond, Lucy and Lia walk quickly out of the girls' barracks, all but sprinting, like they're running away from something—or, at least, speed walking away from something.

"Uh, hey girls. What's up?" I ask curiously. They both look over at me with startled expressions, like they didn't notice us before.

"Nothing," Lucy responds, looking back at the door to their barracks, the look on her face a mixture of disgust and discomfort. "Hey, Nate," she continues.

Geez, I know I'm all about Daffy, but I don't even get a hello? Ouch.

Lia grunts in our direction, possibly in some manner of salutation, possibly in annoyance—it can sometimes be hard to decipher when it comes to Lia—then hooks her hand around Lucy's upper arm and drags her past us.

"Uh, we're meeting in the mess hall for a debriefing!" I call to their retreating forms and Lia raises a hand in acknowledgement without looking back. She says something to Lucy as they turn the corner and walk out of sight.

"Huh," Nate says.

"Yeah," I agree, "I wonder what that was all about."

"No idea," he replies as Daffy wanders out of the girls' barracks, looking all cute and sleepy, plus she's in a tight tank top, without a bra, and is wearing short shorts, so woohoo.

"What's with all the yelling?" she asks, looking perturbed.

"I was telling Lucy and Lia something," I answer since Nate walked away in the direction of the mess as soon as Daffy came into sight. I don't know what his problem is, she's totally hot.

"Well, you, like, messed up my beauty sleep." Daffy pouts and I'm not ashamed to say her lower lip sticking out like that makes me seriously wanna suck on it.

"Don't worry, you don't need it," I say, and she looks confused.

"Need what?" she asks.

Right. I guess that could be part of the reason Nate can't stand her.

"Beauty sleep," I reply and she still looks pretty confused so I figure I may as well just spell it out before she breaks her brain trying to figure out what I'm saying. "Because you're already beautiful..." I trail off and suddenly the light of understanding breaks across her face and she grins happily.

"Aw, thanks. You're, like, so sweet?" she says, although it sounds like a question.

"Thanks. So, we're supposed to get everyone to the mess hall for a debriefing," I tell her as she walks over to me. I know it's really not necessary for her to be there but she'll be good for morale in any case. Well, she'll be good for my morale anyway.

"That sounds, like, dirty. Fun and dirty," Daffy replies. Now it's my turn to be confused, although I'd bet I don't look nearly as cute as she does.

"What?" I ask, trying to figure out what's dirty about a debriefing.

"Debriefing. Isn't it, like, taking someone's underwear off?" she asks and I have to focus hard to get past the image this statement conjures up.

"Uh, no. It just means we're having a meeting and the scientists are gonna tell us what they figured out last night," I answer and she pouts again as she strokes my arm.

"Too bad," she whispers and I swear I almost pass out. It's been way too damn long.

"Connor!" Luca's shout rings through the hallway as he comes up behind us.

Uh-oh.

"See you at the debriefing," Daffy whispers, blowing me a kiss as she flounces away—in the opposite direction of the mess, but I figure with Luca here it's probably best to just let her go.

"What in *el nombre de Dios* are you doing, Connor?" Luca asks, his glower almost to full strength. Goose bumps.

"Sorry, Luke, I got distracted, but did you see how she was dressed?" I plead, hoping he'll be lenient and stop calling me Connor—it's never a good sign.

"*No me importa* how she was dressed, Connor. We really need to focus right now. It needs to be S.O.P. You can't get distracted. Do you have any idea how outnumbered we are? *Dios mío*, this is no time to be thinking with your cock!" he snaps and I look down, ashamed for real this time. He's right. I should at least try to focus. She's just so damn hot...with her long blonde hair and her nice tits and that ass...

"Connor!" Luca's irate voice snaps me back to reality again.

Crap.

"Were you thinking about her again?" He asks, and I'm torn between lying, which he hates, or admitting I failed at following orders ten seconds after he gave them to me, which he would hate even more. Luckily, I'm saved from having to answer as Luca's comm crackles to life with the sound of Darryl's voice, which is just shy of being completely panicked.

"Sergeant?" Darryl's voice screams through the tiny speaker.

"What is it, Cho?" Luca asks, sounding concerned. I'm worried, too. Darryl is usually one of the calmest guys I know, so to hear him sounding this close to losing his shit is pretty goddamn terrifying.

"The zombies got Locklan!" Darryl shouts. "And I am very fucking surrounded. I can't get to him. I need reinforcements A.S.A.P, sir, or I think I'll be taking a dirt nap." The comm crackles again as Darryl stops talking and I feel my stomach drop with dread. I'm not all that upset about Locklan being zombie food, to be honest, but Darryl is a good man, a really good soldier and it would really fucking suck if the zombies either turned him or ate him.

"Retreat, Cho, retreat!" Luca shouts into the mike, his voice worried and urgent.

"I can't, sir!" Darryl shouts through the speaker again. Man, I knew he was brave, but he hates Locklan as much as we all do; he's sure picking a weird time to become stupidly heroic.

"Cho, there's nothing you can do for Locklan now, save yourself," Luca responds, the urgency in his voice even more intense now. "That's an order."

"I'm not being heroic, sir, the zombies are blocking the fucking door and closing in on me!" Darryl yells amidst spurts of gunfire as he tries to fend the zombies off.

"What's your location, Cho?" Luca asks, growling with frustration and worry as he rakes his free hand savagely over his face, awaiting the answer.

"Just outside the western door, sir," Darryl answers, the panic even clearer in his voice as he shouts something indiscernible and fires off more shots before the comm goes quiet again.

Luca doesn't even pause, just barks loudly into the comm, "Kane, Church, to me at the northern door; everyone else to the southern door. Donahue is the lead on team two. We meet in the middle on the west side and deep-six those *putas.*"

My pulse is racing like crazy as Luca and I start running for the northern door, not waiting for Link and Preacher to catch up; going by the panic in Darryl's voice, there's no time for that. We sprint to the northern door and stop, taking out our SIG Pro 9mms and unlocking the door. We pull it open slowly and glance around the immediate area for signs of zombies. It looks to be all clear, the majority of the zombies in the vicinity likely distracted by the prospect of eating Locklan and Darryl.

I click the safety off my gun and put a bullet in the chamber, getting ready just as I hear yet more gunfire from outside as well as the sound of running feet as Link and Preacher join us. Luca nods at them then puts his index finger to his lips, telling us to be quiet so we don't catch the attention of the zombies before we're ready to destroy them.

We move toward the sound of screeching zombies and gunfire, holding our pistols at the ready. As we round the corner, my brain doesn't know what to concentrate on first in the midst of the chaos. I see a few zombies crouched on the ground chowing down on the bloody remains of what I assume used to be Locklan. It's hard to believe that the pulpy, gory lumps of gooey flesh and barely discernible bone used to be a person, but it must be him.

After my brain boxes up this horrifying image to be dealt with later, I notice a gaggle of zombies surrounding Darryl, with a few lying dead on the ground around him. Out of the corner of my eye, I see Marco, Jimmy, Rafe, and Carl, come around their corner, silent with their guns drawn, a mirror image of my unit as we move in sync towards the zombie munch and attack fest. I can't see Darryl all that well through the zombies and at this point, I can only hope he's still alive, with no bite marks that won't even have the chance to turn into scars before he turns into an extremely violent, not to mention extremely undead, version of himself.

Once we're in position, just fifteen feet away on either side of the zombie mini-horde, Luca whistles loudly, to get the zombies to notice us and hopefully give Darryl a chance to get away as safe and sound as possible. Rafe does the same on their side and the zombies start to shift away from Darryl a little, lifting their faces to the wind like wolves. It appears to have the same result as a wolf scenting for prey since they get excited at the prospect of more food, screeching eagerly while turning fully away from Darryl and dropping to all fours, crouching like the zombie chicks in the lab video, getting ready to launch themselves at their newfound food source.

Now that they're no longer swarming around him, I can see Darryl fending off a remaining zombie, pushing it away from him as it tries to grab his head and pull him closer. I lose sight of the struggle as the zombies nearest my unit start launching their shrieking selves at us. I can't distinguish between all the different shots that are going off, but someone must've been able to shoot the fucker 'cause the next time I catch a glimpse of Darryl from behind the row of zombies nearest my unit, the zombie that was attacking him is dead and on the ground. But it's not all good news; Darryl's also on the ground, crumpled in a heap and I can see a lot of blood.

God, if you're there, please don't let him have been bitten, I promise I'll try to be a better Catholic if you spare him from turning into one of the shambling undead.

Uh-oh, no more time for prayers, the screeches of the zombies that were attacking Darryl have attracted the zombies that were cruncha-munching down on Locklan and some more from the surrounding forest besides.

Exhaling, I aim for the rotting head of the zombie nearest me. I feel a momentary shock as I realize it's the fatty I had so much trouble evac-ing yesterday.

Jesus H., did anybody make it out alive?

I shake my head as I realize the zombie fatty is quickly getting closer to me and I finally just pull the trigger. Feeling the familiar cracking sound of the bullet leaving the chamber resonating in my chest brings me completely back into soldier mode and I rapidly take out several more zombies in my near vicinity. The forest rings with the sound of gunfire and so many zombie shrieks while the very air seems to shimmer with blood and brains as we work as a seamless unit, obliterating zombies left, right, and centre and before I know it, all the zombies in the surrounding area are crumpled on the ground, no longer a threat since they're all missing large parts of their heads and grey matter thanks to our hollow-points.

I re-holster my gun and head over to Darryl, who's still crumpled on the ground himself. He hasn't moved at all, which is probably a bad sign.

"Darryl?" I say tentatively. He doesn't answer, doesn't even grunt. I nudge him with my foot and he still doesn't stir, but I can see that he's breathing at least, though passed out cold. That last zombie must've knocked him unconscious. I can now also see the reason for all the blood: he has several deep scratches down the left side of his face and neck, all the way from his forehead to his collarbone.

Uh-oh.

I take my jacket off then strip off my shirt and slip my jacket back on. I bend down and press the shirt to Darryl's face and neck, hoping to stop some of the bleeding. Luca and Rafe do a quick check of the zombies we killed and make sure none of them are going to be getting back up again, and then they join me and everyone else at Darryl's side.

"We should get him inside," I say.

Carl comes forward first and helps me stand him up. More blood flows out of the wounds on Darryl's face and neck and I tie my shirt tightly around his wounds, trying to stop the worst of it.

We head inside before any more zombies can attack us and as we walk, I can't stop my eyes from returning to the deep scratches along his face and neck, can't stop myself from noticing the way the skin is torn so ragged. Even with my shirt pressed to the wounds, the blood just keeps pumping out, trailing down his face, dripping off his chin and staining the shirt and his uniform a red so dark it's almost black.

There's a part of me that's wondering if we should have shot him along with the rest of them, but he doesn't seem to be bitten, and we don't know if the scratches will turn him or not, so I guess it's better if we wait and see what happens. I just hope we don't regret it 'cause I feel like if this were a movie, he would be turning zombie any second and would end up biting someone just after we got safely inside, probably me, since the funny ones almost never make it to the end.

If we do have to kill him, it would be better if it weren't done in front of the civs; they've already seen too much, gotten much more involved than the higher-ups would be happy with. They don't need to see us killing one of our own, too…even if that one is a zombie.

"Mac, was he bitten?" Luca asks.

"I can't tell yet," I answer while more blood trickles out of Darryl's wounds, looking even redder than normal against his paled face. He looks so bad, if we don't bandage him up soon, I don't think we'll have to worry about whether or not to kill him anymore, he looks like he could keel over and just not get back up any second now.

"Is everyone okay?" Elliot's nervous-sounding voice blurts suddenly out of the comm on my belt. Luca nods at me, giving me the okay to answer.

"More or less. We lost Locklan, though," I answer. Probably not exactly what Luca would've said, but he doesn't seem annoyed by my response. Mama always said I had a certain, awkward, way with words.

"Um, what does 'more or less' mean?" Elliot asks.

Luca frowns; he hates the way civs ask questions and don't just wait to be given the information—or not—like a good soldier would. He looks back at me again, nodding at me to handle it, and I say into the comm, "You'll see in just a minute."

Luca shakes his head furiously at me and takes my comm away. "*Qué diablos?*" he asks, which I'm pretty sure is Spanish for "what the hell?" or "what the fuck?" or something along those lines anyway. "We can't have him around the civs like this, if he turns and one of them gets bitten, it will be a huge *problema* for us."

"Elliot can fix him up at least a little and if he's not about to undergo zombification, he needs medical attention or we'll have rescued him for nothing," I reply and Luca's face twists with annoyance, but he knows I'm right: he hands me back my comm with only medium glower power turned up.

"*Bien*, but we keep guns trained on Cho at all times until the time limit for turning has passed," he orders. I certainly won't argue with that.

A minute later, we're approaching the mess, where everyone should be waiting for us. Luca pauses and glances back at me, then at Darryl, still passed out and hanging off me and Carl. He mutters an angry "*Dios mio*" under his breath then turns around and opens the left door, signalling Rafe to hold the other one open so Carl and I can help Darryl into the room.

As everyone gathered in the mess sees Darryl's ruined face and throat, a round of surprised gasps and horrified murmurs are exhaled by the civs and the scientists alike. Carl and I walk towards them and lay Darryl on the nearest table as the civs move out of the way quickly, except for Elliot, showing more courage than I would've expected from that skinny frame. Gregory all but runs away, almost tripping himself in his panic. Coward.

"Was he bitten?" Elliot asks anxiously.

"We don't know," I answer.

"You should probably make sure," Elliot suggests.

Luca nods in assent and glances at me and thankfully, I get his clear intent this time as I ask the civs to wait outside and he nods his approval. Darryl is a good soldier and he deserves his privacy.

After the civs file outside, with Daffy asking "What's going on?" the entire time, Carl and me start stripping Darryl down—an awkward job, but since he's covered in blood, it's impossible to tell if he was bitten or not when he's fully clothed and since he's not exactly awake right now, someone has to do it for him.

Just in case, Luca moves to where he could get a clear shot of Darryl's head without hitting Carl or me and he nods to the others to do the same.

Darryl's dead weight is complicated to manoeuvre as Carl and me pull first his boots and trousers off, then his jacket and undershirt. We leave him in his underwear since there's no blood visible in that area so there's no need to remove it, and also I just really don't want to.

"This would be a lot more fun if he were a chick," I say, then noticing the funny looks I get, I elaborate, "You know, also if he were conscious and not gross and bloody…and a chick."

"Homo," someone, I think Link, mutters.

"Nuh-uh," I say, "I specifically said it would only be fun if he were a chick, how does that make me gay?" I ask and he doesn't answer, just shakes his head at me.

So immature.

But I'm glad some of the homoerotic tension is broken as Carl and me continue to check Darryl's inert body for bite marks. There aren't any visible on his legs, arms or chest. As we pull him up into a sitting position revealing his bite free back, my tied shirt comes undone and falls from around his neck allowing yet more blood to seep out of his wounds. Darryl slumps over and the blood drips onto the table with a strangely loud sound.

"Mac, get Elliot back in here now," Luca orders, keeping his gun trained on Darryl's head as I go get Elliot, who obviously impressed Luca enough by not running away that he graduated from being called a "skinny geek," which is pretty high praise coming from Luca.

Carl waves Preach over and together they ease Darryl back into a prone position and pull his pants back on as I return with Elliot and Terry in tow. Darryl doesn't move, doesn't make a sound as more blood trickles down his face and into his mouth, bubbling back out with each breath.

It's an unpleasant sight.

"So, no bites?" Elliot asks as he comes level with the table carrying a first aid kit in one hand and a bucket of soapy water in the other. Terry's following him, carrying some towels and a trash can.

"No bites," I confirm then ask, "will the scratches turn him?"

"I'm not sure," Elliot answers as he sets the kit and the bucket down on the table behind Darryl's head.

"Has he lost too much blood?" I ask.

"I don't think so, it looks like the zombie just missed his carotid artery. Barring the possibility that he turns into a zombie, the main thing we have to worry about is infection. I wouldn't think that the zombie's nails would be all that clean."

And with that, he gets to work, taking a towel from Terry and draping it over Darryl's chest. He then opens the kit and pulls out rubbing alcohol, cotton swabs, some bandages, tape, and a shitload of gauze. After he has everything set up, he leans over Darryl and examines his wounds. If he's nervous about being so close to Darryl when he could possibly turn zombie at any minute, he doesn't show it, and I raise my estimation of his guts a little more. Luca looks impressed, too; he's probably done calling Elliot "the geek" for good now.

Elliot dips the gauze into the soapy water and starts cleaning out the massive scratches. Darryl jerks a little and opens his eyes, making a pained noise. "Could someone hold him down for me, please?" Elliot asks. Carl, Preach, and I step forward again. I grab Darryl's right arm, Carl his left and Preach holds down his legs. "Thank you," Elliot says then gets back to work.

The water in the bucket is soon a dull brown, stained with Darryl's blood. He's awake now, struggling against the hands holding him down as Elliot finishes with the water and swipes the rubbing alcohol a few times through each furrow. He tosses the last of the gauze into the trash and makes a sympathetic face as he stares down at Darryl.

"I know that was painful, but we're almost done," Elliot assures him. Darryl sort of mumbles something then passes out again, relaxing onto the table. Elliot doesn't seem concerned, just continues with his work. He spreads some anti-infection goo into each of the furrows with a cotton swab then tapes a huge bandage to the side of Darryl's face, another around his jaw, and one more along the side of his throat. He steps back to survey his work.

"Aren't you gonna stitch him up?" Marco asks.

"No, the edges of his wounds are much too ragged, stitching wouldn't work. Simply bandaging him up is the most effective thing to do with this kind of injury," Elliot answers.

"That was all really impressive, Doc," I say, adopting the nickname Terry uses for him, as I let go of Darryl's once again limp arm. "Where'd you learn to do all that?" I ask.

"Um, med school," Elliot says, looking confused and turning awkward again now that his job is done. And also maybe a little 'cause it *was* a dumb question. He removes the blood and water soaked towel from Darryl's chest and mops up the rest of the bloody water mixture from the table-top with it. He grabs two fresh towels from Terry and puts one underneath Darryl's head, the other he drapes over his chest again.

"So, Doc, you gonna tell us 'bout your plan now?" Link asks, copying me with the nickname usage; the others will probably start calling him that, too, now that he's saved Darryl's life…assuming he won't turn into a zombie.

"Oh, well, yes, but we should get everyone back in here now so that I can tell everyone at once," Elliot answers clumsily.

I look at Luca for confirmation.

"*Sí*, bring everyone back in. Donahue, Cooke, Cantolena, and Halley, keep your sights on Cho in case he wakes up dead," he orders and everyone moves to obey him.

I'm not exactly happy Locklan's dead, but we definitely work better as a unit without him around, being a smart ass and constantly questioning every little thing Luca says.

Elliot walks away from Darryl and goes to stand a few tables away. Terry follows him and they start talking quietly as the others come back into the room, following me.

Link, Preach, Luca, and me join the civs as they sit down at the table nearest Elliot. Daffy is staring blankly into space and has already captured the attention of most of the guys in the room without even doing anything, myself included.

I can't help it, she's just so hot.

Gregory and the other guard, Jake, don't sit with the rest of us; Gregory goes to stand with Elliot and Jake stands by the far door, smoking a cigarette.

"So, what's this plan of yours, Doc?" I ask, trying to make my voice sound a little deeper so maybe Daffy will stop staring blankly into space and start flirting with me again. A guy's gotta distract himself from the zompocalypse somehow, doesn't he?

Elliot

My hands have started shaking again. They stopped while I was cleaning up and bandaging Master Corporal Cho, thank God, because the soldiers already intimidate me enough without me making it worse by embarrassing myself in front of them and screwing up when I'm supposed to be helping their friend. I just hope that what I did makes a difference and he doesn't just turn into a zombie anyway. It would be nice to know that I made a difference in the helping instead of just having a hand in the beginning of the possible end of the world as brought to you by zombies.

And hopefully my plan makes a difference too. It's the only thing I can think of that might. I don't know what else to do and Gregory certainly isn't helping at all. It's like the only thing he cares about is not getting blamed for the entire thing. Although I don't understand how we could not get blamed: we *were* the ones developing the drug after all, not to mention monitoring the test subjects; we should've seen that something was wrong beyond the normal possible side effects. I just hope that there's still time to fix it and contain it somehow before any more people are hurt or killed because of our mistakes.

I shake my head to clear it the best that I can and I realize that everyone is staring at me, waiting for an answer to the question Corporal McCoy asked me quite some time ago.

Crap. I hate it when I do that. The guards used to tease me about it all the time before...before.

"Sorry, what was the question?" I ask, hating my voice for trembling, hating myself for letting it happen in front of Daphne, and most of all, hating the way my hands start shaking even more when she giggles in response to my absent-mindedness.

"I was just asking what your plan is, Doc," Corporal McCoy repeats patiently. He's probably my favourite of the soldiers because he's the nicest to me and he doesn't make me feel stupid when I don't understand all of their military jargon.

"Right. Well, the most basic part of it is that we have to get back to the SymbioVitaTech lab as soon as possible because I think I know how to reverse the infection...or at least the reanimation process," I amend when people start muttering excitedly at the mention of reversal, the hope of a cure. "Once they've turned, there's no way to make them human again, but we *can* make them give into the natural process of, um, decomposition so that they're no longer undead."

"Yeah, I have a way of fixing that whole undead thing too, Doc; it's called shooting them in the fucking head," one of the soldiers, Private Cantolena, I think, shouts out from where he's guarding the still unconscious Master Corporal Cho, much to the apparent amusement of some of the others since more than a couple of them laugh appreciatively. Sergeant Ortiz and Corporal McCoy both give him a dirty look for interrupting, but he does have a point, I should clarify.

"Right, yes, that does work, but my solution would be much more efficient and less dangerous. It would allow us to dispose of the zombies en masse as opposed to singularly, in combat," I say and I'm pleased that almost everyone looks intrigued. The only ones who don't are Gregory, but he's just a curmudgeon, who, as a rule, hates any ideas that he himself didn't come up with, and Daphne, who's unfortunately busy exchanging flirty glances with Private Cantolena. This makes me dislike him even more than his apparent attempts to replace the recently masticated Private Gates as the resident smart aleck.

"That's all well and good, Elliot, but why do we have to travel all the way back to your lab? Isn't there something you can do here?" Sergeant Ortiz asks and I try not to show how pleased I am that he seems to have learned my name. Hopefully, this means that he'll stop calling me "the skinny geek." He simply refers to Gregory as "the British one," which seriously ruffles his feathers and amuses me.

"I wish there was, Sergeant," I reply, "but there is none of the necessary, um, tools or ingredients that I'd need here. Not to mention, we know from Lia and the others that containment wasn't successful"—seeing the soldiers starting to look defensive, I quickly amend my statement—"which was no one's fault, it must have already been too late when you started. But because containment failed, we have to try to develop a cure. It's the least we can do."

"Uh, won't getting back there be kinda problematic, Doc?" Corporal McCoy asks. "Isn't it like fifty kilometres from here or something?"

"Um, yes, it's approximately fifty-five kilometres away, but we do still have the helicopter Mithras sent and it will fit almost all of us. Those that it doesn't fit can stay here and hold down the fort, um, as it were," I finish awkwardly, feeling strange about how literal that statement was. I'm hoping that no one thinks I was trying to make some sort of joke (and failed miserably), but luckily, everyone is soon distracted by Gregory stepping in with his "concerns."

"In my opinion, attempting a return to the laboratory is a foolhardy plan. It is far too dangerous and you do not even know for sure if your little experiment will work," he says pompously, not even bothering to look at me while he says it, he just plucks at some imaginary dirt on the pristine lab coat that he won't take off even though we're no longer at the lab.

I don't know if it's his tone of voice that finally gets me, or the fact that my head still hurts from where he smacked me with his pipe yesterday, or that I want to look confident and manly in front of Daphne, or if it's as simple as the fact that he so obviously doesn't care about anything besides what happens to him and his precious career and reputation, but suddenly, it's too much, I have to fight back for once.

"You selfish asshole!" That gets his attention. He stares at me in disbelief as I continue, "We have to at least try! It's our fault! Ours! Don't you get that? Or are you just so damn self-involved that you can't see just how bad this could be for anybody but yourself? It's too bad that you weren't one of the ones who turned back at the lab because you'd do less harm as an actual zombie than as the reprehensible human being that you are now." I finish angrily and I'm surprised to realize that my hands aren't shaking anymore.

But Gregory is a different story. His face is white with fury as he scowls at me and the next thing I know his hand is coming up fast and he's backhanding me across the face.

Ow.

He can hit a lot harder than he looks like he could. I hit the ground and the next thing I know, so does Gregory and after yesterday's pipe incident, I would've thought Terry was the cause, but he's busy helping me up. It was Corporal McCoy who threw the punch. Gregory makes an enraged noise and cups his hand to his clearly broken nose. I'm more satisfied than I probably should be by the way the blood pouring out of it has stained his obsessively white lab coat immediately, but I don't care, he deserved it. Gregory gets up unassisted and stalks furiously from the room.

"You okay, Doc?" Corporal McCoy asks once I'm standing again.

"Yeah, I'm fine," I say, touching my cheek and coming away with blood from where that stupid ring Gregory always wears gouged me. "Thanks," I add, meaning for both his concern and his defending me. He nods and shrugs, making a face as if it's no big deal, and for him it probably isn't considering he's obviously tough and proficient at the defensive arts.

I look at everyone else gathered in the cafeteria and they're all just staring at us. I feel myself blush and I clear my throat awkwardly, not really knowing what to say.

"So, basically, your plan is for us to get back to your lab, make some kind of antidote and what? Mass distribute it to the hundred or so zombies hanging around there? I don't think it'll be too easy to get them to take some kind of pill or something." Private Cantolena pipes up again and the fact that Daphne laughs at his joke makes me feel more inclined to violent tendencies than I'm generally used to.

"*Cállate*, Cantolena. Keep your eyes on Cho or if he wakes up dead and bites you, it will be your own fault, and I won't think twice about putting a bullet in your *cabeza*," Sergeant Ortiz growls angrily and Private Cantolena does as he's told. He may be acting like Private Gates did, but he sure can't stand up to one of Sergeant Ortiz's angry stares like Private Gates seemed to be able to.

"The antidote will obviously not be in pill form," I say, trying to regain some control and get my whole plan out so that we can start making preparations as soon as possible. "My plan is to make it into a gas or vapour so that it can be distributed to multiple zombies at one time."

Corporal McCoy makes an impressed face then seems to consider something. "So, Doc, how many zombies do you think we'll have to fight off to get you to the actual lab? Considering you said there was over a hundred people working there and just you guys made it out for sure," he says, not looking angry or worried, mostly just curious.

"Right. That part could be problematic, but I don't see any other options," I answer honestly and he nods as if it doesn't matter, he just wanted to know. "So, um, does anyone else have any questions?" I ask, hoping Private Cantolena won't use this as another opportunity to make Daphne laugh at me. But before he or anyone else can answer me, there's a burst of chaotic noise. It sounds like an explosion mixed with gunfire with no discernible pattern of release.

"What the fuck?" Corporal McCoy asks at the same time as Sergeant Ortiz orders, "Get down!" and we all hit the floor.

As the sound of gunfire becomes more sporadic, the loud and distinctive thrum of helicopter blades fills in the silences. I check the spot where Jake was standing earlier, but he's gone. The soldiers make concerned and confused noises as they too recognize the noise.

"*Mierda!*" Sergeant Ortiz swears angrily.

"Where's Jake?" I ask urgently.

"No idea. Why?" Corporal McCoy asks, looking around the room for him then glancing back at me before returning his gaze to the locus of the helicopter's noise.

"He's the helicopter pilot," I answer and already the urgency's gone out of my voice because it's too late and I know what happened. I should've seen it coming.

"*Mierda!*" Sergeant Ortiz swears again, realizing that it's worse than just Gregory attempting to high-jack the helicopter. Since the gunfire has now stopped, Sergeant Ortiz gives the all clear for us to get up and after quickly ordering those guarding Master Corporal Cho to stay where they are, he runs out of the cafeteria, presumably heading for the stairs that lead to the roof. The rest of us not on guard duty follow him even though, judging by the way the sound of the helicopter's blades is already fading, it won't make any difference.

We run out of the stairwell onto the roof and my prediction is coming true, the helicopter is already far enough away that I can barely make out either of their faces, leaving us to come up with a plan B.

Chapter Nine
If everything went according to the original plan in a zombie apocalypse, it wouldn't be very apocalyptic, now would it?

Daphne

Ugh. It would be such a nice day today, but there's all this icky smoke in the air. So not good for my lungs or my pores. I have no idea why we all, like, ran up to the roof and now I'm even more confused because it's so not awesome out here. I'd love to work on my tan by being outside but—oh, ew, I just peeked over the edge and you can totally see zombies splatted all over the place down there—nasty! I know they were busy, like, rescuing their friend or whatev, but they could have at least cleaned up a little bit before coming inside, it's just good manners. "Why are we on the roof?" I ask 'cause it was so not clear. Everyone else just started running and I definitely didn't want to be, like, left behind, plus, yay free cardio time, so I came with, but I don't know why everyone looks so pouty.

"Are you fucking kidding me?" Lia grumps at me. She's so mean. I'm totes sure everyone else knows why we're up here...not.

"No, I just came up here 'cause everyone else was doing it," I explain because sometimes Lia can be a little slow.

"Oh, for Christ's sake," she grumbles and totes just walks away. So rude! I try to think of something mean to say back to her but before I can think of an awesome comeback, the skinny and totes geeky guy who will just, like, not stop staring at me—not that I can blame him, but come on, he's got to know that I am, like, way out of his league—clears his throat (ew) and steps a bit closer to me (double ew).

"Gregory and Jake just stole the helicopter and, by the looks of things, blew up the garage with the trucks, which means it's going to be a lot more difficult to get back to the lab." He says like I should know who those guys are and care about getting back to some gross, boring lab.

"So what?" I ask, 'cause I do not see the problem. I would so not mind staying here with all the cute army boys that I can totes have my pick of because it's, like, so easy to see that they're all into me, which is so not surprising.

"There is the beginning of a zompocalypse happening here, and if we can get back to Elliot's lab, we might be able to find a way to combat the zombies more effectively," Mac, the cute red-headed one, says.

"Who's Elliot?" I ask. "And what's the zompo…that thing you said?"

"I'm Elliot," the geek answers me. Ew. "And I believe that the 'zompocalypse' is a contraction of zombie and apocalypse, right Corporal McCoy?"

"Yeah, and I told you, man, call me Mac, everyone does." Yay, it's much funner to focus on the yummalicious Mac and not the icky Elliot. I'm about to flirt with Mac again 'cause I so need a distraction from the geek staring at me like we have some sort of connection—ugh, so not—but before I can, that scary prisoner looking guy starts barking orders again. He is so freaky, I had to stop my flirting with Mac earlier this morning, too, 'cause he was, like, so mad I thought he was totes gonna, like, shiv me or something. I've seen prison movies, I know how those kinds of guys act when they get around women again, especially pretty ones.

"We don't have time for this *mierda*, we need to figure out what we're going to do," he says in a mad voice. I don't know why he's so grumpy all the time, everyone always does what he tells them to, which is so weird but whatev, if people always did what I told them to do, I would be, like, super stoked! I mean, how fun!

"I guess we're just gonna have to leg it to the lab, eh, Sarge?" the big, black one says. I forget his name 'cause he, like, completely ignores me so why would I bother?

"*Sí.* I'm gonna kill that *cabrón* if we ever see him again," the angry one agrees and I'm, like, so glad I realized he was probably super violent before I made the mistake of thinking he was cute because he is obviously totes dangerous. And I'm so done with that whole bad boy phase; they never have enough money to make it worth it for the long run.

All of a sudden, there's some rumblies in my tummy and I remember I haven't eaten since, like, yesterday, which would be fine if I were dieting, but I'm so not right now. "I could really use some food," I say and point to my perfectly flat belly. "My tummy is grumbling."

"*Dios mio*," the scary one says.

"Thank you!" I say because I'm sure it was a compliment and I don't want to upset someone so scary looking by not being grateful. But he just looks at me and shakes his head. Whatev, I was just being polite.

"It is a good idea, Sergeant Ortiz, it would be better if we were well fuelled for when we come into more contact with the zombies," the geek says.

"Fine, whatever. Mac, you deal with finding food for everybody, and get the *chicas* to help you. The rest of us will try to think of other ways to get to the lab that don't involve walking the entire *chingada* way," the scary guy says—he's so bossy!—and he and the others start heading back inside.

"Okay, folks, it's time for breakfast, apparently, so let's get to it," Mac says and my tummy is very happy to hear this.

Nate

She went about it in her usual idiotic way, but I have to admit I'm glad that Daffy got the idea of breakfast out there. I didn't even realize I was hungry till she started whining, but once she brought up food, I couldn't help but remember that I haven't eaten since yesterday. True, everything that happened yesterday didn't really leave much time for worrying about food and I certainly wasn't hungry, but dear old Dad always taught me that food is fuel and if you want to continue to thrive at the top of the food chain, you have to be well-fed. Hunger has it uses sometimes but overall it just makes you mean and desperate. And I've found that being attacked by zombies makes you desperate enough without adding hunger desperation to the mix. And I don't need any help being mean.

I look over at Lucy to see how she's reacting to Daffy's relentless idiocy and I'm rewarded with a commiserating eye roll. I smile in response and consider telling her about what I did for her this morning, but I figure it's probably not the time yet. I need to get to know her better first to figure out for sure whether or not she'll fully appreciate my gift before I reveal anything.

I have a feeling that she would, but you never know what women will do, they can be so unpredictable. Besides, it's better if the others don't know about my present to her. I doubt they would understand. Although, perhaps they would, none of them seem very upset about the loss.

Even though I decide not to tell Lucy what I did for her, I would like to talk to her, so I'm disappointed when Lia grabs her arm and drags her back inside. Away from me. Like she did earlier today. Hmm. I'll have to keep an eye on this development.

The door slams shut behind them and I'm alone on the roof. I wish Blaine was here. Some of my anger resurfaces as my thoughts unwillingly turn to where he is now, lying dead and buried in that clearing. When I make it out of this, I'll go back for his body, at least that way I'll have something to give his parents for closure, since I can't exactly explain to them how he died. At that thought, my rage bubbles almost uncontrollably as the memory of his death and the circumstances leading up to it flash across my eyelids again. I let out an involuntary snarl. I wish

Tifani was here, too, just so I could kill her all over again, the stupid bitch.

The screech takes me off guard. Dad would be so disappointed. I look quickly to my right and see a zombie staring at me as it perches on one the outstretched limbs of a tree nearest the roof like a bizarre, real-life gargoyle. It settles its weight backwards a bit and I know what's gonna happen next and not for the first time I'm grudgingly thankful to Father for drilling me with the edicts of always being prepared and never being caught off guard unarmed.

I flip my SKS off my shoulder and into my hands, flicking off the safety and staring down the sights, concentrating on the greenish-grey patch of skin that hangs loosely between those deadened eyes, showing glimpses of coagulated blood and white skull behind it. I squeeze the trigger, and as the bullet exits the chamber with a familiar bang, the cartridge spinning up into the air and landing a few feet away, I don't have to look to see if I made the shot; after all the years of training, I can just feel it when I make a perfect one. Besides the certainty of my finely honed instincts, the slightly liquid sound of the zombie's body hitting the ground confirms that I was successful. But just in case, always just in case, I walk to the edge of the roof and scan the ground below. It's easy to tell my kill from the others from the zombie fight this morning because, as opposed to the exploding power contained within the hollow-points the soldiers obviously used, my full metal jackets go right through obstacles without stopping, and there's only one dead zombie on the ground whose head is mostly intact, though damaged enough that I don't feel the need to let loose a back-up shot into the diseased brain therein.

I check the foliage surrounding me, which suddenly became much more threatening, but I don't see any more gravity defying zombies, so I head back inside, where I lock the roof access door, feeling glad that it's metal. Just in case, though, I'll get one of the soldiers to help me bar it more securely once I get back to the others. I flick the safety back on and adjust my SKS so it's hanging backwards over my shoulder again.

As I start walking, heading to the mess hall, where I figure the others will be, I can't help but notice that the rage has calmed down to the lower simmer that is my usual default setting. I breathe a sigh of relief; there's nothing to be gained from losing control at this stage. I need to stay as focused as possible, at least for now. Later, when we're at the lab and have a lot more zombies to deal with, then I can loosen control and just embrace the carnage. But till then, it's best if I keep my head.

I walk into the mess hall and as I glance at the horizontal openings cut into the far wall, giving a sightline into the kitchen, I see that despite Luca's orders, only Daffy is helping Mac with preparing breakfast. Lucy and Lia are sitting at a table and Lucy is patting Lia's arm as Lia engages in what is clearly an exasperating call on her cell phone. Elliot is at a table with Terry and Preacher, near to the one on which Darryl's still lying unconscious, and they look to be in deep conversation with his guards.

Luca is nowhere to be seen and since I don't yet know the chain of command under him, I just head over to Mac 'cause he's the one I've talked to the most and despite his unfortunate viewpoint that Daffy is actually somehow attractive, he seems alright.

"Hey, man, what's up?" he asks as I walk into the kitchen and Daffy giggles like he made some awesome joke. He looks confused, but pleased, then glances at my SKS. "Did I hear a gunshot about two minutes ago?"

"Yeah," I answer, "there was a zombie in one of the trees near the roof. We should probably bar that door, just in case." His eyes widen in reaction to this. I grab a piece of bacon and pop it in my mouth, my stomach growling in anticipation of food.

"Uh, yeah," he answers haltingly, "that, uh, would probably be a good idea. I thought it sounded like they were in the trees when I woke up this morning. Fuckin' vultures." I nod in agreement and snag another piece of bacon.

"Are we gonna bar it soon, then?" I ask and he shakes his head and comes out of whatever trance he slipped into.

"Right, yeah. I'll ask Preach and Terry if they'll do it," he says and walks out the door I just came through. I watch him walk over to the group surrounding Elliot but look away when I feel eyes on me. I turn around to find Daffy staring at me.

It's almost as creepy as a zombie...actually, no, it's probably worse, because for whatever reason, civilized society dictates that I can't kill someone just because they annoy me. Pity.

"What?" I ask impatiently.

"So you had to, like, take one out all by yourself? Were you scared?" she asks in that vapid voice that makes me have to remind myself that shooting her would be a waste of a perfectly good bullet.

"No. Are you seriously trying to flirt with me right now?"

"No time like the present." She winks at me and giggles.

Good God.

"Get the fuck away from me," I growl at her.

She immediately starts pouting and crosses her arms, looking like she's going to throw a tantrum any second. She opens her mouth to let out some more useless drivel, but she's distracted by the door on the west side of the mess hall slamming open in announcement of Luca and Link walking into the room, both of them looking a little less pissed off than the last time I saw them. I leave the kitchen to get a better view of what's going on and, of course, Daffy follows me.

"What's up?" Mac asks.

"We—" before Link can explain further, Darryl suddenly snorts gracelessly and sits up, looking groggy. The attention of the room shifts to him as he feels the bandages wrapped around his face and neck.

"Uh, Darryl?" Mac says tentatively.

"Yeah?" Darryl responds, still looking pretty out of it.

"Are you a zombie?" Mac asks.

"Not to my knowledge, sir," Darryl answers, returning to his soldier's courtesy as he notices that the guys behind him still have their guns trained on his head.

"Um, I think if he were going to turn, he would have done so by now, guys," Elliot points out and after Luca nods his agreement, they lower their guns and a few of them smack Darryl on the shoulder happily.

Just then, Terry and Preacher walk back into the room from the north door and pause when they see Darryl sitting up.

"Where were you two?" Luca asks.

"We went to bar the door to the roof because Nate was almost attacked by a zombie that climbed a tree, sir. Did you figure out any easier ways to get us to the lab?" Preacher answers.

"The zombies can climb?" Link asks just as Terry says, "Darryl's not a zombie?"

"Praise the Lord," Preacher says, smiling as Darryl confirms that he's still human.

"Praise the Doc," Terry retorts, clapping Elliot proudly on the back, though Elliot's skinny frame sinks under the weight of the affection.

"Easier way to get to the lab? Won't we be taking the chopper?" Darryl asks, cutting off Preacher's indignant reply while Luca crosses his arms over his chest, looking annoyed with the chaos.

"Okay, just so everyone is in the loop and on the same page," Mac pauses and shakes his head, seemingly thrown off by his mixture of clichés, before continuing, "the zombies can climb trees, the roof is no longer safe, we have barred the door, the chopper was stolen by Gregory and Jake, the trucks were destroyed, also by Gregory and Jake, so we need to find another way to get to the Doc's lab, and Darryl is awake and does not appear to have zombified." He takes a deep breath when he finishes recapping everything and I feel a smile tugging at the corners of my mouth. It's really too bad he has the bad taste to have a hard-on for Daffy or I think we could be friends.

"Is that everything?" he asks Luca, who nods in response, looking slightly amused, too.

"So we're basically screwed right?" Marco pipes up. "We have no chopper, we have no trucks...how the fuck do you propose to get to your lab now, Doc?"

Before Elliot can answer, Terry suddenly asks, "You. Lia, is it?" Lia looks over at him and nods. "Don't you have some kind of van or something?"

"Brown Sugar's out of gas," she answers then, seeing the questioning looks across most of the faces now turned her way, elaborates, "Brown Sugar is the name of my van."

"Of course, it's out of gas," Mac says, dropping his face into his hands and sitting down on the bench beside Rafe.

"Everyone, *cállase*. Here's what's going to happen: we're going to have breakfast and we're going to talk about the plan Link and I came up with and we're going to find a way to kill all of these undead motherfuckers, and if we run into the old man on the way, then I wouldn't say no to killing him either, but, *ahora*, I need everyone to calm the fuck down and I need some food, in that order," Luca says and he sits down at the table nearest him.

Everyone moves quickly, obeying him without question. Mac stands up and heads back towards the kitchen. Most of the others move over to join Luca at his table and when Luca notices that Lia and Lucy haven't moved yet, he says, "This concerns you *chicas*, too, unless you're planning on staying here by yourselves." They both stand up and walk over to him, though Lia looks aggravated about it.

"Hey, Nate, man, could you help me with bringing the food out?" Mac asks from behind me and I follow him back into the kitchen, leaving Daffy standing by herself muttering something inane about how rude Luca is.

Once everyone is served and we're all crowded around the table, we start discussing what to do next. I guess it's time for plan C now. But if everything went according to the original plan in a zombie apocalypse, it wouldn't be very apocalyptic, now would it?

Lia

I swear if that asshole orders me to do something one more time I'm going to punch him in the nut-sack, consequences be damned. I really don't need his fucking chauvinism when I'm trying to deal with this fucked-up zombie situation, the disturbing memory of finding out that Daffy sleeps naked (what is this, some sort of bordello? We live in a society, people, come on!), trying to keep Lucy away from the very possibly psychotic Nate, and the continuous ridiculousness that is my mother. Honestly, can't a girl catch a break? Does everything need to go wrong at once? Really, what could I have done in a past life to deserve this shit storm?

I spear another forkful of Mac's surprisingly delicious scrambled eggs as my gaze is drawn to Daffy, sitting across the table from me. It's like watching a car accident: I don't want to look at her, but I can't turn away. She's not even listening to what they're planning, that much is obvious. I guess I'm not really paying attention either since I'm alternating between watching the Daffy car-wreck and focusing on trying to make Lucy look at me using just the power of my stare so that we can marvel at how awful Daffy is together. It doesn't seem to be working. Nor does it seem to be working for Nate, who is also staring at her intently. I feel a chill skitter across the back of my neck at the look in his eyes. I don't want to say "hunger" because it sounds way too overly dramatic, but I honestly can't think of a word that is more apt to describe it.

I don't know why Lucy doesn't have her horror movie paranoia radar up about this guy, but I guess that's what happens when you go too long without getting any. The first stupidly hot guy that enters into your life and acts all enamoured with you...I guess that's bound to give almost anyone lady wood. Still, she should know better; nothing is *that* pretty without something being flawed, which in this case, I'm pretty sure is his sanity.

Adding to my stress from the shambling undead, asshole soldiers, and a temporarily (hopefully) lust-fogged best friend, I have to deal with the messages Roz left on my voicemail at some point. Five in total by the way. If I don't call back soon she'll have a fit, but if I call she'll know I'm lying about something and if I tell her the truth...well, actually, even if I did that she'd think I was lying...or she'd just tell me to try not to get any blood on the nice new sweater they got me for my birthday. Too late for that, sorry Mom.

Sigh. Lucy was right after all, this weekend was a terrible idea since we've somehow landed right smack in the middle of an "ominous situation." To say the least.

"Lia?" My head jerks up when I hear my name spoken and I feel an unwelcome blush spread over my cheeks as I realize everyone else is quiet and staring at me. God, I'm getting as bad as Lucy; sometimes I think her reverie induced zombie-ism is as contagious as the normal kind.

"What?" I ask, trying to act like I'm not embarrassed.

"You were muttering to yourself...um, pretty loudly," Elliot says,.and even though he doesn't say it in an unkind way, it still makes my blush deepen.

"Sorry," I mumble. "What's the plan?" I ask, hoping to divert some of the attention away from myself.

"Right now the plan is to make it to the lake and use one or two of the boats there to get to the other side, which will take a lot of time off of our trek to the lab," Elliot answers, smiling kindly at me and despite the fact that I think he's an idiot for being so obviously besotted with Daffy, I can't help but notice that he's actually kind of cute.

"I still don't get why we have to, like, go all the way to your dumb old lab. If it's gonna be dangerous, what's the point?" Daffy asks and Elliot blushes and mumbles something incoherent in the face of being directly addressed by her. Yeah, he seems cute and then that happens. I can't respect a guy who doesn't respect himself enough to realize when a chick—or anyone, for that matter—is treating him like crap. And I just cannot find guys that I don't respect attractive.

"Staying here is dangerous, too, you moron. Have you ever seen a zombie movie, ever? They'll get in eventually. It's a rule," I answer before anyone else can and I can't help but feel a little better as a grin creeps over Lucy's face while Daffy makes random offended noises.

"Right, well, there is the fact that it won't be safe here forever, but also if we have a chance to stop it, we can't just sit back and do nothing while they continue to kill innocent people and spread the mutation unchecked," Elliot finds his voice and expands on my answer in a much gentler manner. Not that it matters, though, since Daffy seems to have lost interest in the reasons for the current plan as she's gone back to mooning over Mac, batting her lashes at him and giggling for no apparent reason. Elliot makes a disgruntled, embarrassed noise and stops talking as he looks enviously at Mac. Mac, for his part, looks divided between being pleased with the attention and seeming to be sorry that Elliot is so obviously dejected. Stupid, stupid boys.

"When do we leave?" I ask, partly to break up the obsess-fest surrounding Daffy and partly because I really want to know; I hate just sitting here when there's zombies that need killing wandering freely outside.

"That's a good question, *chica*—" Luca starts answering me but I cut him off abruptly.

"My name is Lia. I wouldn't accept being called 'girl' in English so don't think that saying it in Spanish makes it any cuter or more tolerable," I growl and Luca glares back at me.

"Whoa, okay, well, it was a good question and one that I think the Doc should answer," Mac says quickly.

"Um, well we can probably stay here for another day or two while we plan the route and figure out what we're taking with us so that we can be as prepared as possible and yeah…" Elliot trails off uncertainly, looking anxiously back and forth between the asshole and me since we still haven't broken from our angry staring contest.

"Yeah, I think that's a good idea, Doc. Uh, why don't we clean up these dishes and then study the maps some more and we can start figuring those things out," Mac offers and after he elbows Nate, who's sitting beside him, Nate breaks his stare away from Lucy and voices his agreement then stands up to help with the dishes.

"Luke?" Mac says hesitantly as he stands up, too, and Luca breaks our stare to look up at him. Ha, I win. Secure in that knowledge, I stand up, as well, and join Nate in collecting the breakfast dishes, even though a part of me is wondering if I should since I wouldn't be surprised if doing so confirms Luca's opinion that I should be and now am doing "woman's work," but I decide that since I'm already standing, not to mention holding a number of plates, it would be weirder to stop suddenly than to just do it and find some way to prove him wrong later.

When I'm alone in the kitchen with Nate and that hungry look is gone from his eyes, I can almost convince myself that he's just a normal, extremely good-looking guy. Were I not worried about Lucy's safety, that might be an actual possibility. But that look in his eyes. Who knows what he might be capable of?

"So," Nate says, breaking the silence.

I grunt in response and continue focusing on cleaning the dish in my hands. Maybe if I ignore him, he'll go away.

"You don't like me much, do you?" he suddenly asks and I am thankful for my yoga training, because without the controlled breathing techniques I've learned from it over the years, I don't know if I would've been able to stay so calm and nonchalant when faced with this situation.

There's nothing in this question or his tone that is overtly threatening, but something about his presence and his...aura, I guess you'd call it, is off, even worse than yesterday and, goose pimples immediately crop up along my arms.

"What makes you think that?" I ask, glad that my voice is completely steady and bordering on indifferent.

"Just a feeling," he answers and this time, the tone of his voice sends intense shivers down my spine. I turn to look at him and my heart starts beating faster at the look on his face. It's...hunger again, I guess, but different than the hunger I saw on his face when he was staring at Lucy. That hunger was like a more intense version of lust. This hunger...the only word that comes to mind is "predatory."

"I like you fine," I answer and give myself a mental high five that my voice is once again steady and kind of bored sounding. "I'm just a little distracted right now, with all the zombie action, and I'm not too focused on socializing properly. Sorry if I came off rude or anything. I'm just in battle mode, as Lucy would say." Now I mentally kick myself for bringing her into the conversation. I meet his eyes, trying not to seem like I'm challenging him. I hate feeling like I'm backing down from a fight, but I figure psychos are probably an acceptable exception to my rule.

He tilts his head to the side a little bit, studying me. I force myself to blink a couple of times as I work on keeping my face as impassive as possible. If I let fear slip into my expression, or even wariness, he might see me as prey. If I let defiance or obstinance slip in, then he might see it as a challenge and that's probably the

166

last thing I need right now. After a few more seconds of studying me, his face clears and he flashes an easy grin.

"Don't worry about it. I understand about being in battle mode. Sorry for overreacting," he says, still smiling and looking like a completely normal person. That's not at all disturbing. I force a smile back in return and go back to scrubbing dishes.

As I pick up the nearest plate, I hear someone walk into the kitchen behind me. I turn around to see Mac and I give a mental sigh of relief. I am definitely cool with not being alone with Nate any longer than I have to be. The only thing worse than this is him being alone with Lucy.

"Hey, guys, I just thought I'd bring in the last of the dishes," Mac says, raising the stack of plates balanced on his right hand like we might need proof of this statement.

"Thanks, Mac," I say, feeling grateful for his goofy presence.

"No worries," he answers, flashing his own easy grin, which, when compared to the memory of Nate's from only a few moments ago, drives home the high creep factor that Nate has. Mac's grin is natural and wide, and so obviously not fake, when I recall the image of Nate's attempt at the same thing, it seems like nothing so much as a degraded copy that's a pale comparison to the real thing.

"Listen, I'm sorry about Luca, he's just used to being in charge, you know? And civs kinda stress him out," Mac says, easing the dishes into the sink, turning to me and smiling in a way that seemed so charming only moments ago when he wasn't defending someone who seriously makes me get my rage on. Though, right now, I'll definitely take being annoyed versus being completely freaked out so I turn all my attention on Mac.

"Yeah, he's kind of...intense, I guess is a polite way to put it," I say.

Mac makes a face that is half embarrassment and half sympathy, "I know. I'm sorry. I mean, he'd kick my ass if he knew I was in here apologizing for him, but I just—I mean, it is the zompocalypse, right? Things'd go a lot more smoothly if we could all just get along." Mac makes another face as he finishes talking, this one closer to disgust. "Wow, that sounded cheesy, sorry." He shakes his head at himself. "I just mean that if we can't all," he pauses as though trying to think of a less clichéd way to make his point before gritting his teeth and giving up, "get along, then at least we should try to tolerate each other."

"Yeah, he's doing a bang-up job of tolerating us '*chicas*,'" I say, unable to stop the retort even though Mac's amusing awkwardness is lightening my mood considerably. To use a cliché myself, laughter really is the best medicine.

"I know," Mac sighs and looks down-right sorrowful. I hold back a giggle and shake my head at him. He glances up at me and half-smiles before pressing on, "He's just...really terrible at dealing with people who don't blindly follow his orders." He shrugs.

I barely hold back an eye roll at this rationalization. "Huh" is all I can think of to say and luckily I'm saved from having to say anything more by the appearance of Daffy, which normally I wouldn't be thankful for, but I'll take the distraction she offers now.

"What's everyone doing in here?" she asks and her stupid squeaky voice quickly does away with any appreciation I might have been feeling for her sudden appearance.

"Washing dishes," I say, acidly. "What does it look like?"

"Oh. Do you, like, need any help? I could help wash or dry, 'cause I'm, like, totes equally comfortable with getting wet or with rubbing things down," she says, adding a hip shimmy-thing that has Mac's attention completely ensnared. And that's all I can handle of that.

"They're all yours," I say and turn to see if Nate's left the room yet because nothing causes him to vacate somewhere faster than if he's faced with a Daffy interaction. Not that I blame him for this Pavlovian response to her presence, but still, if I didn't think Lucy would kill or at least maim me, I'd somehow try to get Daffy attached to Lucy, because then I wouldn't have to worry about keeping Nate away from her.

Oh shit.

Nate has indeed vacated the room; he probably left as soon as Daffy came in. I walk through the door of the kitchen, striding back into the cafeteria and whipping my gaze around the room, searching for Lucy. As I look around, I am unpleasantly surprised to find a certain red-head and a certain potential psycho missing from the bunch.

"Has anyone seen Lucy?" I ask, hearing the worry I suddenly feel clearly in my voice.

"Nate offered to check out how much damage those *cabrones* did to the garage, and see if anything in it is salvageable. Lucy went with him," Luca answers and I swear, I could strangle him, I'm so angry. And worried. I'm wongry.

"What?" I ask, unable to suppress the rage in my voice.

"Relax, *chi*—Lia," he corrects himself after a murderous glance from me. "There won't be many—if any—zombies out there now; we killed a large number of them when we were retrieving Master Corporal Cho. And in any case, Nate is a very good fighter; she'll be more than safe with him. I also gave them a comm unit in case something does go wrong."

"I don't trust him," I spit, my tone venomous.

"You need to calm down, everything will be fine."

"What a terrible thing to say!" I growl, and then stalk out of the room, but not before grabbing my battle axe off the table I left it on.

"Lia, wait," a voice entreats from behind me as I stomp into the hallway. I whip around and Elliot steps out of the way of my swinging axe blade.

"Sorry," I mutter, returning the axe to my side and gripping the handle firmly.

"It's fine, no harm done. Can I ask, what's going on with you and Nate? What do you think he'd do to Lucy?" he asks. I grumble something unintelligible and look down, studying the glint of my axe's blade in the fluorescent lighting.

"I'm sorry, I didn't catch that," Elliot says without any traces of sarcasm or impatience. And definitely none of the oh-so-infuriating "hysterical woman" viewpoint that I just saw on the faces of the majority of the soldiers.

"I just...don't think he can be trusted. He's dangerous."

"Okay," Elliot says, sounding completely non-judgemental. "Do you know where the garage is?" he asks.

"Sort-of," I say.

"Alright, I'll help you look for it and Lucy, if you want," he offers and I look up quickly, bracing myself for any signs that he's just trying to calm me down and placate me, but he looks earnest and sincere, totally genuine in his offer of help.

"Sure," I answer, grateful for his authenticity, but distracted by trying to avoid panic until I know it's necessary. However, I am unable to resist my anger. She should know better even if she does have major lady wood for this guy. Going off alone with a dude who may very well be a psychopath when there's something sinister going on? Rookie mistake.

Lucy

Nate and I reached the now smoldering garage without incident and now I'm waiting outside while he investigates.

"There's nothing here that can be saved. Let's head back," Nate says as he pops back up beside me. I jump a little; I didn't even hear him coming.

"Sorry, didn't mean to scare you," he says.

"It's fine, I'm just jumpy."

"There's plenty of reason to be right now." He smiles at me and my stomach flips over.

"So, nothing worth recovering?" I ask, trying to distract myself from this ridiculous crush angst.

"No. Some things might have made it through the explosion and the fire, but when the ammo stores lit up, the bullets took out the rest."

"How did they even manage to blow it up so quickly?"

"I only took a quick look, but from what I could tell, they did a variation of the Molotov cocktail with a rag in the gas tanks of the trucks. It's dangerous as hell, but efficient."

"I hope they get eaten by zombies," I say and he smiles again, making my stomach get all acrobatic once more in response. I know I should probably be more cautious around him, especially because of the concerns Lia raised last night. And this morning. And yet again after the helicopter was stolen and the garage was blown up. But he's just so hot. And while I know in my paranoia centre that this is not a valid argument or defence, I can't help myself. I adjust my sunglasses, feeling embarrassingly grateful for their dark lenses. I mean, my eyes are sensitive and it is bright out here, but I'm mostly wearing them because it makes it easier to stare at him and have it go undetected...God, I'm the worst. And yet I can't tear my eyes away from taut lines of his cheekbones, the curve of his lips or the hard angle of his jaw, made all the more distracting as he clenches it and the muscle jumps in response.

I try to think about something besides the bad things I want to do with him, which would be irresponsible and inconvenient given the situation, but my mind refuses to drift in any sort of useful direction. The conversation dwindles as we start walking back across the short expanse of land that separates the main fort from the garage along with a small storage shed and I try to think of something else to say to Nate besides "So, zombies, huh?"

Damn crushes. Really make me feel about as intelligent as Daffy. Whatever. I decide to just dive in and hope inspiration strikes as I start talking. "So..." I say and turn to look at Nate, hoping for a cue to aid in my improvised conversation attempts.

Only Nate's not there. My heart leaps into my throat and I stop walking, gripping my machete handle tightly as I look around my immediate area, but I can't see him, nor do I get any indications of where he might have gone. See, and this is what I get for following my hormones instead of my paranoia.

I hear ragged noises to the left of me and turn my head slowly, hoping I won't catch a glimpse of an injured Nate.

Nope. Zombies. Okay, that's worse.

An ear-piercing shriek rips through the air and two zombies are charging at me before I have any time to think. They cut me off from the fort and I make a split-second decision and start sprinting for the shed since it's the closest building to me that's not a smoking ruin. I know they say you shouldn't run from predators 'cause it'll only make things worse, but in this situation, I'm pretty sure not running would be a worse plan.

I'm about five feet from the shed when something hits me hard in the side and I tumble to the ground, trying hard to fall without impaling myself on the machete. To this end, I go down swinging, my machete connecting with flesh and bone and inciting further zombie shrieks. As soon as I hit the ground, I scramble to my feet as quickly as I can and whip around, swinging the machete as I go. I feel the blade slice into the head of the zombie nearest me and thankfully, it keeps right on going, shearing off the top part of its head, spraying me with thick, clotted blood that smells, for lack of a less obvious description, like death. The zombie drops to the ground and the remaining one shrieks and lunges at me again. I stumble backward and feel the doorknob jab into my shoulder blade painfully. That'll definitely bruise...though of course it won't even have the chance to do so if I get my zombie on. I hear shots from somewhere nearby—Nate probably, nowhere near enough to be of any help now. I'm on my own and I need to make my getaway and quick.

I brace myself against the door and thrust my machete blade forwards as hard as I can. It smashes into the centre of the zombie's face and I feel skin, muscle, and bone collapse as my momentum carries me forward and I topple to the ground with the zombie beneath me. Sticky, viscous blood, black with decay oozes out of the zombie's crushed face and I gag at the smell. I work at disentangling myself from the zombie, its decomposing body squishing unpleasantly under my weight as I right myself and free my machete, pulling free some bone and muscle attached by a thin webbing of skin along with it. And yup, that's a nose. There's no time to even suppress a shudder at this because yet more shrieks are ripping through the air.

I turn back to the shed and leap for the door; I twist the knob and say a silent prayer of thanks to the universe that it opens, as I fall inside with the force of my lunge. As gravity takes over, a hand suddenly grasps my ankle tightly and something else gets tangled in my hair. I fall hard, bashing my knee and straining my neck as my head snaps back, anchored by what's tangled in my hair. I don't even think, I just grasp my hair with one hand and pull as hard as I can while kicking my leg out with all of the force I can muster. I pull my hair painfully free as my foot connects with something that's solid yet gooey at the same time and there's a sickening crunch as the hand loosens its grip. I yank my leg inside and slam the door shut, driving the lock home before anything else happens.

I lean my face against the door for a few seconds, the cool metal soothing after my almost unsuccessful escape. I breathe deeply in and out a few times, trying to catch my breath and calm myself down—the zombies screeching and clawing at the other side of the door makes this rather more difficult. I step away and flick on the light switch I find to the left of the doorframe. A single, dangling bulb lights the small space. I push my sunglasses to the top of my head and glance around the dimly lit shed quickly, scanning the room for any indications that something else might have come in here while the door was unlocked. My breathing gets closer to its normal rhythm as I confirm that I'm alone. I'm almost hysterically relieved that the shed's light is working, dim as it is, because I do not need to be any more scared than I am right now and full darkness gets me every time.

I comb my fingers through my hair, stomach twisting as I feel remnants of zombie skin and blood amongst the tangled strands. I tie my hair up quickly, twirling it into a hasty bun with the spare elastic I usually keep on my wrist, remembering too late the advice I read in Max Brooks' *Zombie Survival Guide* about making sure you don't have loose bits of clothing or hair flapping about that a zombie could easily grab. My heart belatedly pounds again as I think about what would've happened if I hadn't gotten free in time.

Shaking free my mind of these non-productive horror movie images, I walk to the back of the shed, putting as much distance between me and the zombies as is possible in the small room. I skirt around a decrepit-looking riding mower and I drop to the ground behind it so that my back is against a bench covered haphazardly in various tools. My hands are trembling.

That was so close. Way too fucking close. Where the hell did Nate go? I feel the beginnings of tears climbing up the back of my throat and putting pressure against my tear ducts. I can't tell whether they're tears of relief, tears of anger, or simply left over tears of blind panic. Maybe it's all of the above.

To help stop myself from losing it, I pull out my omnipresent iPod, which I'm very glad to see survived the latest zombie attack; I flick through it for a while before finding a song to help calm my nerves, but before I can press play, I hear two shots fired from somewhere close by outside the shed. The zombie screeches cut off abruptly and then I hear the doorknob being jiggled, then unlocked and turned.

As the door opens, I grab my machete and try to ignore Lia's voice in my head, scolding me for running off with a possible psycho and apparent flight-risk when we're in the midst of a horror-movie type of situation. I know it's probably one of the soldiers because they used a key to get in, but my fight-or-flight response is still in overdrive so I remove my earbuds and try to be as quiet as possible, resisting the urge to break yet another rule and ask, "Who's there?" like some horror movie bimbo that everyone knows won't make it to the end credits.

"Hello?"

The person entering the shed, who is thankfully not a zombie, I never would have heard the end of *that* if I was able to survive and get back to Lia, does not adhere to horror movie survival rules when he hears me knock something metal—and loud—off of the bench behind me when I shift position abruptly due to an unfortunately timed calf cramp.

"Oh good," Mac says upon seeing me, "I was worried I might've stumbled across a zombie."

"Then why did you say 'hello'?" I ask, wiping hastily at my remaining tears. His face scrunches up in confusion.

"That is an excellent question," he says, "and one that I do not have an answer for." At this, I can't hold back a smile despite how freaked out I still feel, and he smiles in return before continuing, "Lia's really worried about you. She hated that Luca sent you off alone with Nate, so he sent me to find you guys before Lia went after you; he didn't want any more civs walking around out here than there already were," he pauses, then asks, "Where *is* Nate?"

I shrug and start to explain about how I heard shots being fired nearby and for some reason, this movement and trying to speak causes fresh tears to flow and I put my face in my hands, trying to calm myself down.

"Oh, hey, it's alright," he says quietly, stepping forwards, closer to me. A second later, I feel his arms slide around me, pressing me to his chest. After a few moments of him holding me, the tears subside and I am able to pull away and breathe mostly normally. I wipe the remaining tears from my face and Mac squints at me in concern.

"You do know there's a zompocalypse happening right now, right?" he asks, his voice gentle and soothing somehow as he jokes with me.

"Nope, hadn't noticed," I say, trying to appear nonchalant by shrugging and curling my left hand around the handle of my machete. But truth be told, it is a hell of a lot harder to be nonchalant when you've just broken down and cried like a little girl in front of someone you barely know.

He smiles kindly and his greenish-grey eyes crinkle up at the corners. "Okay, well did you also know that going off by yourself during a zompocalypse is generally not the best idea? In light of this reckless behaviour, I'm afraid that I'm gonna have to implement a buddy system," he says and his smile widens.

"Says the person who gives away his position when he doesn't know what could be lurking in the shadows. Not to mention, *you* came here alone," I retort and his smile turns into a chuckle.

"Alright, touché, but see, now we're together, so the buddy system works," he says and I laugh involuntarily again. "So what happened?" he asks gently.

"I don't really know," I say, shifting my machete and hopping up onto the bench. "I was walking back to the fort with Nate, everything was fine, and then, all of sudden, he was just gone and next thing I know, I'm being ambushed by zombies."

"Jesus," Mac breathes, swiping a hand over his face, "are you okay?"

"Yeah, I mean, it scared the hell out of me, but I wasn't bitten or anything."

"Good," he says and squeezes my hand. "I'm gonna radio Luca and let him know what happened before we head back, okay?" I nod my agreement; he smiles in response and hops up onto the hood of the riding mower, sitting across from me as he radios Luca. Our knees touch slightly in the space between the mower and the bench.

"Hey, Luke, I found Lucy. She was ambushed by some zombies, but she's okay. Nate is MIA."

"Where the fuck did he go?"

I jump in surprise as Lia's enraged voice blares through the radio's tiny speaker.

"No idea," Mac replies for me when I gesture that I don't want to answer her. I'm mad enough at myself for my stupid error in judgement, I don't wanna deal with Lia's anger, too, at least not until I'm back in the relative safety of the fort and the zombie ambush isn't quite so fresh in my mind.

"Goddammit, Lia!—Mac, get back here ASAP, *si*?" Luca's growl replaces Lia's voice as he talks over top of her.

"Sure thing, Luke, we'll be right there," Mac answers and clicks the radio off.

"Can we just wait a few minutes?" I ask. "I need to calm down a bit more before I go back out there."

"No problem," he says, "I go when you go, because, you know, if we lose the buddy system, we could descend into total anarchy and I'm not sure we wanna take that chance." His voice is grave but his eyes are crinkled at the corners again and yet another unintentional smile curves my lips up.

"Well, we wouldn't want to contribute to anarchism, what with having to worry about the zompocalypse and all," I answer and he grins.

"My point exactly."

There's a lull in the conversation and I say, "I'm glad your friend isn't a zombie."

He grins again and I feel my face mirror his. I can't help it, his smiles are contagious. "Yeah, me, too. He's a good guy, that would've sucked," he responds simply before saying, "you seem to know something about horror movie rules...so I gotta ask, what's your favourite scary movie?"

"The movie that line came from, actually. I love me some *Scream*."

"Yeah, Wes Craven is generally a pretty safe bet for decent horror," he says and I nod my agreement.

"Speaking of horror movies," I say, "can you believe we're actually near a place called Crystal Lake?"

"I know, it's crazy. I swear to God, I'm so paranoid that Jason's gonna come out of nowhere and slash us all with his, well..." he trails off and gestures at my machete, which I must admit looks very like the one favoured by the Voorhees, and I also must admit that's partly why I love it.

"Yeah, ditto. Glad I'm not the only one," I answer. "I mean, we might as well just move to Woodsboro and change our names to Sidney Prescott."

"Or go to Elm Street and take a nap," Mac adds.

"Find the video from *The Ring* and watch it," I say, enjoying this game.

"Get a doll and name it Chucky."

"Buy a car and name it Christine."

"Tease a girl named Carrie."

"Go skinny dipping off Amity Island."

"Stay at the Bates Motel."

"Hang out in Haddonfield on Halloween," I say and Mac smiles.

"All the horror movies in the world can't prepare you for the real thing though," he says after a beat.

I'm pretty sure he just changed the subject 'cause he couldn't think of anymore examples, but I can't help responding anyway because this is exactly what I've been thinking since this whole thing started. "Yeah, no kidding. I mean, Jesus, I've watched a ton of zombie movies, I had a tentative survival plan in mind, just in case, but I never actually thought that I'd be in the midst of a zombie attack. Especially because, you know, in a lot of zombie movies, they act like Canada is impervious because it's so 'cold.' Like in *Land of the Dead* or *I Am Legend*, they say stuff about how the virus or whatever can't survive in the cold so people are safe further north. So many lies."

"Exactly. It's like that thing about hearing hooves and thinking horses not zebras, but instead, I mean, generally you hear shuffling, you think LMFAO, not zombies."

I snort a laugh at this assessment of our current situation and Mac grins appreciatively back at me. I would've been happy for the conversation to continue in this vein, with horror movie banter to distract me from my issues, but, unfortunately, it is not to be. The walkie-talkie on Mac's belt crackles to life, Elliot's voice coming hesitantly through the static this time, "Um, guys, I hate to interrupt, uh, if I am interrupting, but Lia's getting pretty worried. It'd probably be good if you came back soon."

There's the sound of a struggle and then Lia's voice, which sounds pretty damn pissed off, is raging out of the tiny speaker.

"You are breaking so many rules right now, Lucy Malone, I am at a loss for words." A statement which is soon proved false when she continues to rant, "You better get your ass back here now, and I mean now, before I have a heart attack or you get eaten by zombies. I'm serious Luce, get back here now!" And with that, the walkie-talkie goes quiet.

I look at Mac and he's staring down at the walkie-talkie like he can't quite believe what just happened.

"That was a little terrifying," he finally says and a somewhat hysterical giggle bursts out of me. He glances up, looking concerned and perhaps my giggle was more hysterical than somewhat.

"I guess we should go back," I say.

"We can wait a little longer," Mac says, acting completely nonchalant, shrugging his shoulders and crinkling his eyes again.

"She sounds really mad," I protest, albeit feebly. If I'm still in a confessing mood, and it would seem that I am, I have to further admit that the idea of just hanging out here with Mac for as long as I can, isn't exactly repulsive, whereas the idea of facing an utterly pissed off Lia? It's pretty frightening, so I just smile back at him once again, grateful that he's giving me an out and I settle into the wall behind my back.

"Thanks," I say, as an afterthought, suddenly a bit ridiculously grateful that he's the one who found me.

"No problem," he answers, "she scares me just a little bit so I'm cool with putting off the showdown with her."

I open my mouth to continue our horror movie discussion, but, before I can, Lia's voice growls out of the speaker on the walkie-talkie again, "Seriously? You're not even going to answer me? You need to at least let me know you're not dead, and—you know what? No, if you don't answer me in the next two minutes, I'm just going to come looking for you," her voice breaks off for a second and when she speaks again, I feel like a total bitch for how much turmoil I've obviously put her through by endangering myself. "Please, Luce, I just need to know you're okay, I need to see it for myself, just please come back. You're scaring the shit out of me." The walkie-talkie goes silent again and I look past Mac to the door of the shed.

"Yeah, I guess we should head back, eh?" Mac says, following my gaze.

I nod mutely, grabbing my machete in my left hand and not saying anything as I slide off of the bench and stand up. I can't think of anything to say so I just continue staring past him, feeling my heart pounding in my chest as I contemplate the look on Lia's face when we get back to the main building of the fort. Not that I blame her for being upset, how would I feel if it was the other way around? Terrible, angry and panicked, that's how.

Mac slides off the hood of the mower and stands beside me. To my surprise, I feel his hand slide into mine and squeeze as he brings the walkie-talkie to his mouth and says succinctly, "On our way." He doesn't say anything to me afterward, but he doesn't let go of my hand as we head for the door, skirting around the mower as we go. Once we're standing in front of the door, he pauses for a moment, tugging on my hand until I don't feel that I have a choice but to look up at him, so I do, questioningly.

"You good?" he asks.

I drop my sunglasses back down onto the bridge of my nose, squeeze his hand back and answer, "I'm good."

He smiles and flicks the lock on the door with his free hand before pushing it open and walking out into the sunlight with me right behind him. Perhaps, it's the sunlight that makes it so surreal, from watching horror movies, you almost never expect anything bad to happen in the daytime, but standing there, in the middle of the day, we are faced with a pack, a herd, a passel, whatever you want to call it, a group of zombies hanging about between us and the fort.

"Well, fuck," Mac says, pretty much summing up the moment.

"Yup," I say, "we're such horror movie buffs, we should've seen this coming."

He snorts a little laugh then shuts up when some of the zombies glance in our direction. Luckily we're downwind so they don't seem to have pegged us as a food source just yet; we have some time to think of a plan.

"You know, since this whole thing started, there's something I've wanted to try…" Mac says, looking over at me and raising an eyebrow as though asking for permission.

"Okay," I respond, shrugging.

He smiles in a way that strikes me as completely adorable and I feel weirdly happy that he doesn't let go of my hand as he reaches into his pocket with his free hand and brings out his phone.

"Just a sec," Mac mutters as he flicks through the options with some difficulty due to being one-handed, but he doesn't seem too keen to let go of my hand either and he soon finds what he's looking for, making a triumphant noise when he does. "I just always wondered if this would work in the event of a zombie attack," he says by way of explanation and before I can ask what he plans to do, "Thriller" is blasting out of the surprisingly powerful speakers and I can tell you that whatever he thought might happen, what actually happened? Not the plan.

At the sound of the familiar strains of the song that we all know and love, the zombies, who seem to have a dissenting opinion about the love part, start screeching in a way that I've never heard. Not only that, but they start charging at us.

"Oh, fuck!" Mac swears and after a moment's hesitation, he throws the cell phone away from us. It distracts about half of the zombies, who change direction startlingly quickly and run after the apparently offending cell phone. This leaves us with five zombies to take care of.

"I'm sorry," Mac says, squeezing my hand one more time and then letting go, he shifts away from me and pulls out his gun. I'm not at all sad about this development, I'm just glad that my lead hand is now free and I can defend myself better.

I slash my machete as hard as I can through the first zombie face to come near me, and I don't even have time to revel in the clean cut that severs the top of its head and brain from the rest of its anatomy or indulge in feeling some squeamishness about the resulting blood and brain matter that splatters against my torso in a distinctly icky way, before a second zombie is shrieking at me while it scuttles towards me.

I distantly hear the cacophony of gunfire as Mac defends himself while I hack at the reanimated beast currently trying to munch on me. My machete catches it awkwardly on the side of the face and instead of the decapitation that I was going for, my attack only results in ripping off a chunk of its face and spilling the decomposing ooze of its left eyeball down the side of its now exposed cheek. Gross? Yes, very. Effective for anything other than making me feel like puking? Not so much.

The torn skin clings to my blade as I hit the ground, instinctively protecting my head with my left hand as I continue to slash at the zombie now straddling me with my right. The zombie carries on screeching and doesn't notice or care that its left cheekbone is now completely exposed—albeit covered in a gooey blackness that covers most of the white bone, making it look even more perverse and wrong, especially in conjunction with the blank pit where its left eye used to be.

It thrusts its face close to mine and I barely hold off gagging as the smell coats the inside of my nostrils and the back of my throat. As I push against its chest, keeping its snapping jaws away from my tender flesh, a drop of sludgy blood drips from its empty eye socket and lands smack in the middle of the right lens of my sunglasses. My heart does a frantic jitterbug against the walls of my ribcage as I send out a thank you to any power in the 'verse that I wore my sunglasses today. The zombie lunges for my face again. It's time to get this motherfucker off of me and send it straight to hell.

I shriek back at the zombie, wondering if the ruse will work again and it pauses for a moment, seeming confused that its own sound is emanating from its prey and in its moment of hesitation, I twist my hips up at the same time that I push off of the ground with my right arm and soon I'm straddling it. I feel the decaying flesh squish wetly under my weight and before I can let myself contemplate the full horror of my current situation, I grasp my machete handle with both hands and bring the blade down as hard as I can into the spot just above the centre of its ruined face. It goes still instantly and I know I've found the sweet spot. The true death spot.

Blackened blood flows sluggishly out of the wound around my blade and I rock back onto my heels, grasping the machete tightly and pulling it out of the zombie's face. There is a squinching sort-of sound, a sound like cutting through raw chicken and yet more blood and brain matter splashes onto my shirt, hands, and neck. I should've worn the shirt from yesterday, even if a halter top isn't the most practical fighting gear, at least it was already bloody and gross; at this rate, before long I won't have any clean clothes left at all.

With my machete now free, I stand up and whip around in a circle quickly, checking my vicinity for any more immediate zombie danger. None are nearby at the moment, and the good news continues as I spot Mac, still standing and looking relatively unscathed.

"You okay?" he asks, sounding worried.

"I'm fine, covered in ick, but fine," I answer, feeling mostly back to normal again despite the gore already tightening the fabric of my black t-shirt and the surface of my bare skin as it starts to dry. I really need another shower as soon as possible, this whole bloody thing does not work for me. But otherwise, I actually am fine; I don't feel nearly as terrified as when I was engaged in my earlier solo zombie battle on this spot. Probably because I had back-up this time around and wasn't defending myself all by my lonesome.

"Are you okay?" I ask Mac but he doesn't answer right away. His gaze is lowered and he only briefly raises his eyes to meet mine when I say his name.

"I'm so sorry. I didn't think that would happen," he mutters, as he resumes staring at the forehead wound sporting zombie corpse nearest him.

"Yeah, 'cause I thought your plan was to get them to attack us," I say and he glances up at me again, smiling faintly this time. His smile fades quickly, however, because suddenly there's silence as the final notes of "Thriller" fade and the zombies that were attacking his cell phone are now focused back on us.

"Double fuck!" Mac swears again before grabbing his walkie-talkie and shouting into it, "Open the door! Open the door! Open the door!" as he waves me over to him and breaks into a jog towards the fort. I follow suit and start to run.

"Which door?" Luca's voice now crackles through the walkie-talkie, his tone urgent.

"West!" Mac shouts back before tossing the walkie-talkie away and grabbing my wrist as we approach said door, shifting me behind him as he pulls his gun and backs me towards the door until I feel my shoulder blades touch the metal. The no longer distracted zombies are focused solely on us and closing fast. I can hear them shrieking and scuttling, scrambling as they trip over themselves in their desperation to reach us and chew us limb from limb.

I hear and feel Mac fire a couple of shots, but since I am currently pressed against his back, I can't tell if they hit their marks or not. I feel like I should be helping and yet I'm weirdly distracted by the muscles in his back and the way he still smells good despite being in the midst of a zombie attack. He smells like just after it rains...in the middle of a zombie attack. How is that even possible? I don't know, but it's enjoyable. Before I can start to freak out over whatever the hell I'm feeling, Mac swears violently and I realize that he's out of bullets.

I shift our positions, so that I'm now in front and though he tries to pull me behind him again, I ignore him and focus on the zombie closest to us. I push Mac back with my left hand and swing hard with my right, angling the tip of my machete inwards so that it's aimed at the zombie's temple. I make contact, burying the blade in the zombie's skull. Its deadened eyes shutter as I hear the metal door behind us swing open and Mac and I fall backwards into the fort.

The dead zombie and a few other ambitious zombies fall with us, but luckily, Luca brought back-up and they are dispatched quickly as Mac rolls off of me and stands up, reaching down for my hand as soon as he's holstered his gun. Luca locks the doors against the remainder of the zombies as Mac pulls me to my feet, asking if I'm okay.

I retrieve my machete from its place in the zombie's brain, shift my foot so it's out from under a recently re-deceased zombie arm, and nod my head, feeling a little off balance from the impact of having the full weight of Mac, plus a few zombie hangers-on, crash into me.

"There you are!" Lia's voice shatters the silence and as I look up to see her and Elliot coming towards us. I feel suddenly distinctly aware that I'm still holding the hand Mac used to pull me up. I drop it quickly and say, "Hey," as nonchalantly as I can, given the circumstances.

"What the fuck happened?" she asks, taking in the small pile of re-dead zombies and the blood covering me as she walks up to us. When she reaches me, I only have a second to notice that she's replaced her battle axe with its smaller cousin, the tomahawk, before she hugs me so hard that all of the breath rushes out of my lungs and just as I'm about to beg for mercy, she lets go and shoves me, hard. I stumble over the deadened zombie nearest me and fall back, crashing to the floor in a rather ungraceful and slightly painful way. I sit there for a second, looking from my machete, which is now a short distance away since it spun out of my hand during my fall, to the zombie I'm currently sprawled on top of, to the puddle of cold, sticky blood my right hand is resting in, and finally to the look on Lia's face, which is a combination of anger and love. And I couldn't tell you why, but suddenly, I can't hold back a laugh. For a moment Lia looks angrier than ever but soon she's chuckling, too, and she pulls me up to standing again and draws me into another, much less painful, hug, one which I'm happy to return. Neither of us mentions the blood now staining her clothes, too.

When we release each other, all the guys surrounding us look a bit bemused, to say the least. "Alright..." Mac says slowly, shaking his head as he bends to pick up my machete. He hands it to me and mouths, "You okay?"

I nod, smiling, and take my weapon from him with my left hand as I wipe my blood soaked right hand on my already stained shirt—it doesn't help all that much.

"So, what the fuck happened?" Lia asks, although it's in a good-natured way this time.

"Just what I would like to know," Luca adds, sounding annoyed. He glares at Mac and Mac cringes a bit, looking stressed and shamefaced.

"Uh, I was curious to see if 'Thriller' made zombies react the way it does in the music video..." Mac says, trailing off and staring at the ground in a way that makes me want to hug him. "It didn't," he continues after a breath, "It just seemed to enrage them. It was really weird," he finishes, still looking at the ground.

"Like the music video?" Elliot asks, incredulously.

"I was just curious," Mac retorts, defensively.

"You could've gotten the both of you killed," Lia snaps angrily.

"I know that!" Mac growls, glancing at me with a pained expression before returning his gaze to the zombie littered floor. "I didn't mean to...I'd never..." he trails off again and this time doesn't resume talking.

"Well, we weren't killed," I pipe up. "Everything's fine." Mac glances at me again and I smile reassuringly, he smiles back weakly and Lia scowls, looking between us. I feel a mild shame spiral from seeming so boy crazy lately and I resist the urge to take Mac's hand again.

"Fine, whatever, just don't do it again, Mac," Luca says, looking at Mac with an expression that is oddly similar to the one Lia was wearing when she first saw me a minute ago.

"You don't have to worry about that," Mac answers, "I'm not that dumb and besides, I'm pretty sure they ate my phone." The smile that I'm now associating with Mac's very presence tugs at the corners of my mouth and I can't hold it back. He's just so...incongruously innocent. It's sweet and endearing.

Lia scowls at him again and snaps, "Jesus, between you and Nate, it's a wonder she's not a zombie right now!" Mac reddens and stares down at the floor looking ashamed. This time I don't fight the urge, I just reach out and squeeze his hand. He doesn't look up but he squeezes back. Lia shakes her head at this and asks me in an only slightly less angry voice, "You're okay, you weren't bitten?"

I shake my head and look down at my bloody torso, saying, "I'm pretty sure none of this is mine." Mac and Lia both get very concerned looks on their faces and I wave them off, accidently using my machete in a weird form of punctuation and splattering yet more blood on the gory mess at our feet. Not to mention quite a few droplets against the wall. "Kidding, sorry, I'm fine, I promise," I amend quickly.

"Not funny," they say at the same time, resulting in them looking at each other incredulously.

"Oh, come on," I protest, "you've got to retain your sense of humour in a zombie attack or you'll go insane before you ever have the chance to make it to the sequel."

This statement earns me a few more disbelieving stares until Luca slowly says, "*Bien…* we should get rid of these bodies. Mac, Rafe, Link, help me throw them off the roof. You *chicas* should go get cleaned up, it's probably best not to go on being covered in the blood, right Elliot?"

"Oh, right," Elliot answers vaguely as he breaks off his stare that was fixated on the zombie pile oozing on the ground.

I am most definitely down for cleaning up. Is it girly to say that I'm getting really sick and tired of being covered in blood? Even if it is, I don't care. I'm sick and tired of being covered in blood. I start to walk away towards our barracks and washroom. "Wait up," Lia says and I do, glad she doesn't seem too upset with me anymore. She hooks her right arm through my left and as we walk away, I'm pretty sure that I hear Luca say behind us, "*Ésas chicas están locas.*"

Lia

"Did you hear that?" I ask angrily and I attempt to turn around so that I can give that asshole a piece of my mind. I may not be fluent in Spanish but I know enough to know that he was insulting us. Unfortunately, I'm prevented from doing anything by Lucy tightening her arm against mine and keeping me to our path.

"Let it go, Li, we're covered in blood, and it's not worth it," she says. I make a "hmmph-ing" noise, but I stop struggling and continue walking with her. Though a part of me still wants to strangle her for being so stupid, I can't help but be so grateful that she's safe that I just squeeze her arm and say nothing. She looks over at me and smiles as she flicks her machete absent-mindedly through the air, sending a couple of bloody drops against the wall each time. And yes, though it technically belongs to me, there can be no doubt that the machete is now hers. I feel another surge of affection and squeeze her wrist again.

"You really scared me," I say.

"Sorry," she responds ruefully, stopping outside our barracks and looking down at the ground abashedly. "I don't know what I was thinking. Who knew being boy-crazy was so dangerous?" She shrugs and pulls a self-deprecating face. "I really did not foresee him just abandoning me out there, though. It was so random."

"Yeah, well, he's just lucky that he didn't get you killed," I answer gruffly and pull her into another hug, which is unfortunately made gross by a latent drop of zombie blood trickling from her machete and sliding down my back. "Ugh," I growl and pull away.

"What?" she asks.

"Zombie blood," I answer, pointing at the machete blade.

"Oh, sorry," she says. "I guess I should clean it off, eh?"

"Maybe," I say, stretching my arms around my back, trying to reach the wet spot. I can't. It's gross. "Okay, and now I really need to get cleaned up, too. Damn zombie blood."

"Sorry," she says again as we walk into the room and come upon something even more disturbing than the reanimated dead…Daffy posing in front of the mirror in her underwear. Say it with me now: blech. As if finding out she sleeps in the nude wasn't bad enough.

"What the hell are you doing?" I ask, unable to keep the repulsion from my voice, not that I care.

"Just making sure that I'm still as hot as I was yesterday, duh. I want to make sure that I have my pick of the yummy army boys," she answers and yes, that's definitely a bit of homicidal rage I feel in my gut. It's exacerbated because after hanging out with Elliot this afternoon while looking for Lucy, I now feel majorly pissed off that she's such a cold-hearted bitch when it comes to him. He's actually pretty cool when he's not drooling all over that sickening carrot skinned, overly blonde waste of space. He likes the *Shadowlands* series, which pretty much makes him automatically awesome.

"There's something wrong with you," Lucy says casually.

"I was just thinking that," I agree and Lucy smiles at me, amusement showing through despite her obvious disbelief at Daffy's continuously escalating vapidity and narcissism.

"What? Where? I look perfect, don't I?" Daffy squeaks, sounding terrified that she might have missed a glaring imperfection during her whacked out body inspection.

"There's seriously something wrong with you," I say, rolling my eyes at Lucy; she smiles, then walks over to her cot and retrieves some clean clothes from her bag. I do the same and we leave the room as Daffy spins around in circles over and over again trying to locate any sort of imperfection. Man, it's just too easy, I actually feel a little bad. There's just no sport in this.

When we get into the bathroom, Lucy huffs an angry noise and growls, "That chick is so friggin' messed up."

"Uh, yeah, I hate to borrow a line from someone so vapid but, duh. What's new? And what's up?" I ask, quirking an eyebrow at her to let her know I'm onto her.

"Nothing, I just…she's such a psycho hose beast," she asserts, putting her hands on her hips and frowning.

"Well, yeah, but it's not like that's news, why is it suddenly bugging you so much?" I ask, quirking my eyebrow even higher. "Does this have anything to do with your bonding session with Mac?" I ask, actually hoping she developed a thing for him, since it would be much preferable to her crushing on Nate…although Mac thinks Daffy is hot so he might not exactly be the best crush replacement. But considering Nate left her alone with zombies afoot, it all might be a non-issue anyway…

"Who says we bonded?" She asks, now crossing her arms over her chest for a moment before she blushes and walks over to the sink, trying to hide it from me as she cleans off her machete. Of course, this isn't the best thought out plan of action since I can still see her blush clearly in the mirror.

"Um, the fact that you were holding his hand when we got to the doors, not to mention him constantly asking if you're okay, and the fact that you're blushing right now...someone like Daffy might not have noticed something going on, but in case *you* haven't noticed, I'm no Daffy," I say, meeting her eyes in the mirror as she looks up, then quickly back down at the bloody machete.

"So I see you switched your battle axe for the tomahawk...," she says, obviously trying to change the subject.

"Yup, this is more lightweight and easier to carry with at all times while still being totally deadly," I answer, touching the head of the small axe that's tucked into my belt, reassuring myself it's still there. "And don't think I didn't notice your not-at-all-subtle subject change, missy. Don't think you can throw me off the trail that easily. What's the deal with you and Mac?"

She sighs resignedly. "He's just...sweet and funny...and nice," she offers, shrugging and refusing to meet my eyes again as she drizzles some soap onto the blade and scrubs at the zombie gore staining it.

"Does this mean you're over Nate?" I ask, trying to sound casual.

Lucy makes a face, continues to scrub the blade even though it's pretty much cleared of blood at this point, and says nothing for a moment, then she heaves a big sigh and turns around, dripping water onto the floor. She makes a discontented noise and grabs a nearby towel. As she dries the machete, she looks at me and shrugs helplessly.

"I don't know, Li. I mean, I know he abandoned me today and he is possibly psychotic, probably not at the crazy manifesto writing level or anything, but still possibly psycho, but...he's just so hot." Her voice is petulant, whiny.

"Oh, for Christ's sake," I growl, "can you get over that? He obviously can't be trusted and honestly, you're really putting yourself in danger by acting like you're in high school or something."

She sighs and makes a pout face. "You're right. I know. Besides, Mac does make me laugh and he certainly doesn't seem to have any latent homicidal tendencies. And you know that I do love me a good ginger."

"Look, no offence, and Mac does seem like a fairly decent guy, but maybe the impending zombie apocalypse isn't the best time to be worrying about this kind of stuff? It might be for the best if you just, you know, ignored the instincts of lady town for the time being..."

She thinks about this for a second then says, "That is an excellent point actually." She shakes her head. "Besides, Mac does think Daffy is hot, so that's probably dodging a bullet of a whole nother kind."

"No shit," I agree, feeling relieved.

"Okay, now that I've had some sense knocked into me, thank you—"

"Any time."

"I really need a shower. And I'm running out of clothes," she says, looking down at her blood-spattered outfit then turning to grab a towel.

"Oh, that reminds me, I found a laundry room earlier when I was looking for you with Elliot," I say as she steps into a shower stall and pulls the curtain shut behind her.

She tosses her bloody clothes over the top of the curtain rod and they land on the floor with a thump. I'm starting to wonder if she heard me when she calls, "Wait, who?"

"That doctor," I answer, raising my voice so she can hear me over the flow of water as she starts the shower up.

"The British one?" she asks.

"What? How? He left. The other one."

"Oh, right, duh...sorry. I think all that zombie fighting scrambled my brain a bit. But that's perfect," she says then falls silent.

"Lia?" I hear my name being called from behind me so I walk to the door and stick my head out, spotting Elliot immediately. "Oh, there you are," he says.

"Here I am," I agree.

He smiles briefly before continuing, "Sorry to bother you, but I thought you might be interested to know that they found Nate."

"Is he dead?" I ask.

"Um, no, he's fine."

"Not for long," I growl, "because that would've been the only excuse I would've accepted for him ditching Lucy the way he did. Where is he?"

"In the cafeteria, with the soldiers," Elliot answers, not batting an eye.

"Okay, give me a minute," I say and duck back into the bathroom.

"Luce?" I call.

"Yeah?"

"I've got to go take care of something, okay?"

"Wait, don't leave me," she protests.

"Why?" I ask.

"Um, the rules? Duh."

I roll my eyes. "It's zombies, remember, not some '80s slasher villain. You'll be fine."

"Whatever, it applies. Just give me a sec and I'll join you."

I sigh in frustration. If she knows what I'm planning she might try to stop me.

"You do know that when you took a shower last night, you were in here alone and you were just fine, right?"

"That doesn't mean my luck will hold a second time around," she argues.

I make a face and walk over to the bench where she left her machete along with her clean clothes. I pick both up and walk over to her shower stall.

"Here," I say, "your clothes and machete are right outside; nothing bad is going to happen."

"Oh, my God!"

"What?"

The water shuts off and she steps out of the shower, flinging the curtain aside as she does so. She's wrapped her towel around herself and she puts her hands on her terry-clothed hips, glaring at me as her hair drips onto the floor.

"What?" I repeat.

"I already broke the no shower rule and you just broke the saying nothing bad will happen rule. There's no way I'm staying in that death trap."

"You are so weird," I say and she makes a face at me. "Whatever. You're out now, so I'm gonna go take care of my thing and I'll meet you in the cafeteria, okay?"

"Wait, what about laundry?" she asks.

"I'll get one of the soldiers to come and show you where it is."

"Fine, whatever, just go and do your mysterious errand. And you say I'm weird."

"You are," I assert as I head for the door and she sticks her tongue out at me. I roll my eyes at her and leave the room, stepping out into the hall where Elliot is still waiting for me.

"Let's go," I say.

Elliot

Lia starts off down the hall, her stride purposeful. I would not want to be Nate right now. Lia looks so angry, it doesn't take much of an intellectual leap to see that his life might actually be in danger. I don't blame her for being angry that he deserted Lucy and almost got her killed in the process, but I figure we have enough bloodshed to worry about without factoring in killing each other so, as deftly as I can, using the skills I learned when I had my magician phase, I remove Lia's tomahawk from her belt just as we reach the cafeteria. She might not appreciate what I'm trying to do right now, but hopefully, she'll forgive me in the future.

We walk into the cafeteria—well, I walk in, Lia stomps in and captures everyone's attention as she slams the doors open with a loud thwack. She pauses for a moment, her gaze sweeping the room until it lands on Nate, who's standing amidst the soldiers in the middle of the room. Lia stomps over to the group, everything about her countenance displaying her rage: her shoulders are tensed, her back is ramrod straight, and her hands are balled into fists. I follow behind her, glad that I thought to remove her weapon when I did.

She stops in front of Nate and glares at him intensely. "Well?" she demands, looking expectant.

"Well, what?" he asks.

"I was hoping for some kind of explanation or perhaps abject apology after what you did, you son of a whore, but I guess that was too much to ask!" Lia growls and reaches for her tomahawk, making me glad all over again that I decided to take it. When her fingers come up empty, Lia looks down, confused, pauses for about a half-second then shrugs and takes a swing at Nate. Her fist connects with his jaw with a loud thud and Nate reels back a step. He rights himself and looks at Lia with a deadened, blanked out facial expression that gives me chills. I expect Lia to step back or at least react in some way, but she just stands her ground, looking ready for a fight. That girl is either really brave or just a bit crazy.

Nate tenses and I realize just in time that he is going to hit her back. I don't even think, I just step in front of her and ready myself for the blow. At least getting beat up in high school had one use: I can take a punch a lot better than people would think. A few seconds pass and I realize that I haven't been hit yet and I also realize that I have my eyes closed.

That's a bit embarrassing.

I snap my eyelids open and survey the scene. Nate still looks strangely blank, but a little animation has entered back into his face and he doesn't seem like he's going to hit me. I relax a bit just as the rest of the room explodes in a verbal frenzy.

"*Qué diablos está pasando?*" Sergeant Ortiz roars just as Corporal McCoy yells, "Can everyone just calm the fuck down!"

Lia pushes me out of the way growling, "What the fuck is wrong with you?"

At first, I think she's talking to Nate again but then I realize that she's glaring at me, her heated gaze going back and forth between my face and her tomahawk in my hand.

"Um..." I say, and then trail off, not exactly sure which action I should try explaining first.

"I had it under control," she says.

"Oh, *sí, chica,* you had everything under control," Sergeant Ortiz says condescendingly and Lia balls her hands into fists again.

"Okay, seriously, everyone calm the fuck down! Use your words, people," Corporal McCoy says loudly.

"Fine. I'll use my words," Lia spits out, and then turns to glare at Nate again. "Why the fuck did you fucking abandon my friend and leave her to fucking die?"

"I was trying to protect her," Nate growls, looking angry now.

"Oh, really? How did that work exactly? What, were you trying to teach her to survive better by forcing her to fend for herself?" Lia asks sarcastically.

"I saw some zombies watching us and I figured I'd take them out and get back to her in no time, but there were more than I expected."

"When he found him, he'd killed, like, twenty zombies, it was pretty impressive," Master Corporal Donahue says.

"Yeah, that is pretty impressive," says Lia, clearly unimpressed, "but it would've been even more impressive if you didn't almost get my best friend killed, you jackass."

"I wasn't trying to put Lucy in danger," Nate replies, his voice tense.

"God, imagine if you tried," Lia growls, then whirls to face me, sticking her hand out. I'm confused for a second, but then I nod and deposit the tomahawk in her hand. She makes an indignant noise and stalks from the room.

"Geez, that was a little frightening, except actually a lot," Corporal McCoy says. "Good thing you took that axe away from her, Doc." He claps me on the back and I stumble forward a half-step.

"Thanks," I mutter. "I'm just going to go check on her."

"Be careful, Doc, you're more useful alive than dead and she looks to be on the warpath."

"Aren't most people more useful alive?" one of the other soldiers asks as I'm leaving the room and I only hear the first half of Corporal McCoy's retort ("Okay, you know what?") as the doors shut behind me. The hallway is silent now and I take a deep breath in the silence, readying myself to go find Lia. I know that she's mad at me and might not want to see me, but she's my friend and I need to make sure that she's okay after that confrontation with Nate. Even if she scares me just a little bit, it's what Hunter would do for his friends.

I square my shoulders and start down the hall. As I'm passing the briefing room where we showed the soldiers the video from the lab, I hear some disgruntled mumbling. I stop and listen for a moment, but I can't distinguish any actual words so I poke my head around the door frame and glance inside the darkened room. Lia is inside, sitting on top of one of the desks, spinning her tomahawk in her hands and muttering angrily to herself, perhaps continuing or maybe simply replaying her argument with Nate.

"Lia?" I venture, ready to take cover if she decides to throw the axe at me. She looks up sharply and narrows her eyes when she sees me.

"Oh," she says, her voice low and tense, "it's you."

I nod and step a little further into the room, figuring if she was going to try to kill me, she would've done so already. "I'm sorry for interfering back there, but I really didn't think that more violence and bloodshed was the answer."

She lets out a disgusted snort and stands up, crossing the room quickly and coming to an abrupt halt right in front of me. I do my best to not step back. I manage to hold my ground and while I may cringe a bit, I manage to hold her gaze, too. She exhales angrily and glares at me.

"He almost got my best friend killed!" she growls.

"I know," I say. "He obviously can't be trusted completely, but he *is* very adept at killing zombies; we need him on our side for as long as possible. But I agree that none of us should be alone with him from now on." She opens her mouth, but snaps it shut again when she can't seem to think of anything to say.

"I hate him," she finally asserts, tucking her axe back in her belt and crossing her arms irritably.

I hesitate for a moment, distracted by the movement of her breasts, then I clear my throat and my head and say, "I doubt anyone would blame you for that. He's not one of my favourite people either, but he is good to have around when the zombies attack. Despite this, I do agree that none of us should entrust our lives to him."

She makes a somewhat satisfied "humph" sound and says, "Yeah, well..." as she steps around me and exits the room. I am still unsure whether or not my company is welcome so I don't plan on following her until she sticks her head back through the doorway and says, "You coming?" I smile and follow her out, falling into step with her as she walks away from the cafeteria.

"You know," she says, "you didn't have to step in and try to take Nate's punch for me. I can take care of myself."

"I know," I say, "it wasn't exactly on purpose, I just kind of...did it."

"Well, next time...don't. I don't need anyone saving me," she says firmly. I nod but don't make any promises. We continue walking in silence for a few moments when Lucy suddenly comes around the corner in front of us and stops dead.

"There you are!" she exclaims.

"Um, yeah..." Lia responds, sounding mildly confused.

"So what of your mysterious errand?" Lucy asks.

"Oh, it was nothing," Lia says.

"'Nothing'?" Lucy asks. "'Nothing'! First you just about abandon me to my watery grave and now you're telling me that it was for 'nothing'?" Lia rolls her eyes, but it's in an affectionate way.

"What have I told you about using air quotes?" she asks and Lucy waves her off. At first I thought that she was genuinely upset with Lia, but judging from Lia's reaction, Lucy's just being sarcastic.

"So besides leaving me to die and not even having the decency to tell me why—" Lucy pauses "—I didn't mean to rhyme. Anyway, besides that, you also didn't send anyone to show me where the laundry room is and you know that if I tried to find it on my own, I'd probably get lost in here. Do you even want me to make it out of this alive?"

"You're being ridiculous!" Lia says.

"We can show you where it is," I offer and Lucy smiles.

"See," she says, gesturing towards me, "helpful. You?" She points at Lia. "Not so much."

"Oh, shut up," Lia says. "Let's just go, okay?" Lucy shrugs in response and we start walking again, heading to the girls' barracks. Once we're there, Lucy and Lia go inside to grab their dirty and bloody clothes. Lia is finished first since she has a few less bloodied items than Lucy. She walks back over to me and I feel my mind wandering inappropriately again as the bundle of clothes she has in her arms pushes her breasts up and makes them even more distracting than usual. I feel her gaze on my face and I look up quickly, flushing embarrassedly as Lia raises her eyebrows at me, looking amused.

Speaking of distractions, Daphne chooses this moment to walk past us, looking as gorgeous and distracting as always. Lia turns to see what's caught my eye this time and she snorts in disdain when she sees her. For her part, Daphne doesn't seem to notice either of us as she flounces down the hallway.

"You would deserve better if you would just realize that she's not worth the time of day," Lia says sharply and my attention is brought roughly back to her. "She's a bitch and she's stupid, pay attention," she finishes, then shoves past me and walks away. Lucy, only just exiting the barracks now, follows after her quickly, glancing at me as she goes, but not stopping.

I stand there for a moment, not sure what to do. There's a part of me that's indignant on Daphne's behalf, the part that thinks someone that pretty could only be misunderstood by the people who think she's not just as pretty on the inside. But there's another, smaller part that wonders if Lia may be right. Either way, I'm alone in the hallway and there's no one to either argue or agree with.

Still unsure about what I should do, I decide to head back to the cafeteria and reconvene with the soldiers and Terry. At least with them, I don't feel quite as off-balance as I do when I'm around women.

I walk into the cafeteria and everyone looks at me. I notice that Daphne is in here, too, and is currently wrapped around Corporal McCoy, although he doesn't seem all that involved in the flirtation anymore.

"Doc, you're back," Terry says and I simply nod since no answer really seems necessary. "I was just telling the guys about your idea for teaching the civs how to shoot," Terry continues, adopting the soldiers' slang for those of us without training.

"You know, I think that's a great idea," Corporal McCoy says, disentangling himself from Daphne and walking over to us. Daphne trails along behind him but she spares a moment to wink at Private Cantolena. Huh. Funny what you notice when you pay attention.

"Not everyone agrees, fire-crotch," Private Cantolena argues, "We're supposed to be defending the civs, not dragging them into dangerous situations, you know, like playing a Michael Jackson song because you think it will make the zombies dance and instead almost get everyone killed."

Corporal McCoy's face creases in an aggrieved look. "I didn't mean to," he says, turning his attention back to Private Cantolena. "I was just curious..." he trails off, staring intensely at a spot on the table in the middle of the group. His cheeks are burning a red to match his hair and his freckles have all but disappeared beneath the embarrassed and angry flush. Despite feeling jealous of him for the attention Daphne gives him, I can't help but feel bad for him right now, he just looks so uncomfortable, I can't stop myself from trying to help.

"It can only improve things, making sure that everyone knows how to defend themselves as well as possible," I say.

"Maybe not everyone," Nate says, gesturing in Daphne's direction, "but the capable ones, yeah."

Daphne doesn't seem to realize she's being made fun of because she's too busy making googly eyes at Private Cantolena again, behind Corporal McCoy's back. As for Corporal McCoy, the support of Nate and me seems to have loosened him from his embarrassment paralysis because he uncrosses his arms and speaks up, "Exactly, you wouldn't want them not knowing how to shoot coming back and haunting us in the ass, now would you?"

What?

"What?" almost everyone in the group vocalizes my confusion and Corporal McCoy shakes his head, and screws up his face as though he is confused, too. "You know what I mean," he growls, though when no one confirms this, he shakes his head again and continues, "I meant to say either come back to bite us in the ass or come back to haunt us and they both came out at the same time, big fucking deal," he finishes, waving his hands in a sarcastic way. "Anyway," he continues gruffly, "It's a good idea, Doc. We should get started right away."

"Right," Private Cantolena responds, "wouldn't want anything haunting us in the ass, now would we?"

"Oh, shut up," Corporal McCoy growls and Sergeant Ortiz seconds this sentiment, ordering Private Cantolena to be quiet.

"Where are we going to do the training?" I ask, trying to break up some of the tension with a distraction.

"The roof?" Master Corporal Kane suggests.

"What about those gross things, can't they, like, fly or something?" Daphne interjects.

"Huh? They can climb, but they can't fly. How the hell would they be able to fly?" Master Corporal Kane asks, staring at her in disbelief. Daphne shrugs and looks unconcerned about the logic constraints of zombie aerodynamics.

Master Corporal Kane continues to stare at her as Corporal McCoy speaks up again, saying, "Besides, when we went up there to get rid of the zombie bodies, we didn't see any more in the trees and it's probably the safest place to teach people how to shoot. If more *do* climb up the trees, we should be able to spot them fairly easily and get rid of them."

Daphne tuned out at some point during his explanation of the relative safety of the roof and is now making eyes at Private Cooke; she certainly appears to have a wide range of tastes, though nerd doesn't seem to be one of them.

I involuntarily think of Lia telling me to pay attention. I look away, feeling anger rumble in my chest. She's not the only one who could use an outlet for aggression right now. It's not something that I've ever needed before, but I'm not going to fight the urge; something tells me I'll need to learn how to use my previously dormant aggression as soon as possible.

Chapter Ten
I do miss the good old days—namely yesterday—when all I had to worry about was the ravenous undead

Connor

"So, where are the other, more capable, civs?" I ask, trying to sound blasé.

"They went to do some laundry," Elliot answers. "They both have some pretty bloody clothes."

"Yeah, no kidding," I say, wishing I could stop thinking about what happened earlier today. Although I don't think that's really possible, it's not like anyone will actually let me forget my boneheaded move of accidentally enraging those zombies. At the memory of that mistake, I feel the blush I hate spread over my face again. I can't believe I did something so stupid. I can't get the image of Lucy fighting with that zombie that was sprawled on top of her out of my head. I feel idiotic about putting myself in danger with that stupid idea, but I kind of wanna shoot myself in the face for almost getting her killed. She looked so defenceless, struggling with that last zombie...you know, until she impaled its face. But she's just so small and adorable, it kills me that I took such a chance with her safety. And now, as if things weren't complicated enough, with that whole reanimating dead person issue we have going on, I find myself in a weird triangle situation with Lucy and Nate, 'cause I suddenly can't stop thinking about her and I'm starting to wonder why I ever thought Daffy was at all worth my time. But, in all honesty, I still think she's hot, so I guess she's included in the love triangle, too...or wait, what does that make it? Like a love rhombus? Man, Luca's right, civs are nothing but trouble in the end.

"Mac...?" I tear myself out of my love shapes stupor to find Daffy standing in front of me, looking all pouty 'cause I've been ignoring her. I run my gaze down her. Yup, still hot, and yet...I can't stop my attention from wandering to the equally distracting and not at all mind-numbingly stupid Lucy.

"Mac!" Daffy pout-growls, leading to a very interesting facial expression.

"What?" I ask, yanking my focus back to her, with no small degree of difficulty.

"Why do you keep, like, wandering off in your brain? If you're, like, fantasizing about me, which is totes understandable, well, it doesn't have to be imaginary. We could sneak off while the others are playing with their guns. 'Cause I am totes interested in playing with your gun."

"What? Then why would we sneak off?...Oh!" I can't help exclaiming as Daffy reaches for the waistband of my pants. Glerk. I back away from her, partly because I don't want to earn a glower from Luca for being so easily distracted again and partly because of how I think Lucy might react if she saw what was going on right now. Or I guess how I hope she'd react; it would suck if she saw this and was completely indifferent.

"I think we should probably stay with the group," I say, batting her hands away from me, something which takes a lot less will power than I would've guessed. "And, uh, I have to go," I add, backing away from her and speed-walking out of the room before anyone can stop me.

I head to the laundry room to find Lucy and Lia. We should really give them a comm unit or two so we don't always have to go searching for them. But I find I don't mind the excuse to get away from Daffy now that I find her attentions pretty unwanted so I'm not complaining.

As I make my way to the laundry room, I check the locks on the entrance doors, making sure they're secure. Considering all the zombie shrieks I can hear coming from the other side, I figure it's a smart move to double check them so we have less chance of a security breach. But I'm sure it's only a matter of time anyway; I've seen the movies, they always get in in the end, that's how it goes.

After checking the western entrance door, my boots sticking slightly in the still drying puddle of zombie blood as I walk by, I reach the area that houses both the gym and the laundry room.

Walking inside, I stop just outside the door to the laundry room, where I can hear the girls talking within.

"So, you *are* over that whole Nate thing, right?" Lia asks and I'm grateful for my convenient timing; I'm curious about Lucy's answer myself.

"Yes, I told you, I've seen the light, he's not to be trusted, blah blah blah," Lucy says and I smile. Maybe it's not such a rhombus after all.

"I'm being serious, Luce," Lia says.

"I know, Li, so am I. I swear, I'm on board with your plan to avoid him; doesn't mean I don't still enjoy looking at him," Lucy responds and I feel a twinge of jealousy.

"You're impossible, you know that?" Lia says.

"Yeah, yeah, whatever, you know you love it."

"Not right now I don't. Not when it puts you in danger," Lia argues.

"I'm not in danger." Lucy pauses. "Well, okay, obviously I am, what with the whole zompocalypse thing, but we're all in danger from that. From Nate? No. I promise, I'll stay away from him whenever possible and I won't ever be alone with him again; I swear, *mom*."

"Ha-ha, very funny. You know, it's not like I'm being unreasonable."

"I didn't say you were. You're just being very protective."

"You'd do the same if the situation was reversed and you know it," Lia says.

"Yeah, I would," Lucy agrees.

I really wish Lia would bring my name into the conversation, I'd like to know Lucy's thoughts on that topic. "Mac? *Dondé estás?*" Luca's impatient voice practically blares out of the comm unit. Maybe it just seems that way because I'm eavesdropping, but the silence from within the laundry room does not bode well for me being unnoticed. I decide to just cut my losses and walk into the room.

"Hey, ladies!" Oh my God what is wrong with me? That's just as bad as saying "folks." Maybe if I just keep talking I can pretend it never happened. "So I just got here and uh, wanted to let you guys know that we're gonna be doing some gun training on the roof. Excuse me for a second; I have to tell Luca that I found you." I grab my comm and try to ignore the looks Lucy and Lia are giving me. It apparently doesn't work because I spaz out and drop the comm unit. It hits the ground with a loud thud and the battery pops out, just to make it all that much more embarrassing. I can feel my face flushing that god-awful cherry colour. Damn Irish blood. Okay, so that whole being stealth thing didn't work at all. I cross my arms and focus on the ground, staring down at the traitorous comm unit.

"So..." I say, trailing off, not really sure what to do or say.

"Wow, you're spastic," Lia says.

"That thing is really slippery!" I say defensively.

"Dirty," Lucy says. I look up at her, smiling tentatively. Both girls look amused instead of angry, which is something, but I still just made a total ass out of myself. Lucy crouches down and retrieves the comm unit and battery. She stands back up and hands them to me.

"Thanks," I mumble, feeling like a complete idiot.

"So, we're gonna learn how to shoot?" Lucy asks.

"I know how to shoot," Lia says.

"It never hurts to brush up?" I offer, shrugging and then turning my attention to the possibly broken comm in my hands. I push the battery back in and press the mike button.

"Luke?" I try. There's no response, just some static. "Well. We should head up to the roof then and meet up with the others, before Luca starts freaking out," I say.

"*Everyone's* meeting on the roof?" Lia asks and Lucy gives her a questioning look. If I were a betting man, I'd guess that Lia hasn't shared the details of her earlier altercation with Nate.

"Yup," I answer simply, figuring Lia wouldn't exactly appreciate me spilling the beans. Lia looks at me and nods, looking mildly appreciative.

"Well, I guess we should head up, eh?" Lucy says slowly, still looking suspiciously between the two of us.

"Yeah, we can just leave our stuff to dry," Lia says, though she still seems reluctant to see Nate. I wonder if she's scared of him or just doesn't want Lucy to find out what happened. On second thought, considering the stand-off she had with him, I wouldn't bet on her being scared of him. To be honest, I'm a little intimidated by him, but she's pretty intense herself so I guess maybe it evens out.

The closer we get to the stairs leading up to the roof, the more Lia tenses up. By the time we actually reach the door, her back is excessively straight and her hands are balled up, her mouth a thin line. Actually, she looks pretty much like the first time I saw her when she was pissed at Locklan for taking her axe away.

Lucy gives me a questioning look and I look away quickly, trying for innocence 'cause I really don't wanna get on Lia's bad side. Lia slams through the door with a look on her face like at any second she could go off the rails and start attacking anyone who looks at her cock-eyed. I feel some goose bumps rise on my arms and I resolve once again never to piss her off if I can help it.

I take a breath and am about to follow Lia through the door when Lucy grabs my arm. I look at her, hoping she won't ask what I'm sure she's going to.

"What's going on, Mac?"

Damn it. She did. Now what?

"Uh..." I say, and then pause, taking a minute to try and figure out what I can say that won't have Lia out for my blood, too.

"There you are! I've totes been looking everywhere for you?" Daffy says, turning the exclamation into a question. Lucy's eyes narrow at Daffy. I have a feeling this is gonna be a fire/frying pan type of situation.

"You don't have to be shy, Macky, I promise I'll be totes gentle with you?" Daffy says in a breathy, yet still squeaky voice. Lucy's eyes narrow even further and she lets out a disgusted noise, then turns on her heel and slams through the door just like Lia did.

Shit. Although I'll admit a small part of me is happy that she doesn't seem indifferent to Daffy flirting with me; that she's pissed is a good sign.

I frown at Daffy and turn to follow Lucy up to the roof hoping Daffy doesn't follow me, though once I reach the upper door, I look behind me to see if she's there so I don't accidentally slam the door in her face. I may not be all that into her anymore, especially since she might have just cock-blocked me with Lucy, but I'm still a gentleman. And she is following me, looking like a hot, slutty, sulky puppy or something. I would maybe feel bad except the way she's been exchanging glances and flirtations with Marco, Jimmy, and Rafe leads me to believe that she will only be upset about my rejection until she sees someone else who has a penis and gives her the slightest bit of attention walks by.

"Connor!" Luca growls when he spots me. Uh-oh. "What in *el nombre de Dios* happened to you?"

"Uh, I accidentally dropped my comm, no big deal, but I may have broken it," I say, looking down with what I hope is the appropriate amount of chagrin as I try to subtly scan the rooftop, looking for Lucy.

"*Madre de Dios*," Luca snarls. "Again? You have to be more careful, Mac."

"I know, I'm sorry," I say, but he's already stalking away from me. I'll have to fix that later, but right now...I glance around the rooftop, checking for zombies in the trees but also trying to finally locate Lucy. I see Lia first, posed in an impatient stance while Rafe explains the features of the rifle in his hands. Her expression very clearly says, "just give me the fucking gun already," which would be funny if I wasn't still worried she'd use the thing on someone living and not undead.

Lucy's laugh alerts me to her whereabouts and I see her standing with Link at one of the far corners of the rooftop, smiling while he apparently says something just so damn witty. Damn it, I just stop having to worry about Nate as competition and now I have to start worrying about Link? Am I back in a rhombus?

"Careful, Doc, watch where you point that thing," Terry says, batting Elliot's hand down so the pistol in it is pointing at the ground.

"Oh, sorry, Terry, I got distracted," I expect him to be referring to the sudden presence of Daffy in his near vicinity, but his attention seems to be captured by the angry figure of Lia now standing alone at the edge of the roof, shooting down at the zombies gathered below without any hesitation. Spooky.

The shots ring out loudly amidst the shrieks of the zombies on the ground and I'm suddenly worried that we'll just attract more zombies to our whereabouts with this exercise. I guess we should try to kill as many in the area as possible before we make for the lab, but it does seem a tad counterproductive if it makes it that much harder for us to get to the lab.

I'm considering raising the issue with Luca when Lucy's laugh once again echoes across the roof along with a self-deprecating comment about not being very good with guns and could he show her how to do it again. Goddamn Daffy! I could be the one showing Lucy how to shoot right now if Daffy hadn't screwed things up for me.

Nate appears to have a similar thought process and he starts across the roof, heading towards Link and Lucy. Out of nowhere, Lia spins around and points her gun straight at Nate.

"Stay the hell away from her!" she commands, her voice tight with anger. Nate pauses for a second and then raises his rifle and points it back at Lia.

Oh, goddamn, shit just got real.

Everyone else on the roof has gone silent and I'm trying to figure out what the hell to do to diffuse the situation before anyone gets hurt—or worse. I glance at Lucy and see that her gun is raised, too, and pointing at Nate. Nate turns his head a little and looks at Lucy, when he sees that she's aiming her gun at him, he gets a look on his face that makes my blood go chilly.

I really don't think this is going to end well. I was kinda unsure about the guy after he up and left Lucy like he did, but now I can see why Lia doesn't trust him. There is something that's just off about him. I put my hand on my gun and consider joining the fray, even though I'd probably just make things worse at this point.

Suddenly Luca steps in and, thank God, I feel like I can breathe normal again. "Enough!" he snarls, stepping up beside Lia quickly. Before she can react, he smacks the gun barrel up to point harmlessly at the sky. He shoves her with one hand while grabbing the gun with the other causing her to fall roughly to the ground, fortunately relinquishing the gun in the process. Luca then grabs her arm forcefully and drags her to her feet. He pushes her in front of him and steers her towards the door, not giving her a chance to change course. As they pass by me, Luca tosses me the rifle without looking and keeps right on walking, pushing Lia on in front of him. Once they're through the door, Luca slams it behind him and for a moment, no one says anything in the ensuing silence…well, silence except for the now usual ambient zombie noises.

Elliot is the first of us to move; he walks by me and heads for the door.

"I wouldn't…" I say, but he ignores me and keeps walking. I wouldn't wanna risk one of Luca's major glowers by going down there right now, but that's just me.

Elliot

Jesus Christ, that was intense. I hope Lia's okay; she was so upset. I don't blame Corporal McCoy for warning me away when Sergeant Ortiz is obviously furious, but I want to make sure that Lia is alright. Sergeant Ortiz scares me, but Lia is my friend and that alone makes the decision easy.

Going down the stairs, I can already hear the sounds of a heated exchange coming from the hallway. I open the door at the bottom of the stairs quietly and slip out, intending to head back upstairs once I know that Lia's not in any danger or anything since she still seems a little miffed at me and I don't want to make things more stressful for her.

I see the two of them standing a ways down the hall. Lia is leaning against the wall with her arms crossed over her chest and Sergeant Ortiz is facing her, looming over her and getting right in her face.

"What the hell is the matter with you?" he bellows.

"I wasn't actually going to shoot him," Lia growls defensively, then mutters, "Probably."

"Oh, that makes everything fine then, doesn't it? Did you even have the safety on?"

Lia doesn't say anything, she just stares angrily down the hall in the opposite direction from where I'm standing.

"I don't know what's going on between you and Nate, and I don't care, but if you endanger my men or yourself on my watch, then I have to care and that is infuriating. You cannot just aim a loaded gun at someone because you're angry and throwing a goddamn tantrum!" Sergeant Ortiz pauses and takes a deep breath, exhaling loudly before continuing, "Whatever drama you have going on with him, deal with it, or all of you civs will be on your own. This is not even close to being worth the trouble so don't think for a second that I would regret leaving all of you to your own devices."

Lia glares up at him then suddenly moves towards him. At first I think she might smack him, but instead, she whirls him around, pushes him up against the wall and starts kissing him like there's no tomorrow...which I suppose is the smart way to kiss someone when there really might not be a tomorrow, but it still catches me off guard and I accidentally let the door slip from my grasp and it snaps shut with a loud bang.

Lia and Sergeant Ortiz spring apart and stare at me for a second. Sergeant Ortiz looks thunderstruck, but Lia just closes her face down, sliding a weird expressionless mask into place as she turns around and stalks away in the opposite direction.

"Um," I say, without knowing what else I plan on adding when the door abruptly re-opens, sending me stumbling as all of the others come rushing into the hallway.

"*Qué paso?*" Sergeant Ortiz asks, rubbing a hand over his head and down the back of his neck while walking towards the group.

"Zombies!" Corporal McCoy answers between heavy breaths, slamming the door shut again.

"Mac, we already knew there were zombies," Sergeant Ortiz says.

Corporal McCoy gazes at him dubiously for a second then shakes his head. "What? No. Of course we already knew that. I mean they attacked us."

"How?" I ask.

"They came out of the trees again," Nate answers, barely looking spooked, which is definitely not normal. The normal response is to be spooked when zombies start dropping from up above, not acting like it was a mild inconvenience.

"*Dios mio.* Was anybody injured?" Sergeant Ortiz asks.

"No, we're all fine, except for being a little shaken up," Corporal McCoy says.

"Speak for yourself carrot-top, those fuckers don't scare me," Private Cantolena says, glancing at Daphne to see if she's impressed by his bravado.

"Well then you're a fucking moron, but we already knew that," Corporal McCoy snaps.

"So did they jump down at you?" I ask, partly trying to break the tension and partly because I'm curious.

"No," Lucy answers, "it was really weird, actually, they kind of just dropped, like they'd slid off the branches on accident or something. There were all these random zombie heaps and then they righted themselves and started launching themselves at us."

"It was so rude," Daphne adds, leaning back against Private Cantolena, who's got his arm around her stomach and is staring lecherously down her shirt. I may not have minded if he had gotten bitten.

"What is wrong with you?" Lucy snarls, glaring at Daphne. Before Daphne can answer, however, Lucy rounds on Corporal McCoy and continues, "And you? What is wrong with you?"

Corporal McCoy looks confused, which I think is valid. "Me? What did I do?" he asks.

"How can you be attracted to someone who looks like five cents a dance?"

"What is that supposed to mean?"

"Oh, never mind!" Lucy responds hotly.

"No, really, I don't know what that even means!" Corporal McCoy protests.

Lucy ignores him and glances around the hall. "Where's Lia?" she asks.

"I'm not sure," I answer. "She stalked off after I accidentally interrupted her and Sergeant Ortiz, um, kissing..." I trail off abruptly, not sure how to finish because I'm suddenly certain that it was a bad idea to say this.

"What?" this response comes from pretty much everyone at once, except for Daphne who's busy wondering, "Wait, I thought she was a lesbian, isn't that why she's so, like, jealous of Nathan?"

"No one is a lesbian!" Lucy growls at Daphne.

"That is totes untrue, Lucy. There are such things as lesbians and I don't think it's very, like, sensitive of you to say that there isn't," Daphne retorts.

Lucy stares at her for a second before apparently deciding it's not worth it to try to clarify her statement and just shakes her head, saying, "Whatever." She rakes her hands through her hair and turns to Sergeant Ortiz. "Why were you two kissing?" she asks.

"That is no one's business but mine and hers." He frowns at me and I feel an uncomfortable tingling in my spine, like a Spidey sense only not at all cool or superhero-esque.

"Um, Lucy, why don't we go and find Lia?" I suggest, looking away from Sergeant Ortiz's intense gaze.

She seems to realize she won't be getting a better answer out of Sergeant Ortiz so she shrugs and says, "Yeah, fine, good idea." I lead the way, following in the direction that Lia went, glad to escape from the uncomfortable situation in the hallway.

Connor

"What is going on?" I ask, throwing my hands up in exasperation as I watch Lucy walk away with Elliot.

"Women, man, they're nuts," Link answers, shaking his head at me.

Daffy disentangles herself from Marco's arms and sidles up to me saying, "Girls like her are so complicated, but I am totally simple."

"Yeah, no shit," Nate growls, glowering at her.

I push Daffy away from me saying, "Not now!"

"Fine," she retorts, "I know when I'm not wanted, even though it's totes rare."

"I don't think any of what you just said is true," Nate says.

Daffy pouts with even more commitment and flounces off without another word—for once. A weird noise gargles out of the back of my throat and I ask desperately, "Seriously, what is going on right now?"

"This is exactly why I never wanted them here in the first place," Luca says, just adding to my confusion.

"But, according to the Doc, you were just, literally five minutes ago, making out with Lia!" I say.

"She started it," Luca answers with a shrug.

"What—" Suddenly, there's a shriek and a thump against the door and turning to stare at it, we all shut up.

"When you guys came in, did you shut and bar the roof access door?" Luca asks, pinching the bridge of his nose with exasperation since judging from the noises coming from the stairwell, it's obvious the answer is "no."

I glance at Nate and the rest of the guys. We all stare at each other for a second. "Well this is definitely a face palm moment," I say.

"It might be just a bit worse than that, Freckles," Marco retorts, going for an extremely low blow by using the nickname Luca used to have for me.

"You know what, why don't you go fuck yourself, Jersey Shore?" I growl, using his own nickname and getting ready to throw down until there's more shrieks and thumps from behind door number one. Right, we have bigger problems right now.

"We need to secure this door," Luca says.

"And we should find Lucy, Lia, and Elliot," I add.

"And Daffy," Marco puts in, looking pointedly at me.

"Whatever," I reply, shrugging.

"You're both right, unfortunately. We should all be in the same place right now; things are getting more dangerous. Some of you will go find the Doc and the *chicas locas* and the rest of you will help me secure this door," Luca says.

"I'll go after Lucy," Nate volunteers before I have the chance to do it first. I am now on board with Lia and I don't want him anywhere near Lucy. He seems calm, but there's a weird sort of energy radiating from him. He's almost vibrating and it's giving me chills of an entirely different sort than those induced by glower power.

"I can do that," I argue.

"Why don't you go look for Daffy? Because I really could not care less if she doesn't rejoin the group."

"I wanna make sure Lucy's okay, she seemed pretty upset," I counter, hoping Luca will take my side.

"*Cálmase, chicas*, you can both go and find the little one. Remember your buddy system idea, Mac? It's probably a *buena idea* if we stop splitting up so much, *acuerdas*?" I nod in response but stare at him hard, hoping he'll somehow pick up on my vibes. He doesn't. I really wish I was psychic so I could tell Luca about my realization regarding Nate without Nate figuring out I'm on to him.

"Terry, you go with Nate and Mac to find the Doc, Lia and the little one. Church and Kane, you two find the *chica idiota*." Marco and Jimmy, as well as Preach and Link voice protests to Luca's assignations.

"*Cállase!* We do not need any more distractions *ahora*, so, no, Cantolena, Cooke, you cannot go looking for the blonde *idiota*. Church, Kane, I trust you two can keep your thoughts in your brains and not in your *pantalones*, *sí*?" Preach and Link agree, though neither looks pleased with having to locate and escort Daffy. Jimmy and Marco are still grumbling but a good dose of some extra potent Glower Power from Luca shuts them up and they settle for glowering back but not saying anything more.

More thuds emanate from beyond the door, which Darryl and Carl are now leaning against as a stop gap.

"*Bueno, vaya*," Luca says to the search teams. To those that are staying behind, he says, "Let's get this secured before we really have a *problema* on our hands."

Terry, Nate and I head in the direction Lucy and the others went. We walk in silence for a few minutes and then Terry suddenly nudges me. I look at him and he asks, "Where did Nate go?" I whip my head around looking for Nate, but Terry's right, he's gone.

Shit.

"Come on," I say and start walking faster down the hall. I hope we find them before Nate does 'cause the thought of him finding them first is really unpleasant, to say the least.

Nate

The thrumming in my chest is reaching overdrive. I need to vent some of this rage soon or I'll go into a blackout and those never end well. Unfortunately, there's nowhere to vent it just now since killing or maiming either Terry or Mac would not be advantageous for optimum survival. Besides, neither of them has done anything to earn it and I don't plan on breaking that code unless I have no other options.

I quietly slip away from them and step into one of the storage rooms so I can practice some of the calming techniques Blaine taught me. I don't want to lose control until I'm ready. I close my eyes and take a few deep breaths. It's beginning to work, but then I feel the spot where Lia punched me throb mildly, see Lia pointing her gun at me and Lucy following suit, and the thrumming starts up again, more insistently this time. The roaring is in my ears and it's so loud that for a second I feel my head might split open from the pressure of it. I think of punching a wall to release the pressure—an old standby—but I don't want to alert the others to my location so I go for the last resort instead.

I take out my hunting knife and roll up my left sleeve. It's dark in the closet so I go by feel, counting the previous scars like rosary beads as memories of the reasons for their existence flash through my mind. I find an empty space and set the knife tip to my skin. I press down hard and drag the blade slowly across. It hurts more if you do it slowly and more pain clears my head faster. I feel the skin unknitting as the blade cuts through it and although it's too dark to see the blood, I know it's there from the slight wetness that now slicks the metal. It's less blood than they always show in the movies. A slight bubbling rather than an aggressive flow.

As the tip of the knife reaches the inner part of my forearm, I pull it away from my skin. That's the danger zone. The difference between an injury and possible death. I have no scars on my wrists—this is about clarity, survival, not suicide.

My arm throbs in the familiar way and I can feel my heartbeat localized at the site of the cut. I wipe my knife off and stick it back in its sheath. I roll down my sleeve, the fabric of my shirt sticking to the edges of the fresh wound. The thrumming has dissipated, leaving just my normal heartbeat pattern, and the roaring is gone; I can hear again. I take a relieved breath, glad to be back in control.

Now to find Lucy and the others. I need to observe them without them knowing so I can accurately judge their threat level, the way my father always taught me to do with anything that might pose a risk to me. I've never been caught truly off guard by a possible threat, and there are abundant reasons to stop it from happening now.

Lucy

At first Elliot and I walk in silence as we search the halls looking for Lia, but after a few minutes I have to ask.

"Okay, seriously, what was Lia's 'errand' earlier today? I know it had something to do with Nate 'cause now they're in a weird Mexican stand-off and I need to know what is going on because there is enough to deal with right now without adding in this nonsense!" I finally take a breath and Elliot stares at me, looking mildly alarmed and also quite uncomfortable. Clearly, he's reluctant to tell me what happened. "Come on, Elliot! This obviously concerns me, so I deserve to know what the hell is going on!"

"Okay, okay, I'll tell you. But it might annoy Lia," he says.

"If you're worried about pissing her off, I don't blame you, especially considering recent events, but I think she probably has other things on her mind, what with the aforementioned stand-off and the totally random make out session with Luca," I say and Elliot looks at me for a moment then nods.

"Good point. Okay. So when you were finishing your shower, Lia went to confront Nate about abandoning you this morning. When we got to the cafeteria, I was worried that she might do something she'd regret out of anger so I got her tomahawk away from her without her noticing. It was a good thing I did because when she saw him, the first thing she did after yelling at him was to reach for the axe. When she couldn't find it, she just took a swing at him."

"She punched him?" I ask incredulously. Although, if the situation were reversed I would probably have done the same thing, so I guess I should be more credulous.

"Yeah, and I think he was planning on hitting her back, but I got in the way."

"Brave," I say.

"I can take a punch better than people think," he says.

"Yeah, I know. We all saw you get bitch-slapped by that jack-hole, Gregory—you took it well. I meant trying to protect Lia, she doesn't exactly respond well to that. She likes taking care of herself."

"I have noticed that," he says. We lapse into silence again and I contemplate the scene from the roof.

"Do you think Nate is some kind of psycho killer?" I ask, wanting a second opinion that's less biased. I'm more inclined to be on board that train with Lia now, but I'm still curious about what an outside observer thinks of the whole thing.

"I haven't been around him enough to form a concrete opinion, but I definitely agree with Lia that he's not to be trusted," Elliot answers.

"Yeah, now that I'm less blinded by his hotness, I definitely am picking up on a creepy vibe myself," I say, then ask, "So what do we do?"

"I'm not sure. He's an invaluable asset when it comes to fighting off the undead, but with the threat he himself seems to pose, the trade-off is beginning to seem detrimental. Unfortunately, I am not certain that the soldiers would agree with us and we are at their mercy right now."

"Good point. So I guess we just try to stay away from him as much as possible?"

"I think that's probably all that we can do for the foreseeable future. And perhaps we should work on trying not to anger him worse?" Elliot suggests.

"Another good point. Like how you're not supposed to poke a sleeping bear, right? We should probably try not to poke the psycho. Though try telling that to Lia, eh?"

"We should tell that to Lia," he says adamantly.

"Well, we can try, but have you met Lia? She's kinda the go in guns blazing type," I say.

"Yeah, I've noticed," he answers and his voice is tight, worried.

We pass the girls' bathroom and I duck my head inside, calling Lia's name. There's no answer. Our barracks are similarly empty, so we carry on.

"I thought that Lia didn't like Sergeant Ortiz," Elliot suddenly says.

"Who? Oh, Luca? She doesn't. She thinks he's 'a chauvinistic misogynist who thinks women are to be seen and not heard,' and that's pretty much verbatim," I say.

"Then why did she kiss him?" Elliot asks. I glance over at him, but he purposefully avoids eye contact and I notice a pink tinge to his cheeks. Mayhaps someone is a wee bit jealous.

"Honestly, that's something you'd have to ask her about. She reacts weird to stress sometimes. And on that note, I think I know where she went. Come on."

Lia

The world has shrunk down to my fists smashing against the heavy canvas punching bag, the persistent squeak of the chain that holds it up, and the blood rushing in my ears. At this point, I probably wouldn't even notice if a zombie were sneaking up behind me—as much as they can sneak anyway. All I can see, all I can feel is this red hot rage that has been boiling up inside of me all day, waiting for a chance to finally manifest itself.

Thwack, thwack.

The bag swings away from me and I adjust my stance and throw out my gloved fists to meet it as it swings back again. A guttural noise escapes from my throat as I continue to pound the bag again and again. The dull ache growing in my hands, wrists and shoulders barely registers against the overwhelming and all-encompassing rage that has taken me over.

There is a sudden tap on my right shoulder and without any thoughts registering in my brain, I whip around and land a solid punch on the face of the person behind me with my left fist. There are two grunts of surprise, one from me and the other from my innocent victim.

Elliot is now sprawled on the ground, one hand covering his nose, which is bleeding profusely and the other adjusting his glasses, which were knocked askew. "Holy cats!" Lucy exclaims, crouching down beside him, looking concerned. She helps him up and frowns at me. "Jesus, Li! You really hurt him."

"Sorry," I grumble, knowing I'll feel bad later, but not feeling much remorse right now since I'm still in a combat frame of mind and the rage has yet to cease being in control of my body.

"That's okay, it was an accident," Elliot says, then seeing what I'm guessing is a still enraged expression on my face, clarifies, "Right?"

"I didn't know who it was," I state simply. "You should've announced yourself."

"We tried calling your name about five times, but you didn't seem to hear us, so I figured I'd try tapping your shoulder to get your attention. It was either that or try throwing something at you," he answers with a shrug.

His behaviour is starting to make a dent in my fury and I can't hold back something that, while it would probably not be construed as a smile under normal circumstances, is as close as I'm likely to get in the near future.

"Are you okay?" I finally ask.

"Oh. Yeah," he answers, the words slightly muffled by the blood dripping down his face.

"Your face sure isn't having a good day," I say as I take in the damage I've just done in combination with the injury inflicted by Gregory earlier.

"It'll be fine," Elliot says, doing his best to wipe the blood off of his face, but since it's still generously pumping out of his obviously broken nose, he just makes the mess worse, so that the lower half of his face is a bloody mask. He glances in the mirrored wall of the gym and upon seeing that his efforts have been unsuccessful, he stops trying and simply shrugs.

"The real question is, are *you* okay?" he asks me and on reflex, the anger quickly transforms into a sort of defensive shield.

"I'm fine. Why wouldn't I be?"

Lucy snorts and I toss her an angry look. Elliot only shrugs, thankfully not bringing up my waving a gun in Nate's face, my impromptu make out session with Luca or my ensuing flight, and simply answering, "I was just worried about you. Going off on your own…it's pretty dangerous right now."

"I can take care of myself," I say.

"I know that. But you're my friend and I was worried," he states this so simply and sincerely that varied emotions like being grateful and wholly embarrassed flood over me. In order to quash the sudden presence of confused tears, I look up at the ceiling of the gym, only now noticing that someone took the time to plaster it with an innumerable amount of pictures of scantily clad—or, in many cases, not at all clad—women. This annoys me enough so that I can get my errant emotions in check and I say a quiet thanks.

"You're welcome," he answers with a bright smile that looks vaguely sinister in combination with all the blood covering his face. Lucy looks back and forth between us and raises an inquisitive eyebrow at me. I mouth "shut-up" at her and she smiles in a way that is pretty damn irritating.

At that moment, Stewie's voice invades the silence of the gym and I can't hold back a groan as the insistent British voice announces the presence of Roz via my cell phone once again.

"What's happening?" Elliot asks, unsurprisingly looking confused since my cell phone is currently taking up residence inside my bra. I fish it out and even though I knew it was her, the confirmation of her face filling the screen makes me roll my eyes skyward to the pornographic ceiling once again.

"It's my mother," I explain.

"You gonna answer it?" Lucy wonders.

"It's kind of a damned if I do, damned if I don't type of situation. If I answer, she'll freak out at me for not answering earlier, not to mention rag on me for anything and everything, but if I don't, it'll only be worse when I finally do talk to her again. Plus, there's always the chance that she'll call the police or something if I take too long to respond to her. Although, actually, that's not a bad idea, we could use the backup."

Elliot offers, "I could talk to her if you want. Parents love me."

This suggestion is frankly so mind-boggling that I simply hand the phone over to him as it starts to ring again, Stewie's rant starting anew. Lucy looks at me again and this time I raise my eyebrows back at her and she just shrugs, not seeming to know what to make of Elliot's actions either.

"Hello?" Elliot answers.

"Ophelia, is that you? You sound very male all of a sudden." I can hear Roz's strident voice through the phone and I can't help rolling my eyes again. If I'm not careful, one of these days, my damn retinas are going to detach from sheer incredulity. Lucy smiles and a giggle escapes. I put my finger to my lips and step closer to Elliot so I can hear better. This is going to be good, I can tell, and I could certainly use an entertaining distraction from the confusing emotions overwhelming me right now.

"No, this is a friend of Lia's," Elliot responds pleasantly, not even pausing to tease me about my Shakespearean name.

"What friend of Ophelia's? I thought she was just going camping with Lucy."

"I'm a new friend, we only recently met."

"Only recently? Isn't Ophelia in the woods?"

"Yes, ma'am, that's where we met." I can't help but face palm at his answer, which is so not going to go over well. Lucy giggles again and I swat her arm, trying to keep her quiet.

"You met in the woods? I told her to stop making friends with strangers she meets in the woods...are you actually a friend or are you some kind of serial killer?"

Elliot glances at the phone quizzically and then back at me, not seeming to know what to do. "Give me the phone," I say, holding back a giggle myself. The laughter is contagious. "Hi, Ma, it's me," I say after a breath.

"Ophelia! What are you doing making friends with strange men in the woods? Do we need to have another 'stranger, danger' talk when you get home? Or is he a serial killer and you're being held against your will? That would almost be less disappointing actually because then you'd have an excuse for being with a stranger in the wild."

"Wow. No, Ma, he's not a serial killer and I still understand the merits of 'stranger, danger.' It's kind of hard to explain, but you don't have to worry, I'm safe, I promise." Elliot smiles ruefully at this lie and I wave him off. Lucy finally just bursts out laughing and ends up kneeling on the floor, holding her stomach as she laughs uncontrollably.

"What about Lucy? Let me talk to her, too," Roz commands.

"Lucy, um, can't talk right now, Ma, but she's fine, too," I answer, working hard to keep myself from succumbing to a laugh attack of my own.

"Well, where is she?"

I lose my ability to speak as the laughter takes me over following a particularly strange gasping noise of Lucy's. Elliot reaches over and takes back the phone. "Mrs...um, Lia's mom, I assure you everything is fine with both Lucy and Lia. Lucy is just busy right now."

"Well, that's good to know. Now where'd Ophelia go? I want to say goodbye to my daughter."

"You know, she actually just stepped out," Elliot answers and both Lucy and I launch into another round of hysterical laughter.

"Stepped out? But you're in the woods."

"Yes, ma'am, we are...listen I have to go now, but it was nice to make your verbal acquaintance. You have a lovely daughter." I crow with laughter at this and Lucy snorts.

"Yes, I do. Even if she doesn't call her mother as much as she should. Tell her I love her."

"Yes, ma'am, I will," Elliot says as he hangs up. "Lia? Lucy?" he ventures, his voice hesitant. "Are you guys okay?" he asks and Lucy takes a few deep breaths, trying to get herself under control.

"We're fi-ine," she manages before bursting into another gale of laughter, which sets me off again. The muscles in my stomach and my face are starting to hurt, but I finally feel the tension that's been building in me all day release and I collapse onto the floor again, laughing quietly.

Our laughter finally subsides and Lucy struggles to her feet. "My face-*hic*-hurts. Oh-*hic*-great. And now I've-*hic*-got the hiccups," Lucy says as she rubs her face.

"Feel better?" Elliot asks as he hands back my cell phone and smiles kindly. I barely notice the weird juxtaposition between his sweet smile and the half-dry, half-wet blood caking his face as I return his smile and take back my phone.

"You know? I really am," I say, and then pause for a moment before turning it off and putting it back in my bra.

Elliot

Lia replaces her cell phone in her bra, which I guess would be a handy place to keep it, and I try to be respectful and not stare since I'm pretty sure the last thing she needs right now is to be ogled. I glance skyward instead and soon realize that this isn't a good idea considering that the ceiling is covered with pictures of women in various stages of undress and that is not conducive to keeping my mind off of Lia's womanly parts.

Lia crosses her arms over her chest, which is also not helpful for trying to refrain from ogling her, so I just lower my eyes to the ground. As I catch sight of her gloved hands again, I have to stop myself once more from saying anything about her coping mechanisms. I'm just glad that she seems to have calmed down since her laughing fit with Lucy. I suppose laughter really can be curative.

My face is aching from her punch and I'm pretty sure my nose still hasn't stopped bleeding. I reach up to test this theory and Lia follows the movement of my hand with her eyes. "We should probably get you cleaned up."

"Probably. I do look awful," I answer, glancing at myself in the mirror again as my hand comes away with fresh blood, confirming my hypothesis. "Should we tell everyone what really happened, or should I just say that I walked into a door to avoid further questions?" I ask and Lucy giggles and hiccups again.

"Well, since telling people you walked into a door would probably incite its own barrage of questions, let's just go with the truth," Lia answers as she whacks Lucy on the back.

"I told you, that-*hic*-doesn't cure hiccups," Lucy says, batting Lia's hands away from her.

"I would try scaring you, but since it would be like adding one more thing to an immersion therapy session, I doubt that would work," Lia counters.

"Well-*hic*-hitting me-*hic*-certainly doesn't! *Hic*!"

Just then, Terry and Corporal McCoy walk through the door, stopping abruptly when they see my bloody visage. "Whoa, Doc, what the hell happened to you now?" Terry asks.

"I walked into one of Lia's punches when I surprised her," I say, deciding to combine the two explanatory options we discussed. Lia glances at me, but she doesn't refute my account of what happened, she just half-smiles and crosses her arms again.

"No offense, man, but you look like shit," Corporal McCoy says bluntly, "and kinda whacked out."

"Yeah, we were just talking about how I should go get cleaned up."

"Since people keep running off by their lonesomes, Luca has now fully implemented the buddy system so we've got to stick together," Terry says.

"That reminds me," Corporal McCoy says before bringing his walkie-talkie to his mouth and speaking into it, "Luke, it's Mac, just letting you know Terry and I found Lia, Lucy, and the Doc and everything is copacetic."

Sergeant Ortiz's response crackles out of the speaker on the walkie-talkie, "*Bueno*, Mac. We're in the briefing room." A pause and then Sergeant Ortiz asks, "But where is Nate?"

Corporal McCoy screws up his face in consternation and glances first at Lucy and then at Lia, both of whom look suddenly grim—although the effect is ruined somewhat by Lucy's continued hiccups.

"We kinda lost him," Corporal McCoy says and then tenses as though bracing himself.

"What? *Dios mio*, Mac, what the hell is wrong with you?"

"It's not my fault, he's like a ninja!" Corporal McCoy protests.

Sergeant Ortiz swears in Spanish some more then barks, "Just get back here ASAP with the civs that you did manage to keep track of."

"Sure thing, Luke. Are the others back yet?" Corporal McCoy asks, ignoring the brusque tone in Sergeant Ortiz's voice.

"Church and Kane have yet to find the *idiota*."

"What happened to Daphne?" I ask, then wish I hadn't when Lia tenses. I wish I could explain to her that I'm curious simply because I want as many people to make it out of this mess alive as possible. I don't have any residual fondness left for Daphne. It's all focused on Lia now.

"She threw a hissy fit when she didn't feel she was getting enough attention and she ran off not long after y'all went after Lia," Terry answers.

"Women," Lucy deadpans, getting a laugh from everyone.

"She wasn't in the girls' bathroom or barracks so who knows where she is now," Corporal McCoy says with a shrug. I'd say that any of his residual fondness for Daphne looks to be gone, as well; he seems to be focused solely on Lucy now.

"We should probably head back," Terry says a moment later.

Lia says, "We should get Elliot cleaned up first, though."

"Agreed, 'cause, dude, you look almost as bad as one of the zombies," Corporal McCoy says and Terry grunts in agreement. I'd take offense, but they're right, I do look kind of insane.

We head out of the gym en masse and walk down the hall to the bathrooms.

"Because of the buddy system and all, I think we'll have to dispense with you girls staying out of the guys' bathroom," Terry says and Lucy and Lia nod their agreement, following us in.

I head over to the line of sinks and turn the water on. Lia grabs a towel from the shelf and follows me. "Here," she says after wetting the towel, "let me." She starts cleaning off my bloody face and it's all I can do to avoid cringing and yelping in pain. I manage to remain silent and quite stoic and I'm probably a tad inordinately proud of myself for doing so. Most of the blood that was covering my face is gone within a couple of minutes, but my nose is still stubbornly dripping. Looks like I'll have to go with the old sticking toilet paper up the nostrils solution.

But, first things first, I say a quick thank you to Lia for her help and then, while watching my progress in the mirror, I adjust my nose as best as I can to avoid it looking too crazy once it's healed. This time I can't hold back a loud groan of pain as I shift the cartilage back into a rough approximation of its usual positioning.

"Ow," I say as even more blood starts to leak out of my nose.

"No shit," Corporal McCoy says while Lia hands me the towel to stem the bleeding. I press it to my face as Corporal McCoy continues, "That was pretty hardcore, Doc." I shrug as indifferently as I can; glad the towel is hiding my grin at someone so tough thinking that I'm "hardcore."

I walk over to one of the toilet stalls and grab a large amount of toilet paper. I drop the towel and then stick as much paper as I can into each nostril. I turn around and walk back to the others once I'm done and sneak a glance in the mirror, though I quickly wish I hadn't. Even with the blood now gone from my face, my t-shirt is still soaked with it and my nose looks about four times its normal size. That, in combination with my eyes, which are quickly turning black, and my cut, bruised, and swollen right cheek and the already crimson toilet paper sticking out of my nostrils gives me a very strange and grisly look.

"I should probably change my shirt before we meet up with the others," I say, trying to act unaffected by my frightening appearance. My attempt at being cool is ruined not only by the fact that I am decidedly uncool, but also by the way the toilet paper shoved into my nostrils makes my voice come out sounding incredibly nasal.

"Yeah, that'll help," Terry says, a little sarcastically.

I start to laugh, but I stop quickly because of how much it hurts my face. I walk back to the stall and pull out the now sodden and useless toilet paper from my nose and then I refill my nostrils with a fresh batch. I grab some extra and stick it in my pocket for later.

"Good to go?" Terry asks as I return to them once again and I nod, patting my toilet paper filled pocket.

We leave the bathroom and start walking towards the room Terry and I were sharing with Jake. Once we reach it, I feel some slight anxiety about taking my shirt off in front of Lia, but remind myself that with the buddy system, I can't ask her to wait outside and besides, I don't want to ruin Corporal McCoy's new impression of me being "hardcore."

So, first I strip off my no longer white button-up and then peel off my slightly less gory t-shirt. I try to act normal and almost trip over my bag in my efforts to remain casual. Just once, couldn't the universe help me out and not make me look like an idiot in front of a pretty girl? I sigh and squat down to rifle through my bag, pulling out a clean shirt and a hoodie, opting to wear that in favour of donning an over shirt again. I pull on the shirt and then the hoodie, finally turning around and hoping that my injuries will cover up any signs that I might be blushing, because I'm quite sure that blushing is not hardcore.

"So you guys have no idea where Nate is?" Lia asks as we exit the room.

"It was an accident!" Corporal McCoy proclaims defensively.

"Whoa, calm down, I was just asking," Lia says.

"Sorry, I just"— Corporal McCoy breaks off and glances at Lucy—"I was hoping to be able to keep an eye on him." Lia turns to look at Lucy, too, and before I know it, we're all staring at her. She stops walking and stares back at us.

"What?" she asks then hiccups again.

"I think we're all on board with the notion that it may not be entirely safe to be around Nate anymore," I say and Corporal McCoy nods, Lia mutters something about that being an understatement and Lucy hiccups and then nods, too. I look at Terry.

"I trust your judgement, Doc, if you say he can't be trusted then I'll back you," he says and I smile a little grimly, once again thinking about how all it took was the potential zombie apocalypse to turn Terry into a decent guy. Who knew?

"Thanks, Terry. The only problem is, I'm betting the soldiers, besides Corporal McCoy obviously, won't really agree. So right now all we can do is to further implement Corporal McCoy's buddy system idea and be on the lookout not just for errant zombies, but also for Nate. Agreed?" Everyone nods in reply and we start walking again, heading towards the briefing room in silence.

As we walk, I can feel the waves of tension rolling off Lia as she continuously bites her nails and makes loud sighing noises every couple of seconds. Terry and Corporal McCoy have noticed something is amiss: they keep glancing over at her and back at either Lucy or myself. Lucy and I both just shake our heads and luckily, neither of them asks Lia what's wrong, since that wouldn't be helpful to her mood.

Another bad idea would be to try to comfort her, although it's hard for me to resist doing so. I have to fight very strongly against the urge to pat her shoulder or to try squeezing her hand or something else that would most likely only result in me having yet another injury to explain to people. And while my face isn't exactly up to the quality of say, Ryan Gosling's, I don't want it to be too unrecognizable should I ever get home again; my mom would have a fit.

We reach the briefing room quickly and I can't stop myself from glancing at Lia before we go inside, she catches me looking and scowls darkly…it was definitely a good idea not to attempt comfort via some kind of reassuring touch. I just smile back at her, even though it makes my face ache even worse. Unsurprisingly, her scowl only darkens and she immediately stops biting her nails, then she throws the door open and stomps inside.

I walk in behind her, followed closely by Terry, Corporal McCoy, and Lucy. Sergeant Ortiz nods at us and his gaze lingers on Lia. My stomach clenches but relaxes again when she doesn't even notice or return his look. I know that I have no right to be jealous, it's not as though I have any sort of claim on Lia and she'd be angry if she knew that I was feeling in any way territorial or possessive about her, but I can't help picturing them kissing and every time I do, I feel a little like hitting something. I usually tend towards nonviolence so this is all foreign to me.

Connor

"Everyone sit down," Luca commands and we all find seats. Lia sits down on one side of Lucy and I sit down on the other while Elliot sits on Lia's other side. Nate sidles into the room and I feel Lucy tense up beside me. Nate barely spares a glance for us and merely waves a dismissive hand in acknowledgement of Luca asking him where the hell he went. Most people wouldn't just ignore a question like that from Luca, but I can definitely see now that Nate is not like most people.

Rafe plops into the empty chair beside me. "Preach and Link aren't back yet?" I ask him, trying to distract myself from the worrying presence of Nate, who's now gone to sit at the back of the room; I can feel Lucy squirming a little beside me in reaction. Without really thinking about it, I slide my hand around hers and squeeze, she squeezes back as Rafe answers me, "No, they can't find Daffy."

"Where's Marco and Jimmy?" I ask.

"Luca sent them to help find her."

"Huh," I say. That seems like a terrible idea.

"I know," Rafe says. "I think mostly Luca just wanted to get them out of his hair while we figure out our strategy for tomorrow."

"Makes sense. Those two are almost as bad as Gates was."

"No shit. Maybe even worse considering there's two of them."

"*Bueno. Primero*, tonight we will all be sleeping in the men's barracks, together," Luca says, quieting what little conversation was going on in the room. "The situation is getting too critical to keep separated." He casts a look in Lia's direction, probably expecting some kind of outburst. I almost want to break out with one myself, the thought of Nate sleeping in the same room as Lucy is stressing me out and, judging from the way she's squeezing my hand even tighter now, I'm not the only one who feels that way.

When he sees that no obvious protest will be forthcoming, Luca continues, "*Segundo*, tomorrow morning at dawn, we will be starting out for the laboratory. *Tercero, ahora*, we are going to plan our route to get to the lab and *cuarto*, after Church, Kane, Cantolena, and Cooke finally return with the blonde *idiota*, we will have dinner and then we will get everything packed up so we can leave A.S.A.P. *en la mañana. Preguntas?* No? *Bueno.*"

Luca turns around and pulls down the map of the surrounding area. "The map is old so it doesn't have the lab on it, but if you had to guess, Elliot or Terry, where would you put it?" he asks. Elliot stands up and walks to the front of the room, joining Luca in front of the map. They start talking in low voices as they plan the best way to get to Elliot's lab.

Since I don't really have to pay attention for the time being, I glance over at Lucy, wondering how to reassure her without getting Nate's attention. She looks back at me and smiles faintly and I notice her hiccups are finally gone.

"Uh, Sarge?" Link's voice abruptly comes out of the comm on Luca's belt.

"What?"

"You might wanna rendezvous with Preach and me, STAT."

"*Porqué?*"

"'Cause we found Daffy."

"So? Just come back to the briefing room."

"She's kinda busy right now."

"What are you talking about?" Luca asks impatiently.

"Marco and Jimmy found her first and uh...well, it ain't pretty, sir."

"*Qué?*"

"They're sinning against God!" Preach's strained voice replaces Link's.

Luca sighs then asks, "*Dondé estás?*"

"Outside of the women's bathroom, sir."

"Come back to the briefing room."

"Yes, sir."

"Donahue, Cho, Halley, *conmigo.* Everyone else, stay here," Luca commands, his voice tight. "Mac, help Elliot with planning the route so we can accomplish something while I'm taking care of those *chingada idiotas.*"

"Sure thing, Luke." I squeeze Lucy's hand again then let go, standing up and walking over to Elliot and the map as Rafe, Carl, and Darryl join Luca and leave the room.

"So, where abouts is your lab?" I ask Elliot once they're gone.

"It's around here," Elliot says, indicating the top right corner of the map, a little over fifty kilometres away from the fort, like he said.

"Easy walking distance then," I say, grimly.

Elliot smiles humourlessly then winces.

"Lia packs one hell of a punch, eh?" I say.

"She does at that," he says and winces again. I clap him on the back and we return to studying the map. In between the lab and us is the huge and in my opinion, unfortunately named, Crystal Lake.

"There's a boat house on the lake," Elliot says.

"Of course there is," I answer, thinking about the Voorhees. Elliot gives me a funny look, but I wave him off and he continues.

"If we can find a boat that will fit all of us, or even a couple of boats, and we use them to get across the lake, it would really shorten the distance that we have to go."

"Mmhmm," I agree, although I still have to fight the urge to argue. I know it'll cut a lot of time off the journey to the lab, but it's hard to ignore the voice inside me that's a mite paranoid from watching what, some might say, is way too many horror movies.

I know it's pretty unlikely that Jason Voorhees will suddenly show up and join the fray, but it's not like we need another undead, seemingly impossible to kill monster on our hands. I mean, most people think zombies are a pretty unlikely occurrence, too, but here we are.

This paranoid train of thought is interrupted when Preach and Link suddenly appear in the doorway. "What was going on with Daffy and those two jackasses?" I ask once they're inside the room.

"They were sinning against God," Preach says again, fiddling with the cross hanging from his neck.

"Yeah, got that part," I say. "What the hell does that mean exactly? I mean, there are a lot of things people do that you consider sins against God, so it might be handy if you narrowed it down a bit."

"They were having a three-way," Link says.

There is a chorus of disgusted noises from Lucy, Lia and Nate—and I don't necessarily disagree with them. I'm not surprised considering how idiotic Marco and Jimmy are and how *friendly* Daffy is, but, it's not really the time or place for such shenanigans.

On the other hand we *are* facing an end of the world sort of deal, so I guess I can kind of see their side, but just no. Not to mention the fact that Luca is pretty much going to kill them when he gets there. If he was pissed off at me for flirting earlier, I don't even know what he'll do now that he's faced with an honest to God devil's threeway.

I glance over at Elliot, curious about how he's taking the news, but it's hard to read an expression on his battered face. "You okay?" I ask and he looks at me and raises an eyebrow, then winces.

"I'm fine," he answers. "I'm just trying to think of what we can do if there aren't any boats left at the boat house when we get there. We don't want to leave ourselves without a back-up plan in case something else goes wrong."

"Yeah, good idea," I say, then, "Listen, Doc, I gotta ask..."

"Mmm?" he grunts, still studying the map intently.

"Are we gonna have to worry about zombified deer and that kind of thing?"

Elliot stops studying the map and stares at me, looking surprised. "Have you seen any yet?" he asks.

"No, but I was just curious 'cause it'd be pretty damn inconvenient if we had to worry about that, too."

"True, but I don't believe that the mutation would transfer species; not to mention, animals tend to be a lot faster than humans and I have a feeling that the animals would run as soon as they smelled one of the zombies coming. More likely than not, the animals have all fled the area."

"So, you don't think there'll be any, but there might be?" I clarify.

"I suppose it is possible, but I think that if there were animals that had mutated, we would've seen them around, don't you?"

"Yeah, I guess," I say, unconvinced. Human zombies are one thing, but animal zombies? That's a whole nother level of fucked up and creepy.

"Don't worry, Corporal McCoy, the nervous systems of animals are very different from ours, very few sickness or mutations can travel in between them. And there are none that would affect all animals as well as all humans," he says.

"Okay, well that's good to know. And please, call me Mac."

He smiles. "Alright...Mac."

"Thanks. So, *do* you have a back-up plan?" I ask.

He sighs. "So far, the only ones that are viable are either swimming across the lake or simply walking the entire way. With no other vehicles, those are the only other options."

"Damn. We really need a boat."

"That we do," he agrees.

Just then, there's an eruption of noise as the others return. Marco enters the room first with Rafe behind him, prodding him forward with the butt of his rifle. Next comes Jimmy, who's being herded along by Darryl. Carl walks in behind Darryl, and he's followed by Daffy, who's being pushed along by Luca. He has his gun trained on her and she looks majorly sullen.

Rafe nudges Marco into a chair at the front of the room and Darryl does the same with Jimmy, but at the opposite end of the row. Luca grabs a chair from the middle of the first row and slams it down in the front corner of the room closest to the door.

"Sit!" he commands, gesturing at Daffy. She hesitates and he levels his gun at her. She pouts even more exhaustively and plops down in the chair.

"You have some major anger issues!" Daffy exclaims.

"Shut the hell up and don't move! I am this close to throwing you outside and leaving you to your own defences, so I suggest you don't give me any more motivation to do so."

Ooh, this is bad, he's bypassed the angry Spanish stage and is fully into the speaking very clearly in English so the person he's pissed at doesn't miss a thing stage. I am really glad I'm not the one he's mad at.

Marco and Jimmy pipe up with protests, saying that Luca can't do that, she's a civ under his protection, et cetera. "Don't for a second think that that threat did not include you two. As far as I'm concerned, you're as useless as she is," Luca says, his voice a low, dangerous rumble. That shuts them up real quick and Luca just stands there for a moment, breathing hard and pinching the bridge of his nose. After a few silent seconds, he gestures at Daffy and tells Carl to keep an eye on her. He walks over to me and Elliot.

"Do we have a plan for tomorrow?" he asks. Elliot nods, but before he can explain anything about the plan, Luca says, "Good," then louder, to the whole room, "it's time for dinner." With that, he stalks out of the room without looking back.

"Okay," I say, acting like nothing crazy is going on, which, when you think about all of the crazy that is going on, is pretty damn impressive. "I guess it's time for dinner, let's go." At that, Carl hauls Daffy to her feet and pushes her along in front of him, following in Luca's footsteps. Darryl follows with Jimmy and Rafe does the same with Marco. Elliot nods to Terry and they head for the door, too. Lucy stands and walks over to me, I smile at her and she smiles back a little half-heartedly. She looks around for Lia and I follow her gaze. Lia is standing and she's turned so her back is towards us, but she hasn't moved otherwise. She's just standing there staring at Nate.

And he's staring right back. I try to find something human in his eyes, in his expression, but, I swear, there's nothing. It's like he's been hollowed out. His eyes are blank, his head tilted slightly to one side as though he's watching something—no, that's not quite right. It's like he's studying something with a clinical disinterest. He looks like a scientist waiting to begin a dissection. A shiver passes through me.

"Lia?" Lucy's voice is surprisingly strong considering I can feel her trembling beside me. Lia doesn't move, doesn't act like she heard Lucy at all. "Lia!" her voice is even stronger now, more insistent and sure. Lia turns her head slightly but doesn't break her stare with Nate. "It's time for us to go to the cafeteria now," Lucy says, her voice tight, but still strong and even. I reach over and squeeze her arm, hoping to help.

All of a sudden, Nate breaks from the stare down with Lia and focuses his gaze on me. The weight of that blank, empty stare hits me like a semi, but I don't let go of Lucy's arm. Instead, I slide my hand down the inner part of it until my hand is clasped with hers. Nate's stare sharpens and something sparks behind his eyes. Something I can't quite identify.

Lia looks between us and lands on Lucy's hand in mine. Her face darkens, though, for the life of me, I couldn't tell you why; I thought she at least liked me better than Nate—not exactly a highly set bar, but still.

"Guys! Come on, you heard what Sergeant Ortiz said, it's time for dinner and I don't think he's in the mood for any more tomfoolery," Elliot's voice breaks the silence and thank Jesus Homeslice, some of the tension, too. It feels like we all abruptly unfreeze and return to normal, which isn't saying a whole lot for this group, but at least it's something.

Nate moves first, walking past Elliot and out the door, a more human expression on his face now, but there's still a darkness visible beneath the surface. Lia was dead on about him, that's for sure. Now if only Luca would get on board, that would be great.

Lia moves next, following in Nate's footsteps, too fast for anyone to say anything to her. After she leaves the room, Elliot surveys Lucy, looking mildly accusatory. "Remember our conversation about poking the psycho? I'm pretty sure you guys just did a lot more than poking him," he says and Lucy mutters, "Dirty," in response. I can't quite hold back a laugh, but I cut it off quickly in the face of Elliot's obvious annoyance.

"I'm being serious!" he snaps.

"I know. I'm sorry. It's just habit," Lucy says, looking chastened.

"Let's just get in there before one of them pulls a gun again. And you should stop that before we go in," he says, gesturing at our entwined hands. "That's part of the whole poking him thing— and don't say it!" he warns Lucy before turning away and stalking out of the room.

"I wasn't gonna," Lucy says under her breath. Then she looks up at me and says, "Remember when all we had to worry about was the homicidal undead? Good times." She squeezes my hand and lets go, saying, "Come on," as she heads out of the room.

I follow her and we walk into the mess hall a few seconds later. It's strangely quiet, but after a moment, it's easy to see why: almost everyone is at separate tables while Link and Preach are in the kitchen. Marco is at a table with Rafe, Jimmy's at one with Darryl, Carl, poor guy, is sitting with Daffy, Lia is sitting at a table with Elliot and Terry, and Luca is sitting at yet another table with Nate. I'm guessing Luca's still not on the whole Nate is a psycho train, which is not good.

Lucy goes to sit with Lia and I plan on joining her, but Luca calls me over to his table. With Nate, which is just awesome. I sit down beside Luca, across from Nate. That deranged, blank expression is gone from his face and he looks mostly normal. I'm not sure why, but I think that's almost more disconcerting for some reason.

"What did you and Elliot come up with for tomorrow?" Luca asks me.

"Shouldn't we wait and tell everyone at once?" I ask, trying to distract myself from the way Nate is looking at me. I never thought I'd say this, but his stare is actually worse than Luca glowering at me.

"I'll just brief everyone before we go to sleep tonight," Luca answers.

"Right. Good plan. And speaking of that, I was thinking it'd be good if we set up a watch rotation. We don't know how secure that door to the roof access stairs is." This is true, but my ulterior motive is to make sure Nate never has a chance to be alone with Lucy while she's sleeping.

"*Sí, buena idea*, Mac. Now, the plan for *la mañana?*"

"Right. Elliot says there's a boat house on the lake—" I begin.

"There is," Nate cuts in, confirming this.

"So our best bet is to find a boat, preferably a bigger one so we can all go together. If we can cross the lake, it'll cut our journey by more than half."

"There's usually a couple of fishing boats around," Nate says. "One of those would be big enough to hold all of us." Look who's suddenly being Mr. Helpful. Like that's fooling anyone. Alright, so he's fooling Luca, but I think Luca's just blinded by Nate's superior fighting skills. And probably by the fact that he hasn't thrown a hissy fit yet—unlike the other civs.

"Perfect," Luca says and before he can say more, Link and Preach are coming out of the kitchen, bearing bowls of something that smells damn delicious.

Within minutes, everyone is served and eating happily, or at least quietly. But, of course, the silence doesn't last. Daffy is grumbling something about how she's "on a totes restricted meal plan" and the food seems "like, way fattening."

Link, offended that she's refusing his food, mutters, "It's a good thing for you jizz isn't fattening; your social life would disappear." Lia grins at the insult. Daffy doesn't respond. Either she didn't hear Link or she just doesn't care about what he said.

Lia doesn't seem content with Daffy's non-reaction to the insult. "You know, Daffy," she begins conversationally, "it would probably be in your best interest to keep it in your pants, just for future reference."

This gets Daffy's attention. "Are you trying to, like, threaten me?" she pout-growls.

Lucy cuts in, "Look, Daffy, the horror movie gods are sadistic, pervy bastards—who are also somehow prudish—they get off on slut-shaming by way of brutal death scenes. You're more likely to make it through this if you just, yeah, keep it in your pants, which goes for you two, as well." Lucy throws meaningful looks at Marco and Jimmy; both just give her the middle finger in response.

Daffy clears her throat to regain Lucy's attention. "If this is, like, supposed to be some sort of safe sex talk, you can just save your breath, 'cause I've totes heard it all before from the guidance counselor when I was in high school. I'm not stupid."

Lia makes a disgusted noise that I'm pretty certain has nothing to do with the food. "'Kay, Lia, you know what? I am so done taking shit from you. I am so not gonna be judged by some slutty girl who makes out with random angry dudes in the hallway."

"You're calling *me* a slut?" Lia asks, standing up and turning around so she's facing Daffy. "If that isn't the pot calling the kettle black, I don't know what is."

"Lia," Daffy hisses, sounding horrified, "that's racist." She inclines her head at Link and then at Rafe as she says this and I am definitely not the only one who does a face palm.

"Oh, for Christ's sake!" Lia growls and takes a step forward, Lucy grabs her wrist and I figure it's time for someone to step in and try to do something before this gets any uglier.

"Ladies, ladies, can't we all just get along?" I say and, ignoring the not at all cleverly disguised groans that the guys tend to make when one of my speeches is forthcoming, I plow on. I like a girl fight as much as the next heterosexual guy, but only when there's mud or possibly JELL-O involved and it's for entertainment and no one gets hurt. When it's like this, all intense, I don't think anyone enjoys it. And it's not like Daffy would stand a chance anyway, so it wouldn't be at all sporting.

"There are zombies, emotions are running high, but come on, we kind of have bigger problems right now, don't we? Like, the zombies? I don't see why we need to give them any sort of advantage over us by having breakdowns in communication within the group. So, can't we just set aside our differences and come together, at least until we don't have the threat of the zompocalypse to deal with?"

I'm actually pretty impressed with my own speech, I thought it was quite inspiring; I don't know why the guys always act like I'm torturing them with my speeches, they always seem pretty awesome to me.

"No." Lia's voice is flat and unimpressed. Fine, maybe that's why my speeches never get the warmest reception, no one ever seems as impressed with them as I am. Daffy doesn't respond, she simply goes back to pouting.

"God, would you give it a rest with the gay speeches already?" Marco says.

"Who are you calling gay?" I ask pointedly.

"What the fuck is that supposed to mean?" he retorts, standing up now.

"Just that, of the two of us, I'm not the one who's ever had sex with another dude."

"Oh that's rich, having my sexuality questioned by a guy who answers to 'Connie,'" Marco chuckles, but the sound is mean and he takes a menacing step toward me. He's held back by Rafe so I focus on my retort instead of getting ready for a fight.

"Only my mama calls me that...and my sisters sometimes. Whatever! You still technically had sex with a guy." At that, Marco lunges past Rafe. I scramble over the bench so I'm clear to fight, but Rafe is faster than Marco and he grabs the back of his shirt as he tries to get by him. Rafe is also bigger and stronger than Marco, so he makes slamming him to the ground look like a piece of cake. Marco lays still for a few seconds, clearly winded.

"Enough! I wasn't kidding about throwing you *idiotas* to the zombies!" Luca snarls.

"Which people?" I ask, figuring clarification might come in handy.

"At this point, anyone who pisses me off!" he snaps.

Damn. Full Glower Power. That shit is intense.

"Everyone sit down and finish eating. Or don't. I don't give a damn. But you will sit down and you will shut up until I finish eating. And if there are any more outbursts from anyone, I cannot be held responsible for my actions." Everyone sits back down. There's an uncomfortable silence that reminds me of being a kid and the painful silences that followed me royally pissing off my parents.

Lucy was right, I do miss the good old days—namely yesterday—when all I had to worry about was the ravenous undead. Now we have to factor in a furious and fed up Luca and a guy who's basically a trained killer and who also happens to be all bats in the belfry as my mama would say. I did not appreciate how good I had things yesterday.

Lia

We finish the meal in tense silence, but at least the food is good. I mentioned to Link that I was a vegetarian and luckily he remembered, so he gave me a meat-free version of the stew that everyone else got. He is definitely my favourite of the soldiers. Regardless of what awaits us at the lab, I'm glad we're leaving this place tomorrow morning, I am so sick of most of these people. It'll be nice to be somewhere where they're more easily avoided. Or at least there will be so much else going on that they will have less opportunity to annoy the shit out of me.

"Everyone done?" Luca asks imperiously. Man, I dislike him. Good kisser though. There's some mumbled confirmations that we're done eating and Luca nods, saying, "Let's go then."

"Go where?" Mac asks, voicing my curiosity for me. I guess he's good for some things, but I could kill him for drawing Nate's attention back to Lucy with that hand-holding stunt he pulled in the briefing room. I don't know what he was thinking. Actually, I'm pretty sure it was along the lines of "pretty girl = mine" and that's about where his thought process ended. Men.

"We're going to take an inventory of our weapons and decide what we'll all be taking tomorrow so we don't have to do it in the morning," Luca says.

"Good idea, but should we all go? Not everyone will be totally useful, you know?" Saying this, Mac inclines his head slightly toward Daffy. I guess he does have some redeeming qualities.

"*Sí, verdad.* But you're the one always worrying about us splitting up. What about the buddy system?"

"That's really more for people going places alone, Luke. I mean, do you want us travelling everywhere in one big clump, like that one episode of *Family Guy*?" Mac retorts and I smile a little to myself at the memory of said episode.

"Hey, carrot-top, I'm pretty sure he was making fun of you, idiot," Marco pipes up.

"*Cállate*, Cantolena! Here's what's happening—and there will be no arguments," Luca growls, glaring around the room intently. When no protests seem imminent, he continues, "Most of us will go to collect the weapons for the morning. The ones who won't be going are: Cantolena, Cooke, and the blonde *idiota*. So, *desafortunadamente*, Donahue, Halley, and Cho, you will also be staying here, to make sure they don't do anything stupid." Marco seems ready to protest this, but he resists the urge after Rafe smacks him upside the head. "Everyone else, *conmigo*," Luca commands and then he walks out of the room, followed closely by those of us permitted to join him.

We leave the cafeteria and I'm focused on following the others because I'm curious about where this weapon room is, especially considering that's where they stashed most of my weapons and I would like them back, thank you very much.

All of a sudden, someone grabs my arm and hauls me into a room. I twist around quickly, ready for a fight since my first thought is that Nate is ambushing me.

"What the hell are you doing?" I demand when I see that my ambusher is actually Elliot.

"I'm sorry, but I really need to talk to you," he says insistently.

"Fine," I say, relaxing slightly now that I know I don't have to defend myself. And to be honest, if I did, my opponent would be fairly easy to beat. "What's up?"

"You need to back off of Nate."

"Excuse me?" I growl warningly. "I don't know what gave you the idea that I'm someone who's okay with people trying to tell her what to do, but you are dead wrong."

"I'd never dream of thinking that you'd actually take orders, Lia, but, I mean it, this is really dangerous and frankly a bit stupid!"

"What?" I growl again, giving him a chance to back track before I completely lose my shit. "Now you're insulting me? What the fuck is your problem?"

"My problem is that you're being reckless! You've said it yourself umpteen times: he's dangerous, he can't be trusted, he's not normal. Yet, every chance you get, you're in his face, you're getting his defences up, and you're making it completely obvious that you distrust and despise him. God forbid that you ever back down. Don't you realize how insane that mentality is in this situation?"

Rage is pounding so heavily in my head that taking a swing at him is a pretty attractive idea right now. "So now I'm insane *and* stupid, is that it?" I demand.

Elliot gives a growl of frustration. "You're not listening to me! Can you just tell me how you think it's a good idea to keep baiting a guy whom you yourself have deemed a psychopath? What exactly is your thought process behind that?"

"I don't have to explain anything to you."

"You can be mad at me all you want. You can hit me again. But know this, I'm telling you this for your own good and you can run away and freak out and be angry, but I'll follow you, no matter how furious it makes you. I won't let you be so reckless with your own safety. And you can hate me if you want, but you need to hear this. As strong as you are and as brave, you're no match for him, because he doesn't care who he hurts. As soon as he can afford to do away with you, he will. Can't you see that in his eyes?"

His voice softens a bit, but his breathing is still ragged. "You're my friend, Lia—" and that's the last straw.

"Well, you're not mine. God, I barely know you and you're following me around like a lost puppy because we have a few things in common, and you finally realized that Daffy is a bitch who couldn't care less about you. And maybe she has a point; you really are kind of pathetic. Just because you couldn't defend yourself against anything bigger than a gnat, don't project your insecurities onto me. I can take care of myself just fine."

His face crumples and a small part of me feels terrible, but the rest of me is still so mad that I don't give a damn. I push past him and stomp out of the room. My heart is pounding so hard, I can hardly think. The only thoughts that enter my brain are indignant protests as snippets of Elliot's speech flash back through my mind.

How dare he? I can take care of myself, I've proven that time and time again. Who is he to try and tell me what to do? I've known him for barely more than twenty-four hours. He knows nothing about me. And I could definitely take Nate if I had to. Yeah, he has that whole deranged thing on his side, but I have righteous fury on mine.

I hear footsteps behind me, the sound somehow making itself known through the roaring of my heart in my ears. I turn around, my hand on the handle of my tomahawk, ready to take it out should the merest threat present itself. But it's only Elliot again, trailing behind me. Following me just like he said he would. This makes me incensed all over again and a part of me knows it's because I feel terribly guilty, but that part is not in control right now.

"Jesus, don't you have *any* pride?" I ask, my voice acidic.

"I'm not following you because of a lack of pride, believe me, I heard you loud and clear and I got the message: we're not friends. That's fine. I'm following you because no one is supposed to be left alone," he says.

"Whatever," I say and turning back around, I continue walking. I feel slightly less vindicated in my anger now, but slightly less of a ton still leaves a whole lot so I don't think too much about Elliot's woeful expression. Like I said, we're not friends. He really doesn't know anything about me and he doesn't know what he's talking about at all. So it's not like it's some big loss if he's mad at me now. And that part of me that knows how awful I'll feel about this later can just shut the hell up and go away. I don't need its input either.

Lucy

Just as I'm getting ready to turn back to look for Lia and Elliot, first one, then the other walks around the corner. Luca may have a point about us always splitting up and going off on our own. It does seem to happen a lot.

Uh-oh.

Lia does not look pleased. And neither does Elliot. I'm guessing that he tried to talk to her about Nate and from the looks of things, it did not go well.

"Everything okay?" I ask as Lia gets close to me.

"It's fine. I think I'm just going to go to bed though; I'm exhausted. Pick out weapons for me?" she asks.

"Sure, of course," I say, knowing that pushing to try to get her to tell me what went down is the last thing I should do. If Elliot confronted her, she'll need to cool down before she can process what he said.

"No one goes anywhere alone, not even to bed. Haven't I made that clear?" Luca butts in.

"Anyone else tired?" Mac asks. I expect Elliot to offer to stay with Lia but he stays quiet. Poor guy; he looks so upset.

"Okay, well Link, why don't you stay with Lia and help her move the girls' stuff into our barracks?" Mac suggests and Link agrees. Lia doesn't argue and within seconds, they're gone, disappearing into the girls' barracks.

"*Bueno*, let's carry on then, *por favor*," Luca says sarcastically as he turns around and starts walking again.

"Thanks," I say to Mac as he falls into step beside me.

"For what?" he asks.

"For making sure that someone stayed with Lia."

"Oh. No problem. The buddy system and all that," he says with a smile, nudging my shoulder with his and I feel myself smiling in return, despite still being freaked out to be so close to Nate. God, the look on his face when Mac held my hand earlier. I always thought that whole blood running cold thing was just a saying. Not so much anymore.

We arrive at a door that's in between the guys' room and the girls' across from the western entrance. Luca pulls a key on a chain from around his neck and unlocks the door, steps inside, and turns on the light.

Wow. Too bad Lia's in such a bad mood, 'cause she would love to see this.

"I don't know about you, but I feel like an Irish vigilante right about now," I whisper to Mac.

"Huh? Oh, *Boondock Saints*, right?" he whispers back and chuckles.

This room is easily as packed with awesome as the weapon room in that movie was. There are guns everywhere. All different kinds, too. There are boxes and boxes of ammo and different types of bladed weapons, as well. Not to mention the crate filled with Lia's arsenal.

"This is pretty damn impressive, Sergeant," Terry says as he eyes a particularly nasty looking scimitar that he fished out of Lia's crate.

"That's actually one of Lia's," I say and he looks even more impressed and although Luca rolls his eyes, he looks a little impressed, too.

"*Bien,* we need to be well armed, but remember that we will be carrying all of what we bring with us. Potentially for over 50 kilometres of walking if there aren't any boats at the dock when we get there. Choose weapons you can carry easily and weapons that you know how to use. There won't be any time for training once we get out there and any mistakes could prove fatal," Luca says as he begins taking stock of the supply.

"Something else to keep in mind: the best thing to do to cover all areas of defence is to carry a mixture of guns and blades because they both bring something to the table," Mac notes. "Remember that guns can jam and they always run out of ammo, so blades can come in really handy. Of course, you have to get closer to use them, but nothing's perfect." People nod or grunt in answer then return to picking out their weapons.

For myself, I decide to stick with my machete, of course, and my ever present switch blade. As for guns...

"Which of these is best for someone who doesn't have the greatest aim?" I ask Mac and he thinks for a moment then hands me a pistol and a hip holster to go with it.

"These are really steady and they're fairly lightweight so they don't have too much kick to them but they'll get the job done," he says and then hands me a couple of boxes of ammo. I thank him and start scanning the room, looking for stuff that Lia would like. I know she'll bring her two axes, but some kind of knife would probably be good, too, so I select a rather vicious looking one off of one of the tables, sliding it back into its sheath and adding it to my pile.

I look to Mac to get a recommendation for some guns to get for Lia, but he's busy studying a machine gun and talking to Luca and Preacher. Elliot and Terry are nearby though, and Terry looks like someone who knows his guns. Besides, this will give me a chance to ask Elliot what happened with him and Lia.

"Hey guys," I say as I approach them, "having any luck?"

"Yup. This place is great!" Terry says enthusiastically. Elliot doesn't say anything.

"You okay?" I ask him.

"Yeah, Doc, you're being pretty quiet. I know weapons aren't really your thing, but you can't go out there empty handed tomorrow," Terry says. Elliot smiles but his heart isn't in it.

"Everything's fine. Terry, why don't you just pick out whatever you think I'm least likely to kill myself with?" Elliot says and steps away from us. I follow him and tug on the back of his hoodie to make him stop.

"No one goes anywhere alone, remember?" I say.

"I'm not, don't worry. I'm just trying to get out of the way. Like Terry said, this isn't really my thing."

"What happened with Lia? Did you confront her about," I pause and glance at Nate, who's studying the contents of Lia's crate intently, before finishing with a quiet, "you know." Elliot doesn't answer so I press on. "Because I'm sure she got upset, but she'll cool off. She just really hates it when she thinks people are trying to tell her what to do."

"Everything's fine, Lucy, really," he insists, then steps around me and re-joins Terry.

"Almost done?" someone asks from behind me and for a second I think it's Mac so I nearly jump out of my skin when I turn around and see that it's Nate.

"Yup, almost," I say, trying to modulate my voice so that he doesn't see how freaked out I am.

"Listen, I'm sorry about earlier today. I never meant to leave you alone like that. I was trying to protect you," he says and although this would've made me swoon a bit even this morning, now I just feel like I'm freezing from the inside out. But I am on board with Elliot's insistence that we not annoy the psycho so I nod and try to look as normal as possible.

"It's fine. I know it was just a misunderstanding and no one got hurt so there's no need to dwell on it," I say.

"A misunderstanding," he says and his handsome features tighten almost imperceptibly; my gaze is drawn to the bruise on the right side of his jaw, the place where Lia hit him. "Yes. We're having a few of those today. Like the one on the roof. That was quite the misunderstanding." It's amazing. He's not exactly doing or saying anything threatening but I can feel my heart pounding harder and my breathing is more intense. My fight-or-flight response centre is begging for me to do something, anything but just continue to stand passively near the reason for my encroaching panic.

"Yeah, that was definitely a pretty bad one," I say, trying to smile. He smiles back and my heart pounds all the harder. He smiles like a shark. Like something that's getting ready to hunt and likes it. A lot.

"I guess we're even then," he says and I don't know what to do. He looks appeased, like we've reached an agreement about something.

"Um, I guess," I say because I can't think of anything else.

"Good. I'm glad."

"Me, too," I say, my tone more unsure than I'd like. He doesn't seem to notice though, just smiles wider. I think that smile is going to give me nightmares.

"You guys about done?" Oh, thank God. Mac comes up beside Nate as he asks the question, concern written all over his adorable face.

"Just about," I say. "Do you think you could help me with something though?"

"Sure thing," Mac says casually and we walk away from Nate, both of us trying to be as inconspicuous as possible. Nate doesn't seem to notice, he just seems...pacified. I shudder a bit and Mac makes sure Nate isn't watching us then squeezes my hand. "Do you really need my help with something or did you just want to get away from him?" he asks.

"A little from column A, a little from column B," I answer and proceed to get his advice about which guns Lia might like.

After about another twenty minutes and a short argument about whether it would be safer for Daffy to have a weapon or not (we all agreed it's probably safer for everyone involved if she's unarmed but to give her a knife just in case), we leave the armory, weighed down with the weapons we chose for ourselves as well as the ones we chose for everyone not present.

We walk into the guys' barracks and I spot Lia right away; she's lying down on a cot in the very back of the room. Link is sitting near the door and he joins the group as I leave it. I walk over to Lia and sit down on the cot nearest her. She seems to be asleep and even if she's not, she's pretending, so I know she doesn't wanna talk right now. I deposit the weapons I picked out near our bags and clean clothes, or at least cleaner clothes; those blood and gore stains can be pretty stubborn. She and Link must have gone to get them while we were in the weapons room.

I get ready for bed while Mac radios the exiles in the cafeteria and tells them to come to the barracks and Luca sets up the watch rotation for the night. I have no idea what will happen tomorrow, but I really hope that we make it to the lab and that Elliot is right about his hunch for the "cure." I also really hope that Nate stays pacified and doesn't decide to kill anyone who isn't reanimated. The last thing we need to worry about is him going even loopier and slaughtering everyone just for kicks.

I close my eyes and for a few minutes, all I can focus on is that smile of Nate's and the weirdly mechanical tone in his voice. Random images from the intense day flicker through my mind. I think about that feeling in the pit of my stomach when I realized Nate had left me alone with some definitely unwelcome company. I remember the look on his face when Lia pulled a gun on him up on the roof and the even more intense expression it morphed into when I aimed my gun at him too. A flash of the way his eyes stared into Mac's when he was holding my hand is replaced by that smile again. That predator's smile.

I open my eyes and take a deep breath. Time to focus on something else or I'll never fall asleep and I don't exactly want to be fighting zombies, and possibly Nate, with sleep deprivation messing up my skills.

I try to think about nice, calming things and finally, without totally meaning to, I settle on Mac's smile. The complete opposite of Nate's, it calms me down instantly and as I finally start to drift off, I even feel a slight smile on my own face.

Chapter Eleven
All we can do is keep going; there are no other options

Nate

I wake up before everyone else, not counting those out on patrol. I've always been able to do that: wake myself up without having to use an alarm. It's proven useful more than a few times over the years.

I'm awake, but I don't do anything to give this away yet. I lay still on my cot and listen, getting a feel for what's going on around me. I can hear the shrieks of the zombies that surround the fort. Getting out of here should be interesting.

I hear the sounds of the others beginning to stir. "Alright, *chicas*, time to get up, we don't want to waste anymore daylight than we have to." Luca's voice echoes around the large room.

A groan comes from a cot nearby. "It's not even, like, light out yet," Daffy protests.

"My point exactly. By the time everyone is up and moving and we have some breakfast, the sun will be coming up. Now move your asses!" Luca barks.

I open my eyes and sit up, swinging my legs over the edge of the cot so my feet are on the floor. Around the room, people are in various stages of waking and getting up. Daffy is still whining, though it's under her breath. What a pathetic excuse for a human being.

At least she won't survive the trek to Elliot's lab. If the zombies don't get her, I'll make sure something else does because I'm done putting up with her. She's like an annoying mosquito and it's time for her to be squashed.

I drop this chain of thought for now; there's plenty of time to devise a strategy later. I bend over and pull on my steel-toed boots, lacing them up tight as the others get up and begin gathering their things. Elliot reminds everyone that it'll be colder up at the lab and to dress accordingly. Mild arguments circulate as people decide what to bring and what to leave behind.

"Look, Doc, you can bring those if you want, but you said it yourself, if the boats aren't there, we'll have to walk the 50 k or so to get to the lab and those books will start getting pretty damn heavy real quick," Terry says, gesturing to the stack of books Elliot has clamped in his arms.

I'm a little surprised when I see what books they are. I walk over to them and Elliot balks slightly when he notices me, but not as much as I would've expected; that boy has a bigger pair than you'd think when you first meet him.

"Are those the *Shadowlands* books?" I ask, even though once I'm close, it's obvious that they are.

"Yeah," Elliot answers, his voice hesitant, betraying the uncertainty he now views me with. "Do you read them?"

I almost laugh. "No. Well, sort of. I write them."

"You're Pete Moon?" Elliot asks, looking shocked. His question gets Lia's attention and she walks over to us.

I'll play nice. There's no hurry.

"No way. You're Pete Moon? That's impossible," Lia states haughtily. I sigh and walk over to my duffle bag, reaching in and grabbing the working draft of the latest book. I return to the group and hand the pile of papers to Lia. Her eyes scan the letter from my editor that's clipped to the front page. "'Nate, this is great, I just have a few notes...'" she reads out then trails off, looking up at me in disbelief. "You're really the writer of *Shadowlands*?" she asks, still disbelieving. I can see her urge to be impressed warring with her great dislike for me.

I nod and her gaze returns to the sheaf of papers in her hands.

"This is for the new book?" Elliot asks, stepping closer to Lia and staring intently down at the pages for a few seconds before he glances at her face and seems to change his mind. He steps away from her and returns his attention to me. Lia stares at Elliot and an expression passes over her face, one that I can't quite define; it seems like a mixture of regret and guilt.

"What's this one about?" Elliot asks me as he studiously refuses to meet Lia's eyes. Something definitely happened between them. This divide could prove to be useful.

"It's about—" I begin, but I'm cut off by Lia's strident voice.

"No spoilers!" she commands. I raise an eyebrow and take the draft back from her.

"Then you shouldn't keep reading this," I say and hand it to Elliot instead, "since it's not the final draft and all," I finish and Lia narrows her eyes at me.

"Fine. Whatever," she says, waving her hand dismissively and walking back over to Lucy and Mac. Lia says something to Lucy that I can't quite hear, but I think it has something to do with me being Pete Moon. Lucy looks only mildly interested, so I'm guessing she's not a fan of the graphic novel genre. Too bad. I could use something to get her back on my side again. Right now, she seems to have chosen Mac, which is irritating but not impossible to rectify.

"Can I read this?" Elliot asks, nodding down at the draft.

"Sure," I say, shrugging. It doesn't really matter. It's not like he'll be worried about posting it online when there's so much else to be worried about right now. "And don't worry about bringing the other ones with you; I can send you new copies any time."

He stares at me for a second, and then he says, "Awesome," quietly and immediately starts reading. I walk away from him and Terry and return to my duffle. I'll be bringing the entire thing with me. I've gone back-packing with a lot more equipment so this won't be a problem for me if we end up having to walk the entire way to the lab. And I don't want to leave any of my weapons or tools behind, you never know when they might come in handy.

Lia

Man, Elliot is so mad at me. He'll barely even look at me. Can't say I blame him, but it still sucks. "I can't believe Nate is Pete Moon," I say again, trying to distract myself from my guilt over yesterday's venomous tirade.

"Yeah, it's crazy," Lucy says, as she studies her stuff, deciding what to take to the lab.

"You don't understand! I love these books and now I find out they're written by a psycho that I hate! It's messing with my head!" I say and Lucy "mmhmms" at me. I heave an exasperated sigh. "You're not even listening, are you?" I demand.

"Sure I am, Li, I just don't see what the big deal is," Lucy says.

"Okay, think about it: it's like meeting Neil Gaiman and it turns out he's like Jeffrey Dahmer or something. It's disturbing," I say.

"But the books are still good, right?" Mac asks.

I groan and repeat, "You don't understand!" Then I automatically add, "And they're graphic novels!"

"Okay, sorry," Mac says, putting up his hands in surrender. "But they're still good, right?"

"Yes, but now every time I read them I'll think of big bowl of crazy flakes over there," I say, gesturing at Nate with my head.

"Mac! *Ven aca!*" Luca commands suddenly and Mac walks away from us, squeezing Lucy's shoulder as he goes by her. Once we're alone, Lucy fixes me with an intense stare until I have no choice but to look at her.

"What?"

"Come on, Li, spill. What the hell happened with Elliot? 'Cause when you went over there, even from this far away, I could see some pretty intense shunning going on."

"Really? I hadn't noticed."

"I thought It was pretty obvious." I give her a look and she clues in. "Oh. Right. You were being sarcastic. It's really early and I'm tired," she says defensively. She's quiet for a few glorious seconds and then she asks again, "Seriously, what happened though?"

"I don't want to talk about it."

"Come on, Li, if I don't know what happened, then I can't consult on how to fix it."

"Maybe I don't want to fix it," I growl and turn my back on her.

"Oh, don't be like that. I can tell you feel bad about whatever happened. He's a good guy—"

I can't help interrupting, "Yes, I'm aware of that, thanks." But Lucy is used to me and she continues on, acting like I didn't say anything.

"So, if you apologize and mean it, he'll forgive you."

"Why do you assume it was all my fault?" I ask, feeling cranky.

"I'm not assuming anything. I don't know what happened— through no fault of my own. All I know is that you look guilty and he looks upset," Lucy says all of this in a soothing tone and I feel even crankier.

"Ugh," I mutter.

"I know," she says, full of understanding.

"Oh, shut up," I snarl, shoving her shoulder. She grins at me.

"You know you love me," she says jumping out of the way as I swat at her again.

"Hey, you guys about ready for breakfast?" Mac asks, coming back up behind us.

"Just about," Lucy answers, smiling at him. I roll my eyes then check to see if Nate is watching them, but he's gone. Everyone is.

"Geez, even Daffy is faster than us?" I ask.

"She's still under guard so she didn't really have much of a choice," Mac says.

"Still," I say, "we're such girls."

"I know," Lucy agrees forlornly. "I don't know when this happened." She looks despondently down at all the stuff still strewn across her cot and mine.

"It's just stuff," I say, fingering my Betty Boop pajamas.

"Now once more with feeling," Lucy says.

"If Elliot's cure thing works, we can come back for your stuff," Mac says. "We'll have to come back to clear the area of the zed-heads anyway."

"Good point," Lucy says and I nod in agreement.

"Okay, so just the essentials and we store the rest somewhere safe in case the zombies get in?" I say and Lucy nods. "Now, do you think I should bring the Claymore or not?"

"Li, you've already asked me that like five times."

"Just answer me."

"No. Just like every other time you asked. I know that it's more than a little badass, but it's just too unwieldy to bring all that way."

I sigh in defeat. "Fine. I guess you're right. Let's go eat."

We grab the bare necessities from our stuff and on the way to breakfast; we stop at the laundry room and store the rest in the dryers, figuring that they'll be pretty zombie-proof. From there, we head to the cafeteria. Mac and Lucy talk on the way about horror movie possibilities for the day to come. Sometimes I think those two may have really found each other.

We walk into the cafeteria and the first thing I see is Elliot. He's examining the soldier who got clawed by the zombie yesterday, Darryl. Man, was it only yesterday? It feels like we've been here a lot longer than that.

As we get closer, I can hear Elliot talking. "Your wounds look as good as could be expected, Master Corporal Cho. How are you feeling?"

"Not bad, Doc. Mostly tired and sore, but nothing worse than that."

"Good, good," Elliot says and he finishes cleaning the wounds and re-bandages Darryl's face, jaw, and neck. That guy is going to have some wicked scars. If he makes it out of this alive, that is, which, of course, is not guaranteed...for any of us actually.

"How is he, Doc?" Luca asks as he approaches the table. He glances at me and I feel heat rush into my face—and other places. He is a really good kisser and, despite his asshole tendencies, I would definitely not mind experiencing it again. Especially if I might be eaten by zombies in the near future.

"He's fine. As good as you could hope for with his injuries. There's no sign of infection thus far, which is a very good sign that he'll make a full recovery," Elliot answers Luca and my attention returns to him. Lucy's right, I really should just apologize to him. I know he wasn't trying to attack me, he was trying to protect me, which is actually quite sweet, if unnecessary.

Once Luca is assured about his comrade's health, he says that it's time for breakfast and everyone splits up to sit at various tables. Mac starts bringing said breakfast out, with help from Lucy. I glance at Nate to gauge his reaction but he looks relaxed and indifferent. I don't trust it, especially since he's sitting with Elliot and Terry, looking all chummy and like he doesn't think gutting stuff is a fun hobby. He's got to be up to something.

Mac and Lucy finish serving everyone then sit at my table. Breakfast is good. It's eggs again and toast; good, solid food. This is smart since who knows when we'll get the chance to eat an actual meal again.

As I finish eating, I try to psych myself up to go talk to Elliot, but before I can, Luca stands up and clears his throat, quieting the room. "*Bien, todos*, we're going to get going soon, but, *primero*, we need to figure out how to leave the fort."

"What?" Marco asks incredulously. "It's not like it's hard, you just open the door and walk out. I'm sure you can handle it." What a smart-ass.

"What about the zombies, numbskull?" Mac asks. "They're kind of everywhere." Marco shuts up, looking embarrassed and muttering to himself.

"Exactly," Luca says. "It seems as if we are surrounded, so we need a plan."

"I have a plan," Nate says suddenly and stands up. "We should open the door to the stairs, kill the zombies bottle-necked there, have some people with good aim go out onto the roof and make sure the trees are clear, then clear a path from the doors so people can get out. Then, whoever's on the roof—and I volunteer, by the way—can join those on the ground and away we go."

"That's insane." The words pop out before I can stop them and I receive some harsh looks from Elliot, Nate, and Luca—all for different reasons, I'm assuming.

"Do you have a better idea?" Luca asks. "It's risky, but I think Nate's on to something."

"Every time we've gone out on to the roof, it's always taken a while before the zombies descended so we should have just enough time to clear a decent path before they start climbing the trees again," Nate says, acting like he doesn't have murderous designs on me, but I see right through his reasonable act. "If about three or four people go up on the roof, two could clear the path and one or two could watch for zombie ambushes."

"What if there's a bunch of zombies still on the roof when you get up there? If the ones in the stairwell have been shrieking up a storm since they've been in there, which is likely, then others will probably have come to investigate," I counter.

Luca looks thoughtful but Nate is the one who answers me. "The upper door that opens onto the roof shuts tight if something isn't propping it open, so the ones in the stairwell are likely trapped there and even if they've been 'shrieking up a storm' the ones on the ground wouldn't be able to hear them with the door closed so they wouldn't have any reason to come investigate."

"Okay, fine, but what if a zombie is stuck in the doorway, propping it open? You don't know," I argue.

"These are decent points, Lia, and it's not a perfect plan, but, again, do you have a better one?" Luca asks.

Typical. Siding with the other person with a penis.

Unfortunately, though, I don't have a better plan so all I can do is glare. It's a pretty impressive glare if I do say so myself, but Luca still nods like I've agreed with him and says, "*Bueno*. Nate, since it's your plan and you volunteered, you will be going on the roof. Mac, Kane, Donahue, you three have the best aim so you will be accompanying him."

Lucy looks alarmed to hear that Mac will be going with Nate and whether it's because she's worried about Nate or zombies or a combination of the two, I can't tell. I pat her arm comfortingly and she meets my eyes grimly.

"He'll be fine," I say, nodding at Mac, who's relocated to the soldier table along with Nate while they all discuss strategy.

"It's not him I'm worried about. I mean, I am, I don't want anything to happen to him. But I'm more worried about the fact that Nate will be on a roof, with a gun and we'll be easy pickings if he decides to go all Columbine on us." I feel a slight shiver run through me as I consider this for the first time. I hadn't even thought of that.

"Oh," I say, because nothing else comes to mind.

"Yeah."

"So what do we do?"

"I don't think there's anything we can do, besides just trying to not be out in the open as much as possible; no need to make it any easier for him if he does decide to engage in some 'friendly' fire."

"Remember when all we had to worry about was zombies?" I say and a slightly hysterical laugh bubbles up out of Lucy.

"I remember it very fondly," she says. "At least with them we never had to worry about what their strategy might be since it's pretty much just, you know, leap at stuff with jaws gnashing till you hit something. Those were the good old days."

Ain't that the truth.

Connor

It's really shitty that Luca's blinded by Nate's skills and his lack of tantrum throwing, because he obviously doesn't see the danger in allowing Nate to go out on the roof with his rifle and aim it down where people he isn't exactly fond of will be. Thank God, Luca chose me to go up there with Nate, too; at least this way I can keep an eye on him and try to watch out for Lucy and Lia.

Speaking of, they keep throwing worried glances over at Nate as they talk intensely. They're obviously freaking out and I'm right there with them; this is bad news bears, no two ways about it. As for Nate, he doesn't seem to notice anything at all. In fact, he's acting just like he did when we first met him: aloof, but sane and like he only poses a threat to the undead. I'm pretty confident Elliot can see through Nate's act and overlook that he's Pete Moon (I don't really get why it's such a big deal, but it seems important to him and Lia), but it's a little worrying that he seems to be so friendly with Nate all of a sudden.

"Everyone understand the strategy for getting our shooters up on the roof?" Luca asks and everyone nods or grunts in agreement and we all get up from the table.

"Everyone listen up," Luca says, louder and to the whole room, "we're going to get ready to open the door to the stairs and let the zombies out soon. We don't know how many are in there so I need anyone who can help with killing them to come with us. Halley, unfortunately you're still on guard duty"—Luca throws an extremely dirty look at Daffy as he says this and she immediately starts pouting again, rolling her eyes and muttering under her breath. Everyone ignores her and she sulks all the more intensely. One of these days she's gonna pull something. "So you'll have to stay here," Luca continues. "Doc, you might want to avoid the fray, as well."

At this, Elliot glances at Lia, looking discomfited. Not sure what that's all about. "Yeah, I'm not the best fighter," Elliot says quietly.

"Actually, I was just thinking you should stay out of harm's way as much as possible considering without you, there's no reason to go to the lab since there won't be any hope of a cure," Luca says.

"Oh, right. Okay," Elliot says, brightening considerably.

"You three stay here and block the doors with a table after we leave so you are protected in case some zombies slip past us. I'll radio when it's all clear and you can reconvene with us and wait while the shooters clear a path. Everyone else, let's go."

The walk to the barricaded roof access door is silent for the most part, but along the way, I take Link aside; if I can trust anyone to be on my side and listen to my suspicions without asking questions, it's him.

"What's up, carrot-top?"

I respond without any jokes so he knows I'm being dead serious. "When we're on the roof, I need you to help me keep an eye on Nate."

"What do you mean?"

"I'll explain everything later, just watch for any strange behaviour, okay? Make sure he's targeting zombies and zombies only." It's a testament to our friendship that he agrees without asking any more questions and that he also agrees to tell Rafe to do the same. I feel slightly more relaxed about the whole thing now that I know I'll have back-up.

Once we arrive at the barricaded door, we take a few minutes as everyone makes sure they're as armed and as ready as they can be. The shrieks coming from the other side of the door intensify; the zed-heads seem to know we're here.

"*Listas*? Everyone ready?" Luca asks and we all confirm that we are. "*Bien*, here we go."

We remove the barricade and the door buckles outward slightly as the zombies contained behind it throw themselves at it. We organize ourselves into the pattern Luca decided on, sort of a staggered circle so it's unlikely we'll accidentally injure each other while we're fighting. Luca takes point since he's gonna be the one to open the door. He clasps his gun tightly as he places his free hand on the knob and takes a deep breath.

"*Uno, dos...tres!*" On three, Luca whips the door open and a flurry of activity explodes into the hallway as it's suddenly filled with zombies. The stench of them fills the air in the enclosed space as they throw themselves at us. It's a cloying scent; they smell like death, obviously, but like something else now, too, something I can't put a name to. It's a bit of a different smell than they had before. 'Course, now's not really the time to try and figure it out.

I return my attention to the melee in front of me as a zombie launches itself at me, screeching like nails on a chalkboard, fingers across plastic wrap. I shoot it right between the eyes and the back of its head explodes with a plethora of reddish goo and white chunks of bone.

It's weird, but it's almost like these zoms are moving slower than the ones we've encountered before, because I have time to check on how everyone else, namely Lucy, is getting on in the fight before another zombie comes close to attacking me. I take this one down, too, and return to assessing the situation. Everyone else seems to be having a similar experience; this fight doesn't seem nearly as intense as the others we've had. Before I know it, the whole thing is over.

"Huh," I say.

"Yeah," Lia agrees.

"Did that seem kinda...easier?" Lucy asks.

"I thought it was just me," Link says.

"No, they were slower than before," Nate says.

"*Sí*, it's strange, but let's not waste time. We can ask the Doc what he thinks about this development later. *Ahora*, it's time for my shooters to get up on the roof and inform me about the situation up there," Luca commands.

Nate takes point, which is fine by me. I don't exactly want him at my six, especially considering that rifle of his has a bayonet.

A bayonet, for fuck's sake!

We reach the top of the stairs and I can see Nate was right: the door is shut tight. It must've slammed shut after the zombies followed us into the stairwell, trapping them there. "That's something at least," I say and Nate grunts in reply, and then reaches for the knob.

"Ready?" he asks over his shoulder and when we agree that we are, he turns the knob and flings the door open quickly, moving back a step and holding his gun at the ready, but nothing happens. There are zombie shrieks, but they're distant, coming from the ground, not from anything on the roof or in the trees.

"That was a little anti-climactic," I say as we walk out onto the roof, although I am relieved that we didn't have to try and fight off any zoms while we were bottle-necked in the stairwell there.

No one answers me 'cause everyone is busy checking the trees, making sure no zombies have learned to be sneaky and are just lying in wait for us.

I walk around the roof, checking out the ground below, trying to decide which exit will work best for everyone inside. The zombies on the ground are sort of just milling around, randomly screeching when they run into each other, but not doing much else. They're definitely moving more slowly than before and their movements are different overall: they look more rigid and spasmodic, reminding me of macabre marionette dolls more than anything else. A chill runs up my spine as I watch them stumble erratically around. They just look all the more inhuman now.

"Mac, what's the situation?" Luca's voice clears my head as I remember my mission and I put aside being creeped out for the time being.

"The roof is all clear and the trees look good, too. We're gonna start clearing a path for you guys from the north door," I say. "That one has the least zombies and is also the best place to leave from to head towards the lake."

"*Bueno*, get started and let me know when it is safe to move."

"Yes, sir." I wave the others over so I can give my orders. "We're going to start clearing out the zombies down there now. Rafe and Link, I want you to keep an eye on the trees," at this, I incline my head slightly towards Nate so they remember to keep an eye on him, too. "Nate and me will start picking off the zombies."

Nate and me walk to the edge of the roof and look down. I stand near him but far enough away that I'm out of bayonet range in case he starts feeling stabby. We both lay down and use the slight lip at the edge of the roof for more stability. He starts shooting at the zombies and his aim is scarily impeccable. Every zom he aims for falls and does not get back up. His ammo is different from my hollow points, so while my targeted zed-heads explode into reddish mist with great chunks of their faces disappearing in the process, Nate's kills simply fall to the ground with neat holes drilled between their eyes.

It'd be impressive if he wasn't so damn terrifying. While he's been shooting, he hasn't kept his mask in place, so instead of the affable fellow who's been walking around all morning like he's a totally normal person, I can now clearly see the dark reality beneath the surface. His eyes are focused to the point of being blank. Just blank, as though there's nothing behind them except a killing machine. His jaw is set and it seems to pull the skin more tightly across his face so all the angles seem harsher, like his bones are pressing from the inside out.

"If you can tear your eyes away from me, you might want to tell your sergeant that the way is clear for now and they should head outside," Nate says suddenly, catching me off guard. I pull my gaze from his face and look down.

He's right, all the nearby zombies are dead. I hadn't even realized that I'd stopped shooting, I was so distracted by his transformation. I look back at him and have to stop myself from making any sort of surprised noise. He's back to looking like a normal person—if better looking than I'd care to admit. It's hard not to convince myself that I imagined the whole thing.

"Good job," I say, trying hard to keep my emotions in check. Trying not to show fear.

"Practice makes perfect," he says, enigmatically, as he stands and brushes himself off then extends his hand to help me up, too. I take it because I don't know what else to do.

"Thanks," I grunt as I grab my comm and radio Luca.

"*Sí?*"

"Everything went well, Luke, you guys should start moving before more zombies come. We'll cover your six then join you on the ground once everyone is clear."

"*Bueno.* Good work, Mac. See you soon."

Daphne

I am so over this place. It is not worth the man candy to be treated like this. It's so unfair! I don't get what they're so angry about; they're all, like, such prudes. Or they're just jealous. What am I saying? Of course they're jealous.

"You know, I'm sure this whole guarding me thing is way boring for you...I could make it a lot more interesting," I say, putting my flirt on, which is impressive given the situation I'm working with, 'cause the dude guarding me? So not hot.

The guy guarding me, whose name I've completely forgotten 'cause it so does not matter, doesn't even answer me.

So rude! I give him the opportunity to enjoy the full-on Daffy experience and he doesn't even bat an eye? He must be gay.

Whatev. I'll just focus on the geek who's in love with me 'cause even though he's, like, so not my type or worth my time at all, I could really use some sympathy right now. I point at my guard and roll my eyes but the geek just, like, snorts, and turns his back on me.

What is with this place? Did they put gay stuff in the water? Or maybe they're turning into zombies...that would totes explain their sudden lack of interest.

"Are you turning into a zombie?" I ask my guard. He doesn't say anything, just gives me a full-on nasty look, which does not exactly disprove my theory. He has no manners at all and it's not like the zombies are super polite.

"Halley?" the mean Mexican's voice comes out of the radio thing on my guard's belt.

"Yes, sir?"

"It's time for you to meet us at the northern exit, double-time, we only have a small window."

"Yes, sir, en route now." The guard, Halley—so not surprised he has a girl's name—clips his radio back onto his belt (so blah, these guys really need better accessories) and says, "Time to go."

I stand up, but I guess I'm not quick enough for him 'cause he grabs my arm and hauls me to my feet. So pushy! "Geez, I'm coming, don't be so grabby!"

He doesn't say anything to me, he just yanks me over to the doors they pushed a table in front of and after he and the geek push the table back out of the way, he grabs me again and starts dragging me down the hall.

"I can walk fine by myself, so let me go!"

"You're not walking fast enough. Double-time means double-time."

Wow, so apparently he can actually speak to me, who knew? "Okay, saying it twice won't make me understand your gibberish."

"Double-time means twice as fast; it's not that hard to figure out," the geek says.

"Wow, rude much?" He makes a face at me and Halley grabs my arm again. I swear, if he mars my totes perfect skin with ugly bruises, I'm gonna sue.

"If it were up to me, I'd leave you here, no question, but the Sergeant's orders are to get you out. However, he did not specify how I am supposed to do so. Believe me when I say, I'm not above dragging you all the way there, so move your ass," Halley says and he breaks into a full-on jog.

I like cardio as much as the next skinny person, but I am wearing heels. "Ugh, I liked it better when you weren't talking to me."

"I don't know what makes you think I give a good goddamn what you like, but you're sadly mistaken, now hurry up."

I stop walking. I deserve way better treatment than this. "I'm not going anywhere until you say sorry to me and start treating me way nicer."

"For Christ's sake!" the geek exclaims.

"Yeah, you need to say you're sorry, too. You're both being so rude to me."

"That's it," Halley says and before I can do anything, he grabs me and totes throws me over his shoulder like he's a caveman. He starts running and it's really not comfy 'cause my head keeps banging into his back. And the geek is, like, no help. No matter how loud I shriek, they both just ignore me. Ugh, these people are so awful.

He finally stops running and drops me on the ground. Just drops me! "Jesus, Halley, you could've hurt her!" Jimmy exclaims and finally! It's about time someone was on my side. And maybe Jimmy isn't great looking, definitely not as, like, drop dead as Marco, but he can do some way impressive stuff with his tongue and his hands, which I guess makes sense 'cause he has to, like, make up for his whatever face. Anyway, it's just nice to finally be treated the way I deserve again.

He reaches his hand out to help me up, but the mean Mexican steps in between us and says, "Stay away from her, Cooke. We don't have time for this."

What is with everyone? I get to my feet myself and put on a total pout. I'm not going anywhere until I get an apology, I mean it.

"Sarge, I know this isn't the time, but I officially request to be taken off guard duty," Halley says.

Good riddance.

"Fine, you're off. Church, you're on. Now, everyone shut up and get ready. Here we go."

Great, now I have the weirdo religious guy. Gross. He's, like, even worse than Halley.

The Mexican opens the doors and I was ready to throw a tantrum till they started treating me better, but that's a lot of dead zombies there and more are yelling and they don't sound that far away and maybe it's not the best idea to have the people with the guns be all mad at me. I walk beside the preacher and try not to gag at the smell of the zombies. Puking can be handy for keeping your weight down, but I'm tired of them all yelling at me so I just keep walking with everyone else.

There's some sudden yelling from behind us and I cover my ears and shut my eyes. Some loud shots go off, sounding like they're coming from above us and the screeching stops. I open my eyes to see Mac, Nathan, and the two pretty black ones, like, climbing down the side of the fort. It's a nice change for my eyes after all the icky zombies.

"Nice job," the Mexican says when they're back on the ground. "*Bueno, todos*, we're heading to the boathouse now. Walk fast, but don't run unless you have to, we don't want to attract any more attention than we can help. Keep your eyes and ears open and be ready for any attacks. If that happens, when possible, use a blade to defend yourself because we want to make as little noise as possible and conserve ammo as best we can. Let's move."

I'm not sure what any of this has to do with the Wizard of Oz and I do not appreciate being called a dog, but I totes do want to get out of here so I keep my mouth shut for now and start walking.

I will need such a spa weekend after I get out of this hell hole. I swear, I am never going out in nature again, ever!

The walk is long and I almost twist my ankle, like, infinity times. And every once in a while a zombie or two comes out of the woods around us. Seriously...nature! Ew!

They always kill the icky things pretty quickly. It might actually be a teensy bit impressive if it wasn't so completely disgusting. After, like, forever, we finally get to the boathouse they keep going on about. I don't know what the big deal is. It doesn't look very impressive to me. The boards are all faded and not in a cute, shabby-chic way, and there's a sign half-falling down that says "Crystal Lake Boathouse."

"Damn," Mac says.

"Yeah," Lucy agrees.

"What?" I ask, but they ignore me. God, I am so sick of these people, I can't wait to get away from them.

Nathan opens the doors and we all walk through the boathouse onto the dock. "*Gracias a Dios*, there's a boat," the Mexican says.

"Good size, too," Mac says.

"We're going on a boat ride?" I ask and they all stare at me. "What?"

Nobody bothers to answer me except for Jimmy and when he tries, the mean Mexican holds his hand up and says, "Leave it."

"You're so rude!" I say.

"Cry me a river, *puta*. Get in the fucking boat before I leave you here."

The preacher nudges me forward with his gun so I have, like, no choice but to step onto the boat. Everyone gets on after us and after they untie us from the dock, the big guy who's always following the geek around starts the boat up. Everyone cheers and we pull away from the dock. I stumble (again! Ugh! Some warning would've been nice) and bump into some big, like, pole thing. Something comes loose and drops down into the water. Oops. Well, no one noticed so I'm just gonna walk away before someone yells at me again. I'm sure it won't do anything.

Everyone looks all happy as the boat speeds up. I really don't get what they're so excited about. Boats make me totes sea sick. But at least the wind will make my hair look good. Well, it always looks good, but it will look even better, so yay.

We don't get very far when the boat suddenly, like, grinds to a halt. I almost fall over (again!); I am so suing these people—all of them—when I get home.

"*Qué paso?*" the Mexican asks.

At least I think it's a question. I really wish he would just speak in Canadian all the time, 'cause it's so hard to understand him.

"I think we're caught on something," Mac says.

"What could we be stuck on?"

"I dunno, seaweed?" Mac says.

I look over the edge and try to see what's going on down there. The water is, like, totes murky and I can't see much of anything except some ripplies on the surface. "Hey, look, fishies!"

Lucy

Daffy squeals something about "fishies" and she leans further over the side of the boat. I doubt that it's "fishies" that are in the water, our luck is nowhere near that good.

"The fish hook, it's caught on something!" Elliot says and he tries to reel in whatever it is. If this were a movie, this would be the part where the ominous music starts playing. Cue the *Jaws* theme song. I know it's not the right time for movie quotes, but nonetheless, I can't help muttering to myself, "We're gonna need a bigger boat."

Mac goes to help Elliot and they make some progress. I grip my machete tighter and glance at Lia. She looks as tense as I feel, which makes me feel worse, 'cause now I know that the ominous feeling isn't just in my head. The lake is too still, much too still. Besides Daffy's idiotic exclamations, Mac and Elliot struggling with the fishing reel, it's completely silent in a way that lakes almost never are. There are no bird calls, no sounds of fish jumping out of the water, nothing. I clench my jaw and squeeze my machete handle all the more tightly.

The fishing rod suddenly comes free with a strange squelching sound. Elliot and Mac both fall backwards, partly because of their momentum and partly because of the thing that's struggling on the hook. A horrific zombie is shrieking loud enough to end the world, I swear. This one is horrendous even compared to the ones we've seen before. The water has made its skin soft and pliable, soggy, so that it looks like a mess of wet, grey paper. Its face is a ruin; there are no eyes left to speak of, just hollow sockets. I can see its teeth through the rotting sides of its face. In many places, the flesh has simply sloughed off its bones, leaving strands of tendons and muscles out in the open, clinging to the strange gleaming whiteness of the bone beneath. Its ribcage is clearly visible, its heart and lungs pressing against the ribs as it swings forward, succumbing to gravity.

It swings around, still caught on the hook, the pointed end jutting out just beneath its sternum; its limbs are flailing jerkily, the movements so alien and wrong, I have to work hard not to panic at the sight. As it swings, we all duck...except Daffy, who doesn't notice until it's too late. Much too late.

You know, in books and movies they always describe horrific things as seeming to happen in slow motion. But this...it happens in the blink of an eye, in the space between panicked heartbeats, in just the time it takes to form a barely coherent thought of "oh, God, no." In this infinitesimal span of time, the zombie careens towards Daffy, the hook piercing its torso smashes into the right side of her face, impaling her cheek and thrusting her face-first into the decayed entrails of the zombie. The intestines pressed against her mouth muffle her screams. She claws desperately, helplessly at the zombie, trying to free herself. Under her onslaught, chunks of skin come loose and fall to the deck, but she can't get free.

The zombie continues to thrash wildly, causing the rod to swing in wide arcs across the deck. Jimmy is the first one, the only one to break free from the horror-stricken paralysis that seems to have rooted us all to our spots. He dashes forward to help Daffy— too fast. The violently flailing limbs of the zombie and Daffy connect with Jimmy in his headlong rush and he loses his balance, continuing forward right over the side of the boat. He hits the water with a loud splash and his shrieks suddenly rip through the air as he screams for help. Apparently, there are more zombies in the water. I can't see what's happening to him and I am obscenely grateful for this small mercy because seeing what's happening to Daffy right now is bad enough. I feel sick, knowing there's nothing any of us can do. At least Jimmy's death is quicker and therefore more merciful than Daffy's long, drawn-out torture. She's still trying to get free, writhing dreadfully and still screaming into those decomposing organs.

The zombie continues to screech and flail, the movements causing the hook to move around in the side of Daffy's face with a gruesome, wet, squishing noise, like someone walking through sticky mud. No one can get at the zombie and no one can help Daffy. I feel beyond sick. The boat suddenly rocks to one side and more zombie shrieks join the cacophony.

"We have to get it down and we have to move, they're trying to climb onto the boat!" Luca shouts and he stands up from where he's crouched just as the boat rocks again. Carl rushes forward and grabs him, stopping him from going over the edge, but Carl's own force carries him too far forward and he pitches over the side before anyone can do anything. His screams are indistinguishable from the zombies that are trying to climb up onto the boat.

Mac edges over to Luca and pulls him back down into a crouch. Luca shakes his head and regroups. He aims his gun at the flailing zombie and fires several times in a row, the shots echoing across the lake. None of the bullets meet the intended target of the zombie's head, but plenty of them find purchase elsewhere, spraying thick drops of gooey blackened blood, bits of bone, strands of muscles and tendons, and chunks of viscera all over the deck. At least a few shots have also grazed Daffy, so Luca finally stops shooting and growls in frustration. The zombie keeps thrashing and with the combination of its wild movements and the damage done by Luca, its left foot dislodges and lands on the deck with a loud splat. I feel breakfast making a move towards my esophagus and take a deep breath. Now is not the time to break, not till we're safe...or at the very least, safer.

Preacher suddenly runs forward and slashes at the zombie with a sword he picked out in the weapons room last night. His slash goes wild and instead of severing the head from the body, he barely misses Daffy and only manages to slice the zombie's throat open. He falls to the ground as his momentum continues to carry him forwards. Decaying blood oozes slowly, hideously slowly, out of the wide gash in the zombie's neck, dripping down onto the top of Daffy's head. The slash must have damaged the vocal chords because its shrieks sound different now, raspier and rougher. Less like nails on a chalkboard and more like a rusty hinge opened slow.

For a second I think one of Luca's wayward shots must have killed Daffy because she's suddenly gone very still. Then she abruptly starts jerking around again, the hole in the side of her face growing bigger as she writhes on the hook.

"Enough of this," Nate says suddenly, and then he steps forward and shoots. As the zombie jerks and twitches, the first shot goes a bit wide, taking out what's left of the zombie's right ear. Nate breathes out heavily, and then goes very, very still. He does nothing for what seems like a long time but is probably only less than a minute, and then he suddenly pulls the trigger again and this time he hits his mark perfectly. The bullet goes straight through the zombie's brain, leaving a neat hole in its forehead. As the zombie finally stops flailing, Nate pauses, takes another deep breath, aims, and pulls the trigger once more. This time, the bullet goes through the back of Daffy's head and she abruptly stops moving, too. The rod slowly comes to a halt; it seems to groan with the effort of going still, a dull rasping sound that finally ceases as the lake descends into eerie silence. The zombie and Daffy both hang motionless on the line, the only sound now coming from the fat dollops of blood that splash onto the deck with dull thuds.

The silence is broken by the zombies in the water resuming screaming and scraping at the side of the boat. Nate walks forward and grips the hanging corpse of Daffy around the middle, pulling her off the hook and walking the few feet to the edge of the boat, where he tosses her unceremoniously over the side. He walks back to the still dangling zombie and grabs it around its hips, what's left of them anyway, and lifts it up, pulling it up off of the hook. Its skin tears with the movement and squishes with the pressure of Nate's arms, several chunks of flesh and ruined organs slide from the corpse with wet, slurping noises. They slip down Nate's back and arms but he doesn't seem to notice, just walks back over to the side of the boat and heaves the dead zombie over the edge. He turns around, grabs the zombie's foot and throws it over the side, as well. He looks down at himself and makes a face at the greasy gore covering him. He takes his shirt off and tosses it in the water, too.

I'm grateful for the chance to think about anything besides what just happened to Daffy, so even though I know he's a bit crazy and totally dangerous...wow. Just wow. Psychos should really not be that hot. It's not fair.

He walks over to his duffle and as he turns his back, I have to work not to gasp at the massive and intricate-looking scar on his back. Above the mess of scar tissue is a tattoo that reads "*Iacta Est Alea,*" which, if I remember my Latin correctly, means "the die has been cast." Creepy. Yet still hot. What is wrong with me?

And while it is definitely not the time—or the subject, considering he's bat-shit crazeballs—for such thoughts, the mild lust has cleared my head, giving me a reprieve from my panic and nausea and I feel like I can breathe again. I look at Lia and she makes a stern face at me; she is way too good at reading my mind. I wave away her concerns as Luca stands and takes charge again—

though he still looks a bit shell-shocked. He walks over to Nate just as he finishes putting on a clean shirt.

"What the hell is the matter with you? Why did you shoot her?"

Nate looks at him with his head cocked slightly to one side as though Luca has done something interesting. If Mac did that move, it would look adorable, like a puppy, but on Nate, it's just downright scary. "She'd obviously turned just now. Which isn't surprising considering her mouth was stuffed full of zombie guts."

"You can be sure she turned?" Luca asks.

"I've seen it enough by now to know what it looks like. And even if she hadn't turned, she would've died soon anyway, that damage was too great to survive—not that she would've wanted to survive, with so much damage done to her face; she was too vain. And why do you care? You hated her, too."

Listen, I know he's crazy town banana pants, but I agree with him, there's no way Daffy would have wanted to live with that amount of damage done to her face (honestly, I'm not sure I would either) and it did seem like she turned anyway.

Luca seems to agree, too, and doesn't bother denying that he hated her; he doesn't say anything else for a moment. Then he just asks, "Why didn't you do it sooner, then?"

"I was distracted." His tone is so cold, his expression so empty, Luca looks half like he wants to yell at him some more and half like he finally sees what the rest of us do when we look at Nate.

"We need to get out of here," he says and walks away from Nate. Nate looks unconcerned, his face slipping back into a non-threatening expression.

"On it," Terry says and he disappears back into the cabin that houses the controls for the boat; he does something I can't see from my angle and the boat mercifully starts up again. It moves forward with a jerk, the motor making a disconcerting garbled noise as we pull free of the zombies clinging to the boat. We head into deeper waters, the zombie shrieks fading as they sink back underwater. We all breathe a collective sigh of relief.

"You okay?" Mac asks as he walks up beside Lia and me.

"We are. I'm sorry about Carl and Jimmy." Lia murmurs her condolences, too, and Mac tries to smile at us, but it won't stay on his face. I slide my machete into the sheath at my belt and pull him into a hug. After a few seconds of squeezing him tight, he finally squeezes me back, and then pulls away.

"Thanks," he says, "they were good men. Jimmy might not have been the sharpest tool, but he was still a decent guy. He didn't deserve to go like that. None of them did." I nod and Lia grunts in agreement. I slide my hand into Mac's and clasp it firmly. He returns the pressure and shakes his head. "Man, shit got real just now."

I can't hold back a somewhat hysterical giggle at this understatement. "That is most definitely true." He smiles at me and it stays more solidly on his face this time.

"Is everyone okay?" Elliot asks and I have a feeling it's his way of asking if Lia is alright without having to actually ask her because he's looking at her as he speaks. There are some general confirmations from around the boat. The twelve of us that are left seem to have gotten away from that debacle pretty well unscathed; besides sporting some new gore that splattered on us during Luca's frenzied shooting.

"Preach, what's up, man? You okay?" Mac suddenly asks and I follow his gaze to where Preacher is standing. He looks...strange. I'm not really sure what it is, regretful maybe. Scared, I think, and something harder...angry. His eyes flick nervously towards us and he grasps his right forearm with his left hand, the movement seeming unconscious and involuntary.

"Something...happened..." he trails off and won't meet Mac's eyes. I notice he's covered with a sheen of sweat even though the breeze that flows over the deck as the boat motors along is chilly, verging on downright cold. As I continue watching him, I notice his breathing is laboured and heavy.

Damn. This is not going to end well.

I glance at Mac and around the deck, taking in the other survivors of Crystal Lake, wondering if they've picked up on what's happening yet. Mac meets my eyes and his grief is obvious and sharp. I squeeze his hand hard, wishing I could somehow make it better for him. He closes his eyes for a second as I let go of his hand and brush my fingertips across the handle of my machete. I glance at Luca as he exchanges a sorrowful look with Mac then nods once, his face sliding into an unreadable expression.

"Uh, Preach?" Mac begins haltingly and he hesitates further as Preacher suddenly stares intensely at him. I step around to Mac's other side so I can take his hand again while still keeping my lead one on my machete in case Preacher turns suddenly. Mac wraps his fingers tightly around mine and carries on, asking. "Did you get bit, man?" Preacher flicks his eyes away again and grasps his right forearm more firmly, almost protectively.

My spirits sink to have it confirmed. Damn. My heart is breaking for Mac.

"It's fine. I'm fine," Preacher mumbles, his gaze darting feverishly around. "God will protect me, he always protects me," he finishes, the words rasping through his heavy breaths. His protest makes my spirits sink even lower and Mac squeezes my hand so hard it hurts, but I don't let go. Mac looks helplessly at Luca and he nods again.

I don't know what their plan is, before either of them can do anything, Nate suddenly walks forward and stops in front of Preacher. His face is impassive, his jaw set.

"God will protect me," Preacher asserts again and his left hand suddenly lets go of his wounded arm to grasp the cross hanging around his neck. The wound is clearly visible now and it's a bad one, the skin is torn wide open and is already slightly green at the edges of the wound. The zombie must have grazed him when he tried to cut its head off.

Nate says nothing, he just brings his rifle to his shoulder and pulls the trigger. I brace myself for the loudness of the shot and the repercussions that will follow, but it doesn't come. I glance at Nate's face wondering if he had a change of heart, but his expression only shows that he's mildly disgruntled as he examines his jammed gun. He shrugs and before I can follow through on any actions that might have been born from my horrific realization of what he's about to do, he flips the bayonet out, steps forward quickly—so damn quickly—and, closing the distance between himself and Preacher, he stabs the blade into the centre of Preacher's forehead. He didn't pause or hesitate even once.

Any lust is definitely gone now, although I finally do completely realize that that should've happened a long time ago.

Crimson blood, so different from the zombie's black goo, bubbles and begins to flow profusely. Preacher's face is soon invisible; it's covered in so much blood. Nate presses against Preacher's chest with one hand and pulls the blade out. It makes an awful, awful sound that hideously reminds me of scooping out the insides of a pumpkin. Preacher crumples to the ground and Nate makes sure that he's dead, completely, no chance of coming back. He nods to himself and picks Preacher up. No one has a chance to react, he tosses the body over the side of the boat and we're going fast enough that within seconds I can't even pick out the spot where he went in.

Luca finds his voice first. "What the fuck?"

"What?" Nate asks, looking genuinely surprised that Luca is upset. "Didn't you want me to react faster?" he throws Luca's words from earlier back at him and Luca's face turns ugly with rage as he lunges at Nate; Link and Rafe hold him back and Nate continues talking, unperturbed. "Should I have waited until he turned? Maybe even bitten one of us? What protocol am I supposed to adhere to? Because the rules I'm working with are all about survival. Optimum survival at any cost."

His points are reasonable, which makes it all so much worse somehow. Luca curls his hands into fists and Link and Rafe restrain him more tightly. He's fighting so hard to get to Nate and Nate barely moves, barely reacts, but whatever he does, it suddenly turns him into a predator again, making it obvious that he is ready to fight if he has to.

"You didn't have to do it like that," Elliot blurts out.

"My gun jammed. But it was quick, he was dead before he could feel anything," Nate speaks like this is all oh-so-reasonable and I shudder because he's right, but it's still atrocious, what he did.

"You're nuts. You're fucking nuts!" Luca spits angrily. "They tried to tell me and I didn't listen. But they were right, you are a *follando psico*!"

"Maybe. Probably. But I'll survive this. Will you?" Nate answers simply and while it's not exactly a threat, something about the way he says this, the way he's so damn calm, makes me shudder again and seems to finally get to Mac.

"And what the hell is that supposed to mean?" he shouts, letting go of my hand and stepping forward threateningly. I hear rumbles of agreed intent from the other soldiers.

Nate seems totally unconcerned. "Nothing." He shrugs. "Just that I'll do what I have to, whatever I have to, to survive all of this. Can you say the same?" The tone of his voice when he says "whatever I have to", chills my blood all the way to my core.

"Yes, but I still plan to be able to look at myself in the mirror when this is over," Mac answers, livid.

Nate snorts and wipes his bayonet on his pant-leg, ridding it of Preacher's blood. This seems to be the last straw for the soldiers and they rush him. Link and Rafe let go of Luca and the three of them join the fray. Nate moves so fast, so incredibly fast, I can't believe my eyes. He drops into a crouch and sweeps Link's legs out from under him, the next second he leaps up and slams into Rafe, knocking him flat. His momentum carries him forwards and he quickly rolls back up onto his feet then turns and jumps back into the fight.

He elbows Luca hard in the face and a loud crack precedes the flow of blood by a few seconds. Mac, Marco and Darryl all jump on Nate at the same time, but it doesn't even seem to slow him down. He head butts Darryl in the face, rams his fist into Mac's gut and finally, horribly, pulls out his hunting knife and brings it down towards Mac.

I scream and fumble with one of my pistols, trying to get it free, trying to do something, anything to help. Marco steps in front of Mac at the last second and Nate stabs him in the chest.

As the three of them fall to the ground, Nate yanks the knife out of Marco's chest and as I finally get a shot off, I notice Lia aiming at him, too. Her gun goes off a second after mine and Nate stumbles slightly but keeps moving, crouching slightly to grab his rifle on the way, and then sprinting over to his duffle bag, which he grabs by the handle before launching himself over the side of the boat.

It's all over in minutes, and although Elliot finally screams at Terry to stop the boat, it's not nearly soon enough; Nate is gone. I can't see him anywhere in the vast expanse of the lake. I have no idea whether or not either of us actually hit the bastard, there's so much blood on the deck now, it's impossible to tell who any of it belonged to.

The boat rumbles to a halt and Elliot crouches beside Marco, pressing his hands firmly against the wound in his chest, trying to stop the bleeding. He stops after just a few seconds though when he sees that it's a lost cause.

Marco is dead. Nate must have gotten his heart when he stabbed him. Elliot sits back and brushes his hand over his brow, smearing his face with blood. He shakes his head then starts checking out the people that are still alive. I re-holster my gun and go crouch beside Mac, who's still a bit winded but otherwise none the worse for wear. I can't help but feel glad that Nate stabbed Marco instead of him, even though the thought makes me sick at myself. I kiss Mac's forehead, then move to Elliot's side.

"What can I do?" I ask, wanting to help.

"Check on Rafe, he hasn't moved since Nate knocked him down." He turns back to Darryl and presses some more gauze against his mouth. The poor guy got some teeth knocked out and a wicked gash in his lower lip when Nate head butted him. He wasn't drop dead gorgeous or anything to begin with, but he was nice looking; now, however, with the damage done by Nate today and the carnage left by the zombie yesterday, his face is a Picasso-grade mess.

I head over to Rafe and am relieved to see that he's breathing and has his eyes open. "Are you okay?" I ask as I kneel down beside him.

He groans and starts to sit up. "Don't do that yet!" Elliot commands as he rushes over to us. I glance back at Darryl, who's being looked after by Mac now that he can breathe again. "I need to check on you before you start moving. He hit you really hard."

"Really, Doc? I didn't notice," Rafe growls. Elliot ignores him and performs some checks to see how much damage Nate did. I move over to check on Link and Luca. Lia is already there.

"Link seems fine, but Luca's nose is broken, like, bad," she says as I approach them. Luca mutters something angry in Spanish; it comes out really garbled due to all of the blood that's flowing into his mouth so I can't make it out. Terry is rushing around, fetching supplies for Elliot as he needs them and pretty soon, everyone is standing again.

Except for Marco, of course. I can't stop looking at his body just lying there. Can't stop thinking about how close that came to being Mac.

"Arrgh!" Luca lets out a pained exclamation as Elliot shifts his nose back into place. I'm selfishly grateful for the distraction this provides.

"Sorry. It won't heal pretty, but you'll be able to breathe." Luca waves him off and marches to the back of the boat.

"Where is that piece of *mierda*?" he bellows, bringing his hands down on the side of the boat with a loud thump.

"He's gone, Luke, come on, we have to keep going," Mac says. "He'll drown, there's no way he could swim that far, with all of his equipment."

"*Él es la lefa que su madre debió haber tragado*! Drowning is not enough for what that *escoria* deserves!"

"No, it's not. But we still have to keep going." Luca looks at Mac and nods after a few seconds. Elliot quietly tells Terry to start us moving again. Mac walks back over to me, pausing as he nears Marco's body. He looks down at the prone figure and shakes his head. I don't think I've ever seen anyone look so sad. He continues over to me and pulls me snug against him. I mumble that I'm sorry against his chest. He doesn't say anything, he just presses his lips against my hair and holds me closer.

I hope Nate runs into some underwater zombies and gets torn to pieces before he dies. That's the kind of death he deserves. I press my face against Mac's chest and try not to think about how few of us are left now for the final trek to the lab. Mac is right; all we can do is keep going. There are no other options.

Elliot

I stand beside Terry in the small cabin of the fishing boat we commandeered. In the distance I can just see the first signs of the shore ahead. I'm focusing as hard as I can on that speck of land because if I don't, if I let my mind wander, all I can see is the horror that ensued just minutes ago. The faces of those who died keep vying for attention in my brain, especially Private Cantolena's because he's the one on whom I wished violence just yesterday, for something as petty as the fact that I had feelings for someone who liked him better. It all seems so insignificant now. Of course, it was insignificant then, too, but we still had the luxury of being petty, of not realizing just how bad things were going to get.

"Hey." The voice breaks through my whirlwind of thoughts. Although the fact that the voice belongs to Lia starts my brain down another whirlwind. But after everything that happened today, I just don't have it in me to stay actively angry with her so I drop the silent treatment.

"Hi."

"So...a lot of people just died and even though I always had a feeling that Nate was mental, it's a lot different to actually see him acting like a total psychotic killer and I just..." She pauses and I turn to look at her. Her face is grey and drawn; she looks incredibly tired. "Anyway, I'm sorry for what I said and how I acted. I know you were just trying to help keep me safe and you didn't deserve any of the things I said to you. They weren't true and I'm just...sorry." She looks almost like she's bracing herself, waiting for me to start ignoring her again, but we just had a catastrophic real life example about how there are other, more important things happening right now. And I've never been very good at holding grudges and staying angry anyway.

"Okay."

There's silence for a few beats. "Does that mean 'okay' as in you forgive me, or 'okay' as in you heard me, but are still processing, and are still mad?"

I can't help smiling at her, although I wouldn't be surprised if it comes out more like a grimace, with my injured face. "We're cool. I forgive you." I pause then ask, "Can I ask you something that might annoy you?"

Lia looks at me warily then says, "Okay..." like she's not really sure she wants to be agreeing. And maybe I shouldn't be asking since we only just made up, but I want to know and after everything that just happened, I'm taking a "what the hell" stance on it.

"Why did you kiss Sergeant Ortiz yesterday?" Lia's eyebrows shoot up, either because she's surprised by the question itself or because she's surprised that this is the question that I chose to ask.

"Sometimes I just angry make-out with people," she answers after a few seconds.

"You could angry make-out with me if you wanted," I offer before I really think about what I'm saying.

"You're not the type of guy I'd do that with."

"Oh." I feel strangely disappointed by this. "What type of guy am I?" I have to ask.

Lia takes a deep breath as she contemplates the question. She takes so long to reply that I start to get worried that she just won't answer. Finally, she says, "You're the type of guy I could see myself happy making-out with. Just not right now. There's a lot going on here that we need to deal with first before I could happy make-out with someone."

"Oh, right," I say, trying to appear casual and not let my elation show through. She's right, this is hardly the time. "Good."

"Good," she repeats. Then she asks, "So...what can we expect when we get to the lab?"

I make the decision to put the very attractive idea of kissing her out of my mind until our lives are no longer in danger and re-focus on the tasks at hand. "Good question. I guess I should address everybody at once, eh? To make sure everyone is prepared. Terry, stop the boat for a few minutes, please." Terry brings the boat to a halt and we walk out of the cabin. I silently survey the people that we have left for a few moments. Sergeant Ortiz is sitting beside Private Cantolena's body, his head in his hands. Master Corporal Kane, Corporal Donahue, and Master Corporal Cho are sitting side by side at the back of the boat, not saying anything. Mac and Lucy are standing off to one side and they have their arms wrapped tightly around one another.

"Excuse me, can I have everyone's attention, please." One by one everyone looks up at me. "Lia reminded me that I haven't really told you what you should be expecting when we get to the lab. For one thing, as I said at the fort, it will be colder there because the lab itself is a ways up the side of the mountain and we will be quite a bit farther north. For another thing, it's likely we won't encounter any of the undead until we are at the lab because it was shut down tight for emergency protocols when we left, so none of those inside will have been able to get outside.

"This is both good and bad. It's good, because we won't have to worry about attacks from zombies until we reach the lab. It's bad because once we reach the lab, we will be faced with over a hundred trapped zombies in an enclosed space." Everyone is quiet for a few moments as they consider what I said.

"Hey, Doc, I wanted to ask you something," Mac pipes up, disentangling himself some from Lucy so that he can speak to me more easily. I nod at him and he continues, "Do you have any theories for why the zombies are starting to act differently?"

"How do you mean?"

"Their movements are different—slower and jerkier. And they smell different."

"They smell different how?"

"Well, they always smelled terrible, like dead things, you know, but now they smell a little worse and it's different, more intense. They smell more like rot."

"I would say then that they are decomposing, which makes sense. Rigor mortis is setting in—it seems to occur more slowly in them than is normal for one who is simply dead, which I would suppose is a side-effect of the reanimation process, regardless, they do seem to be deteriorating more the longer they are undead. By that logic, the ones in the lab will most likely be quite rotted and deteriorated because they have been dead for almost three days now."

"What does that mean for us?" Sergeant Ortiz asks as he finally stands back up, his soldier's instincts taking over again as the prospect of battle draws near.

"It's likely to be a good thing because the zombies will have slower reflexes and move more slowly overall; more like the classic movie zombies than the new version of movie zombies, for example."

"So, we're talking the original *Night of the Living Dead* rather than, say, *Zombieland* yeah?" Lucy asks.

"Most likely, but I won't know for sure how the zombies will have reacted to decomposition until we get there." No one has any more questions so I ask Terry to get the boat moving again.

We're almost at the shore when Sergeant Ortiz comes up to where I'm standing with Lia, Lucy, and Mac. "You said there probably won't be any zombies on this side of the lake? Not till we get to the lab?"

"That's right. I can think of no scenarios where there would be any."

"Then I would like to take some time after we dock to bury Marco and pay our respects to him and the others we've lost so far."

"Of course," I say.

"Good idea, Luke," Mac says and Sergeant Ortiz nods then walks away. I look at Lucy, who has a curious look on her face.

"There's no chance of Marco turning, right?" she asks.

"No. He wasn't bitten and the infection doesn't seem to be airborne."

"Good. 'Cause having to decapitate him would put a damper on the funeral a bit." I can't help raising my eyebrows at this flippant statement. "Sorry, I use humour when I'm upset." I smile sympathetically at her and Mac tightens the arm he has around her shoulder. There's a sudden jolt as Terry steers the boat close to the rocky shore and I reach out a hand to steady a stumbling Lia.

"Thanks," she says, smiling as well as could be expected given the situation.

There's no great way to get off of the boat so people take different routes. Lucy and Lia jump off the bow with Mac's help and I follow them down with Terry's help. Master Corporal Kane, Corporal Donahue, Master Corporal Cho, and Sergeant Ortiz all work together to lower Private Cantolena's body down to the ground as respectfully as possible. Terry helps me clean as much of the blood as we can off Private Cantolena, as the others scout for a good burial spot. My knees are starting to ache from kneeling on the uneven rocks of the shore.

Lia comes back out of the woods into which the others disappeared. "We found a good spot. Is he ready?"

I say that he is and Terry picks him gingerly up, as though he might hurt him. I grab the random stuff I gathered on the boat to dig the grave. There's only one actual shovel—a folding one from the emergency kit—the rest of my find is made up of scraping tools, ice scoops from the fish freezer, and basically whatever else I could find that looked like it might be useful.

Clutching the tools awkwardly to my chest, I follow Terry into the brush. Lia falls into step beside me and takes some of the tools so I don't drop any. She seems to just want to be near me now that I'm not ignoring her anymore. I'm not complaining, it's nice to have her be friendly again.

We reach the others in a small clearing just as Terry sets Private Cantolena's body down on the ground as gently as he picked it up. Lia and I hand out the implements and everyone starts digging. No one talks while we work and the eerie silence of the woods seems to settle into my bones. It's difficult work thanks to the semi-hard ground and the random tools, so even with all of the muscle going into it, and it takes us about an hour to finish. The remaining soldiers work together to lower Private Cantolena respectfully into the grave.

Once he's in, Sergeant Ortiz clears his throat and starts to speak. "I'm not the best at speeches and these men should have better than what we can give. Much better. Once we get out of here, we'll make sure they get a proper military send-off, like they deserve, but until then, let me just say that none of them deserved to go like that." He pauses. "Not even Daphne. Let's have a moment of silence for those we lost today."

We fall into silence to pay our respects to everyone who died. Without any zombie screeches to break the quiet, the moment is indeed silent, for the first time in what feels like a much longer time than it's actually been. All I can hear is everyone breathing and the occasional sniffle; the forest seems oppressively hushed.

When the moment is over, Sergeant Ortiz clears his throat again and says, "Now, pray to whatever gods you keep that their souls are no longer suffering and that we find that mother fucker Nate alive, so we can send him to hell like *he* deserves."

There's a collective, intense "Amen" from the group and then the soldiers start piling dirt on Private Cantolena's body. The rest of us stand back so that they can bury their comrade in peace. They finish burying him and Mac wipes the back of his hand across his eyes. Lucy steps forward with some stones she must have collected from the beach and she places one on top of Private Cantolena's grave, then places four other stones in a line beside his, symbolically marking the graves of Daphne, Corporal Halley, Corporal Church, and Private Cooke, as well. She stands up and steps closer to Mac, taking his hand; he smiles half-heartedly at her, his gaze drifting back to the gravestones.

"Okay, Doc, let's get to that lab," Sergeant Ortiz says. I nod and Terry hands me a map and a compass. I find our rocky beach on the map and with help from the compass, start heading in the direction of the lab. Terry walks on one side of me, Lia on the other. Lucy and Mac walk behind us, then Corporal Donahue, Master Corporal Kane, and Master Corporal Cho fall into step behind them, with Sergeant Ortiz taking up the rear.

I don't know exactly what we'll find at the lab, all I know is that I'm not alone in praying that this nightmare is over soon.

Chapter Twelve
Cue *The Twilight Zone* theme music

Nate

The water is cold, above freezing, but very fucking cold. I've been in colder, thanks to training with Father, but it's not a temperature I want to stay in for longer than I have to, especially with two bullet wounds to deal with—though the cold water is at least slowing the bleeding. And luckily both of them were just grazing shots, but they still complicate things more than I'd like.

I tread water for a few minutes, getting my bearings and ignoring the stinging pain in my left arm and shoulder like I was taught to do. My pack is slung across my back; the extra weight is annoying, but it's nothing I haven't dealt with before. I'm a strong swimmer so it's easy enough to ignore. My SKS is slung across my shoulders, too. It's a very resilient gun so the water won't damage it, fortunately—it's one of my favourites. I still have my hunting knife in hand just in case there's anything in the water that decides to get friendly with me.

As I swim, I think about how the boat ride across the lake ended. Or, how it ended for me anyway. I'm not bothered by how it turned out; I was planning on breaking away from them sooner or later because they are obviously not playing for optimum survival and that's my constant goal above all else. So the fact that I broke from them sooner rather than later doesn't make much difference. My only regret is that I had to kill Marco instead of Mac. Marco was nothing. He was inconsequential and no threat to me. But Mac is an annoyance.

No matter. Once I catch up with them at the lab, I'll be free to do whatever I want—there's no doubt in my mind that they'll be easy pickings.

It's surprising that killing Locklan and Marco hasn't really affected me. Considering that they were the first real people I killed—not counting zombies, of course, because they're *zombies*—since my father had to die. But the feeling is never wrong and the instincts of my body are not something to be ignored. That's what he always taught me and it's never steered me wrong. Following my instincts and responding to the feeling allowed me the distinct pleasure of killing that blight upon the earth, Daffy, and that's proof enough for me that I am following the right path. It's just too bad that she was a zombie when I killed her, it would have been so much more enjoyable if she'd still been human.

The swim takes a while, longer than it normally would if I weren't injured and weighed down, which serves to keep my anger bubbling at the surface and stokes my determination. I'm not sure how far ahead of me they are by the time I finally make it to the little stretch of rocky beach they were planning on docking at. The presence of the boat confirms that they didn't change course.

After untying the boat from where they had it anchored and shoving it out into deeper water, I take a few minutes to catch my breath and empty my pack. It has a waterproof lining, but I need to check everything out, just in case, since it was submerged under water. Besides, I could use some water and some food. I take a few swigs from my canteen and eat a granola bar luckily kept dry by the wrapper.

Once I'm sated, I check out the rest of my supplies. My clothes are moist and I squeeze them, draining the water as much as possible. My sleeping bag can wait until later. I can't do much for my wounds right now, I need a mirror to be able to really see how much damage was done so I just wrap a damp shirt around my upper arm and tie it tight, slowing the blood loss further. My shoulder will have to wait.

My tools and extra weapons made it through okay for the most part, my electronic stuff is all waterproof, so there's barely any damage to my equipment, but my pistols are now useless. Luckily, I keep the ammo and cleaning kit for my SKS in a watertight case, so not having the pistols anymore isn't much of a loss. I throw them into the lake, since they won't do me any good there's no sense in keeping them and it's never smart to leave evidence of your presence if you're on the hunt and want to keep a low profile.

My duffle emptied of the unnecessary detritus and repacked, I set to cleaning my SKS. When I've made sure that it's undamaged,

I reload it with ten rounds from a stripper clip and head out after the others.

I've only walked a little way into the forest when I come upon a clearing with what looks like a fresh gravesite and memorial gravestones...a stupid gesture for people who didn't earn the right to be commemorated in any way. It just goes to show that the others will not be much of a threat; they're too soft and emotional. And tracking them will be beyond easy; they obviously didn't even bother trying to cover their trail.

Bad move; don't they know they're being hunted?

Connor

This hike feels interminably long. Partly because it is actually a pretty long trek, of course, but the goddamn silence makes it feel so much worse. No one is saying anything; we're all just following Elliot mutely as though none of us has anything to talk about. I can't stand this silence. It's getting under my skin and making me more and more tense. Not even Lucy's hand clasped tightly in mine is enough to keep me grounded. It's not enough to keep those memories at bay. I keep seeing flashes of everyone who died on that boat. My brain just won't stop running the images across my eyelids. I can't keep walking in this godforsaken silence. Even some zombie shrieks would be welcome at this point, just something to break up the quiet where the only sounds come from the brush we disturb as we navigate through the forest.

We need to talk about something, anything. I need the distraction and I'm sure the others could use one, too. I repeat this sentiment aloud and Link says, "I hear you, man, but what are we supposed to talk about? 'Cause I'm betting we all have similar things on the brain and I'm also betting none of us wanna be talkin' about any of those things."

"So let's talk about something else, anything else. Something stupid, inconsequential. Just anything. It's too goddamn quiet, and I can't stand it."

"Now would be a good time for a break anyway, we're about halfway there," Elliot says as he comes to a halt. We all stop walking behind him and take up positions in a rough circle, sitting on fallen tree trunks or the ground. We refuel with protein bars and water and everyone looks at me sort of expectantly. I don't want us descending into that awful quiet again so I say the first thing that pops into my mind that doesn't have to do with zombies or Nate.

"My aunt Nettie is a klepto." Everyone stares blankly at me. I figure at least it's a decent distraction, so I keep talking. "She's been at it since forever, can't seem to stop herself. My mom's given up trying to make her stop, so every time Aunt Nettie comes over, my mom hides all her knick knacks and puts out stuff she thinks would look good in my aunt's house. She's been decorating it for years." There's a sort of stunned silence and then Lia lets out a laugh.

"My mom still wants me to ask for her permission every time I go out of town and I haven't lived at home since I was seventeen," she says.

"My mom calls me chickadee," Terry says.

"My brother once tried to skateboard with rollerblades on," Lucy contributes.

"The movie *E.T.* scared the bejesus out of me as a child; that part where he says, 'Elliot'...it gave me nightmares for years," Elliot says.

"My grandma insists that our toaster is haunted...our toaster!" Link adds.

"My little sister refuses to accept that Pluto isn't a real planet anymore. It was always her favourite," says Rafe.

"My wife thinks that 'irregardless' is a real word and that Apple is at the head of a conspiracy to get the entire world addicted to technology," Darryl puts in, smiling, then wincing as the movement stretches all of his numerous facial injuries. Poor Maria is gonna have a heart attack when she sees his face again.

If she sees his face again...no, can't think like that.

I look at Luca, hoping he'll add a little story, too, to distract me again. He's quiet for a beat and then, grinning, he says, "My father used to swear up and down that he almost caught Bigfoot once."

"Carl swore he saw a yeti in the mountains when he was a kid," Darryl says, seemingly without thinking about it. He drops his eyes and puts his head in his hands.

"Jimmy carried a lucky rabbit's foot everywhere," Rafe adds in a quiet voice.

I can't help myself. "Marco was afraid of rabbits ever since he saw *Monty Python and the Holy Grail* as a kid. And Preach said that movie was blasphemous but he knew every single line."

"Gates knew all the moves to the Macarena," Link says, laughing for a second before dropping silent again.

"Daffy thought that veganism carried over even if you were turned into a zombie," Lucy says, smiling and shaking her head.

"We should start walking again," Luca asserts suddenly. But after a second, he softens this abruptness by saying, "We can keep talking as we go."

So Elliot resumes the lead as we all fall in around or behind him and we start off again, but this time it's better because it's peppered here and there with more quirky anecdotes about someone's family, such as Lia's admission that her dad is an unabashed believer in UFOs or my confession about how me and my cousin Kato used to constantly search for buried treasure when we were kids. There are also more reminiscences about the people who've died: "Carl always said that he could tell when it was going to snow, that he could feel it in his elbows," remembers Darryl. Or sometimes just random stuff people admit about themselves, like Lucy saying, "I literally cannot wash my face without thinking someone or something is going to be coming up behind me and will be there when I open my eyes. Same thing if I close my eyes in the shower...it's ridiculous." The random flow of the conversation seems to make this leg of the journey go a lot faster than the first one and before I know it, we're there.

A two-storey building seems just to appear out of the blue, even though we've been hiking up the side of a mountain for about two hours to get to it.

"This is the lab? The infamous lab where this whole thing started?" Lia asks, incredulous. "Shouldn't it look more sinister?"

It does look pretty innocuous, minus the remote location.

"Remember, a lot of times in horror movies, the more innocent something looks, the worse it is," Lucy says.

"You know that we're not actually *in* a horror movie, right?" Lia asks teasingly and Lucy swats at her, saying, "You know what I mean."

"There's more to this place than meets the eye," Elliot puts in as we draw nearer to the plain grey building. "There's four subterranean levels where the more secretive stuff goes on, testing and the like. That's also where the more...priority people live. The floors you can see house departments like administration and security, that kind of thing."

"Subterranean floors? Definitely getting a more sinister vibe now," Lia says and Lucy rolls her eyes. We approach the door, which looks as innocuous as the rest of the building; it's just a plain white door, no bars or nothing.

"Wow, not too worried about security up here, I guess," I say and Elliot looks at me, one eyebrow raised in a question. "The door doesn't even have that great of a lock on it."

"It's more secure than it seems. That door actually has a steel core and you can't get inside without knowing the code."

"I can't even see a keypad."

"It's hidden."

"Geez, what were you guys making in here?" Lucy asks then says, "Oh, right, zombies."

"That was an accident," Elliot mutters, frowning. He steps up to the door and places his palm flat right above the handle. After a second, a hidden panel slides open and a keypad is now visible. Link whistles and says, "Fancy," under his breath. Elliot turns around and says, "Now, we don't know what to expect when I open this door so everyone be on your guard." Everyone readies his or her weapon of choice and Elliot punches in the code. There's a small click and he reaches for the handle, takes a deep breath and opens the door.

The door falls open away from us and...nothing happens, except that we can now hear an awful screeching noise that for once doesn't belong to zombies, but rather to a very loud and grating alarm. Coupled with the alarm are some red-hued emergency lights alternating with pitch blackness. We all look around at each other and then back at the empty doorway leading into the gloomy interior.

Cue *The Twilight Zone* theme music.

"Dark," Lucy says.

"Yeah," I agree.

"So, the lights?" Lia asks and Elliot glances at her.

"The emergency lights of the alarm that triggered the building going into lockdown."

"Oh good, 'cause this definitely wasn't creepy enough before we had to go into the shadowy abyss with ominous red lighting!" Lucy practically shouts.

"*Cállate*, if there's something in there it will hear you," Luca commands.

"'Kay, first of all, I highly doubt they could hear me over that alarm and second of all, if there were zombies in there, they probably would have made themselves known by now considering they'd be attracted to the movement of the door opening and the smell of us," Lucy defends herself.

Luca frowns slightly but nods his head in acquiescence. "Good point. *Bueno*, this room is likely clear but we'll do a sweep of it just in case before you civs go in."

"It's strange that there seems to be no one in there," Elliot says, "there are so many employees."

"Would people have gone home for the long weekend?" Lucy asks.

Terry and Elliot gaze slack-jawed at her. "It's a long weekend?" Elliot asks. Lia confirms that it is and a look of massive relief comes over Elliot's face; he looks happier than he has in days. "With the end of the project coming up I've been living here full-time, so I completely forgot. Thank God."

"What does the long weekend have to do with anything?" Luca asks, looking impatient to get on with the sweep.

"We would've had just a skeleton crew in attendance: a few administrators, some security and the few doctors and technicians that were working on projects. This means that there will be a lot fewer zombies to contend with and, actually, with the building on total lockdown like this, it's not out of the realm of possibility that we'll even find survivors." Elliot grins at the thought and Lia smiles at him. Good to see those two have made up; they were both sulking pretty bad about it all.

"*Buenas noticias.* Regardless, we'll do a sweep before you civs enter." Luca ignores a protest from Lia and orders Alpha formation and it's easy to slide back into soldier mode.

Still, even knowing there's probably no zombies inside, it's hard to look into the gaping maw of the doorway and see the pulsing red lights beyond and not feel a tingle of dread at the menacing sight.

Our formation is modified from its usual form now that our unit has been halved. Luca and me take point with Link and Darryl in the middle and Rafe at our six. We walk slowly into the darkened room, partly because it's S.O.P. not to go rushing into places with unknown factors and partly because the alternating lightness of the room—one second bathed in that eerie red light and the next pitched into total blackness again—is disorienting.

"NVGs everyone," Luca orders and one by one we put on our night vision goggles. We don't all do it at the same time because we can't take the chance of being caught off guard. Once my NVGs are in place, I'm less discombobulated but the grainy-green wash they give the room combined with the continually pulsating lights doesn't really do away with the forbidding aura the room has.

I glance around the large room, which I think would normally be pretty airy, but the numerous windows are shut tight behind metal shutters. Not much point in a total lockdown if people can just get in or out via the windows, I guess.

Luca gives his orders for the sweep and him and me take one side, Darryl and Link take another and Rafe continues up the middle of the room. It doesn't take long for us to confirm that the room is empty and that the doors leading away from the reception area are locked. I hope Elliot has keys or this mission is gonna get even more complicated than it already is.

We head back outside and the day seems overly bright as I remove my NVGs, though it is a relief to be farther away from the jarring sound of the alarm. That thing is annoying as all get out.

"All clear?" Elliot asks.

"*Sí*, it's clear, but everything is locked up, we can't get past the reception area. And it would be better if we could get that alarm turned off and the lights back to normal. Do you know how to do that?" Luca asks.

"Between Terry and me, we should be able to override the lockdown, but we'll need to get to the second floor to do so, because that's where the security offices are located."

"How do we get past all the locked doors?" Lia asks.

"I have a master key. It's how I got the Doc out Friday morning," Terry answers.

"Alright then. Let's do this thing," Lucy says, gripping her machete in one hand and a flashlight in the other.

I feel myself grinning at the fierce look on her face. Her attitude is infectious and everyone voices their agreement. It's time to get this show on the road.

Lia

"Booyah," I say, agreeing with Lucy and grasping my axe handle tightly to help psych myself up further.

"Hold up," Luca says abruptly as he holds up his hands to reinforce this command. "You civs aren't coming with us; it's too dangerous."

Pompous ass.

"You expect Lucy and me to just sit on our asses and wait out here for you boys like good little girls? That would be a no."

"A hell no," Lucy adds, "especially since there's the possibility of Nate still being out there somewhere. Not to mention, have you ever seen a horror movie? There is no way in hell we're splitting up now. This would be the part in the movie where more characters bite it, so we're certainly not going to help it along by splitting up. That's an amateur mistake."

"You know, *chica*, I think you could use a reality check," Luca intones harshly and Mac opens his mouth, maybe to defend Lucy, but I beat him to it.

"Shut the hell up, you pompous ass, she has a point. And besides, we're not your soldiers, you have absolutely no authority over us, so you can say 'no' till you're blue in the fucking face, but it doesn't matter because we're coming with you." I can tell how just much he annoys me because I'm defending Lucy so stridently even though I've said the same thing to her on numerous occasions. But he really drives me up the fucking wall. And anyway, she *is* right, splitting up never leads to anything good.

Luca growls unintelligibly and Mac pats him on the shoulder saying, "Come on, Luke, we'll need all the help we can get in there; even if there's fewer zeds than we originally thought, there's still gonna be enough to cause trouble. Besides, they've more than proven themselves to be assets in a fight, not liabilities."

That boy continues to grow on me all the time.

Luca mutters something in Spanish, clearly unimpressed with the lack of blind acceptance of his orders. I could not care less...and actually, it's more fun when he's annoyed, so this works out perfectly.

"Come on, come on, let's go already!" Lucy barks and she walks past Luca and heads into the building.

I'm about to follow her when Elliot suddenly asks, "Did you hear that?"

"What?" I answer. "I can't hear much of anything over that horrible alarm." I follow his gaze and run my eyes around the edge of the clearing, looking into the depths of the forest. I don't see anything amiss. It's all as still as it was when we were trekking through it earlier.

"Nothing, I guess, let's go," Elliot says, although he sounds unsure. But then he gives me a quick smile and follows the others into the lab without another glance at the forest behind us. I take one more look around then follow suit, shutting the door behind me just in case. I take a second to get my bearings; the lighting is quite disconcerting. I lock onto the beam of Lucy's flashlight, following it like a spotlight over to where she's standing on the opposite side of the room. As Elliot and I bring up the rear, Terry pulls out a key card and slides it into the lock. Once he opens the door, the soldiers raise their guns and aim them into the empty hallway. Luca and Mac take the lead with Terry sandwiched between them. Lucy and I take a place in the back of the group with Elliot and Luca sends Rafe back to get into position behind us.

"Kind of anticlimactic so far, eh?" I say to Lucy and she nods.

"Still creepy though," she adds, gazing around the shadowy hallway and looking displeased.

"No kidding," I agree, trying not to focus on how the sound of the alarm mixed with the emergency lighting is making me disoriented. Terry opens the next door at the end of the hallway and Lucy mutters something that's lost in a wave of alarm bells.

"What?" I ask.

"I said, 'oh great and now there's an empty stairwell involved...'cause that never turns out badly," she repeats.

"You know, you probably should try to watch fewer horror movies when we get home," I can't help teasing.

"I'm just saying," she growls while we follow the others inside the admittedly sinister looking stairwell.

"Whoa, stop," Elliot says suddenly, coming to an abrupt standstill and putting his arms out so we have no choice but to stop with him.

"What is it, Doc?" Rafe asks, coming up close behind us.

"Can't you hear that?"

"The alarm? Yeah, it's pretty annoying," Lucy says, deadpan.

"I don't mean the alarm!" Elliot all but snaps. "Aren't you ever serious?"

"Hey!" I interject, ready to defend her, but she cuts me off with a wave of her hand.

"It's fine. I'm sorry, Elliot. Like I said, I joke when I'm stressed...or when I'm not...it's just a pervasive type of thing, really. What sound did you mean?"

"Just listen in between the blasts from the alarm." A moment of silence ensues in the intermittence of the alarms and I hear what caught Elliot's attention just as the smell hits me: the smell of rot and death, decay and putrefaction. That smell coupled with the sounds—some scraping noises followed by a sort-of wet, cracking sound that I can't adequately describe—makes all the little hairs on the back of my neck stand up. The alarm blares again and as one, Elliot, Rafe, Lucy and I turn to face the stairs that descend into the depths of the building since the sounds seem to be coming from that direction.

Everything goes dark for a second just as the alarm goes quiet again and in that darkness and silence, a sound comes from not far in front of us. In the weak illumination of Lucy's flashlight, a slimy-looking, green tinged hand comes into view. The red lights flash back on and more of the zombie comes into shadowed focus.

It's pulling itself up the stairs, each movement looking arduous and pained. Its joints creak wetly with the effort and there's a squishing sound as it slides across the floor dragging itself closer to us. Its mouth cracks open almost in stages, a scritching sound accompanying each sequential movement of its jaws. It lets out something like the shrieks we're used to and yet wholly dissimilar from the shrieks we're used to. It's a rough sound, raspier and harsher than the others we've heard, like it takes more work to utter the noise. There's also a wetness behind the rasping and as it attempts to shriek at us, blackish ooze drips down its chin.

Rafe moves first, stepping around us and letting a shot loose into the middle of its forehead. With the close range and what I would guess are hollow point bullets, there's no question about whether or not he's successful in his kill. Brains and more of the black goo spatter the landing and us in pretty much equal measure.

"Blech!" Lucy says, stepping back in reaction even though it's too late for this to have any effect on the amount of splatter she's covered in. I wipe a dollop of something wet off my cheek and look up as the others come running down the stairs. Mac slips in a puddle of zombie gunk but catches himself with the railing.

"What the fuck? What happened to you guys? We turned around and you were gone and then we heard a shot..." he trails off as his attention is commandeered by the ruined face of the zombie at the foot of the stairs. "Are you okay?" he asks, his attention focused solely on Lucy. She assures him that she is.

"The rest of us are fine, too. Thanks for asking," I can't help snarking, though it's mostly due to residual fear from the unexpected zombie rather than actual annoyance with Mac.

"Sorry, I did mean everyone. Are there any more?" he asks, changing the subject and sticking his head cautiously around the corner of the stairwell, gun raised. "Doesn't look like it," he asserts after a second. "Come on." He starts to head back up the stairs but Link's voice stops him.

"Should we make sure there aren't any others?"

"Later. After the alarm is turned off it will be easier to find them without them finding us first," Luca declares. I actually agree with him for once, which is almost as uncomfortable a feeling as the feel of some remnants of the zombie splatter sliding down my chest and getting lodged in my bra.

That's great, just fucking excellent. I can't wait till we've killed all these monsters. I'm so tired of being smeared with gore.

We trot up the stairs and, after two flights, we hit the top floor and Terry pulls out his magic key again. We walk through into a medium sized ante-room and Terry turns to open a door to our left. This next room is large and has a wall of TV screens as well as a row of desks with computers on top.

It smells pretty nasty in here, the question of why being answered when we suddenly hear "Who's there?" in a voice that comes from the far side of the room and we all raise our weapons in response. Except for Terry, who jogs across the room and says, "Benji!" in a happy voice when he sees the person who spoke. Elliot is close behind him once he recognizes the haggard looking guy—I'm sure looking dramatically worse due to the harshness of the red lights—who is pulled into a tight hug by Terry. It seems safe, so the rest of us lower our weapons and cross the room to join them.

"What the hell is going on?" the guy asks once Terry releases him, his voice raspy and tired. "I've been trapped up here for almost three days! No food or water. Nothing." And no bathroom. Immediately Elliot reaches into his bag and pulls out a bottle of water and a protein bar.

"We'll explain in a minute, you need to drink and eat—in that order. I know it's hard but you need to pace yourself or you'll get sick," Elliot coaches the guy, Benji, through refuelling himself and Terry claps Benji once more on the back before turning to the massive computer monitor that's situated in front of the TV wall. He takes something from around his neck and inserts it into the tower; the screen of the monitor suddenly comes to life and he keys in a password. We gather around Terry as Elliot informs Benji of what's been going on, going through the whole "Zombies. Zombies? Yes, zombies," thing that we've all been through before.

"Doc, I need your authentication here," Terry calls and Elliot and Benji join us. Benji still looks pretty dazed; I do not blame him, after being trapped for three days without food or water with those flashing lights and the horrible alarm blaring, I'm surprised he's not climbing the walls by now.

Elliot leans over Terry's shoulder and types something into the computer. "This isn't the normal security protocol for a lockdown is it?" he asks when he's finished and Terry takes over again.

"No, Doc, it sure ain't. I have no idea what that crazy old Brit did, but he implemented a whole lot of overrides to the protocols."

"Like what?"

"Like, he made it so there was no warning before the lockdown took effect. There's supposed to be a minute of emergency warnings so people have a chance to get out, but he made it so the lockdown happened immediately after the emergency alarm was tripped."

"Why would he do that?" Elliot asks, incredulous. "And *how* would he do that?"

"Your guess is as good as mine, Doc. All I know is it's gonna make things tougher than I originally thought."

"Can you still turn off the alarm?" Luca asks.

"I think so." A semi-hysterical noise erupts from Benji and he sinks to the floor. Elliot crouches beside him and starts talking. Between the alarm and his low tone, I can't hear what he's saying, but it seems to calm Benji at least a little. I'm so focused on them that I can't suppress a surprised noise when the alarm suddenly goes quiet and the emergency lights are replaced with the normal fluorescence you expect to find in office buildings. Benji lets out a grateful sounding sob and buries his head in his arms.

"I'll need your password again to work on reversing the lockdown now, Doc."

"That's weird. You're head of security, shouldn't yours be enough?" Elliot asks as he pats Benji on a shuddering shoulder and stands up to type his password again.

"Yeah, it should be. Like I said, I have no clue what that deranged fuck did or why, all I can tell you is he didn't want anyone turning off the alarm or reversing the lockdown. It's a good thing your security clearance is as high as his or we'd be up shit creek for sure." Terry continues to type furiously for the next few minutes, with Elliot assisting occasionally.

Benji finally starts to calm down in the continuing silence and fixed lighting and although he's still sitting on the floor, he's no longer crying; he just sips his water occasionally and takes deep breaths.

Suddenly, a promising sounding beep is emitted from the computer's speakers and the metal shutters on the windows roll up slowly, letting in sunlight. There's a faint click from the two doors in the room and all of a sudden Benji bolts, running for the door closest to us. He whips it open and he's gone before anyone has a chance to react.

"Shit!" Terry growls in delayed reaction. He stands and turns to go after him, but Luca grabs his arm. "We don't have time to go running after him; he'll be fine. Anyone would at least need fresh air after being trapped in here with that alarm going for as long as he was." Terry nods, though it's reluctant. He sits back down in front of the computer and starts typing again.

"What are you doing now?" I ask curiously.

"Trying to get the security cameras up and running again, they would really help with hunting the zombies and planning our route to the doc's lab."

"No kidding."

About thirty seconds later, Terry swears and smacks the desktop with the flat of his hand.

"*Qué pasó?*" Luca asks, startled into using Spanish.

"That demented old bastard," Terry growls.

"What happened?" Luca asks more insistently and in English.

"He did something to the security cam system. There's some sort of virus there. There's no way I can get them working again."

"Fuck," Mac breathes.

I'm sure we're all thinking it. I know I am.

The door that Benji made his dramatic exit through opens unexpectedly and most of the group turns with weapons raised, in case it's something or someone that poses a threat. I'm half-expecting it to be Benji, but instead, it's three exhausted and scared-looking people—a guy and a girl about my age dressed in rumpled work clothes and an older gentleman dressed in janitorial coveralls.

"Doctor Frink?" the young guy says, his voice hesitant in his disbelief.

"AJ, Amy, John, thank goodness you're alright!" Elliot says happily.

"What's going on?" Amy asks, her voice tremulous. They look dazed like Benji did but not quite as wrecked, which is soon explained by the fact that they were trapped in the break room so at least they had food and water and access to a bathroom.

"I'm just glad you guys are all okay," Elliot says after they tell us about their ordeal.

"That's an optimistic take," the older guy, John, says, "but we're alive anyway. Now, can you tell us what's going on, Doctor Frink? We've gone through hell the last few days and we could really use some good news."

Elliot's face takes on a pained expression. "We don't exactly come bearing good news. Something...happened during a round of testing. Something dangerous."

"I knew working in a place like this would come back to bite me in the ass!" AJ exclaims. "What the hell happened?"

"Well..." Elliot begins but stops at Luca's warning noise. Elliot glances back at him and Luca shakes his head slowly.

Ugh, what a dictator.

"Um, just a second," Elliot says then steps back beside Luca. "What?" he whispers.

"Think about what just happened with that guard. I am sick and tired of *chingado* civs running around making my life more difficult. Them knowing what's going on will only make things more complicated."

"We can't just leave them to their own devices, not after everything they've been through."

"What do you suggest then, that we take them with us?"

"What else can we do?" When Luca looks like he's going to get particularly obstinate, Elliot re-evaluates and instead of appealing to his humanity, he goes for threatening him and his mission. "Look, you can't get the cure without me and I'm not leaving them here." He crosses his arms and stares Luca down the best he can, which he surprisingly does quite well, something that I also surprisingly find quite hot.

Luca makes a choking rage-filled noise and barks, "Fine. Do whatever the fuck you want, but if these *putas* get in my way and fuck with my mission, I can't guarantee their safety." He turns on his heel toward the door we came through and stalks off through it without another word.

What a baby. He obviously just expects us to follow him without question so he throws a tantrum if anyone dares to disobey him. Seriously, what an ass...on the other hand what an *ass*; it is a seriously good view, watching him walk away.

"What's going on?" Amy whines, her voice verging on hysterical now, as the other soldiers follow in Luca's footsteps. Elliot looks distressed but not sorry about standing up to Luca.

"It's probably better if we just show them. That seems to be a bit more effective at getting the point across more efficiently," Lucy says, leaning towards him.

Elliot nods in reply then addresses the others, "I'm sorry. All I can tell you right now is that there's something dangerous going on. It would be best if we could just show you—"

"Show us?" AJ yelps. "You tell us 'there's something dangerous going on' and we're just supposed to come with you like it's no big deal? Without even knowing what we're walking into. No. Hell no!"

Elliot looks even more distressed and like maybe he wishes he'd listened to Luca.

I don't blame him. Luca drives me crazy and I always enjoy disagreeing with him but he might have had a point this time. Still, I guess Elliot's probably right, we can't just leave them here.

I step up beside him and squeeze his arm; he shoots me a grim smile of thanks. I lean into him and say, "Go smooth things over with Luca, we'll calm them down." His smile turns more grateful and he pats my hand then walks out of the room.

I know it's not the time for such thoughts but I can't help noticing with some surprise that Elliot has quite a nice rear view of his own.

Once he's gone, it's just Terry, Lucy and me alone with Amy, AJ, and John. I look at Lucy and she nods at me. Before I can say anything though, Terry clears his throat and says, "Look, guys, with this thing, it's really best if we stick together."

"Just tell us what's going on first, Terry," AJ demands, his voice condescending.

"You're not considering going with them are you?" Amy screeches.

Man, this girl is actually making me miss Daffy, at least she was so dumb she pretty much just followed along without asking questions.

"What exactly do you suggest we do instead, Amy?" John asks brusquely. Amy pulls an ugly face but doesn't answer.

"Look, it'll make more sense if you see it for yourselves. There's danger, but we can protect you, although only if you come with us and do what we say," Lucy says calmly.

Amy doesn't argue, but now AJ pulls an ugly face of his own and says mulishly, "*You're* going to protect us?" He pointedly looks both me and Lucy up and down to demonstrate his disbelief of this statement. Lucy's expression goes from calming to seriously pissed off in just a few seconds, and I feel the expression on my own face match hers. I try to remind myself that Elliot obviously wants them to stay alive so he'd probably be upset if I killed AJ right now, which is really a shame.

"Bottom line, man, you really wanna stay here by yourself when you don't know what's going on out there?" Terry asks.

AJ seems to mull this over for a few moments before he finally says, "Fine. But I will be expecting compensation from the company for all I've gone through." Amy voices her agreement, though she still sounds close to giving in to hysteria, she seems to be clinging to AJ's arguments as a way to keep her grip on her obviously fragile mental state; taking them with us might not be the best idea after all. John makes a disgusted face at the both of them.

I like this guy already; thank God one of the survivors isn't a total idiot. It calms me down enough that killing AJ really does seem like a legitimately bad idea. "Come on, they're waiting for us," I say and turn to go. I can hear Amy and AJ muttering behind me but they stay with us as we leave the room.

The others are waiting with bleak expressions on their faces when we meet them in the stairwell. That feeling is one that I'd bet we're all sharing right now. Who knows how these new people might complicate things? And without the info from the cameras we're flying blind, but this is no time to hesitate, not when a full-fledged zombie apocalypse is still a good possibility, so we head down the stairs—into the belly of the beast, as it were.

Nate

There haven't been any signs of movement from within the building for a few minutes now since they disappeared inside. It's too bad my ruse didn't work to separate Elliot and Lia from the others as they came to investigate, but it's not a significant setback. Anyway, it's advantageous to keep one's prey on the fine line between being tense from feeling spooked and being relaxed from feeling safe. Having prey be relaxed is helpful because prey tend to get over-confident and screw up. Having prey be tense is helpful because prey tend to panic and screw up. So a balance is best for making sure things aren't over too quickly. Half of the pleasure is in the hunt itself; what fun would it be if things were too easy?

I start to approach the building. I need to do some recon so I can find a way inside. It looks like it's locked up pretty tight, but there's always a way. Everything has a weakness; you just need to look hard enough to find it.

I'm halfway between the woods and the lab when there's a sudden noise and the metal shutters covering all of the windows begin to slide up with a rattling sound. To avoid being seen from anyone within, I sprint forward and, once I have momentum, I tuck down into a roll, coming to my feet again just in front of the building, near the door.

Idiots. They don't know how much easier they just made it for me to get to them. A part of me is almost disappointed with the lowered challenge level, but I'm soon distracted by the door flinging open and a man a bit smaller than I am running out at full speed.

The predator within me is intrigued by the man's flight and I feel the thrumming in my chest and hear the rushing in my ears. Before I have time to contemplate this new development in my instincts, I am propping the door open with my bag, then turning to run after him. I catch up within seconds and the muscles in my legs bunch like coiled springs as I leap after him, catching him around the middle of his back and slamming him into the ground. An anguished noise escapes his throat and the thrumming increases in intensity.

"Get off me, Terry, I need to get out of here!" the man cries out in an agonized tone.

"I'm not Terry," I say and although I don't think my voice was particularly menacing, the man obviously doesn't agree, since he makes a gasping, choking kind of noise and starts writhing, trying to escape. I raise myself up and kneel on his back. He grunts in pain but hasn't started panicking yet. I slide my knife out of its sheath and lean slightly forward. I grasp his hair tightly in my fist and yank his head up. He tries to scream, but the awkward angle of his throat makes it difficult and only a strangled sound comes out. He tries to buck me off and I almost lose my balance, but I regain it quickly. Locklan was much bigger and stronger than this man and I killed him the same way in which I'm about to kill this man, so the upper hand is easy to retain.

I slick the knife blade against the man's throat and he goes wild, bucking and rocking, trying to unseat me. This gets old fast so I grasp his hair more tightly and smash his face against the ground to shut him down.

The front of his skull cracks against the ground; there's a large rock in the soil that I didn't notice before. I feel his head give and collapse in my hands. He stops struggling. I wait a beat then slide onto the dirt beside him. I roll him over. His face is a ruin, blood everywhere and the smashed bones looking like Silly Putty with bits of gravel imbedded in it. I place a hand against his throat. He's not breathing and his heartbeat is still.

Huh.

Not what I meant to do, but the predator is satisfied with this kill. I shrug and stand up, and then head back to the lab. Halfway back again I pause and retrace my steps. I grab the collar of the man's shirt and drag him along behind me; my injured arm protests and I feel more blood ooze out of the wounds, so I switch to using my right arm instead. When I reach the building once more, I retrieve my bag and step inside, closing the door behind us.

Lucy

As we start down the stairs, I can't help remembering the way that the zombie we ran into before moved, how different its movements were from the first zombies we encountered a couple of days ago. Especially because of the emergency lights flashing, it just looked so surreal. Like the way people look when a strobe light is flickering or the weird stuttered movements of people in old-timey home videos, the ones they're fond of using in certain horror movies. As I recall this, I also can't help wondering what's going to happen when we get to the zombie corpse on the landing below. The three survivors we picked up, minus John maybe, don't exactly seem up to coping with the whole zompocalypse scenario that's happening here. Objectively, I get why Elliot didn't want to just abandon them, especially since he knows them, but I can't help thinking that they're merely cannon fodder. They may as well be red-shirted ensigns as far as I'm concerned.

"Oh, my God, what is that awful smell?" Amy cries. No one answers her although AJ murmurs in agreement. Dollops of not quite dried goo and bits of bone appear on the stairs in front of us.

"What the hell is that?" AJ asks and comes to a dead stop.

The rest of us continue down the stairwell, treading carefully around the splattered zombie on the landing so we don't slip in the still wet ichor surrounding it. The smell is still terrible and seems to cling to the inside of my nostrils and slide down the back of my throat. I try to distract myself so that I have a better chance of keeping my gag reflex under control. Amy and AJ aren't so successful and they lose it once the zombie carcass comes fully into view. They both start throwing up and I step away from them as they heave.

"Seriously, what the hell is that?" AJ repeats breathlessly as he finally stops throwing up and stares down at the disfigured body. Luca throws a disgusted look at Elliot and then growls at AJ, "Keep up or get left behind, your choice."

"But..." AJ begins but the rest of us are busy following Luca and no one acknowledges him. Elliot is looking somewhat cowed by Luca's seeming vindication. So far I'm with Luca on this one, but who knows? Maybe they'll end up surprising us with sudden awesome sauce. But that feels pretty optimistic given what's happened thus far. My mind drifts back to the guard that went AWOL, Benji; I'm betting that it's pretty optimistic to think he's okay, too. Going off by one's lonesome is a really stupid idea right now and I can't help thinking that the next time we see him it will be after he's shuffled off this mortal coil.

"You okay?" Mac's now familiar voice cuts through my worst case scenario imaginings, which are now far more worst case than ever before, though who could blame me?

"Sure," I say, smiling the best I can. It's apparently not very good at all because Mac's face crinkles up with worry lines. His cuteness is definitely a better distraction than my grisly reveries and my smile sticks better on my face now as I say, "I'm fine, just really ready for this all to be over."

"I'm right there with you," he says and slips his arm around my shoulders, pulling me close to him.

"Stop," Luca commands suddenly and Mac jumpily removes his arm from around me, but it soon becomes apparent that Luca is addressing the whole group because he's stopped walking and is holding up his hand in one of those signals you always see military people do in movies. "Shouldn't the smell be lessening the further we get from that zombie?" he asks, looking back over his shoulder at the group.

"Z-zombie?" AJ stutters. "Did he say 'zombie?' That's impossible! There is no such thing!"

"Do you think there are more around this area, sir?" Darryl asks, ignoring him, and Luca nods. "It seems likely. We should try to draw them out so they don't catch us off guard. They might not move as fast now, but that doesn't mean they don't still pose a threat."

I figure now is as good a time as any to practice my newfound skill of zombie calling, so I belt one out, making it as loud as I can. Amy screams and clutches at AJ. Almost everyone else jumps and Lia punches my arm multiple times. "Don't *do* that without warning!" She pauses. "Actually, don't do that ever; don't you remember what happened last time? You almost got us killed!"

"Only because you didn't start driving away quickly enough," I counter, rubbing my arm where she punched me.

"*Cállate*, both of you," Luca snaps and Lia and I both get ready to throw his attitude right back at him but he waves his hand at us and growls, "Listen."

Everyone is quiet and the sounds from within the stairwell are suddenly very prominent. It's like the zombie—or possibly *zombies*—is trying to call back to me but it can't quite manage it. The screech seems to stick in its throat with a thick, soggy sound.

"W-what is that?" Amy asks, voice quavering.

Luca glares at her then orders me, "Do it again."

I take a deep breath and grip Mac's hand, then let out another shriek doing the best that I can to make it as loud and as zombie-like as possible. The zombie—I'm pretty sure there's just the one—makes its rasping, squelching sound again and some additional noises are audible this time. They're the same sounds that we heard from the zombie on the stairs earlier—a creaking, cracking sort of sound that I now associate with these more decayed zombies trying to use their limbs the best that they can despite the rigor mortis, and the squinching sound of putrefied flesh sliding across the floor—drift up from somewhere below us.

Without the distraction of the alarm bells going off, the sounds are much starker and they seem to slide under my skin. I don't think I'll be forgetting them anytime soon. I shudder and Mac slides his arm around my shoulders again. I smile briefly up at him and then concentrate on the noises that are moving closer and closer to us. It sounds like the zombie is only one flight below.

Luca is the closest to the bottom of the stairs since he was leading our group. He continues taking point but motions for Darryl and Link to move up next to him and the three of them turn the corner slowly. As they disappear around the corner, I hear a disgusted sound that is soon eclipsed by the loudness of three guns going off at once; in the enclosed space, it's almost deafening. I nearly cover my ears in reflex but luckily, I remember that my machete is in hand and that there are several people standing near me before I do. I settle for wincing and leaning into Mac, which is definitely preferable to simply covering my ears anyway.

"All clear," Luca calls from below us and we descend the stairs to join them. Once we do, I can see why someone couldn't contain their disgust. The zombie's head is pretty much gone, but, of course, that's not the reason since that was caused by the gunshots. What's particularly disturbing about this zombie is that its insides are hanging out, strewn around its body like the contents of a really fucked up piñata. Even worse than that, the skin around the exposed viscera, along with the organs themselves, looks to have been chewed on. Pretty obvious how this one was killed and turned.

Ugh. I am gonna need industrial strength brain soap to get rid of all these horrible mental images I've unintentionally been stocking up on for the past few days.

Amy emits a squeak then crumples into a ball and starts rocking back and forth. AJ absent-mindedly pats her head, but he doesn't look to be in much better shape himself. His face is the colour of skim milk and he looks about two seconds away from throwing up again. For his part, John looks relatively calm, so hopefully, he at least, will turn out to be an asset.

"Alright, Doc, I need you to make a decision," Luca says, breaking the sickened silence and paying no heed to the distressed members of our group. Elliot tears his eyes away from the mutilated corpse, looking faintly green himself. Lia squeezes his hand and he smiles unsteadily at her then turns his attention back to Luca.

"A decision about what?"

"We're obviously going to be running into more zombies and without the cameras we have no idea what we're walking into. Do you think it's best if we do a search of the complex and try to find and kill as many as possible before you get to work on the cure or do you want to head for your lab now and just kill any zombies we find on the way?"

Elliot pinches the bridge of his nose with his free hand and adjusts the one gripped in Lia's hand so that their fingers are intertwined.

I know that it's so not appropriate right now, but I can't hold back an "aw", at least not mentally.

He lets out a breath then says in a slightly shaky voice, "We should get to the lab as soon as we can. Taking them out will be easier once I get the compound figured out and...as much as I hate the thought of doing it, I will need some zombies to experiment on while I'm figuring it out." Elliot looks sick at the thought and I don't blame him. It's easy for me to see them just as zombies because I never knew them, but these were people he worked with, disconnecting mentally must be so much more difficult for him.

"*Bueno*, where is your lab?"

"Um, the fourth sub-level. The basement."

Of course it is.

Chapter Thirteen
This is the part where the audience starts screaming, 'Look behind you!' at the screen

Elliot

Getting to the lab, while not uneventful, is at least not terribly arduous either. The few zombies that we encounter along the way are slow moving and give themselves away with their various noises and odours. So far, we haven't encountered any more survivors and I'm grateful for this in a way that makes me ashamed. But in my defence, Amy and AJ are already making things more difficult and slow-going and it's hard to quell the discomfort I feel at the enraged looks Sergeant Ortiz keeps throwing my way. Still, I have to believe that I did the right thing, if perhaps not the smartest thing.

I don't know any of them very well, they are really just faces I've seen at work, names I memorized because my parents taught me that it's important to remember people's names—they're big on manners. Regardless, I can't stand the thought of any more people I know dying. I can't help wishing that my parents hadn't been so insistent on the remembrance of names because every zombie we do come across, I see their faces and even with the decay, their names flash unrelentingly across my memory and I can't help picturing them when they were still alive and still human. It's jangling my already rattled nerves. The only thing that helps keep me from going out of my head is that Lia hasn't let go of my hand once since she grabbed it on the stairs. It's like she's giving me strength somehow and, thanks to her, I can focus on what needs to be done. I can always go into therapy later.

We finally reach the basement and I have to punch in my pass code to get into the lab. This is the area where the more secretive and/or potentially dangerous testing and development is done...or I guess, was done, who knows what will happen now. I wondered why Gregory fought to work on our tests here rather than sub-level two, where our type of testing was usually done. Now, it seems more and more likely that what happened to our subjects may not have been completely accidental. Clearly, Gregory was planning something, though I still can't figure out what his endgame was...or is, I guess, considering that he's still out there. I grip Lia's hand more tightly to distract myself from this train of thought. It's unhelpful and irrelevant to what I need to do. There's nothing to be gained from agonizing over it right now.

After I punch in my code on the keypad, Sergeant Ortiz motions for Lia and me to step back and out of the way. Lia stiffens and looks ready to argue but then she looks at me and is reminded that while I'm not unarmed, I'm not exactly the best fighter either and she steps out of the way with me.

"Sorry," I say.

"What? Why?" she asks as Sergeant Ortiz and the others get into formation.

"Don't you want to go on ahead?"

"No, it's fine. Think of it like me being your bodyguard." She smiles at me. "It's all good." I smile back at her and try to ignore the ardent feelings that bubble up. Those kinds of things are irrelevant right now, too.

"Goddammit! Shut her up!" Sergeant Ortiz snaps suddenly, whirling away from the door before opening it and turning on Amy and AJ. I didn't notice before now, I guess I was blocking it out, but Amy is letting out this high, keening noise that I now find impossible to ignore.

AJ gestures helplessly at her but he's too shaken to attempt to reassure anyone else. John makes a "tsking" sound and grabs Amy roughly by the shoulder. "Amy, calm down!"

This only seems to agitate her further and the keening gets louder.

"Jesus," Lia mutters beside me. I pinch the bridge of my nose, just below my glasses and shrug feebly at her. She squeezes my hand again and whispers, "It'll be alright." She glances at the inconsolable Amy and amends, "Probably."

"Someone do something before I have to. This is ground zero. We're not going in there with her freaking out like this," Sergeant Ortiz barks. John shakes Amy again and tries to get her attention but she just keeps shaking her head as tears slip down her face. Lucy walks over to her and grabs her face—not hard, just firmly.

She forces Amy to stop shaking her head and Amy's eyes focus blearily on her face.

"You have to relax. You have to calm down. I know this is bad, but it's only gonna get worse if you don't calm down." Amy blinks her eyes and tries to extract her head from Lucy's grip but Lucy tightens her hold. "Look at me. No, look at me. You need to calm the fuck down, okay? Or we can't protect you. So get some ovaries and woman up, damn it!"

This is evidently the wrong thing to say since Amy's freak out cranks back up a notch. She wrenches her head out of Lucy's hands and backs away from her, arms flailing. She stumbles and falls back onto the stairs where she curls up into a ball and resumes wailing.

Lucy turns around. "Well, that didn't work. Now what?"

Lia makes an aggravated noise and takes her hand from mine before striding over to Amy's crumpled form. She yanks her up out of her fetal position and smacks her across the face. "Snap out of it!"

This feels a little extreme to me, but only just a little. Amy's not exactly up to the standards I've grown used to from being around Lucy and Lia. Amy doesn't "snap out of it." Instead, she sort of just goes limp and quiet. Lia straightens up looking alarmed.

"Jesus, I didn't hit her *that* hard."

"You've killed her!" AJ shrieks, reminding me again of just how obnoxious he can be. Lia throws him an extremely dirty look.

"Of course I didn't!" she snaps, but she leans down and presses her hand against Amy's throat, looking slightly disconcerted, then relieved. "She's fine. She just *fainted*." This last word is said derisively.

Lucy snorts. "Regular damsel in distress, this one."

"What is the matter with you people?" AJ cries.

"Oh, for God's sake, he's just as bad as she is," Lia groans.

"I'm sorry," I say, feeling like I should apologize.

Lia looks puzzled. "It's not your fault. We don't blame you."

"Speak for yourself," Sergeant Ortiz mutters and I look down at my shoes, feeling uncomfortable.

"You are such an ass!" Lia shouts.

"That's enough! Fuck! This is ridiculous. Calm the fuck down! Let me reiterate how we have bigger things to worry about right now than the fact that we don't all get along!" Mac yells. Everyone lapses into silence and to my surprise, Sergeant Ortiz actually looks chagrined.

"*Bueno*, Mac. You're right. But we are not going into ground zero with these useless *putas* in tow. Unless they get their *mierda* together, they have to go somewhere else."

"Where do you suggest they go?" I blurt out before I can stop myself.

"I don't give a fuck as long as they stop fucking with my mission."

"Stop talking about us like we're not even here!" AJ exclaims, his arm around the still unconscious Amy. "We deserve a vote in what happens to us!"

Sergeant Ortiz's face tightens in annoyance. "No. Only competent people deserve a vote. Here's what's going to happen: you are going to leave this area, you are going to go upstairs somewhere and you are going to lock yourselves in until someone comes to get you." AJ's mouth drops open. I can't tell if it's from shock or if he's planning on protesting something Sergeant Ortiz said, but either way, the result is the same: Sergeant Ortiz holds up his hand and growls, "End of discussion."

"What happens if we run into more of those—those things?" AJ asks, not willing to call them by name. "She's not even conscious; what do you expect us to do?"

"That's your problem, not ours."

"Luke, man, come on," Mac protests.

"No. I've had enough of this; they can fend for themselves."

"At least let me escort them back up, man; let's try to keep the death toll to a minimum, eh?"

Sergeant Ortiz's jaw tightens and he glares at Mac, drags a hand across his jaw, and throws a livid look at AJ and Amy. "Fine. Take Cho with you; you might need back-up and these two obviously don't qualify." He turns his attention to John. "You, can you shoot, handle yourself in a fight?"

"Yes, sir, I can. I'm ex-military."

"*Bueno*. At least there's that. Mac, Cho, go now and get them out of my sight before I change my mind and just kill them myself so they're out of my way for good." A sharp intake of breath comes from AJ, but I'm pretty sure Sergeant Ortiz wouldn't actually kill them just for being difficult. Probably not anyway.

"Mac, radio us when you're finished with them and on your way back."

"That won't work," I say. When he looks at me confusedly, I elaborate, "The building is built and wired so that frequencies and cell signals don't work in here. It's to help protect against corporate espionage and that kind of thing."

"Come on, guys, of course our communication devices won't work, that would just make things way too easy," Lucy says, throwing her hands up in the air in exasperation.

"'See that, Vitus, even the phones are dead,'" Lia adds.

"Exactly," Lucy says, pointing at Lia emphatically.

"You two need to stop with this nonsense; you're giving me a headache!" Sergeant Ortiz snaps then, ignoring them both giving him the finger, he says to Mac, "Get going now and come back here as fast as you can. Since we don't have radio contact, I'm sending Kane with you, too, so you have more eyes."

Mac nods his assent and they set out. Amy is semi-conscious again, half-looking like a zombie herself. Between the two of them, Master Corporal Kane and Master Corporal Cho herd her up the stairs. AJ trails along behind them looking dazed. Mac follows, taking the rear position. As they walk out of sight, the rest of us settle in to await their return.

Lucy and Lia are talking quietly, though animatedly, to each other. If I had to guess, I'd say that their conversation is about the pros and cons of our group splitting up right now. I'd also bet that their thoughts fall somewhere in the middle. I know how they feel about the whole splitting up thing, but I'm sure that they're not sorry to see AJ and Amy go. Right now, I'd have to say that I agree with that viewpoint. After their stellar performances, I'm almost wishing that I'd sided with Sergeant Ortiz in the first place and just left them on their own.

But I had to try. So many people have died already. I just want to prevent any more deaths if at all possible. But the way things are going, who knows what kind of survival rate is possible anymore.

Connor

All the way back upstairs, AJ mumbles to himself. I could probably pick up what he's saying, but his tone is enough to let me know that it's probably not flattering to us or positive about the situation he's found himself in so I don't bother. I can't blame him, but that doesn't mean I'm not happy to see him go.

Amy's a different story altogether. I'm not unhappy to be getting rid of her either, but I feel bad for her. She's barely responsive at all: Link and Darryl practically have to carry her between them and she doesn't acknowledge any verbal prompts. So, I feel a little guilty about sort-of abandoning them—especially her—like this, but I've got my orders and besides, our mission will go a hell of a lot smoother with them out of the picture so I wasn't gonna argue with Luca. Well, besides arguing to escort them, obviously. But we couldn't just have them wandering around by themselves—that would have caused more harm than good for sure.

By the time we arrive back at the break room, Amy's started moaning again and I'm more than a little relieved to be leaving her and AJ behind, despite some residual guilt.

"Okay, lock yourselves in here till someone comes to get you. You've got food and water and access to a bathroom so you'll be fairly comfortable and you'll be safe."

AJ mutters something dark in response and as far as I'm concerned, that's our cue to leave. I indicate as much to Darryl and Link, jerking my head toward the door and we make our exit, sound-tracked by Amy's distressed noises.

We head back downstairs, taking the central staircase down one floor to the reception area 'cause it's closer and this way we don't have to deal with navigating through the maze of offices again. We exit the stairwell and I feel a creeping sensation settle over my skin. I've had this feeling before and it never leads to anything good. I raise my fist in the air, signalling to Darryl and Link to hold up behind me.

"Mac?" Link ventures.

"Something's wrong."

They fall silent behind me and I peer around the room, which is now as airy as I predicted earlier, but the seeming innocuousness of the room only serves to unsettle me further. I try to locate what set off my alarm bells and then, out of the corner of my eye, I see it: a booted foot sticking out from behind the receptionist's desk.

I signal silently to Link and Darryl, they follow my gaze and then, following my further signed instructions, they cover my six while I go investigate.

As I get closer, I can tell what triggered my instincts. I smell the rusted iron scent of blood that I've gotten used to in the past couple of days, which would be why I didn't realize what got my attention at first. I turn the corner of the desk and the body comes fully into view. Despite everything I've seen, especially lately, my stomach heaves a little when I see the poor dude's face...or what's left of it.

His head is a mess of skull fragments, vivid with blood, torn muscle, and chunks of brain, all of which are loosely held in place by the remaining skin. Because of the destruction, I wouldn't have recognized the guy, but his uniform lets me know that I'm looking at the recently deceased Benji. I wave Link and Darryl over so they can see what we're dealing with.

"That's fucked up, man," Link says.

"How do you think he died?" Darryl asks, leaning closer to examine the ruin of Benji's face.

"Pretty obvious, don't you think? The dude got his face smashed all to hell," Link answers.

Darryl stands up straight again and looks seriously at Link. "I meant, do we think it was a zombie...or something else?" He doesn't say it, but I gotta admit I was thinking it, too: Nate.

"I don't know. We'll reconvene with the others and see what Luca says. That's all we can do at this point."

"What about the civs, sir?" he asks. I know he means Amy and AJ, because it's been a while since anyone except Luca thought of the others as merely civilians.

"They're secure. We need to continue with our main mission; that's priority number one."

He nods in agreement and we set out, heading cautiously for the far stairwell since we don't know what—or who—might be lying in wait for us.

Nate

I watch them go. They didn't seem to enjoy the surprise I left for them, but they're continuing on anyway, which is what I was counting on. None of what I have planned works if they change tactics and start trying to hunt me. They wouldn't be successful, but it would mean having to alter my strategy and that would be inconvenient.

It's good to be on their radar again. It makes them twitchier and more fun to watch.

They leave the room, heading for the stairs, and I turn my attention to the tasks at hand: ministering my wounds and getting rid of the spares.

I head into the bathroom I found when I explored earlier after placing the body in the reception area. I set my duffle on the ground and lock the door behind me just in case. I don't enjoy surprises either.

I pause for a second, examining the bruise on my jaw from where Lia hit me yesterday. I allowed her to get the punch in because I didn't want to activate the alerts of the systems, but now I'm wishing I had gone with my instincts and just punched her instead. There'll be time for that later, I have more pressing things to focus on right now.

I remove the still damp shirt that's wrapped around my upper arm, then take my shirt off and turn to look over my shoulder in the mirror, assessing the damage. It's not terrible, but it's worse than I'd like. I don't like things that slow me down.

I wash my hands then grab some pliers from my pack and wash them, too. Looking over my shoulder, I dig into the wound on my shoulder blade. It was only a glancing blow, but the bullet is lodged under my skin and against the bone and I need to remove it. Lucky for me Lucy didn't have a more powerful gun or better aim.

The pain of removing the bullet throbs through my body and my heart starts beating faster in response. Thankfully, I'll soon have an outlet for the anger that grows in tandem with the pain: killing the spares will help to clear my head and get me back in the game.

I finally pull the crushed bullet from my skin with a slurping sound as the wound starts bleeding freely again. I drop the bullet on the counter and dig through my bag until I find my watertight emergency first aid kit. I remove the rubbing alcohol and my medical grade needle and thread. I soak a cotton pad in rubbing alcohol and swipe it over the needle, making sure it's sanitized. I get a fresh cotton pad, soak it in alcohol, and press it to the wound. It stings like a motherfucker. I catch my breath and focus, shutting out the pain like Father taught me, and start to work on closing the wound. The angle is awkward, so sewing up the edges of the injury takes longer than I'd like.

Once I'm finished, I gauge the damage done to my upper arm. It's shallow enough that a bandage will suffice for now. I clean it out with rubbing alcohol, too, and convert the pain into more potent fury. I use my cauterizing gauze to stem further bleeding then return my pliers and emergency kit to my bag. I pull my shirt back on then grab the bullet off the counter and lock it up in my ammo case. I'll want to return it to its owner at some point.

I sling my duffle over my shoulder again and leave the bathroom, pausing to check my surroundings and make sure that I'm still alone, and then I jog to the staircase Mac and the others exited from earlier. I run up the stairs, making up time I lost stitching up the wound. A short while later I reach the room Mac and the others deposited the strangers in. I take a moment to ready myself. I'm sure they won't present a threat, but as my father always taught me: you get over-confident, you end up dead. So I always make sure I'm prepared before I enter a new environment.

I don't think I'll need the SKS for this one and I won't take the chance that the others could hear this attack. I don't want them knowing for sure that I'm here until that part of the plan comes to fruition. Surprises are so much more entertaining.

In keeping with my goals for both a relatively silent kill and another scare tactic, I select my axe and my best hunting knife. I check both of the blades for sharpness, nicking my thumb slightly, though not enough to break the skin, on each weapon. Perfect.

Because I overheard Mac telling them to open the door when someone comes for them, I know getting into the room won't require any excess force, so I just knock on the door and wait.

"That was fast." The man they escorted opens the door, faint surprise showing across his face when he sees someone he doesn't recognize. "Who are you?"

In answer, I shove him back into the room with the head of the axe and shut the door behind me. He stumbles back and catches himself on a chair. Standing up straight again, he shouts, "What are you doing? You can't do this!" I smile at him in response and he actually relaxes. This is disappointing. There will be no sport with this one, I can tell.

To test my theory, I step forward and slash the knife casually across his chest with my left hand. Father made sure I was ambidextrous so I don't have the weakness of a lead hand reliance—one more thing to be thankful to him for. If nothing else, he did make sure I could take care of myself, which turned out to be to his detriment in the end.

I bring my focus back to the present, mulling over the past is sloppy, but as predicted, the man is no threat, so I haven't screwed myself over by being temporarily distracted. Blood flows out of the relatively shallow wound across his chest and pools darkly in the fabric of his shirt.

"What the hell?" he demands, wiping his hand through the blood disbelievingly. He stares at his bloodied hand and doesn't attempt to defend himself or even to escape.

I'm bored with him.

I bring the axe up with my right hand and swing it down on his neck, angling it up slightly so the cut is clean despite the height difference between us. Blood spurts out as his head is separated from his body, splashing me as I slice through the sinew, tendons, and bone. His body collapses and more blood surges out of the stump of his neck. His head gets a few seconds of air from the momentum of my swing and then it hits the floor with a wet thud, splattering me further with blood as it lands in the pool surrounding his decapitated body.

I shake my head. That was just so easy. At least the others I'm hunting will put up a fight. It just feels wrong to kill something that doesn't fight back, doesn't try for survival at least by running away...but now isn't the time for an existential crisis.

I turn my attention to the girl curled up in the corner. She hasn't stopped sobbing since I entered the room, but I don't think that has anything to do with me actually being in the room. She doesn't seem to realize that I'm here and doesn't seem to know what just happened to her associate. I walk over to her and she doesn't move or react in any way. This is even worse than the pathetic lack of effort from the man.

I nudge her foot with mine, but she still doesn't react. A part of me wonders if killing her won't be crossing some sort of line. It's hard to justify killing something that is so utterly helpless. I don't feel any of the signs that usually point to it being time for me to kill something. There is no rushing in my ears and no thudding in my chest. My heartbeat and breathing rates are both at normal levels.

I crouch down in front of her and set down my axe, then grab a handful of her hair and force her head up, wanting to be sure before walking away. Her eyes are unfocused and glazed with tears. She doesn't seem to register that anything is happening to her. She's catatonic.

I tilt my head to the side as I consider my options. I let go of her hair and her head flops back down. I stand up and stare down at her.

It's decided. A mercy killing, then. It's unlikely she'll ever get over what she's experienced and witnessed, so I'll be doing her a favour. Since it's a mercy killing, I'll kill her the quickest, most painless way I know how.

After retrieving my SKS, I walk back over to her. She still hasn't moved or stopped crying. What I'm about to do is for the best. I place the muzzle against the top of her head and squeeze the trigger. I didn't want to risk the loudness of a gunshot but it's a sacrifice I'm willing to make in order to do the right thing.

The bullet goes straight down through her body, killing her instantly with almost no blood lost. The only change in her posture is that she slumps a little further down. I leave her where she is and return to my bag. I clean the blood off the blades I used and take a moment to sharpen them up again. You've got to respect your tools.

I put the axe back in the bag and swing it over my shoulders, following it with the SKS. Once my knife is back in its sheath and my hands are free, I grab the man's head with one and the collar of his shirt with the other.

It's time to get moving. I have more work to do.

Lucy

Lia and I are engaged in an intense round of time wasting while we wait for the guys to come back. We started with playing an old patty cake type game with the Kit-Kat song, one we used to play when we were younger, and we've now moved on to thumb wrestling. It seems to supremely annoy Luca, which is probably amusing us more than the actual games we're playing.

"Just fucking cut that out! *Dios mio!*"

Lia sticks her tongue out at him and I say, "Oh, I'm sorry we're not sitting here all solemn like the world is ending." While I'm distracted, Lia pins my thumb and I growl in frustration, demanding a rematch.

"It could be the end of the world, and you two are acting like it's just another day. You should be taking this more seriously."

"I am so sorry we're actually having some fun and not being a total downer like you!" I snap as I just barely evade Lia's thumb. "Haven't you ever heard the saying that sometimes you just gotta laugh?"

"Especially when things aren't funny," Lia finishes the statement as she beats me again.

"Bah. I'm terrible at this, let's do something else," I say.

"That saying doesn't make any sense," Luca interjects while Lia and I try to decide on a new game.

"You just don't get it because you're the worst," Lia counters as she holds her hands out for me to try to smack and we start a round of the slap game.

"You didn't seem to think so when you threw yourself at me yesterday."

Ooh, low blow.

Rafe chuckles and Luca smiles smugly. Lia's distracted by being aghast and I slap the tops of her hands. She throws me a Lia Glare that she turns on Luca and cranks up a few notches after I mumble an apology. "You are such an asshole!" she snarls and gets to her feet. Luca gets to his, too, and whips out his own intense glare.

You know, we've really had a lot staring contests this weekend.

322

I see Elliot, who was sitting on the other side of Lia, tense up, although I can't tell if it's because he doesn't like the memory of Lia making out with another dude or because he's worried that there's trouble a-brewing.

Mac, Link, and Darryl suddenly come trotting down the stairs and interrupt the strained atmosphere. I'm almost sorry that Lia doesn't get a chance to finish her outburst because they can actually be pretty entertaining when you're not on the receiving end. But, really, I'm just happy to see that Mac's returned safely. And Darryl and Link, too, of course. Mac's eyes go straight to me and then take in the rest of the scene, bringing a halfway involuntary smile to my face.

"What's going—never mind," he interrupts himself before continuing, "we might have a situation."

"An ominous one?" I can't help asking. Lia makes an aggravated noise at me, taking her attention from Luca. Elliot relaxes slightly and Luca ignores all of us, turning to Mac. "What do you mean? Did the civs give you trouble?"

"No. Uh, it's just that we found that guard."

"Benji?" Terry asks, looking happy to hear this. Mac gets an uncomfortable look on his face at Terry's excitement.

Uh-oh. Methinks this does not bode well.

"Yeah. Uh, he—he's dead, man, I'm sorry."

"What happened?" Elliot asks, getting to his feet beside Lia. Lia takes a break from her irritation at most of the people surrounding her and places a comforting hand on Elliot's shoulder. He reaches his hand up and lays it over the top of hers. Aw.

"We don't know exactly," Mac says, looking even more uncomfortable.

Hmm...yeah, this does not bode well at all; there are definitely doings afoot.

"What does that mean?" Terry asks. "Did a zombie get him?"

"Maybe." Darryl keeps his eyes forward, but Link glances at Mac like he might have something to add to this.

Terry notices the movement. "Link?" Link makes a face and glances again at Mac; though this time, it looks like he's asking for permission.

"Mac, *qué pasó?*" Luca is impatient and mostly looks concerned with getting the mission going again.

"Well, uh, it's possible something else got him."

"Like what?" Elliot asks.

"Or who?" I say, goose bumps popping up along my arms as I point accusingly at the guys. I grip my machete more tightly to reassure myself, but my eyes keep drifting back to the gloomy stairwell. Any second now, I expect Nate to show himself.

"Who?" John repeats, confused.

"We don't know for sure it's him," Mac says to me, attempting comfort. I fix him with my best "bitch, please" stare and he shifts his weight uncomfortably and drops his eyes.

"Who?" John asks again.

"A member of our group who, um, went off the rails," Elliot euphemistically explains, looking tense.

"How did the guard die? What makes you think it might not have been a zombie?" Rafe asks.

"Uh, there weren't any bite marks."

"And his damn head was smashed in," Link adds, seeming fed up with continuing to remain silent. Terry and Elliot both go grey-faced at this news and Mac smacks Link upside the head, glaring disapprovingly at him. Lia switches her position beside Elliot so her arm is now around his shoulders and he leans his head against hers, mourning silently.

I can't take my eyes off of the stairwell, as though if it's in my sightline nothing can catch me off guard. I know this logic is flawed, on par with hiding under the covers or whipping open the shower curtain to see if anything's hiding behind it. I know full well that keeping my eyes trained on the stairs will accomplish next to nothing, just like blankets will protect you from pretty much nothing, and what would you actually do if something *was* hiding behind the shower curtain? Nate's too wily to take such an obvious route when there's still this many of us left alive. Despite this, I can't stop myself—it's really all I can do at the moment and a flimsy protection is better than none at all.

"We move forward with the mission," Luca finally says.

"What? We're just gonna act like he's not here somewhere, hunting us?" I ask.

"We don't know for sure he's here. The best thing we can do right now is to carry on with the mission at hand and get started on the cure."

"You are so naïve. Of course, he's here! And this is the part where the audience starts screaming, 'Look behind you!' at the screen." Everyone turns and looks back up at the stairs. I can't hold back a sigh of exasperation as I explain, "I don't mean that he's literally behind us at this second. It's an expression."

"Since when?" Luca demands.

Mac walks over to me and puts his hand reassuringly on my hip. "Lucy, we checked, he's not up there. I mean, it's possible he's around somewhere but—"

I cut him off. "Of course he is! Falling in a little water is never gonna take out a super villain!" I yell much louder than I mean to because I'm trying so hard to get my point across. There's a beat of silence in the wake of my outburst and if we weren't in the basement of a concrete building, I'd swear that I can hear crickets.

Lia turns from her position leaning against Elliot and says, "Okay, even I'm beginning to worry that you might be starting to get a little unhinged here." She ignores Luca muttering, "Starting to?" and tries to placate me, "Just take a breath, Luce."

"I am not unhinged," I growl defensively, "I am just way too over prepared for this!"

Mac squeezes my hip and says, "I get where you're coming from, but it'll be okay, I promise."

"Worst thing to say, ever!" I throw my hands up in vexation. I count off our problems on my fingers. "There are zombies, we're in a secret lab, and we're being hunted by a crazy person who is literally a hunter! How is any of that okay?"

Mac shrugs his shoulders, seeming at a loss for words before saying, "Uh, fair enough."

He starts to step away, but I grab his hand and pull him back. "I'm sorry. I didn't mean to yell at you. This is all just really stressful."

He smiles that crinkly-eyed smile at me and leans his forehead against mine. "Understatement of the year."

"If you two are finished," Luca gripes. Mac pulls away from me again, but stays close by, muttering, "Sorry, Luke."

"We move forward," Luca repeats. He glares at me. "You can stay here if you want, keeping watch for someone who may or may not be coming after us, or you can stay with us and help us get the cure and finish this. Your choice."

I make a face at him. "I will obviously not be splitting up from the group, I'm not an idiot. I'm just saying that he's out there and he's coming for us. Make no mistake about that. It should be obvious by now that none of us has any semblance of luck. Besides, Murphy's Law is especially apt in horror movie scenarios. Whatever can go wrong, will. The cavalry doesn't arrive in the nick of time, not everyone survives, and things don't get tied up in neat little packages of closure—none that last anyway. All of this very obviously applies to our situation. Closing your eyes to it simply because he hasn't made an explicit cameo appearance yet will only end in tears. And blood."

"Are you done?" Luca asks. I make another annoyed face at him and cross my arms defiantly, which is somewhat difficult with a machete in hand, but I manage it. Luca starts detailing the plan for entering ground zero and Mac gives him his full attention.

I lean over to Lia and say, "You know things are bad when you can sympathize with those dudes wearing the doomsday sandwich boards and tinfoil hats."

She giggles at me, saying, "Unfairly marginalized visionaries, the lot of them."

I nod emphatically and place my finger on my nose.

"Would you two shut the fuck up? *Dios mio!*"

"Shh!" Lia whisper-yells at me. She's really never been good at actually whispering. We both start giggling again.

Luca glares at us. "I mean it."

Once we stop laughing, he addresses the group as a whole again and I lean back over to Lia. "I feel like we're back in high school with Mr. Wilcox," I whisper to her. "Next thing you know he's gonna threaten us with his coming back here to shut us up himself." She snorts a laugh and Luca glares more intensely at us. Lia tries to turn her laugh into a cough, which actually starts Elliot laughing. A domino effect ensues and soon even John is chuckling, but Luca just rolls his eyes.

After a few minutes, the laughter finally dies out completely. "Finished?" he growls.

"You are so dead inside," I say.

"We don't have time for this."

"Pfft. There's always time for laughter," I say with mock-seriousness.

"You're the one who's always going on about how none of us is paying enough attention to the horror movie plot devices you're so obsessed with and now you're advocating that we just stand here, laughing like a bunch of idiots when we could be doing something productive?"

I think for a second. "Yup." At the severe look he gives me, I just shrug and say, "'You gotta enjoy the little things.'"

He takes in the reactions of people who haven't been living under a rock like he obviously has and asks suspiciously, "Is that a quote from something?"

"Maybe."

He shakes his head and drags his hands down over his face, muttering about "goddamn civilians" and adding in some Spanish that sounds very uncomplimentary. He regains his composure and says in one of those tones that strongly discourages arguing, "We're going in now. Do what you want, just try not to get anybody else killed in the process."

I stick my tongue out at his back while he's distracted by outfitting John with some weaponry and everyone else starts moving into the formation he ordered. "Geez. What's Spanish for 'uptight'?" I mutter to Lia and she covers her mouth to keep from audibly laughing before moving into position herself.

Mac and Link stand just behind Luca, taking the lead with him. Terry and John are behind the lead three with Lia and me flanking Elliot behind them and Darryl and Rafe taking up the rear.

I adjust my grip on the machete, as my mood turns serious again in the quiet. I try to keep my mind on the zombies ahead and not the psycho killer behind, but I can't resist one last glance at the stairwell as Luca finally opens the door to the lab. For a second I think I see something, but my attention is soon captivated by the sounds and smells emanating from the now open doorway. One problem at a time.

Here we go.

Lia

Sergeant Ass Clown gets his wish for us to stop laughing as soon as he opens the door to the lab. It's easy to slip back into battle mode as I prepare myself for the new threat we're about to face. Still, my attention isn't solely focused on the fight to come and my heart is pounding more than it has before previous zombie battles. The idea that that psychopath Nate could be in the building with us is worrying, to put it mildly.

But my faster heartbeat is caused only partly by fear, mostly it's beating so fast because I'm seriously fucking pissed off. It's totally inconsiderate of him to still be alive. Why couldn't he have just done us all a favour and drowned? Or died of blood loss? I could've sworn either Lucy or I hit him when we were shooting at him, but he just keeps going, apparently. He's like the fucking Terminator! Or the Energizer Bunny.

Several wet, rasping sounds startle me out of this thought train so for now I force my thoughts away from that crazy in the coconut bastard and think about the task at hand. Better to focus on one bloodthirsty and seemingly immortal foe at a time.

I can't see very much of the room yet because of the five guys in front of me, but I can hear that we've caught the zombies' attention. It sounds like there's quite a few of them and they're all trying to shriek at once but it's not as loud as you might think. The sounds coming from inside the room are liquid and rattling—I think these decayed, subdued noises are actually more disturbing than the screeches of the fresher zombies, those ones are more otherworldly and inhuman, but the moans from these older zombies are that much more obviously the sounds of dead things.

And the smell. Holy disgusting smell, Batman. I have to work, both physically and mentally, to stop myself from throwing up. I glance at Elliot to see how he's holding up. He swallows hard, looking wan, but he gives me a shaky smile that for some reason helps calm me down. I think I kind of just enjoy looking at him. What can I say? The boy gives surprisingly good face. It sort of sneaks up on you, I guess.

Luca and the others finally move farther into the room. I want to go in because I want to get this over with, but hearing and smelling what's going on in there is bad enough, and I have to fight against an urge to avoid adding sight to the mix, too. I swing my axe gently back and forth a few times to help get myself in the spirit of things and I follow the others in.

The lab is cavernous, probably about 80 feet from end to end and about 60 feet across. "Spread out," Luca orders as we all finish filing into the room and we move around so we're not all clumped together.

Ugh. Yeah, seeing it is definitely worse. There is blood everywhere. Blood...and so much else. There's a phalanx of zombies across the room, my brain doesn't transmit the specific number right away—I'm too busy trying not to ralph. That smell is so much worse now that I'm in the room, which is saying a lot. Not only is it stronger, but it seems somehow thicker in here, too. The rusted copper smell of the blood is the best of it, the other smells are worse, way worse.

The zombies are slowly making their way over to us. A few are upright and shuffling along, looking every bit like traditional movie zombies. Some are sort of hunched over and crawling. But the most disturbing ones are dragging themselves across the floor, their movements jerky and juddering. They look like broken spiders.

I'm so focused on the approaching zombies that I don't think about why they might all have been concentrated on the other side of the lab until I hear a sad-sounding exhalation from Elliot. I look over at him then follow his gaze. There's a glass walled room across the lab and inside this are three bodies, not zombies, just dead, but it's no wonder the zombies were congregating there, they were the only source of fresh food—or any type of food—until we came in.

"Doc, how many do you need for your experiments?" Luca asks over his shoulder. "Decide quick because they are getting closer."

Elliot drags his attention from the bodies in the glass room and stares at the oncoming undead. Now that my brain's more adjusted to the smell of the room, I count thirteen zombies. "Um, maybe all of them. I don't know how many tries it will take to develop the antidote chemicals correctly."

"*Bueno*, we'll need to separate them so we can gain control without them having the chance to overwhelm us. Split up so they have multiple targets distracting them."

We break into several little groups and skirt around the edges of the huge lab until we're spread out sporadically. The zombies pause in their forward march now that their targets are in different places.

"We need to contain them. Everybody lead a few zombies into each of these smaller rooms then evade them and retreat. Lock them in and do not kill them unless you don't have another option," Luca orders.

Lucy does her zombie shriek and the rest of us follow suit in our own ways in order to get the attention of whichever zombies are closest to each of us. Elliot and I lead three of them into a nearby room. As we back inside the room, luring the zombies in after us, I feel my boots sticking slightly to the floor with each step. I look down to see why and notice that the room is covered in blood.

Elliot notices my sightline and says, "This is the room where it all started." I suppress a shudder at the thought and I have to suppress another when one of the zombies following us catches my eye. She's dragging herself along the ground and half her face is gone—it's now a mass of congealed blood and ragged strands of muscles and tissue. I can see parts of her cheekbone and her jaw through the wreckage. Her throat is a tattered mess, too: the inside of her esophagus is visible, making the gleaming whiteness of her exposed collarbone stand out even more starkly. I tear my eyes away from the ruin of her face and neck and focus on getting back out of the room without them getting close to us. As we edge around them, the one with the messed up face makes a swipe at my legs but it may as well be in slow motion, it's so easy to avoid.

We step back into the main lab area and I shut the door behind us. I ignore the muffled, disgruntled zombie sounds coming from within as I look around the room, checking that everyone made it back without issue. We're all accounted for, so I turn my attention along with everyone else to the glass room.

"Poor bastards," Rafe says as we approach the room that Elliot informs us was used as a quarantine area to keep people safe in case of emergencies. It looks like it didn't work out so well for the people inside—they escaped the zombies but, from the looks of it, not each other.

"Better than being a zombie," Link says and no one argues.

Elliot looks sadly down at the floor and I ask him if he knew them. "Yes. The woman was a lab technician on our project. Her name was Anne. The others were test subjects for another product that was being developed. I didn't know their names."

"I'm sorry," I say, taking his hand once again. He just shakes his head, seemingly unable to find any words. I'm grimly and selfishly glad that we didn't find any more survivors—it didn't work out well the first time and I wasn't looking forward to having to deal with hysterical people again.

Looking around at the group, I can tell that Lucy, for sure, shares my view of the situation and it looks like most of the others do, too, except for Terry and John, the other people who knew them, I guess.

Lucy

Honestly, I'm relieved that we didn't find more survivors. Thus far, with the exception of John, survivors have only been good for being cannon fodder, at best, and total time wasters, at worst. I hate to sound like a broken record, but I *have* seen the movies and you're lucky if you get one competent new addition to the group when new people show up, let alone all of them being anything more than useless. And since John has already proven himself competent, it didn't bode well for what new survivors might have brought to the table.

I study the grisly scene within the glass-walled room again. My brain doesn't want to keep looking at the images, but I can't seem to stop myself. Like looking at a car crash or reading about a starlet's latest fuck-up, it draws the eye. From what I can tell, it looks like Elliot's lab tech—Anne, he said—went berserk and stabbed the two test subjects, then killed herself. The scene is bloody and, although it's not as gory as a lot of what I've seen lately, it still makes me queasy. And sad. Even though the idea of dealing with the unknown dynamic new survivors would bring was stressing me out and is something I'm glad we don't have to deal with, this just drives home how many dead people we've seen and I'm sick of it. I'm just so sick of death. I turn away from the window.

"With the zombies squared away until you need them, this place should be nice and secure for you to get working on that cure, Doc." Mac's voice catches my attention and the current conversation finally breaks through my melancholia. A loud and derisive snort catches everyone else's attention and it's only after everyone turns to stare at me that I realize it came from me.

Whoops. I really need to learn how to keep my outbursts more in control. I feel my cheeks heating, but I put my hands on my hips defiantly and say, "I stand by my contemptuous noise. A false sense of safety doesn't lead to anything good. Or have none of you learned anything from our weekend of horror?"

"Lucy—" Mac begins in a tone that's half-consoling and half-reprimand, but Luca interrupts him.

"She's right." He shoots me a look and adds, "for once." I give him the finger, which he ignores and resumes talking, "We don't know for sure if we have something to worry about besides the zombies"—I snort scornfully again, intentionally this time, at his continued insistence that there's a possibility that Nate isn't in the vicinity and he glares at me for a moment—"but we should still be on our guard as much as possible." He raises his eyebrows at me as if to ask if I'm satisfied.

To me, this isn't enough, not nearly enough, but due to my exhaustion, stress, and fear, I don't have any concrete suggestions to offer, so I remain silent, which Luca takes as acquiescence. He turns his attention away from me and back to Elliot, questioning him about what he needs to begin work on the cure.

Mac walks up beside me. "You okay?" he asks, sliding his arm around my waist once Luca is distracted by strategizing with Elliot.

"I'm fine."

"You seem pretty on edge," he says, with his characteristic smile, like he's trying to calm me down. I don't know if it's everything that's going on or the dread that keeps pricking the back of my skull, but this time, it only serves to set my nerves off further. I feel stretched as tight as piano wire.

"Right. 'Cause there's no reason for me to be."

"Geez, it's like you're looking for a reason to be mad at me."

I stiffen against his arm and step out of his grip. "Do you not get how serious this situation is? There are multiple zombies still alive, just in this area, plenty more back at the campground that we're gonna have to deal with at some point, and whether you guys will admit it or not, a maniac running around just waiting for us to mess up so he can start picking us off one by one. And what? I'm supposed to be totally cool with all of this?"

The others stop talking and turn to look at the two of us as my voice gets louder. Mac raises his hands in surrender. "Alright, Jesus, I'm sorry. I was just trying to lighten the mood."

"Maybe the mood just needs to stay heavy for once."

"What does that even mean?" he asks and I wave him off, turning to walk away for a cooling off period. I only make it a couple of steps before the dread that has been a dull ache crawling up the back of my head ever since I found out that Nate was still around suddenly contorts into some new and improved panic.

Something is wrong. Something is different.

It's the door. It's open—propped open.

We didn't do that.

"Lucy? Lucy!" Mac's voice finally cuts through the sound of my heart pounding in my ears. "What the hell just happened? You look like you've seen a ghost." I feel like all colour must have drained from my face and my breathing is stuttered. I think this must be a panic attack. I've never had one before, but this definitely feels like my panic is literally attacking me.

Lia appears suddenly in front of me and I step back in alarm. I was so focused on the door I didn't notice her approach. "Luce, what the hell? You're scaring me, now, come on," she says, stepping forwards and gripping my shoulders tightly. Her fingers dig into my skin and I shake my head roughly, brushing her hands and the hand Mac had placed against my back away as I clear my head.

If I panic, he wins. He cannot win. "Sorry. I'm fine."

Lia makes a noise of disbelief in response and crosses her arms. "What happened?"

"Yeah, what was that?" Mac asks. I look at him and take another alarmed step back as I finally notice that everyone else is gathered behind him, looking on in unease.

"Did you finally snap?" Luca asks and my annoyance clears the last of the panic from my system.

I throw him one of the dirtiest looks I can muster and say, "Fuck you. The door is open."

"Is that some sort of riddle?" he asks disdainfully.

I sigh in frustration. "No. Literally, the door to the lab is open. Something is propping it open." I look at Rafe and Darryl. "Did you guys do that?"

They look at each other, and then turn to look at the door. Everyone else looks with them. "No," Rafe says. Darryl confirms that he didn't either.

"Okay, that's probably not good," Mac says and I look at him and shake my head.

"Now, *that's* the understatement of the year." He gives me a sheepish look before turning his attention back to the portentous door.

"It's probably just caught on something," Luca says.

"Like what?" Lia asks, incredulous.

"Why don't you go over there and find out?"

"No one should go over there and find out. It's obviously a trap," I say.

"A trap? You're paranoid."

"By definition, to be paranoid means that one's fears are unfounded. We've all seen what he's capable of. My fears are not unfounded, ergo, I'm not paranoid, you're just a dick, and I can guaran-damn-tee that that door being open like that is a trap. It's just an invitation to death."

"Fine. No one goes near the door then. Can we get on with making the cure now?"

"I'm sorry, but who is it that you think is out there again?" John asks and Luca moans, "Do not get her started on her horror movie theories. We do not have time for this."

"Whatever. Do what you want, but with that door open, he has easy access to us any time he wants," I say.

"Who has access?" John asks just as Luca snaps, "'Don't go near the door, but the door can't stay open'...what exactly do you suggest then?"

"I suggest you go fuck yourself," I growl as I walk away from the group, trying to organize my thoughts as I keep my eye trained on the door, watching for movement.

"Very mature," Luca calls after me, but his voice is easy to ignore as something at the bottom of the door catches my eye.

I stop walking abruptly again and almost fall over as Lia steps quickly up beside me. "Are you having another panic attack?"

"What? No. Just—what is that?"

"What's what?" she asks, eyes following the direction I'm pointing in. "Huh. What *is* that?"

I take a few steps closer, trying to make out what I'm seeing. From this far away, all I can see is that it's something that looks to be palely flesh-coloured and covered in blood. Alarm bells are going off inside my head as I edge a bit closer, still about half the room away, which still seems like a safe enough distance, and the object suddenly comes into focus as the elements of what I'm seeing fall into place.

"Oh, God."

Lia is right on my heels and has her freak out a few seconds after mine. "Fuck."

"What now?" Luca grumbles from behind us.

"It's a head."

"Ahead of what?" Rafe asks.

"No. It's a head. The thing propping open the door. It's a decapitated fucking head," I say, grasping my machete so tight it hurts.

"*Qué?*"

"What?" John echoes Luca, sounding concerned.

"Who's head?" Terry asks.

"Didn't get close enough to tell for sure, but if I had to guess, I'd say AJ's," Lia says. I grunt in agreement and remind myself to breathe. It's probably safe to assume that Amy is dead, too. Just cannon fodder, that's all they were. They may have been useless, but they didn't deserve to die just so some whack-job could cause more panic and put his actual intended victims more on edge before he kills them...us.

"There might be another explanation besides Nate," Luca says.

I whirl around and stalk over to him. "Right, I'm sure it's just our friendly neighbourhood decapitated head fairy! When are you going to get it through you're thick skull? He's here, he's hunting us and right now, he's toying with us!" Luca exhales and looks to be gearing up for another fight when he's distracted by Lia's voice. "Terry, wait! Don't go over there!"

I whip around to see Terry approaching the door. My heart starts pounding even faster. "No." I want to shout it, scream it, but it comes out as a whisper in my suddenly dry throat.

"It *is* AJ," Terry confirms as he leans down, grasping AJ's hair in one fist.

"NO! Terry, get away from there!" I yell, my voice finally coming out the way I intend and before I can think about the intelligence of what I'm doing, I'm sprinting over to Terry. He turns his head to me, looking alarmed, so I get to see in heart wrenching detail the sudden shock and pain on his face as the knife blade hits home, slamming into his chest with a sickening thunk. He falls backward, AJ's head still clutched in his fist as he hits the ground. The door falls shut just as I reach Terry.

The sound of running feet behind me heralds the approach of the others as I crouch beside Terry. He's still alive, but barely. His eyes are rolling back in his head and he's coughing up blood.

"No. Goddammit!" I hear myself say as I place my hands on his chest, barely noticing that my hands are now covered in blood.

I know there's nothing I can do at this point, but I can't seem to just stay still.

"Terry, no," Elliot pleads as he kneels beside me, looking heartsick as he stares down at Terry.

Terry's eyes focus on Elliot's face for a second. "Sorry, Doc." His voice takes on a strange tone around the blood oozing from his mouth and he shudders a last breath before falling silent and still. His grip on AJ's hair relaxes and the head rolls against my foot. I smack it away, not paying attention to where it lands.

"Goddammit!" I cry again, standing up abruptly and punching the door. Pain sings through my knuckles and I bring my hand to my face, ignoring the metallic scent of Terry's blood and trying to calm my breathing. It's only then that I realize I must have dropped my machete at some point since it's not in my hand. I see it now, on the ground beside Terry. No. Beside Terry's body.

My eyes drift over to Lia, who's kneeling beside Elliot with her arms around him, as she whispers, "I'm sorry," over and over again in his ear as he cries noiselessly, seemingly unable to tear his eyes away from his dead friend.

A choking rage takes me over. I walk over to the body and yank the knife out of his chest, spraying blood. I ignore the surprised and outraged cries of people around me, not even paying enough attention to see who made them. I'm focused on one thing and one thing only. I stalk up to Luca and smack the bloodied knife into his hands.

"This is Nate's knife. Any other bullshit explanations now? Or are you finally ready to get your head out of your ass and deal with the fact that he's here, he's fucking with us and he's planning on killing every last one of us?" Tears of outrage slip down my cheeks and I beat them away furiously, smearing blood across my face and not giving a single fuck.

Luca stares down at the knife and shuts his eyes for a second. "*Lo siento.*" He pauses, and then repeats himself in English, "I'm sorry. You were right."

I stare at him, trying to get my anger under control, knowing, if only abstractly right now that the hatred I'm feeling is really for Nate, and that Luca is simply the next best closest thing at which I can direct these vitriolic emotions. I finally get myself under enough control to speak, although my voice still shakes wrathfully as I say, "I'm not the one you should be apologizing to."

Luca looks past me at Elliot then nods at me. He walks over to the trio made of Elliot, Lia, and Terry's body and crouches down beside them as he starts talking in a low voice.

"I'm sorry, too. I just really wanted him to be dead," Mac says quietly, coming up beside me and tentatively putting his hand on my arm. I nod without saying anything. I'm too angry still to want a hug, but I can tell Mac needs one and needs to give me one so I lean into him and slip my arms around his waist. He relaxes against me. "We'll get him," he says, tightening his arms around me.

"Yes, we will," I say, surprising even myself a little with the fury in my tone. Mac pulls away from the hug a bit and studies me.

"Man, I wouldn't wanna be him for a lot of reasons, but right now, it's especially because of that look on your face." I give him a smile that, judging from his reaction, does nothing to soften the effect of my anger. He smiles nervously at me, like you might at a wild animal and pulls me back into the hug, repeating, "We'll get him." I nod against his chest and calm myself by picturing Natc's death and mentally repeating myself.

Yes, we will. And if I have anything to do with it, he'll die screaming.

Nate

That went pretty much as well as planned. It would have been even better if Mac or Lia had taken the bait, but we can't have everything. At the last second, I was worried that Lucy might somehow fall into the trap, but she's too smart to fall for something like that. I knew she was, but I can't hold back a wave of relief that she wasn't the one who investigated the head, it would have ruined everything, since I couldn't have killed her, despite the fact that she could probably be my undoing if the others would pay more attention to her and listen to her more often.

When I was waiting on the landing for them to enter the lab, I was sure Lucy would notice me. But the risk of the closeness was necessary for my plan. Otherwise, entering the lab would have been much more difficult, maybe even impossible since I don't know the code to get in.

Father's lessons may have been arduous at the time, but they're certainly coming in handy now. Darryl and Rafe didn't even hear me as I walked behind them and caught the door, propping it open with the man's head. And the idiots, it took them forever to notice and, if not for Lucy, they might not have noticed at all.

It was an exercise in patience waiting to see who would take the bait. But it was worth it. I didn't see their reactions, of course, but I know how they think. How they react. The knife will scare them more than if I'd shot him. I don't understand why that is. Someone shot to death is just as dead as if they were stabbed, but something about a blade frightens people more than bullets. It doesn't matter. The more scared they are the more it serves my purposes anyway.

The loss of the knife is regrettable—it was one of my favourites. But I have so many knives, I guess it doesn't really matter in the end. And seeing it hit my target so perfectly almost makes the loss worth it. Yet another thing to thank Father for, all those years of target practice made my aim flawless. I would thank him, too. If he were still alive.

But there are so many more important things to think about right now. I have to focus. They're not coming after me immediately. I knew they wouldn't. They'll be in a state of shock and anyway, now that they know for sure I'm here, they're likely to proceed with more caution, which will finally make things more interesting. Until then, it's time to wait again.

Patience is a virtue.

Chapter Fourteen
If this *were* a horror movie and not just my suddenly screwed up life, portentous music would definitely be playing right about now

Elliot

My hands are shaking and I've lost my train of thought again as the vials in front of me go blurry. I feel a hand against my back and Lia's voice breaks through the numbness. "Hey, breathe, okay, just take a breath." Her hand rubs in slow circles around my back and I clench my jaw against the memories of Terry lying there dead, Nate's knife jutting out of his chest. I lean in against her, trying to clear my head as much as possible.

"I can't believe he's gone."

"I know. I'm so sorry." She leans her head against mine. I take in a shuddering breath and re-focus on the work in front of me.

"We need to keep going."

"Yeah, but you can take a breather. This was a hard one."

I shake my head and turn to look at her, focusing on her beautiful ocean-coloured eyes with everything in me. "No. I have to do this. This is the best thing I can do to make things right. When this is finished, we can focus on getting Nate. That's what matters."

Lia breaks into a fierce smile and presses her forehead against mine. "Damn straight. He's not going to make it out of this alive."

"I fear none of us will."

Lia straightens and gives me the fiercest look I've seen on her face yet, which is saying a lot. "You can't think like that. This, all of it, is for nothing if we just give up. If you fight to the end, even if you still lose, at least you know you did everything in your power to stop it from happening."

Her ferocity is infectious.

"You're right." I breathe deeply again, in and out, and stare hard at the materials in front of me. "Okay. Let's do this." I will force myself to pour all of my concentration into developing an antidote; I can't afford to lose it now. I look over at Lia and remind myself that there are still people I need to help and protect for as long as I can, in any way that I can.

"What is it exactly that you're doing, Doctor Frink?" John asks as he comes up behind us.

"We need to come up with a chemical compound to counteract the mutated effects of Inner Thin."

"This...was all caused by...a diet pill?" he asks, incredulous.

"Ironic, right?" Lia says with a half-smile on her face.

John doesn't return the smile. "You caused this? You did this?" He gestures helplessly around the room, the sweep of his arm encompassing the gory remainders of the devastation.

"Watch it—" Lia begins warningly, but I interrupt her, squeezing her arm to take away the sting of cutting her off. "That's not important right now. We need to find a way to create a sort of antidote, in gas form if at all possible, so that we can neutralize multiple zombies more effectively. That's what's most important right now."

"Why can't you just kill them? There's not that many."

"We don't know exactly how many are left in the building, but that's beside the point anyway, there's many more back at the campground we escaped to...and then from."

"There's more?" John asks. "This sure is a shit-show you've created, Doctor."

"It wasn't *his* fault!" Lia growls defensively.

"Lia, it's fine—"

"It is not!"

John shakes his head and starts walking away, waving us off in a way that suggests it's not worth the effort to continue talking to us. I can see Lia gearing up to vent some of her wrath at him, but I tug on her hand until she turns to face me.

"It's fine, really"—she opens her mouth to argue, but I continue talking—"he's right. One way or another, I had a hand in this. Now I just need to do whatever I can to fix it."

Lia exhales and nods, then squeezes my shoulder. "Alright. What can I do?"

"I need you to gather equipment and ingredients while I study my experiment notes." She nods in assent and walks away as I sit down on the stool behind me, glancing at what I gathered in my haste to get started. Not much is of use right now, so I simply start re-familiarizing myself with everything we put into Inner Thin in the first place, so I can figure out exactly what I need to neutralize the chemicals that mutated.

Despite what I said to Lia, John's disgusted face when he realized that I'd had a hand in this destruction keeps running through my mind, and it's hard to not let the guilt overwhelm and distract me. I need to focus. The sooner I get the antidote developed, the sooner we can go after Nate, and the sooner we can make him pay for the things that he's done. And he will pay.

Connor

Elliot and Lia are busy working on the cure and the rest of us—Rafe, Darryl, Link, Luke, Lucy, me, and John—are busy making plans for hunting down Nate.

"I still say we should go right now, go after him and bring him down," Luke says, glowering heatedly at Lucy. He's more inclined to listen to her since Nate killed Terry, but it's obvious he still hates the way she challenges his authority.

"Look, I get that. You don't think I want him dead, too? But your plan means splitting up—"

"You're saying we should wait till the Doc is finished with his cure, without knowing how long that might take or what Nate could be planning next? Do you think *that* is a good plan?"

A dark look crosses Lucy's face and her mouth thins, but after a few deep breaths she says, "Fair enough. So, what then? What do we do?"

"We go after him. He can't get in here without knowing the codes and there's no way he could know them. Why else would he have had to prop open the door?"

"Scare tactics," Lucy counters.

"Okay," Rafe says, "yeah, but he still probably doesn't know the codes. How could he?" Lucy shrugs then growls in frustration.

"What?" Link asks.

"I just—every instinct tells me that we shouldn't split up."

"If we don't, we're just sitting ducks, waiting for him to make the next move," Darryl points out and Lucy nods, staring intensely at the floor.

"He's just a man," John adds, "he doesn't have super powers and he's not invincible. Six or seven of us against one man. I like those odds."

I expect Lucy to say something about him obviously not seeing enough horror movies then, but she's quiet and her gaze keeps drifting over to Terry's body, covered with a spare lab coat. That's the best we could do given that all the adjoining rooms are filled with zombies right now and we don't want them chowing down on his body.

"If you're scared, you don't have to come with us," Luca says and, knowing him the way I do, I know he's attempting to be comforting, but it just comes off sounding condescending and I wince as Lucy's eyes snap up to meet his, full of fire once again.

"I'm not scared," she spits the word out, then sucks in a breath and reconsiders this statement. "Or, I am, of course I am, but I don't run from fights when I'm scared. I'm just frustrated that none of our options seem like good ones, and I'm tired and I am so sad for Elliot and I'm so angry and rage is just exhausting. I want him dead, so, so bad. I just wish that there was a way to accomplish it without giving him a chance to kill any more of us."

"Times like this, you just have to pick the best of the bad options. And as far as I'm concerned, that's going after him, now, on our terms. You can come with us or you can stay here, but that's what we're doing," Luke says, his voice somehow more reassuring this time. I wish Lucy would stay behind, she'd probably be safer here and I don't wanna be worrying about her while we're looking for Nate. I know she can handle herself in a fight, but that's not really the issue. Anyway, now that Luke's said it I can't disagree and if I did, she'd be pissed, so it's probably best to just keep my mouth shut, something I am occasionally capable of.

"I'm coming with you."

I try to rearrange my features to be supportive, but by the look on her face, Lucy caught the disappointed look on mine. I wanna explain, but I can't, not with everyone else here. She turns away from me and focuses on Luke. "It's gonna be tough to get Lia to agree to this, though."

Luca makes a face at the prospect, and then says, "Let's get it over with."

We head over to where they're working and Luca tells them our plan.

"No. Hell, no! What the hell, Luce, you agreed to this? Being against splitting up may as well be against your religion and you're just suddenly on board with this insanity?"

Lucy takes a deep breath and explains it the way Luca explained it to her. "It's the best of the bad plans. You see that, right?"

"Fine. But you stay here." I'm glad Lia's on my side with this one; it makes me feel less like I let Lucy down.

"No. I'm sorry, but I'm going with them. I want to help. I can't just stay here and wait."

"Like you're asking me to do?" Lia says, voice tight.

"You're helping Elliot. He needs you. I need to do this."

"Why?"

"Because what if it had been you? What if next time it is you? Or Mac? Or Elliot? You tried to warn me and I didn't listen, and now I just want him to pay."

"But what if next time it's you?" I can't help asking.

"Exactly," Lia adds. "You can't get angry if we want to protect you when you want to protect us and are willing to die to do so."

"Look, it could be any of us. Staying here and waiting could be just as dangerous as going after him, so this argument is irrelevant. We're going. Doc, you need to finish that cure. Lia, if you're helping him, then you stay and continue to help. Lucy, I think you should come with us. You know more about the way he thinks and could prevent us from walking into a trap," Luca says, his voice taking on the tone he uses when giving direct orders, which are not to be questioned. Lia's glower only deepens at this and I feel my stomach knot up in shared displeasure.

"I'm still not agreeing to this," Lia says, and then to Lucy, "how would you feel if it was reversed?"

"Terrible. I know. I just, I have to do this. I'm sorry."

Lia inhales and stares hard at Lucy, taking in the determined look on her face. She sighs and growls, "If you get yourself killed going after him, I'm gonna kick your ass." Lucy smiles ruefully and hugs Lia tight.

"I'll be right back," she says, pulling away from hugging Lia and attempting to joke. My gut clenches at the numerous horror movie scenes this phrase calls to mind.

"Don't say that," Lia says, her voice tense. Lucy mumbles an apology.

"Be careful," Elliot says to Lucy, then, "all of you. Be careful."

Lucy locks eyes fiercely with him and says, "For Terry."

"For Preach," I say.

"For Marco," Link adds.

"For everyone, we'll get him," Lucy says. "Let's finish this."

"Hoo-ah," Rafe adds.

I nod at him and add my voice to his. "Hoo-ah."

"Let's go. Time to deep-six this *hijoputa* once and for all," Luca barks and amid the general responses of "hell, yeah!" we turn to go.

Luca leaves Darryl and Rafe behind so they can each watch one of the lab doors and Lia and Elliot can keep working. Luca takes point as we approach the door and he pauses for a second before opening it cautiously, and then whipping it open and aiming his gun into the space beyond. He lingers in the doorway for a second and I peer around him to see why. Sitting propped up against the bottom stair is the rest of AJ. His headless body is slumped over and covered in blood.

Man, Nate is one sick fuck.

I glance at Lucy to see her reaction to the maimed corpse. I wish this would be enough to make her turn back now, but though she looks pale and slightly sick, she also looks more determined than ever.

Damn.

Once it's apparent that Nate won't be jumping out at us from around the corner, Luca gathers himself and gives the all-clear signal and we follow him like we always do. I would follow Luke into oblivion. I just wish Lucy weren't here when it feels like we could be doing just that.

Nate

I've made my way back up three floors when a noise from behind a door leading away from the landing causes my curiosity to flare up. It's alien, yet familiar and I want to see what's making it. I try the doorknob, confident about my chances of entering unhindered since there's no key pad. The knob turns easily and I slip inside, keeping my guard up. As I step inside the room, my foot catches on something and I trip. I turn it into a roll and am back up on my feet in a heartbeat. I turn around to see what I tripped on, but now that the smell has hit me, it's unnecessary.

A decayed zombie drags itself slowly toward me as it moans roughly. That alien but familiar sound. I could kill myself, I'm so furious. I let out an infuriated noise as I flip the bayonet out from the barrel of my SKS and stab the zombie directly through the top of its head. I bring the blade down a few more times to make sure it's dead and to release some of my frustration.

How could I have forgotten what I was hunting in the first place? I got so caught up in pursuing the others, in the thrill of the hunt that I forgot about the primary threat. Father would not be pleased. And he would be right to punish me for such carelessness. What if I had killed Elliot? Then there'd be no chance of a cure, no chance to reliably take out multiple zombies at once and with efficiency. I stab the unmoving zombie one more time, trying to control my emotions.

I just have to admit it. I made a mistake. I fucked up. I just had to amuse myself by playing the game. Such an amateur mistake. And now they could be hunting me, trying to find me. What if they put off making the cure because of it? I let out a growl and shake my head to clear it from this useless train of thought.

There's no sense in obsessing over what ifs; what's done is done. I made my mistakes, all I can do now is to try to fix things as much as possible, and go back to focusing on my original prey. The others can wait. They don't have the potential for becoming a long-term threat, unlike the zombies, so that's what I need to be focusing on. And since they're the ones who will be making the cure, that's what they need to be focusing on, too.

I leave my bayonet blade out, covered in zombie gore and blood, and take a moment to cover the blade of my second favourite knife in the same way— it's all part of my new plan. I stomp on the zombie's head as I walk over it and exit the room.

It's time to start fixing my mistakes.

Lucy

My heart is in my throat as we walk slowly up the stairs, watching for any sign of Nate. I know what I'm doing is stupid. I also know that it's probably our best chance to find him. His motivations may have changed, but I'm willing to bet—my life if I have to—that if anyone will be able to draw him out, and provoke him into a direct confrontation rather than him continuing to pick us off, well, it'll probably be me. Which I'm pretty sure is the only reason Luca let me come with them in the first place and if Mac knew, he probably would've locked me up to stop me from doing this. And if Lia knew...I can't even think about that right now.

I grip my machete more tightly and I feel Mac step closer to me, his breath on the back of my neck as he asks, "You okay?"

I nod and clench my jaw. It's harder to keep determined to follow my plan through when he's being all sweet and adorably worried. I can picture the look on his face just fine and it's bad enough without seeing it firsthand. That little wrinkle he gets between his eyebrows when he's concerned could just break my heart right about now and I have to keep my focus.

We reach the main floor and just as we're approaching the staircase to continue upstairs, there's a noise from behind the door leading to the hallway that feeds into the reception area. Luca stops, looking tense as he turns to face the door. He looks back at me, a question on his face. I nod, marvelling at how cooperative he's finally being. And all it took was me tacitly offering myself as bait to catch a psycho. Who knew it would be so easy? And since I *am* bait for a murderer anyway, I figure at this point, what the hell? Let's go investigate the strange noise. Besides, I think the rules change when you're the one hunting versus just being hunted.

Luca approaches the door and Mac hisses from behind me, "You're not gonna argue about this? You've seen even more horror movies than I have. How can you be okay with this?"

I hold my breath as Luca eases the door open and a chill crawls up my spine as I see the darkness within the room ahead. Great. It definitely looks like we're getting closer. First, we have a strange noise and now, a creepy, shadowy room; the super villain will most definitely be close by.

"Lucy," Mac hisses again and I realize I didn't answer his question.

"It's like Luca said, this is just the best of the bad plans," I whisper this over my shoulder. My attention is still riveted by the darkness ahead and besides, I still don't want to see the look on Mac's face. I may be ready to face off with bat-shit crazy Nate, but I just can't take Mac's puppy-dog eyes right now. "It'll be okay," I add, feeling like I just sealed my own fate.

"What?" Mac practically yelps then falls silent as Luca shoots him a murderous glare. Mac grabs my arm and whirls me around to face him. I swear silently to myself and raise my eyes to meet his. The damage to my heart is even worse than what I was expecting. The betrayed and scared look on his face makes me feel like my heart is made of paper and has just been torn into tiny pieces so I can barely catch my breath. "Lucy, what are you doing?" His tone is heavy with emotion, even as he's whispering. His eyes flick to Luca's back and the pain reflected in their green depths makes me want to run myself through with my machete, although I guess that would kinda make using me as bait pretty pointless. I can't take it anymore and I seek refuge from his accusing stare by locking my gaze onto the floor. "Lucy." His tone is pleading this time and I can barely stand it.

"This is the best way, the only way." My voice comes out sounding harsh, tinged with emotions I'm trying to keep under control, and it sounds close to when I do my Batman impression. I'd laugh if I could be sure it wouldn't turn into tears.

"Hey, *ven aca*," Luca growls quietly from behind me.

"I'm sorry," I whisper softly to Mac as I turn around, still avoiding his gaze.

Luca is watching us intently. I dip my head in apology and return my focus to what lies ahead. Luca shoots a look at Mac, one I can't quite decipher, but it stops any further protests and we prepare to head into the abyss. Normally, I'd be worried about Nate having heard us...or I guess, normally I wouldn't be in this situation at all, but anyway...objectively, I'd generally be against giving away one's position to a crazed serial killer, but since we want to draw him out, I suppose it's not necessarily a bad thing right now.

We put on our night vision goggles and I'm suddenly very glad that Darryl and Rafe handed theirs over to John and me in case we should need them. It's one thing to try hunting Nate in the light, but I've always had issues with things that go bump in the dark so I gladly slip my pair over my head and flick the switch, ignoring the goose bumps that crop up along my arms and the back of my neck as the eerie green wash replaces the shadowed interior of the hallway.

I fight to keep my breath steady as the door shuts with a soft click behind us. I remind myself that this is the best way to protect the people that I care about and whom I put in danger when I trusted Nate in the first place. It was his damn face and his stupidly cool name that got me. It's just not right that someone so hot and with such an awesome name turned out to be so completely bonkers. It's not fair. He's like one of those pretty insects that attracts birds with their beauteousness and then bites their heads off or something.

The walk down the hallway is soundless and uneventful, which only serves to raise my blood pressure all the more. If this *were* a horror movie and not just my suddenly screwed up life, portentous music would definitely be playing right about now. I'm just imagining the creeptastic strains that would be echoing from the theatre speakers when Luca eases open the door leading into the reception area, complete with a horrendous creaking sound that I do not remember happening earlier. I have to forcibly stop myself from jumping out of my skin and I'm just barely successful.

"Did it make that sound before?" Mac whispers, confirming my theory.

"Nope," I answer, marvelling at Nate's brand of crazy. If my friends and I weren't the ones in danger from his machinations, I might actually be objectively impressed with his creativity. Luca's waving arm catches my attention and I realize that he's motioning for me to go forward.

I walk up past the others and, as I draw parallel with him, he quietly asks, "Trap?"

"Definitely."

"Are you ready?"

"Sure," I say, and he glances at me. "Well, I don't know if this is something one can ever truly be ready for, but, yeah, I'm good to go. Let's get this bastard." He nods and we slowly enter the reception area.

The few shapes around the room are blurred around the edges, rendered amorphous by the night vision, but it's obvious that Nate isn't in plain sight. I can make out what looks like a person on the far side of the room, but the figure is prone and is likely the poor guard that Nate killed, Benji. Still, you never know, and if Nate is anything, it's crafty, so we should check it out. I'm about to say as much to Luca when the lights suddenly come back on, making the night vision goggles suddenly a hindrance, as the sudden switch in polarity makes us all momentarily blind. I reach for mine, intent on getting my vision back as soon as possible when an arm slides around my stomach, pulling me back against someone's muscular chest. I can't tell who it is at first, but as their free hand grasps the wrist of my machete-wielding arm and twists until I feel an agonizing snap, I know it can only be one person.

My machete drops from my grip as the overwhelming pain shoots up my arm. A hand covers my mouth, effectively cutting off my cry of pain and pinning my head back against his chest. In this uncomfortable position, verging on excruciating thanks to my surely broken wrist, I am dragged backwards and into an adjoining room—something I only ascertain because of the sound of a door quietly closing. My night vision goggles are still making me blind and the agony from my wrist isn't helping; black spots are dancing across my vision and it takes me a second to notice that I can see again when the goggles are removed from my head. I look up and see Nate towering over me, making the main problem of being bait for a crazy person abundantly clear: it is very hard to predict exactly what crazy people are going to do next.

I reach for the gun holstered at my hip. Dazed by the pain, I forget for a second that my lead hand is now useless and, as the movement jars my mangled bones, I can't hold back a scream, but Nate clamps his hand over my mouth again, moving so damn fast, I can barely process it. My surprise mutes me as effectively as his hand does.

He lowers me onto the ground, crouching beside me as he whispers, "Shh, relax. I'm not going to kill you." I'm still so off-kilter right now that I can't even muster up a sarcastic remark. "Well, I'm not going to kill you directly. If they don't come up with a cure in time, then you'll die, but I'd rather you didn't. I really hope you don't die."

My heart is pounding painfully fast as I try to work out what he means through the agony that is muddling my brain. He edges around behind me, keeping his hand over my mouth. "This shouldn't hurt too badly," he says as he grabs my right leg and draws it into my stomach, putting me into an uncomfortable and quite helpless position. He draws my pant leg up and as I see the flash of a blade, my instincts kick in, overriding the internal chaos caused by the pain in my wrist. I flail wildly, wrenching my head back and clipping him with the back of my head. The impact blurs my vision momentarily and he pauses for a second before tightening his grip.

"Stop it! I can do this to you or I can do it to Mac—or maybe I should find Lia." I go still even before I make the conscious decision to do so and Nate laughs softly. "I thought that might work. It's admirable the way you care so much for others, but you should be careful, it opens you up to weakness." The blade of his bayonet flashes again as if to punctuate this remark, and a new pain races through my synapses as it slices across my shin and a little way into the side of my calf when it goes deep and glances off the bone. I gasp and Nate huffs impatiently. "Sorry, it's sharper than I realized." I stare at the blade, now noticing that there's more than just my blood on it; there's something darker and thicker looking adorning it, as well.

"What did you do?" I ask, fighting off panic, not very successfully if my intense heart rate is any indication.

"Relax. If they can come up with a cure—and quickly—you'll be fine."

I start shaking as this cryptic response and its implications fully sink in. I stare down at the gash on my leg. "Oh, God." I put a trembling hand to my lips.

"This should give them motivation to do what needs to be done. This is really for the best. The zombies are the primary threat. It's not personal. I actually like you very much. But this is a sacrifice that needs to me made. I hope you survive this." I stare up at Nate, trying to form a coherent thought beyond, "Dear God, I do not wanna be a zombie." I finally find one, born on a thread of pure fury and rage. Using my uninjured left hand, I take my omnipresent switchblade out of my waistband and flip it open. The sounds of the guys recovering and regrouping outside catches Nate's attention and I don't plan, I just throw myself towards him

STAY CALM AND AIM FOR THE HEAD

and bring the blade down. It lands in the meat of his calf and he grunts in pain. My forward momentum continues carrying me and I land awkwardly on my broken wrist and a sharp shriek of pain escapes me.

Nate looks down at me frowning only slightly, a seeming under reaction that sends creeping danger warnings along the back of my neck and makes me shift away from him, as I cradle my injured arm against my chest. Nate doesn't advance on me, he simply bends down and yanks out the knife. Before he can do anything else, the door suddenly swings open behind Nate and he doesn't even hesitate, he drops my switchblade, whips around and stabs his bayonet into the first person through the door.

Connor

The blade erupts out of John's back, droplets of blood spraying out with the force behind the attack. Nate pulls his bayonet back, twisting it as he does, making John's injury worse and almost certainly fatal. He continues holding John in front of him as he walks out of the storage room. Link makes a move towards Nate and John and Nate shoots his rifle, straight through John; his body muffles the shot a little. Link falls back as his arm is clipped by the bullet.

John's slumped position in Nate's grip makes it obvious that he's dead, so I don't hesitate to shoot at Nate by way of aiming at John. John's body jerks spastically with the impact, blood misting the air as a large hole erupts in his shoulder, but Nate seems unharmed. I wish we were armed with something besides hollow point bullets. Nate's full metal jackets go right through John, but ours stop and explode on impact, usually a useful feature in bringing someone down, but right now it's just helping Nate get away unscathed.

Fury boils up inside me, tempered only by my worry for Lucy. Luca continues shooting as Nate retreats behind his shield of John's body, but I turn and go back to the storage room he dragged Lucy into. She's sitting on the floor, thankfully alive, but looking like she's in pain. "Lucy, thank God you're okay," I say, about to rush in and pull her into my arms. I'm so relieved she's alive; I can't thank the Big Guy Upstairs enough.

"I'm fine, just go." I pause and look at her, feeling confused. "Just get him, before he escapes." I nod. She's right, we have to end this. I turn to go, then stop and rush over to her, bending down and kissing her quickly before I have to slip back into the soldier mind frame. Her lips press back against mine for just a second before she pulls away, saying, "Go."

I flash her a quick smile and head back out into the main reception area. My elation at finding Lucy alive is stamped out suddenly by the scene in front of me. John's body has been discarded and Nate now has Luca in an iron grip, a knife against his throat.

"No!" I holler, running toward them, closing the distance as fast as I can and bringing my gun up, aiming it at Nate's head.

"Stop there or I slit his throat here and now," Nate says, bringing me staggering to a halt about ten feet away from them. "Put your gun down on the ground and kick it over here." I look wildly around the room, trying to find Link, hoping for back-up. I see him crumpled on the ground, off to my left. I feel numb as I pray he's still alive. I return my attention to Nate and Luca. "Put your gun on the ground and kick it over here," Nate repeats, slowly, like you'd explain things to the village idiot. I clench my jaw and put my SIG Pro on the ground, kicking it across the floor and standing up straight again. I curl my hands into fists and glower at Nate, putting all my rage and loathing into it.

Nate stares back at me, impassive, before saying, "You have two choices. You can come at me and Luca will die. There's a chance you could bring me down, but it's more likely that you'll die in the attempt, too. And then it will be really easy for me to go back and finish what I started with Lucy." Dread washes over me at the thought of two people I care about so much dying.

"What's the second choice?" I ask, the absolute abhorrence I feel for Nate clear in my voice.

"You let me go without a fight and make sure they finish that cure and you'll all have a chance of surviving this."

"Yeah, I really trust you to keep your word, you twisted fucker."

Nate sighs. "I want the same thing you want. The eradication of the zombies before it turns into an epidemic. I'm simply trying to give you all ample motivation to get the antidote working as soon as possible."

"You're insane."

"I'm just trying to ensure my optimum survival. That's perfectly sane."

"Right. So how exactly did killing Terry or Benji or Amy or AJ 'ensure your optimum survival'?"

Nate sighs again. "I admit, I got caught up in the game—"

"The game? Those were people's lives. You—"

"I'm tired of this. Make your choice. Try to fight me and sacrifice Luca's life as well as your own, and Lucy's, or not," Nate offers, pressing the knife more tightly against Luca's throat and drawing a bead of blood. Luca is mouthing something at me but I can't make it out.

I think about Lucy and what Nate might do to her if he got another chance and I unclench my fists. "Fine. Just get the fuck out of here."

Nate smiles, igniting my fury again and making it close to impossible to stay where I am. "You've made the right choice." He shoves Luca to the ground and grabs his duffle bag, whips the door open and runs out of the building. The door slams shut behind him and Luca grabs the gun I'd kicked over, yanks the door open again and aims the gun outside. "*¡Chingados!*" Luca bellows. Obviously, Nate is gone. I walk over to him as he's getting to his feet. "Damn it, Connor!" he growls as he fixes me with a deadly glower.

"What? What was I supposed to do?"

"Didn't you see what I was mouthing at you?"

"No, you were too far away. What did you say?"

"I said, 'I'm already dead.' And so is Lucy."

Lia

I wipe the blade of my axe against my pant-leg, cleaning off some of the gummy ichor that was the result of the latest cure test going awry. Elliot looks at me, grey-faced.

"This is not going as well as I'd hoped." I nod in grim agreement. "I don't know what I'm missing," he mutters, half to himself.

"You'll get it. I know you will." I give him a supportive smile that freezes on my face as the door Darryl's guarding opens. My heart starts freaking out as I wait to see who comes through and in what condition.

Darryl tenses and my heart both soars and plummets as I see that Lucy is, thank God, alive, but looking to be in pretty rough shape. Her right arm is cradled against her chest and her left arm is around Luca's neck, for support I guess, since she's limping, but it's a strange sight to see them so close together. I notice blood seeping through her right pant-leg; she must be hurt pretty badly. John is not among them, which I'm betting means he's no longer among the living. And Mac is helping along a very woozy looking Link; he himself looks unharmed but distraught enough that my heart plummets even further. It's somewhere around my knees at this point, I think.

I rush over to them. "What happened? Did you get him?" By the lack of triumphant hooting and hollering, I'm sure they didn't, but I have to ask.

Lucy shakes her head and drops her eyes to the floor. "I'm sorry," she whispers in a tone that makes my heart ache for her. I look at the others and my heart takes another nosedive. I don't think it can get any lower at this point. Something in their faces tells me it's worse than Nate just getting away.

"What happened?" Elliot asks and I almost jump—I'd been so focused on them, I didn't notice him coming up behind me.

"He got away," Mac says, his voice empty in a way I've never heard it sound before. Lucy's face almost crumples and I look back and forth between them.

"What else happened?" I ask, the fear I feel coming out sounding accusatory. Lucy's faces crumples further and I feel like a jerk, especially when Luca shoots me a look and says, "Doc, you

359

should check out Lucy and Link's injuries. Link was grazed with a bullet and Nate walloped his head pretty good. Lucy's wrist is broken and her leg is cut up bad."

Elliot rushes forwards. "Of course. I'm sorry, you guys. What about you?" he asks Luca and I just now notice the blood smeared on his throat.

"It's just a small cut, there's nothing you can do for it." The seeming innocence of this statement is belied by Mac's growl of outrage.

"God, just tell them already!"

"Tell us what?" I ask as I feel my heart thud somewhere down into the soles of my feet. I'm getting the distinct feeling that this is a worst case scenario we're dealing with here.

A small gasp from Elliot refocuses my attention on him and Lucy. He's crouched in front of her, examining her cut leg. "It's infected."

"Infected? But it just happened," I say, feeling bemused before the terrible reality sinks in. "What? You're not   you can't be!" I shout and it turns into a feeble command I wish I could make true by saying it emphatically enough.

"I'm sorry," Lucy whispers in that awful tormented tone again. I rush over to her and throw my arms around her.

"No, don't be sorry, it's not your fault." As I hug her, I feel my fear and heartsickness morphing into a wrathful rage just screaming for vengeance. "I'm going to get him for this. I'm going to end him if I have to tear him apart with my bare hands!" I pull away from the hug and brandish my axe.

I will end him.

"Lia, stop. Please. You can't go after him."

"And why the fuck not? He needs to die. He needs to die painfully and he needs to die now."

"I understand the sentiment, *chica*, but you going after him alone won't do anyone any good. He's in his element now and how do you propose to find a hunter in the woods anyway?"

"I don't know, shut up!" I growl, shoving Luca for lack of any better way to vent my staggering ire.

"Hey!" Mac hollers, sounding very, very pissed off. Luca holds up a hand, signalling him to back down.

"Don't you even want to know why Nate did this to us?" Luca asks.

"Um, because he's crazy, maybe? Who gives a fuck? All that matters is he needs to die!"

"Wait, 'us'?" Elliot asks, catching the nuance I missed due to being encompassed with blind, furious hatred. Luca nods and taps the cut on his throat, which, now that I look more closely at it, I can see that the edges are a sickly green colour and that Luca himself is paler than usual.

Oh, fuck.

"He's completely deranged," I breathe, gripping the handle of my axe more tightly like this will somehow stop me from losing it.

"Maybe. That's not the issue right now. He did it because he wanted to speed up the development of the cure. How is the cure coming, Doc?" Elliot's face falls and Luca nods, seemingly accepting his shitty fate.

"You have to try!" Mac yells suddenly. "Stop wasting time and do something that's actually productive!"

Shock cuts through my rage momentarily. Mac referring to helping Lucy as a waste of time is just about as crazy as anything else that's happened recently. I look at Lucy, but her face has taken on a stony expression that doesn't give me any insight into what she's feeling.

"Mac, *cálmate*. I'm sure they'll do what they can, but you need to accept that the outcome will likely not be the most favourable one. We've seen it before—infections that are closer to major arteries make people turn faster, right, Doc?"

Elliot nods slowly, seeming reluctant to agree. "Yes, that does seem to be the case." I feel a surge of possibly-inappropriate-for-the-situation hope for Lucy's chances rise.

"Then hurry the fuck up!"

"*Connor*," Luca warns.

"What? What are you waiting for?"

Luca looks ready to chastise Mac again, but Elliot nods. "He's right." He glances at Luca's cut and his colouring then continues, "We don't have much time—for either of you." Lucy nods sedately, but I feel my wrath renew itself.

I want to kill something. I want to kill many things. Mostly I just want to kill Nate—preferably several times in new and inventive ways.

Lucy

My leg is throbbing, pulsing strangely, as the infection spreads. Luca is sitting beside me, not saying anything but bringing a strangely comforting presence all the same. I think it's probably because he's the only one who can truly know what I'm feeling right now since it's happening to him, too. I look over at him and he gives me a sort-of smile. I do my best to return it, but I'd bet my attempt is even sorrier than his. I shift my attention back to Mac, who's pacing along the far wall of the lab. He hasn't looked at me once or spoken to me directly since he found out what Nate did. And who knows? Maybe his anger is valid. Maybe if he hadn't stopped to check on me he would've been able to save Luca. All I know is that his ignoring me is pretty much coming up even with my injuries for inflicting pain on me right now.

"*Lo siento*," Luca says quite suddenly.

"What for?"

He shrugs. "I guess it's a pretty wide apology. Mostly I'm sorry Mac is taking this out on you. It's not fair."

Now I shrug, not really sure what to say and really not wanting to start crying. He reaches over and takes my uninjured hand, careful not to jostle my be-slinged right arm. I squeeze back and it helps, but it's not the same as having Mac hold my hand.

Luca takes a deep breath and I look over at him. "Lucy."

"Yeah?" I respond, feeling wary.

"I don't think I have much time." My heart clenches in my chest and I feel my breathing stutter. I can see sweat covering his face in a slight sheen and he looks disconcertingly corpse-like already: his eyes are underscored heavily with dark shadows and his skin has an awful greyish-white tinge that I've seen before on people close to turning. He's right. I nod, trying that much harder to hold back tears; I don't have the luxury to cry right now. "Whatever happens, you can't let Mac be the one to kill me; I don't think he would recover"—he's right about that, too, I'm sure—"And I don't want any of my other men to have to do it either." I nod again. "So, if this next test doesn't work, I'm going to do it myself. I don't think they, especially Mac, would recover from seeing me turn either. And I don't want to take the chance that I could spread this further."

Unbidden, a few tears slip past my closed eyelids. I nod. He says, "Okay," and brushes the tears from my cheeks. "Two more requests." I open my eyes. "Can you give this to my family...after? My men can help you contact them." He hands me a few folded up sheets of paper, his goodbye. I take them and slip them into the pocket of my jeans. "*Gracias*. Just one more thing, I know this isn't fair to ask, but I have to. I need you to promise me that you won't let him, any of them, stop me."

I look over at Mac, still pacing frenetically. He might never forgive me for this, but it's a request I cannot deny. "I promise."

"Thank you. And I'm sorry." I give him a smile that's even more half-hearted than before and squeeze his hand again before leaving to check on Lia. Elliot had an aha moment about the cure so she went to get another test zombie, but that was a little while ago and she hasn't come back out of the room yet.

I reach the door just as it opens and Lia emerges, plastered with enough blood and other gooey remnants that I feel my stomach turn.

"What the—"

"They tried to bite me."

I look past her into the room and come very close to losing whatever might be left in my stomach from the protein bars we ate several hours and a lifetime ago. It's impossible to tell that what was in the room used to be human or even human shaped once. The two bodies—I think there are only two, it's hard to tell with all the gore—are so destroyed that it just looks like what's left in a microwave after someone cooks a Pizza Pop for too long.

"Jesus, Li, how many times did you hit those things?"

"I lost count," she says indifferently.

"Man, even Lizzie Borden only gave her parents forty whacks; take it down a notch, lady cakes." Lia just shrugs. "Do you feel better at least?" I ask and she smiles, grimly, but it's there. "And are there more test subjects?"

She gives me an impatient look, "Of course there are. I'm enraged, not stupid."

I hold my free hand up in surrender. "Okay, okay, let's go get one then. I don't think Luca has much time."

Her face loses some of its fire. "Right. But you're not doing anything. I've got this."

"It's not like they could infect me worse," I say, going for joking, but mostly sounding bitter instead.

Luckily, Lia being Lia, she goes along with the intention for joking and says, "Yeah, well, with you being Gimpy Gimperson from Gimpington County right now, I think it's best if you just take a breather." I laugh slightly, exhaling through my nose, and let her take care of the zombie stuff. It's not like I'd be super helpful right now anyway.

I sidle up to Darryl—as much as one can sidle when limping anyway—I could use someone to talk to and I don't want to disturb Elliot. The others are helping him while Darryl is watching the doors in case Nate's exit was a fake-out.

"Hey," I say as I gimp up beside him.

"Hey." His mutilated face scrunches in a way that looks painful as he smiles at me.

"So, you're married," I say, for lack of a better conversation starter.

"Small talk?" he asks with a slight chuckle.

"I just need to take my mind off of...everything." He nods and scratches absently at one of the slowly healing rivets on the side of his neck. He tells me about his wife, Maria, and I focus as much of my attention on his stories as I can, working to ignore Lia leading a zombie towards the group.

Unfortunately, I can't ignore the disappointed sounds coming from the group a few seconds later as apparently nothing happens. I glance over at Luca and he nods at me. My heart is pounding frantically, a resounding bass beat thrumming inside my ribcage.

"Lucy?" Darryl says my name worriedly. "You just went very pale. What's wrong?"

A harsh laugh claws out of my throat. "What isn't wrong? I'm sorry, I have to—" I trail off and turn away, barely registering his nod of understanding.

I walk over to Luca as fast as my injured leg will allow. His breathing is laboured and he's drenched with sweat now as he stands, almost swaying, and clutches his gun tightly. "Just a little longer, please," I beg, not even sure if I'm begging him or some power in the 'verse that I heretofore patently disbelieved in.

"*No...tiempo...lo...siento*," his strained words reverted to his native tongue put the truth to this statement.

"Fuck. Okay, what do you need me to do?"

"Mac...*distrae...por...favor*." I'm confused for a second, high school Spanish being a long time ago, but between his gestures and the promise he made me give him earlier, I get that he wants me to distract Mac. I nod. I turn away then turn back quickly and throw my one arm around his neck in the best attempt at a hug I can make right now. My right arm screams in protest, but I hold on till he squeezes back.

"*Lo siento*," I tell him and he nods, then gestures at Mac with his gun.

"*Vaya...por...favor*."

I walk away from him, hearing my heart in my ears and willing myself not to look back. I walk over to Mac. He'd stopped his frenzied pacing for the results of the last test but he's started up again now, complete with muttering to himself. He stops when he sees me, but by the look on his face, he'd rather just walk around me than stop to talk. I shift my position and he unconsciously mirrors my movements, his back now to Luca, ensuring that he doesn't see him leave the room.

"What?" he asks impatiently in a scathing tone that makes my chest ache.

"I just—" I don't have time to get out any more words before the gunshot rings out and I swear I can feel the impact in my chest, but it might just be my heart.

"'The fuck?" Mac asks, mostly to himself as he spins around. He scans the room and when he can't find Luca, he rounds on me. "What did you do?" He doesn't wait for an answer, just turns away from me and starts running.

Luca didn't say anything about this, but I'm betting he wouldn't want Mac to see his body. I run after him as best I can, trying to ignore the pain in my leg. I catch up to him at the door and grab his arm. "Mac, please. He wouldn't want you to see this, you know that." By this point everyone else has gathered around us, shouting questions, asking what happened.

"He killed himself and she helped him!" Mac says, his tone hateful in a way that makes me feel nauseous, despite the fact that I am suddenly hungry. At least, I hope that the nausea is a result of

Mac's hatefulness, although my sweaty palms make me really afraid that it's the infection taking over.

All of Luca's soldiers are crestfallen at the news of his demise. I feel for them all, but I return my focus to Mac, squeezing his arm more tightly and pleading with him to understand. "Mac, I'm sorry, I'm so sorry, but he made me promise." Mac makes a disdainful noise in his throat and wrenches his arm out of my grasp, throwing me off balance.

Rafe catches me and says, "Whoa, Connor, take it easy. We're all hurting, but this is better than watching him become a zombie. You gotta see that." Mac doesn't say anything, just shakes his head and walks away.

My heart hasn't stopped pounding; I have to admit to myself that my body is starting to succumb to the infection, something made all the more obvious by the new hitch in my breathing and the tightness that spans across my sternum, making my collarbone feel like it's stretched tight as razor wire. I feel light-headed and I sink down to the ground, a remote part of me registers how dramatic this must look, like I'm fainting because of Mac's rejection. But I'm on the razor's edge of life, death, or zombie-ism. I can't escape the fact that this might be it, so I can't muster the energy to care about how I look. I might die in this godforsaken lab in the middle of nowhere without getting a chance to ever see my family again, to tell them that I love them and that I'm sorry I won't be coming home. A sob catches roughly in my throat, sore from trying to hold back tears. I shift my weight and lay my face flat against the cool floor; it's oddly comforting.

"Hey, come on, we'll beat this and Mac will come around and then somehow we'll find Nate and we'll kill him...a lot. Fighting!" I look up to see Lia doing the closed fist hand motion that accompanies this sentiment, made familiar by all of the Korean dramas we've watched over the years. I can't hold back a smile, thanking whatever might be out there or not that at least I have my best friend with me at the end. I return the gesture and let her help me to my feet.

"Um, Lia?" Elliot calls and I gesture for her to go, repeating the "Fighting!" hand motion once more for good measure and to let her know that I haven't completely given up hope. And I haven't, but all the same, I think I better write a goodbye letter of my own. I run my good hand over the handle of the gun still at my hip, my touchstone of escape and prevention.

I know Mac hates me for the part I played in Luca's death, but I think he did the right thing and, if it comes down to it, so will I. I won't have anyone else taking that on. I just hope that Lia will forgive me and that we can still be ghost friends someday. And I hope Elliot gets his cure working even if it's too late for me, at least the people I love will be safe.

Elliot

I'm trying not to get my hopes up, but so far I can't think of any other explanations besides the one where the cure finally worked! And just in time, too—well, for Lucy anyway. Thinking about Sergeant Ortiz dampens my excitement some, but I try to focus on the good aspects of what I think might be happening right now.

Lia approaches me and asks, "What is it? I have to keep an eye on Lucy; I think she might be planning on following in Luca's footsteps."

"It looks like she won't have to."

"What? I mean, thank God, but why?"

I point to the stilled zombie at my feet. "Did you kill it?" She shakes her head, eyes widening at the implication. "I don't think anyone else did either. I think it just had a delayed reaction, which I should have expected."

"Oh, my God," Lia breathes then rushes away, presumably to bring Lucy over to receive the treatment. I'm sorry that this came too late to help Sergeant Ortiz, but if it works on Lucy, then it's done and we can finally get out of here and start doing something about the zombies back at Crystal Lake.

Lucy and Lia walk back over to me, both of them looking tentatively hopeful.

"What's going on?" Master Corporal Kane asks as he joins us.

I point to the zombie again. "I think the cure worked." Master Corporal Kane smiles at the news, but it's obvious what he's thinking: not in time.

"Elliot, hurry, please. If it takes a while to kick in, we don't have any time to spare," Lia says.

"Right, okay." I grasp the spray bottle—we weren't able to make it into a gas, but at least liquid form is better than a pill or an injection—and mist Lucy's face, telling her to keep her mouth open, we want the delivery system to work as fast as possible. I spray her generously then step back, looking for any obvious external changes even though I know that it will be a little while until it takes total effect.

"How do you feel?" Lia asks. "Any change?"

"I'm not sure yet," Lucy answers, looking like she just really doesn't want to let Lia down. As we're waiting to see if the serum works like I hope it will, the others—minus Mac, who's still cooling off—have wandered over to see what's happening. Lucy quails slightly under all of the gazes fixed upon her and drops her own gaze down, studying her hands.

She sits up suddenly with a jolt. "Whoa!"

"What? What is it?" Lia asks.

"My heart suddenly stopped pounding. And I'm not clammy anymore. And my leg has stopped throbbing!" She pulls her knee into her chest and rolls her pant-leg up. She peels back the bandage I'd put on it; the wound, which had previously been festering and oozing, now looks only like a bad gash, as though the cleansing I did to it suddenly kicked in.

"YES!" Lia shouts and suddenly grabs me and kisses me, her lips pressing hard against mine before she pulls away and turns to pull Lucy into a slightly too vigorous hug that has Lucy yelping and trying to pull her injured arm out of the way. "Sorry, just, yes!" Lia enthuses. My head is spinning slightly from the kiss, but I can't process it right now, there's still too much going on, too much to worry about.

Case in point: while the soldiers are looking happy, regret tinges their expressions. I wish it had been in time, too. Goddamn Nate.

"So you're cured." Mac joins the group, his tone is just shy of indifferent and the happy smile slips off Lucy's face. "You couldn't have tried this on Luca?" he asks me, turning his blazing eyes my way.

"I didn't think it worked; it had delayed effects. I didn't want to take the chance that I'd make things worse."

"He's dead. It couldn't get any worse!"

"I'm sorry. I don't think it would have been in time anyway, he was too far gone, the infection was introduced too close to one of his major arteries."

"Is that supposed to make me feel better?" Mac asks, acidly.

I don't get a chance to answer as the door to the lab suddenly slams open, admitting several men armed to the teeth and dressed head to toe in black. They'd look just like normal SWAT officers but for the Mithras Corporation logo on their chests. No timing is right today.

"What the hell is going on here?" the lead man barks.

Lucy suddenly bursts out laughing and I get a sudden worry that the serum is having unforeseen side effects. "Looks like the cavalry has arrived. And just in the nick of time, too," she says emitting a rough laugh.

"I'll ask again," the man says with an edge in his voice, "what is going on and who are you people?"

It takes a while and the introduction of the remaining zombies, but they're eventually caught up. Lucy was right: they're the cavalry, sent by Mithras when turning off the alarm here triggered their own alarms—you'd think that the alarm going off in the first place would have alerted them already, but apparently Gregory messed with that system, as well.

Before we know it, we're all outside as the team searches the building looking for any more survivors and doing away with the last of the zombies. I guess it's almost over. They called for a helicopter to airlift us out and bring us to the hospital so we can all be checked over—Mithras policy. The Mithras SWAT leader already got my formula for the cure and sent it to headquarters, saying that I'd be compensated handsomely for my contributions. As though I could even think about money right now. Everything seems blurry somehow as we stand around at the edge of the forest, awaiting further instructions from the team. It's like my adrenaline is starting to wear off and I can't focus very well on anything. The atmosphere is subdued. It may be almost over, but we lost a lot of people to get to this point so it's hard to revel in the moment.

"Man, I kinda can't believe we survived," Rafe says to Link, breaking the silence.

"I'm as surprised as you are. I thought our black asses would be toast for sure."

Lia smiles slightly at this exchange. She's holding my hand in one of hers while the other flips through her phone. I'm almost ready to think about—and hopefully repeat—the kiss from the lab. Once things are settled, I hope she wants to repeat it, too. "Oh, geez," she says.

"What?" Lucy asks.

"I've got about a million messages from Roz. Wow, this last text is very cryptic—while still managing to lay a guilt trip on me, which is impressive: 'if you're still alive and just trying to punish your poor mother by not answering your phone, at least check the news.'"

"The news?" I ask and Lia shrugs. She does a search on her phone and within seconds she murmurs, "Oh, damn."

"What? What is it?" Lia hands her phone to me, open to a news bulletin concerning several disturbances up in the mountains...bloody disturbances. I read the headline aloud, as well as the brief synopsis detailing the extent to which the zombie problem has spread. Everyone groans. We knew something like this was a possibility since containment failed so miserably, but it would be nice if there wasn't another disaster to face right after we just finished dealing with so many tragedies in a row. I'm thankful that at least we'll have more help this time with the Mithras SWAT team, but I'm exhausted and it looks like we'll have a lot of work to do before we can rest.

Lucy nods and sums up what I'm sure we're all feeling in a brief statement: "Well, fuck."

The End

Or is it?...

Epilogue
Head shots really are the very best

Nate

After I left the lab, I had to stop for a little while so I could stitch up my leg where Lucy stabbed me. It still hurts but it hasn't slowed me down much; I'm used to dealing with pain. I can't blame her for fighting back. It's part of what makes me like her so much.

It's taken me three days to get back to the place where I buried Blaine. A lot of thoughts have come and gone through my mind in that time. There's guilt over what I did to Lucy, followed by my brain protesting that I didn't have a choice, it needed to be done, I needed to make sure they were on task, then more guilt as I remind myself that they wouldn't have been likely to go off-task in the first place if I hadn't screwed things up by playing my idiotic and childish games. I've made a lot of mistakes recently; I should have been more careful, more aware of how Blaine's death was affecting me. But I blocked it out. Father always said that it was weakness to care about others. Pathetic to tether your happiness to anyone else. He was furious with me when I was upset about my mother dying. He would be disgusted to know how much I miss Blaine.

As I slow my pace, then come to a complete stop and sit down on a nearby log, I tell myself it's time for a break, but I know I'm stalling. I don't want to go back to that place. I don't want to see Blaine's dead face again. I don't want to remember him like that. Right now I'm not sure I want to remember him at all. I can't stand the idea of what he'd think of the things I've done. He knew about Father. What I did. What I had to do when I found out what he'd done to my mother. He knew and he didn't care. He said he had it coming. But this, what I've done since he died. I don't think he would understand. I don't want to see his face again because I don't know if I'll be able to take it, his disappointment, his disgust, his fear—all the things I know he'd feel if he knew.

So I wait. I grant myself the mercy of a pause before I see my existentialist judge and jury. To distract myself, I take out my wind-up flashlight/radio and wind it until it crackles to life. I spin the dial until I find a station that's broadcasting news. I don't have to wait long, not surprising with the near-miss of a zombie apocalypse—and it does seem to have been a near-miss, the reporter is now talking about Elliot's cure, although she's talking about it in terms of Mithras, not Elliot.

"The recent crisis in the Rocky Mountains could have been the plot of a horror-movie, but a widespread catastrophe was averted by the quick development of a cure by the Mithras Corporation, owners of the vitamin and supplement development company SymbioVitaTech, among many others. Mithras has also generously donated the time and labour of its private security firm to help ensure the safety of those in the vicinity of the attacks."

The radio runs out of juice and falls silent, but I don't wind it again. I've heard enough. No word on how it all began in the labs of SymbioVitaTech, no mention of Gregory, nothing about Mithras' last minute arrival at the scene—they must have gotten there not long after I left for it to have been cleared up this quickly, but not soon enough to actually do anyone any good, but they paint themselves the conquering heroes. Despicable.

I return the flashlight/radio to my bag and get to my feet. Enough stalling.

It doesn't take me long to get to Blaine's gravesite, just a half hour or so. When I reach the clearing, my guard goes up and I flip my SKS into my hands. Someone's been here. The bodies of Tif and the zombie that turned her are gone. Blaine's grave marker has been moved. I sprint over to the spot and start digging, feeling a frantic hopelessness as I paw at the dirt.

"He's not there, Mr. Townshend."

I don't think, I don't wait for the instinctual feeling to decide yes or no, I just commit to the urge. Grabbing my SKS, I spin around and fire a shot at the space where the man's voice and my finely honed instincts tell me to aim. The butt of the rifle thuds into my shoulder with a comfortingly familiar sensation and I know I hit my target before my eyes confirm it. Dead centre of the stranger's face, a neat hole drips with less blood than you'd think, coming from a kill shot. He collapses in a heap on the ground and I fire again, now hitting the chest of his associate, who was creeping out of the edge of the trees to my left, aiming a gun at me. He collapses, too. I wait, but no one else reveals themselves, so I walk over to him. Blood gurgles from his open mouth as he slips into death. I study his greying face with nothing short of pure hatred. They took Blaine from me once, turning him into an undead thing I was forced to kill. They took him with their sloppiness, their obliviousness to Gregory's madness and his machinations. And then they took him away again, so I can't even give his parents the solace of a real funeral. Can't give myself that solace.

They will pay. They deserve to suffer, to die for what they wrought upon this world, what they unleashed in their ignorance. For what they took from me...I'll make them pay.

I stare into the man's eyes, which are slowly turning lifeless and I lift my SKS and I make sure, just in case, always just in case, and I shoot him once more in the head.

Head shots really are the very best.

The End

Belinda Dunford wrote the majority of her first novel while studying Humanities at the University of Lethbridge. She also makes YouTube videos with rules for surviving a horror movie, which can be found on her channel, bdbeastie. She currently lives in Calgary. For more information, go to www.belindadunford.com

28165073R00214

Made in the USA
Charleston, SC
02 April 2014